THE SEALEATERS, 20,000 BC

BOOK FIVE OF WINDS OF CHANGE, A PREHISTORIC FICTION SERIES ON THE PEOPLING OF THE AMERICAS

BONNYE MATTHEWS
Award Winning Writer of Prehistoric Fiction

PO Box 221974 Anchorage, Alaska 99522-1974
books@publicationconsultants.com—www.publicationconsultants.com

ISBN 978-1-59433-600-3
eISBN 978-1-59433-601-0
Library of Congress Catalog Card Number: 2015959170

Manufactured in the United States of America.

Dedication

For Sally B. Sutherland, long-time treasured friend.

Other Books in the Winds of Change Series:

Acknowledgements

Without the assistance of several people this book, as is true of the others in this series, would not be. These people are first, my brother, Randy Matthews, and then Sally Sutherland, Patricia Gilmore, Robert Arthur, and Pat Meiwes. All contributed far in excess of what could be expected or hoped for based on family, friendship, or love of reading. I also thank my publisher, Evan Swensen, who had the courage to take on this project.

Contents

Introduction

The Winds of Change Novel Series

The novel series views the period from 75,000 BC to the present as representing two overall times: from 75,000 BC to the last Ice Age Glaciation event is the *Time of Peace* among people on earth and from about 26,000 BC is the *Time of War* among people on earth that continues to today. The eruption of Mt. Toba on the island of Sumatra ushered in the *Time of Peace* by significantly changing the environment and possibly reducing the population of the earth at that time. People had to band tightly together not just for companionship but more to the point—for basic survival in their given environment. The last Ice Age Glaciation event beginning around 26,000 BC ushered in the *Time of War* by creating great sheets of ice that covered northern lands, shoving refugees from the northern levels into lands further south, creating conflict between refugees who had to go somewhere and those who considered various geographic areas theirs. Wars erupted to defend or seize territory. The massive glaciation was gone by 11,700 BC, but the *Time of War* continues. Along with earth changes, people changed. The *Time of War* changed values. In general, cunning became a virtue, not a vice, and guilelessness became detrimental to successful living. The first four books in the series focus on the *Time of Peace*. The last book in the series focuses on the transition to the *Time of War*.

Each book in the series is part of the series, but each novel stands alone also as a single read, since they do not ultimately depend on one another.

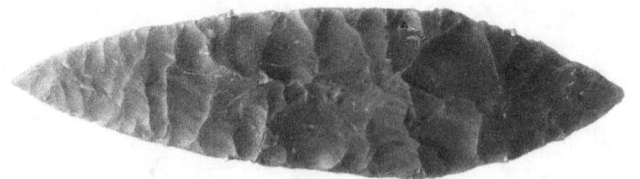

Laurel Leaf Bifacial Spear Point

The SealEaters, Book Five in the Winds of Change Series

Fact: In 1971 the scallop boat, *Cinmar,* was sixty miles off the Virginia Cape. The net brought up a mastodon jaw and a large bifacial spear point from a depth of 240 feet of water. Carbon dating put the mastodon bone at 22,760 years ago. Chemical analysis showed the spear point material originated in France. The two items are thought to have lain in place since the site was above water in the Ice Age. From these and data from the archaeological sites at Cactus Hill (Virginia), Meadowcroft Rockshelter (Pennsylvania), and possibly Topper (South Carolina), the Solutrean Hypothesis originated.

The Solutrean Hypothesis: According to the Solutrean Hypothesis, Solutrean people living in France/Spain during the last Ice Age Glaciation migrated to North America across the Atlantic Ocean. They brought their unique method of tool making with them, most notably the laurel leaf spear point. That tool-making technique became adapted into the laurel leaf design known today as the Clovis Point, which spread through North America. Dennis Stanford of the Smithsonian Institution and Bruce Bradley of the University of Exeter, authors of the fascinating book, *Across Atlantic Ice,* are proponents of this hypothesis.

Clovis Bifacial Spear Point

My view: I am satisfied regarding the plausibility that Solutreans came to what is now the United States and explored the land, leaving laurel leaf spear points. I am also persuaded that there were people living there at the time— not large numbers, but enough for interactions to occur. I see these indigenous people as having come by boat from Asia in the past or from aboriginal Australian people along with Pacific Islanders and people from Africa, moving into North America from South and Central America. *The SealEaters, 20,000 BC* is dated appropriately for Solutrean Hypothesis parameters. Solutreans do, however, pre-date Clovis. It is reasonable to expect that Clovis Points were developed from Solutrean spear point technology. Flaking Solutrean points requires significant skill. If they broke in half during the making, they could be re-purposed as knives or other tools. The base of Clovis points could have been the result of one of the Solutrean points' breaking at the tip of one end. From that it would be possible for a creative mind to see the use of the tool in a different form, altered to attach more easily to a shaft. To reach that creative mind, the one(s) who might have adapted the points, it may have taken the time between the end of the Solutrean points appearances in the area now called the United States and the rise of the Clovis Point.

The Novel: *The SealEaters, 20,000 BC* describes people at the junction of France and Spain in 20,000 BC being squeezed between mountains, ice, and people at war. Their major source of food has become seals that are beaching on their shore. The SealEaters, having realized their food source is diminishing, send explorers across the ocean to North America where they sought a place for their people to migrate. They eat seals along the way. Interacting with indigenous people they find there, SealEaters teach their spear point technique to those who want to learn. The explorers find a place for their people to migrate, and they lead them across the Atlantic Ocean where they are absorbed by people living there.

Genetics? Without a single body of the Solutreans or Clovis Point makers ever having been found, there is no way to study this conundrum in depth.

Bonnye Matthews, December, 2015

For the Reader who wants more information:

Novels in the Winds of Change Series will have DVDs as Introductions. Check Amazon for availability. At this time there are two DVDs produced:

Introduction to *Ki'ti's Story, 75,000 BC, Then and Now in Southeast Asia* and *Cook Inlet, Alaska: Setting of Tuksook's Story, 35,000 BC.*

For other introductory information, see my Facebook Author page at: http://facebook.com/pages/Bonnye-Matthews/484231424985849?ref=hl#

For additional information, see my website at www.booksbybonnye.com.

SealEaters' Genealogical Chart

Wnug + Gemu (d)	Amoroz + Fiuga	Reg + Waywap	Forth + Trupo	At + Merlan	Mongwire + Gunt
Urch	**Murke**	**Blad**	Cudmea	Smam	Lefa
Oppermatu	Akla	Tink	**Wapa**	Litmaq	Morg
Emuka	Momomu	Afte-ba	Kol	**Plak**	Moneo
+ Amegulatuga	Begalit	**Maber**	Dupa	Elaf	Ahm
Sted	Lowat	Ufom	Pligo	Walaf	+ Wewa
Nip	Emu	Egorgo	Gi	Tob	Mulot
Cattu	Kel	Chugu	Meah	+ Elmo	Elu
	Tulib	Bago	Sil	Mo-at	Pella
	Megg	+ Cabell	+ Quapiti	Ta	Yehol
	Comun	Belah	Mii	Grum	+ Mora
	+ Tore	Rezou	Seq	**Vaimo**	Torq
	Mot	+ Ipsatu	Mumo	Pupe	Klamuta
	Azota	Polug	Selat	Bayte	**Wen**
		Gerval	Tup	Klamuta	Moham
			Hag	Lim	Gimul
			Jupo		Rula
			+ Namamat		
			Opa		

The SealEaters

Chapter 1

The SealEaters' Cove

"I wish they'd leave," Lefa whispered anxiously, her fingers pressed tightly against the rock that sloped upwards like a wall in front of where she squatted in a tight hunker of anxiety.

"No need to whisper, Little Rabbit," Litmaq tried to be reassuring. He brushed across her back as he put his arm protectively around her. He didn't try to meet her eyes, which were and had been securely fixed on the shoreline and their home at the Cove, visible from the hill where they hid. He wondered again for an uncountable number of times whether it was wise for them ever to return home. It was a thought he'd not yet discussed with Lefa.

Lefa and Litmaq were nestled low behind some leafy bushes through which they could see. They were just on the downside of the third tallest hill from home. Litmaq had checked to be sure they could not be seen from below. He had planned everything about this escape very carefully. On this day the sun shone brightly. Lefa disappeared during the night of the heavy rain of a few days ago. Her footprints had been instantly obliterated as she ran to the appointed secret meeting place that night. It was part of the plan. From there Litmaq led her to the place he'd prepared and provisioned. He'd chosen a thick forest with a rock shelter and made a well dried and covered woodpile for a very small hearth. It would raise minimal smoke and heat waves.

Standing at the water's edge down below them at the Cove near the boats and leaning on his walking stick, Whug, oldest of the six brothers who were elders, Chief of the SealEaters, surveyed their ever-decreasing land. At sixty-five, Whug was in good health, still very strong. His hair was all but gone at the crown and what was left was thin and lacked luster, but he was capable of doing anything a man twenty years younger could do, and most of the time better. He glanced up at the third tallest hill in the distance to the east. When Litmaq left to hunt, Whug thought nothing of it. When Lefa went missing after the torrential rains, he suspected the two were together somewhere. He couldn't think that Lefa somehow died in the storm. He'd observed Lefa and Litmaq since they were little children. Only he and Gemu had shared the strength of love he saw in Litmaq and Lefa. The two young ones tried to hide their attraction carefully and were fairly successful, but he could see it. They were not husband and wife, but they were one. They could speak with their eyes.

When Reg, the third brother who also was an elder, recently became seemingly obsessed with Lefa's absence, Whug became alert. He finally satisfied himself that Reg's interest in the missing girl had something to do with the recent battle between Reg and Mongwire. Mongwire was Lefa's father, Whug's youngest brother and elder. Whug thought it made no sense for Reg to be so concerned about Lefa's absence. Reg had a vicious habit of leaving disagreements unsettled and seething with brooding anger. He'd grow the anger until he wreaked vengeance on his former opponent. Often, however, Reg tried to inflict pain indirectly on others by hurting someone loved by the target of his vengeance, possibly Lefa in this case, rather than by inflicting pain directly on the target, who would be Mongwire. Whug became more and more convinced that Reg planned to do something to Lefa to hurt Mongwire. He assumed Lefa knew about it and had shared that with Litmaq. That would make sense of all that was happening. Everyone knew Reg was leaving on the voyage. Litmaq only needed to hide Lefa until Reg left, and that would be soon.

Whug suspected Litmaq and Lefa had fled before Reg could do whatever he had in mind. Only Whug suspected their location. He would not disclose his thoughts to anyone, not even to his second wife. He would have shared it with Gemu, his first wife, but she no longer breathed air. At sixty-five, Whug didn't share thought intimacy with his twenty-five-year-old second wife though he treated her well. Whug smiled when he figured out where the two most likely hid. If he were right, they'd be safe there, but he couldn't imagine how they'd have found the place.

The SealEaters looked for Lefa as soon as they noticed her absence. They searched the two highest hills considering that she'd gone to the heights. Having searched the two highest hills, they'd agreed that she hadn't sought the heights but rather had followed the valley, where hunters were presently searching. There was no consensus as to why she was missing. Some thought she'd walked into the water to drown herself, but that seemed unnatural for anything Lefa might do. Lefa was quiet and kept to herself, but she was a happy person. She was not a person the SealEaters noticed, until she was missing. She simply seemed to have disappeared.

Below Lefa and Litmaq, down by the Cove on the coast, the boats were readied. Each had been well supplied with the maximum amount that could be added for safe travel on the sea. Changes of clothing had been carefully stored in bladders that had been sewn or tied watertight. Falling overboard was the biggest safety threat. The mariners had to have at least one dry change of clothing. One could freeze to death quickly unclothed or in wet clothes. Water, known as critical to survival, had not been stored in excess. Ice was readily available. They had some seal oil and small, clean rocks stored in bladders for heating and cooking. SealEaters could always melt ice as they traveled, and they could replenish the seal oil though it took a lot longer. Taking empty bags for melting ice was a better plan than carrying full bags of water. They brought rectangular stone slabs for flame protection against the wind. The voyagers brought some dried meat and grains the women had gathered. Their main food source would be the seals they found along the way. Seals would also be their resource for any needs they had. All provisions had to be secured carefully. The SealEaters were beginning to gather down by the boats.

Up on the hill Lefa watched Reg's boat. It was by far the largest. The tree the men had recently burned and carved out was one of the largest the SealEaters ever made into a boat. The flexible side arm that kept the boat steady in the water was almost as big as the other boats. The side arm was joined by two small tree crosspieces attached through cutouts in the boat and side arm and pegged, so they could provide flexibility but not disconnect. Until Reg insisted on that tree for his boat, no one had been willing to endanger the structures at their Cove by cutting the tree, removing the limbs and roots, and rolling it down the hill. As it was, the tree trunk damaged three structures severely enough that they had to be rebuilt. Men of the SealEaters were happy to help him build it, because they wanted to see how well a wooden boat worked when made of a tree that size. The SealEaters made boats of driftwood frames and seal skins.

Reg ultimately became master of the largest boat. It carried a large load, but it was not as agile in the water as the smaller craft. The boat required more rowers than normal. Lefa wanted to see it leave and know it was gone for a long time—never to return would be far better. It was an amazing boat, but to her it showed all that was wrong with Reg: he wanted for himself the biggest and best of everything no matter the loss that might bring to others. Wishing Reg never to return went against the gods, she knew, but she still had those thoughts and would not deny it to herself.

Down by the water SealEaters were near chaos. People were running about making sure that all necessities were packed on the boats. Reg walked right past Whug, accidentally hitting his walking stick with his backpack. He carried spears, three bladders filled with necessities, cordage, bundles wrapped in seal gut for waterproofing. Whug suspected he'd go back for more. Reg didn't offer an apology for hitting Whug's walking stick. Whug was convinced that Reg wrapped in his self-focus had no idea he'd run into his brother. Had it been intentional Reg would have been looking at the walking stick. Instead Reg's gaze was on his boat.

"She's been gone for four days!" Reg bellowed. "What's the matter with you people that one disappears who cannot be found? Are your tracking skills that poor?"

"Why are you concerned about my daughter?" Mongwire asked, tired of hearing Reg's tirade, while he grieved the loss of his favorite daughter, whom he believed to be dead. "Why haven't you tried *your* tracking skills, if you're so convinced everyone else's skills are somehow inferior?"

"You sniveling youngster," Reg snarled, standing there with numbers of items dangling from cords around his neck, "She's probably still alive. I look for her now, because she asked to go with me on this trip, and I promised to take her."

"You lie," Mongwire spat out the words, outraged. He didn't want his daughter's memory besmirched.

"In the name of Mother Earth, peace between you!" At, their spirit intermediary, called out sharply, concerned for a peaceful launch so as not to anger the gods. At was the fifth brother, also an elder.

"Stay out of it, Go-Between!" Reg hissed, the dangling items dancing in his agitation. "Our youngest elder, Mongwire, has forgotten his place!" he offered as explanation only slightly calmer. Any explanation was rare for Reg. He was becoming quite red in the face, visible despite his early summer's tan. A large vein in the center of his forehead grew large and throbbed.

Women and some of the younger men stood staring, having no idea what would follow the outbursts. Children stood closer to parents. Dogs shrank back, tails between their legs.

"Enough," At said stronger, advancing on Reg. "You could bring the gods' disfavor on this voyage by your strife."

"Very well," Reg said, controlling the volume of his sound, but not the anger passing by his teeth while holding At with his cold eyes. "Vaima, come over here! You'll be privileged to take Lefa's place. Elma, bring her provisions."

Some of the SealEaters finally realized Reg intended to take a female along probably for his needs, not that he had been interested in accommodating Lefa's request. Horror slithered through the group of people at the Cove. Vaima was selected because of At's rebuke. Reg would aim to hurt At by taking Vaima. Vaima was distraught. As strong as she was, Vaima collapsed to the ground in tears. She was only thirteen and not a woman yet. She had no illusions what Reg would do. At knew exactly what Reg would do. Ice knifed down his spine, as he realized too late the burden his daughter would bear for his stand against Reg this time.

At walked defiantly up to Reg and faced him. "You're not taking Vaima on this trip! I give no permission for my daughter to go with you!"

Reg punched At in the face knocking out two teeth and dislocating his jaw. When At fell to the ground, Reg kicked and punched him in the gut with every bit of force he had. At was for a while incapable of making a sound or rising from the ground.

Reg glared at Elma. "I said, 'Bring her provisions!' Do it now!"

Elma, At's second wife, ran to her hut. She put Vaima's clothes in a bladder and tied it closed. She put dried meat in another bladder, tying it tight. She was terrified and frightened witless for her daughter. She complied quickly for fear for her own life, if she failed to do as she was told.

Reg strode over to Vaima and pulled her arm. "Stand up. Go sit in my boat. Now!" he roared.

For the first time in her life, she glared back and defiantly dared to say, "No!"

Reg slapped her hard and told Blad and Afte-ba, two of his sons, "Tie her up and throw her into my boat along with the provisions from Elma."

From the distance on the hilltop, it was a little difficult to be certain who each individual person at the Cove was. Litmaq nudged Lefa. "It looks like they're tying up one of the girls. I can't tell who it is. Well, whoever it is now lies in Reg's boat. Looks like however they tied her, she cannot throw herself out of the boat."

"Beast!" Lefa snarled in a low voice, eyes still fixed on the people below. She wished she had far vision as clear as Litmaq had. "That evil beast! He'd have done the same with me. Just after the big fight he had with my father, when Reg saw me at the edge of the woods and told me I was going on this trip with him. I froze. I didn't know what to think. Then, he just walked off laughing his evil laugh."

"It wasn't you, Little Rabbit," he said using his favorite term of endearment. "Any female would do. Reg just likes to show that he's more of a man than any other. He chose you because he fought with your father. He doesn't care how he affects others, unless he wants to hurt somebody. Reg thinks only of himself. You know that. He wants to make himself stronger, more powerful than any other man. He wanted to hurt your father. Reg knew if he took you, Mongwire would hurt terribly for fear of what Reg would do to you. That's why I had to remove you from Reg's reach. How he became the tallest man by far is a mystery—his strength, probably stronger than any two men or even three—prevents our fighting back. Everyone's afraid of him. So, he achieves his desires. Reg wants to be chief and knows that's impossible. Not being able to become chief only adds dry wood to his fearsome fire."

"Why can't he become chief?" Lefa asked.

"I don't know," Litmaq replied.

Lefa circled his left bent leg in her arms and laid her head on his knee. She still had her eyes on the Cove below.

Back down at the Cove, men who would be on the voyage were taking their leave of family and friends.

"Blad," Reg shouted to his son. "Bring your provisions. I need another rower."

With utter lack of enthusiasm, Blad went to the hut and gathered his provisions. He did not want to take this trip at all. He hoped to take Kol as wife in his father's absence, convinced that his father would block any effort of his to take a wife as long as he was present. Blad knew his plan just died. No surprise.

Merlan, At's first wife, had finished wiping the blood from her husband's face and tried to comfort Elma, At's second wife, whose daughter still sobbed on Reg's boat. The SealEaters walked circumspectly trying to avoid another blast from Reg. Men began to move from their family groups towards the boats. It was almost high sun. They planned that time for leaving to coincide with the outgoing tide and to provide daylight for a good part of the first day.

Whug walked over to the boat his sons, Urch and Emuka, would take. They embraced without comment. Whug stood back looking at his sons.

Each was sturdy of body. Handsome men. Men of good reputation. Sons to make a father proud.

"It'll be good to be away from the seal stink for a while," Urch said to lighten the tension that surrounded their leaving.

"It really bothers you?" Emuka laughed.

"It does. When the wind blows the stink down from there to here, I almost heave up my stomach contents. I also need to leave for a while. It's too hard to obtain a wife. Several of the young women really stir me, Kol most of all. It angers me that elders can have several wives, while we are permitted none. It isn't right somehow." He looked directly at his father.

"Well, you've tried to change that," Emuka said defensively of his father.

"That effort falls on ears that refuse to hear. They all have to agree to our taking a wife. As long as Reg lives, we'll have none, while the elders can take as many wives as they choose—anyone as long as she's not already a wife, simply by demanding it. Even fathers of the girls can't prevent actions of the elders," Urch said, looking pointedly at Whug again.

"I know," his father replied. "I hope to try again while Reg is gone."

Urch said quietly, "My fragile hope is that we find women where we go. Maybe another way of living."

"Urch, what a thought! Do you really think it's possible?" his brother asked.

"I said, *fragile hope*."

"Yes, you did."

Cattu, their half-sister ran to the boat and threw herself at Urch. He hugged her. Then Emuka hugged her.

"Be good and helpful at home while we're gone. Promise?" he asked her, his beard tickling her neck.

Cattu nodded, choked up, not wanting them to leave.

"Now, go back to Amegulatuga," Urch told her. "It's too busy out here. You could be in the way and be hurt."

With tears in her eyes, Cattu turned and walked back to where her mother stood.

"Pretty little thing, if you like red hair," Urch said, smiling at his brother, teasing. They adored Cattu.

"She has the most expressive eyes of anyone here—green as new spring leaves," Emuka said. "I hope when she becomes a wife, her husband will be kind to her."

"Me too." Urch moved away to a large log where he climbed up and stood, stretching his arms wide to the sides.

"Attention," he called in his loudest voice. "Attention."

The SealEaters with the exceptions of Vaima and At moved toward the log.

Urch stood straight and tall. At forty-four, he was still a good looking man. There was no gray in his long, thick curvy brown hair. His body looked like a man much younger. He had never broken a bone. "You will remember us! By Mother Earth's provision and Father Sky's life-giving warmth, you will remember us! With the love of the Pale-Faced Moon, you will remember us. By the Water that always moves and the Hearth Fire that keeps us warmly circled, you will remember us! Be here when we return in the warm time of the year—not next year—but the year after that. Continue your loyalty to our chief. Whug leads you well. Care for the elders who remain. Be loyal. Grow stronger. We hope to find a better land for all of us. Wish us well. Remember us. We are SealEaters!"

Three times those who would remain at the Cove replied, "We are SealEaters! We will remember you!"

The voyagers turned and headed to their boats, pushing the watercraft into the water.

"I need help—over here!" Reg called out.

Urch, Murke, Torq, and Wapa helped Reg push his heavy, wooden boat into the water. The men boarded their boats and headed to sea, not looking back. Most of the SealEaters stood very still watching them leave.

At continued to lie on the ground in severe pain. His snow white beard bloodstained, still brilliant red in stripes that continued to drip. Merlan, his first wife, and Elma, his second wife, were beside him trying to comfort him and decide how to take care of the damage.

"Is his jaw broken?" Waywap, Reg's first wife, asked. She had left her watching place to come to help.

At gave the hunter's hand sign signifying "no."

"Do you want me to try to put it back in place? By Mother Earth, I've had to do this more times than I can count!" The ever present smile in her happy round face put Merlan and Elma at ease. How Waywap could be such a happy person as wife to Reg was a great mystery to all the SealEaters. For her it was simple.

The two women gladly concurred and moved aside. Waywap looked at At's tortured face. "This will hurt worse for a moment, but then it'll feel better."

He simply looked at her, accepting the inevitable.

"Bring some soft leather strips. His jaw needs to be tied in place for a while," she told the women. Elma ran to the hut to gather some soft leather strips long enough to place under At's jaw and tie over his head. Merlan stroked At's hand which she'd already been holding.

With some twisting and tugging and much groaning on her part, Waywap managed to put the jaw back into its proper place. She was a very strong woman, and it was clear she had experience doing what she just did. Merlan began to tie the first strip.

"Make it tight so he doesn't have to clench his muscles to keep it still," Waywap told Merlan. "Then, place him under your canopy. He won't be bringing home a seal today. He should rest. I'll tell my son, Afte-ba, to bring you a seal." She looked at At. "Afte-ba knows what you're feeling, At. I can't count the times . . . ." Waywap muttered turning to head to her hut.

Whug stood with his walking stick in hand. He looked after the boats which were beginning to disappear over the horizon. Whug could not eliminate from memory the sound of Vaima's sobs from where she had been tied up in Reg's boat. What Reg did was so wrong, yet their way of living permitted it. Whug was alarmed, convinced that what they did violated the spirit of Mother Earth and the strength of Father Sky. He was powerless to change it for he'd tried, but with Reg there, young males were forbidden wives, while the elders had as many as they chose—wanting fewer than they had. Whug knew many men wanted to take wives. He did not know how many women wanted husbands. It was, he realized in a flash of understanding, not a good place to grow up female. Whug was glad he was male—and an elder. Shading his eyes against the sun, he turned and the third tallest mountain caught his attention.

"Forth," Whug called to his brother, the fourth son and also an elder. Forth came at his bidding. "What is it, Chief?"

"I think I know where Lefa is. I think I know why she was not here today."

"Why didn't you say something?" Forth replied dumbfounded.

Whug looked away. He turned and looked directly into Forth's eyes. "She loves someone, deeply loves someone," he replied.

"That gives her no right to ask Reg to take her on a voyage and then run away. She should be punished for all the effort she's caused us."

"Forth," Whug said aghast. "Reg lied about Lefa. She wouldn't ask to go with him. Reg was trying to hurt Mongwire for arguing against him several days ago. She's Mongwire's favorite daughter, so Reg decided to take her and use her on the voyage. You know what he'd have done to her, if she'd been here. So did Lefa. Lefa'd be facing the same fate as Vaima."

"Yeah. Reg does lie. It just sounded like fact to me." Forth was feeling a little discomfort.

"I rarely believe anything Reg says," Whug stated, drawing with his staff in the sand at his feet. "It's best with Reg to look for proof of what he says. Reg is not worthy of trust. On a different subject, you've never had any interest in Lefa, have you?"

"Me? By the power of Father Sky, Whug, I have three wives. Do I want another? Not at all. I have trouble keeping peace at my hearth as it is. I only took Nomamat as my third wife because Quapiti, my second wife, said Nomamat was pregnant and needed to have a husband before people discovered it. That's the same way I obtained my second wife. It's crazy."

"That's all Reg's fault. I have some thoughts, but I need to check a little more before I share those thoughts," Whug said quietly. "I need to find Amoroz."

"I saw him heading to the Seal Beach," Forth said trying to be helpful and wondering at Whug's strange comments.

Whug headed towards the Seal Beach. He held his walking stick tighter than he normally did. His knuckles were pale from the stress. From time-to-time Whug glanced toward the hills. He was certain where the two young people were.

"Chief," Amoroz, the second brother, also an elder and Whug's closest friend, called to him. "All have disappeared over the horizon. It seems to be a fair start."

"It does," Whug agreed, though he expected difficulty on the voyage because of Reg. "I have a strange question for you, Amoroz."

"Ask," Amoroz replied.

"Have you any interest in another wife?"

"By the gods, no! I only took Tone to protect her, because she would give birth. You know she could have been drowned for being pregnant while not a wife. I'd prefer to have one wife, not two. Why are you asking me that?"

"I'm doing some thinking and will share when I'm a little clearer about what to do."

"Sounds interesting. I'm eager to hear." Amoroz turned his attention to the seal he'd just killed.

"Do you want help carrying that seal?" Whug asked.

"I'd appreciate your help. Take some to share with your family. It'll feed you and yours for two days at least, now that you're missing two sons, that is."

"I'm grateful, Amoroz."

"Well, I thank you for your help transporting."

The two men carried the seal to the Cove. It had been gutted and they'd finish up back where it didn't smell quite so awful.

When they arrived at the Cove, Amoroz and his wife, Fluga, set about skinning and butchering the seal. Whug headed toward At's canopy over the entry to his hut. The canopy consisted of six seal skins, a barrier to the sun and weather just outside the hut opening. It provided the only protection from the sun, short of entering the hut or going to the forest.

"I'm so sorry to see the damage done to you today," Whug said to At, knowing he could not reply.

"I was crazy," At hunter signed to Whug.

"It's more that we have a serious problem with Reg," Whug said, leaning on his staff.

At nodded.

"I pray that Vaima will do well," Whug said, not at all certain that the prayer would reach any of the gods or receive a favorable response, if it did.

"I was crazy," At signed again.

"Don't blame yourself. It's Reg who's crazy, not you. I have a strange question for you, At. Have you any interest in another wife?"

At signed, "You are crazy!" to which Whug laughed a little too long and loud.

Whug headed toward his hut. He noticed his son, Oppermatu, was down by the water's edge. Whug joined him there.

"Greetings, Father," Oppermatu said with a large smile.

"It will be strange with your brothers gone," Whug said standing tall and straight, his eyes shaded with his free hand against the sun.

"I already feel the loss," his son replied.

"Will you go with me to the hills beyond?" He used his hand to indicate which hills.

"Of course, Father. Will you tell me why?"

"You must discuss this with no one." Whug gave him a knowing look.

"Very well," Oppermatu said quietly and with more seriousness than usual.

"I think I know where Lefa is. I think she is safe with Litmaq."

"You mean they ran off together?"

"No, Litmaq left long before she did. He claimed to be going on a hunt."

"That's right," Oppermatu replied, remembering.

"I think Litmaq prepared a place for her. He must've known Reg's plan to take her. I suspect Reg boasted to Lefa that he'd take her on the voyage, just to make her tremble with fear."

"Sounds like Reg!" Oppermatu spat out the words. He hated his uncle.

"I have a plan," Whug said, "First, I want us to go to where the young people hide, before they do something such as leave the area."

"You think they'd do that? It's not safe. There are fights and wars among the peoples of this land."

"That's why I want to leave as soon as possible. While Reg's gone, I want to make it possible for all you men who want wives to take them without our approval. None of the elders who remain want another wife. That frees up all who are here. We need to make changes while we can."

"That's wonderful!" Oppermatu said, almost overjoyed. He had waited so long. Was it possible, he wondered, that he might finally have a wife? "Father," Oppermatu murmured, "How do you know where they are?"

"When we had the terrible sickness . . . you were not yet born . . . some of us fled to the hills."

"But, we were never hill people. We're told thick forests were predator nightmares and full of evil spirits of sickness," Oppermatu said.

"True, that's why a few of us fled to the hills. We didn't believe what we were told and felt safe there, because others feared it. All of us who fled there no longer breathe air, except for me. There's a rock shelter up on that third largest hill. It was not natural but rather constructed by people before we came to this land. Rocks aren't placed like that by the gods when they made the earth. Whoever placed the rocks were strong people, much stronger than Reg. The rocks are huge. It served us well during the time of the terrible sickness. It was in the thickest part of the forest."

"It still sounds like someplace I'd prefer to avoid."

"Well, that's where we're going to go to find Litmaq and Lefa. Litmaq must've found it during some of his times of hunting alone. I'm sure I've seen smoke and heat waves rising above the place, even though it was almost invisible. We'll find them there, if they haven't already returned or fled from us. Aren't you the least bit curious to see this rock shelter?"

"I suppose—a little. I just have a dread about thick, dark forests."

"I understand, Son. A lot of people believe that's where the terrible sickness came from. I lived where we're going, Op. It's safe. The thing about thick, dark forests is that we are better prey for cats in such places. You just need to keep your hunter awareness active. Otherwise, it's no different from anywhere else."

"When do we leave?"

"Now. Let's gather our spears and some dried seal and be gone."

They gathered their things and began to walk to the path that led into the hills. On the way they passed Amoroz who was pouring water over Fluga's hands.

"Well," Whug said with a smile, "Reg hasn't turned around yet."

The two brothers, Whug and Amoroz had a good, strong healthy laugh. There had to be more to the laugh than just what was said. Oppermatu knew he missed something, but then he had some special connections with his brothers. Oppermatu understood. He was just glad Reg hadn't turned around. It would be very good for SealEaters at the Cove with Reg gone.

After butchering the seals, Amoroz and Fluga carried meat to Amegulatuga as Amoroz had promised Whug earlier. With Whug and Oppermatu gone, only Amegulatuga and her three children remained at Whug's huts. Amegulatuga thanked Amoroz and Fluga profusely for the seal. He cut off some of the meat to cook for that night and carried the remainder to the hut Whug had made for meat storage. Both Sted and Nip helped her with the meat. Cattu stood back trying not to put herself in the way of others. Cattu didn't look like any of the SealEaters. Whug said she had the gold red hair and brilliant green eye color of his mother. It stood out, and because of it, she was often teased or shunned by other children, sometimes by adults. Reg had kicked her once.

Behind the meat hut just in the woods, Emu, Amoroz's son, and Tink, Reg's first daughter, were embracing. Emu placed his hands on either side of Tink's round face which he adored. She was short and looked just like her mother, Waywap. Waywap was strong and knew many things. She was adorably made, always looking young for her age. Her visual facial features made her physical and character strength and knowledge secondary in the thinking places of many. Without fear, Emu looked deeply into Tink's eyes and she shared back the deep look with her own. They enjoyed a moment of freedom, of joy. With Reg over the horizon, they felt comfortable enough to do what they had desired for many years. As time passed, their bravery increased and they entered deeper and deeper into the woods.

The woods into which they moved was the lowland just before the tallest hill. Hunters liked the area because of the occasional deer they found there. Whug and Oppermatu had made good time through the same forested area. The pungent scent of evergreen growth pleased the men. It was a scent that made them think of good, fresh air. They were about to exit it. They headed towards the creek they had to pass to reach the tallest hill from which they'd traverse a valley to the third tallest hill. Whug had the way imprinted since the time of his life there. They were doing well.

Meanwhile back at the Cove, Momomu and Begalit, sons of Amoroz, walked the shoreline. As they'd done as children, they occasionally kicked at the salt water as they walked. They headed south from the Cove.

"I wish I had been permitted to go on the voyage," Momomu said, his brown thinning hair blowing about in the light breeze.

"Not me," Begalit said firmly. "I don't like being at sea. When you can't see land anymore, I become fearful of the great waves that rise up from the deep."

"You always did take the fun out of adventure by reasoning too much what could happen." He poked his brother's arm. "They'll have various forms of sea ice the whole way," Momomu said, repeating what he'd heard the voyagers say.

"Have you ever tried to pull a boat up on sea ice?" Begalit asked with some irritation.

"You know I've never been given permission to go. Until this trip, you always were able to go."

Begalit looked at Momomu. "You have a dreamer's idea of what the voyage will bring. I would be surprised if two people return. If five return I'll have much difficulty believing it."

"Five of thirteen?"

"Yes. They risk much to find us a new land. Most of what they risk is their lives. Just suppose they find ice-free land. There may be people living there. Those people may not want us there. They could make war on them," Begalit stated flatly.

"I hadn't considered others living there."

"If we're considering it, don't even give time to the thought that others haven't thought the same thoughts before we did."

"I didn't think of other people at all," Momomu admitted.

Begalit replied forgetting to keep emotion in check. "That's what's wrong with the voyage! Nobody ever talked about that possibility! I wanted to bring it up at one of our meetings, but father said to remain silent."

"Why'd he do that?" Momomu asked surprised at his brother's outburst.

"I don't know," Begalit replied dispirited.

"Look over there near Forth's hut. Kol is something to see!" Momomu stopped and stared. "She'd be beautiful, if she weren't so thin. She looks as if she'd break in a strong wind."

"She loves Urch," Begalit said with authority. "She started to lose her fat when she found he was going on the voyage."

"What if someone claims her? She has no say in selection of a husband."

"Brother, you need to reason more. You don't want a wife who doesn't want you."

"Well, they don't have a choice," Momomu said confused.

"Do you remember when Reg took Ipsalu?" Begalit asked.

"That was a long time ago." He paused. "That was five years ago by my reckoning."

"You're right. Ipsalu hadn't become woman yet. Reg didn't care. He liked the way Ipsalu looked. Her dark black hair shines beautifully—still does. Reg terrified her. She fought him for a while from fear and anger. He never was gentle with Ipsalu. She hated him and refused even to pretend she wanted him. He broke her spirit because of the way she acted. The emptiness in her spirit comes from fighting a battle she could never win. It was a battle he could have won any time, but he let Ipsalu think she could fight. Reg played with her like a cat will sometimes play with its prey. Ipsalu put up quite a fight at first. Her fight gave Reg the chance to shame her for being a bad woman and her parents for not raising her to know her place. I think he liked the fight in her in the beginning. Then Reg seemed to torture her apparently for the fun of it. He's a very mean man. Now she just seems like an empty shell. The life is gone though she breathes air. I worry for Vaima. He'll probably do the same to her. Reg didn't even claim her as wife—just demanded she go with him. Taking a wife who doesn't want you produces a woman like Ipsalu, maybe lovely to look at but utterly empty on the inside."

"So if I want a wife, I should talk to the woman. I should ask her if she would like to be my wife?"

"That's a very good thought, Momomu." Begalit looked at his brother as if he didn't know him at all.

"Thank you. I'll remember that."

Begalit was shocked at the conversation with his brother. How could he have lived so long and not known to ask a woman, if she'd want to be his wife? Begalit was just astonished. Yet, he realized as he reasoned, not taking the time to consider a woman's feelings might now be normal among his people. He might be the abnormal one. Begalit and Momomu had both seen Whug and Gemu when she was alive. They loved each other. It was a real love, sacrificing self for the other. They considered each other in all things. They were gentle with each other. Their parents, Amoroz and Fluga, had a lot of consideration for the other, but not as much as he saw in Whug and Gemu. Begalit was confident of one thing: the gods approved of the way his parents and his uncle and aunt lived, not the way of Reg. He didn't know how to supply proof of this view, but he was sure he was right. At least, he smiled to himself at the thought, Momomu accepted what he said without requiring proof.

"You know who attracts me?" Momomu asked.

"Who?" Begalit asked, surprised.

"Belah," his brother said with a big grin.

"She's great!" Begalit said, almost relieved. Belah would be a wonderful wife for his brother.

A little further down the water's edge, Cudmea and Kol were gathering sea weeds into a basket Cudmea carried.

"Are you well?" Cudmea asked Kol.

"Yes," she replied flatly. "I just pray Urch returns home alive." She looked carefully at her brother. "You know my secret, don't you?" she whispered.

"Oh, no. You don't mean?"

"I mean I carry Urch's child even now." She smiled a sweet smile just thinking of it.

"What will you do?" he asked. "They could drown you for this." Cudmea was horrified. He and his sister had always been close. This diversion from the norm was disturbing to him and he was trying to recover balance quickly.

"I will ask Whug to take me as wife and give me to Urch when he returns. I just went to find him only to discover that he and Oppermatu have gone hunting for a few days."

"I hope for your sake and for Urch's sake he agrees."

"I also." She smiled and continued cutting meat and greens into pieces the right size for the stew that Forth wanted for dinner that night.

"Does Urch know?"

"No, I didn't tell him. He knew there was a severe risk in the trip. He hoped I'd become a wife, since he fully expects to die on the adventure."

"How awful! He didn't have to go, did he?"

"Reg asked him to go because of his navigational skills. How does anyone refuse Reg? He feared that if he refused, Reg would do to me what he's done to Vaima. And he was probably right."

Cudmea looked to the west. Still he saw no evidence that anyone had turned around. He was unsure that he could feel relief until it had been days that they'd been at sea, and then, they could still return.

Far, far to the west the little boats were edging along the sea ice. They were not tied together, but they were very carefully steered in order to stay together. Reg was the most concerned, because he could not travel as fast as the little boats. His boat also lacked agility.

Out on the water, Reg stopped rowing for a short time and untied Vaima. "Sit here," he said, "You're going to row, now," he declared. "Do your best job. I want to see effort."

Vaima sat where he told her and rowed hard. When she began to tire, she forced her thinking place elsewhere and continued to row despite the burn of her muscles.

Maber and Blad, Reg's sons both breathed a sigh of relief. They had feared what would happen if Vaima fought Reg out on the sea. When Urch noticed it from his boat, he was surprised, but tried to hope that all would be well. He knew it would be a long voyage.

Urch's thoughts were back at the Cove. He and Kol had let their passion have freedom before he left. He wondered whether anything had come of it. He was certain if they produced a child, his father would take Kol as wife to protect her. He groaned to himself just thinking of her. He hated the way they lived. It had to change. He decided if he made it back, he would do every-thing he could to make change so he could take Kol as wife. Nothing else, even his life, mattered. If he had to fight Reg, so be it. He thought back to the beauty of the hills that surrounded the Cove. It looked so peaceful. Under the way it looked on the outside, it wasn't peaceful in reality. The way they lived produced needless misery. It could no longer be tolerated. It had to end.

Back on the same hills that filled Urch's thinking place, Whug and Oppermatu had made it to the valley and stopped by a stream to drink water and eat a bit of jerky. Both men had pushed as hard as possible to reach the rock shelter before night. As far as Whug knew, this path was the only one that led from the hilltop down. It was an animal trail and from the low land it was hard to find, unless you knew it existed.

Quietly they ascended the path to the near top of the hill.

When they reached the rock shelter, it was clear that the two young people were presently in the area, but were not in the shelter. Both he and Oppermatu had made as little noise as possible. Whug signed for Oppermatu to be very quiet. Oppermatu was astonished to see the rock shelter. In quality it surpassed their huts. He took in every detail.

Whug called out gently, "Litmaq and Lefa, it's your chief. Come to the shelter. All is well."

Lefa was startled and jumped at the sound. Litmaq took her arms and pulled her up. "Come, let us talk." He took her hand and they returned to the rock shelter.

All sat on skins around the tiny hearth.

"How did you find this place, Litmaq?" Whug asked.

"One day I decided to track you, Chief. I wanted to know whether I could. I had been working on my tracking skills, and I know you try to leave no trace. When I found this place, you had already left. I don't know how we missed each other. I was stunned, when I saw the stone structure and put the place in memory. It's a special place."

"It is a special place," Whug admitted. "My first child, a girl, died while we hid here from the terrible sickness. We buried her over there under that ledge."

"That was during the time of the terrible sickness? That was long ago!"

"Yes it was. This place is in such a secluded forest and such a thick one, Gemu and I thought we'd be safe from others who might carry the sickness. No one ever found us here. It was a lonely time, but we were saved by staying here. I see you know the voyagers have slipped over the horizon."

"Yes," Litmaq replied, "We watched from the wall. I was wondering whether it was safe ever to return to the Cove."

"It's safe. That's why we're here. I feared you might flee, and we came as fast as possible to let you know things will change. By the way, how did you know when Lefa should meet you?"

"The clouds. When they look like bird toes to the northwest. The way the clouds formed made it clear that we'd have a big storm within a few days. I told her that when the rain began to come down hard to slip away unseen. We had another plan if it didn't rain hard, but fortunately it did. I had her meet me by the meat keeping pond in the rain. I had another way of going to the creek. We took that way. I led her to the shelter through the forest. That was some storm! Now, I have a question. How did you know we were here?" Litmaq asked.

"Gemu and I lived here. I knew about this place and am aware of no other place where you'd be safe in this area. So at night I'd look for smoke and heat waves. It was very tough seeing them. You must have had a very small hearth."

"As you can see," Litmaq used the hand signal for look.

"I noticed that as soon as we arrived. You reason well, Litmaq. Lefa, are you well?"

"Yes, Chief. I am saddened to know that Reg took another girl. Who had to go with him?"

"It was Vaima."

"Why? She's not even woman yet." Lefa wrapped her arms about herself.

"That matters not to Reg. He argued with At and, suddenly, Vaima was tied and thrown into his boat."

"Poor girl. I think At must be feeling awful."

"He feels that what happened to Vaima is his fault. Of course, it's not. It's Reg's fault. At hurts for two reasons. He stood up to Reg. Because of that, Reg dislocated his jaw."

Lefa and Litmaq winced.

"Father, tell them your plan," Oppermatu said with some excitement.

"Of course. That's why we're here. My plan is to gather the elders and others and let it be known that any who want to take wives may do so. Reg is not here to interfere. What we've done is wrong. It's time to change. If Reg makes it back, he cannot change what we do in his absence. Litmaq, you'll be able to have Lefa as your wife as soon as we have the meeting."

For a moment all were startled as Lefa leapt into the ready arms of Litmaq, burying her head in his shoulder. Then, there was laughter among them all.

Lefa said quietly. "Chief, it's always said that the man takes a wife. Can you not make a change that gives the woman some say in the matter? Suppose someone else claims me before Litmaq does. That would make my life unbearable. I am here because I love Litmaq. I have loved him since we were children playing together."

"Agreed. That's also how I knew you were together. I have watched your love for a long time. It's the same love I shared with Gemu. I will propose to the elders that we restore the right of refusal to the woman. Before the terrible sickness women had the right. They lost it when some didn't want a husband after losing theirs to the sickness. All remaining elders will agree to restore the right. I've already asked the remaining elders; not one of them wants another wife. I certainly don't. Vaima's sobs still fill my thinking place. What we do tomorrow will prevent that from happening again."

"How wonderful!" Litmaq said, looking at Oppermatu. Is anyone hungry? I have a roast of deer under that skin. Cut some to please yourself. There's plenty."

Each person cut off what they wanted and ate silently. All but Lefa went back for more.

"We go black here tonight and tomorrow we return to the Cove," Whug said with authority.

Lefa curled up on the skin toward the back of the rock shelter. There were evergreen branches under the skin that softened the sleeping place and gave off a special fragrance. She thought she'd never been happier in her life, until she remembered the thirteen year old girl on Reg's boat. She looked up into the pale face of the full moon. She whispered, "Moon above, through your love, keep Vaima safe and whole. Do not allow Reg to do to her what he did to Ipsalu. Intervene on her behalf, I beg of you."

Litmaq put his arm around her and drew her to him. "Moon above, I ask the same."

"So do I," Whug added.

"I, too," Oppermatu said.

Silence fell upon the group and they went black. Dreams were about to be realized.

Through the darkness and from the land of dreams, dawn rose with a shaft of light aimed at a hut at the Cove. It entered At's hut, awakening him when the light moved to his left eye. A spider lowering itself over his head climbed rapidly back up the strand when the light hit it. At's instant thought was the absence of Vaima. That was a living nightmare to him. His eyes watered. Pain stabbed his jaw muscles. He raised up on his sleeping place and prepared to arise. Another day. His movement awakened his wife, Merlan, who stretched beside him. At stood, wrapped his elk skin around his shoulders, and went to the woods. Merlan would soon follow.

Early risers were beginning their day. A melodious birdsong welcomed the warmth of the sun as it rose over the mountains in the east bringing warmth and light. The bird scratched its head and left.

Returning to his hut from the forest At noticed Egorgo standing beside the path. She was not supposed to be near the men's path into the forest. That was their private place. He signed for her to leave. She snubbed him.

Egorgo was considered exotic. Her sexually attractive appearance arrested most of the men. She had dark brown hair and very dark eyebrows that looked like raven wings to At. Egorgo's skin was exceptionally pale, and she had piercing sky blue eyes. Her full lips seemed to have been stained by red berries, but he knew better. Her lip color was natural. Egorgo stood there with her hips uneven stroking her thigh, looking at him at one time seeming to issue an invitation and the next seeming to display defiance. To At the message was unclear and totally unacceptable. Signing at her to move to an area not reserved for men, he was appalled to see that she continued to remain in place.

At wondered whether she mocked him. Finally, he cared less about her motivation and more about her defiance. With a sharp spring in his step, he grabbed her and wrestled her to the ground to gain a hold on her arms to pin them behind her. Egorgo's strength surprised At. He grabbed the closest limb on the ground he could find and with his knee in her back to hold her down, he pulled the excess branches from the limb and struck her severely with it. He did so repeatedly. In the struggle her head bumped his jaw, sending searing pain. He did not let her go, despite his pain. Her screams awakened any who remained in the black.

Then, At held her arms behind her and shoved her toward Reg's hut. At found Afte-ba, Reg's son, and shoved the girl to the ground at his feet. At signed what had happened. Afte-ba was horrified. Reg would have drowned her for doing that, and he told her so.

Egorgo spat out, "My father is . . . NOT . . . here!"

Afte-ba slapped her across the mouth.

She glared at him.

Afte-ba slapped her harder multiple times to the point that she fell to the ground and wept. "I hope that finally brought the message through to her. Thank you, At. As we all know, she has been somewhat of a problem. She needs a husband but nobody wants her—for obvious reasons."

"I leave now," At signed.

"You're a good man. Sorry about Vaima. My father is another problem."

At turned and looked at Afte-ba with sad eyes. He signed. "Speak gently of your father. He is your father."

Admonished, Afte-ba said, "Thank you, At. I do sometimes need reminding."

At smiled sadly, turned, and left for his place under the canopy of his hut.

Waywap came from the hut and saw her daughter curled up on the ground. She knew what had occurred.

"Daughter," Waywap said. "You disappoint me. You bring shame upon our family. If you continue, someone will drown you. Don't think just because Reg is your father you're safe somehow. What you do is the fecal waste of fools."

Egorgo was in pain. She heard her mother, but she did not respond either in word or deed. She continued to lie there unmoving.

Afte-ba looked at his mother. Then, he said, "Egorgo, arise—now! Go inside the hut and do not leave it for three days. If you disobey, I will drown you."

Egorgo pushed herself up to a sitting position. Her face was bright red. She made no further movement, so Afte-ba jerked her to her feet.

"Do you understand what I just told you?" he demanded glaring at her.

Egorgo nodded affirmative.

"Then, go in there. I don't wish to see you," he said shoving her into the hut. Waywap followed the girl into the hut to clean the cuts on her skin. There were many.

Egorgo was struggling internally. Her brother had never treated her so badly. She wanted to have him hug her to make it all go away, as he had done in the past when her father punished her. Though it didn't show, she was frightened. She was certain her brother was deadly serious. She thought, her father wasn't really gone. He'd just reappeared in Afte-ba. Egorgo stumbled her way to the hut and her sleeping place. She lay down there, thinking of having to stay there for three days.

Egorgo's incident was no secret. Everyone at the Cove heard it. They couldn't hear what At signed, but everyone knew Egorgo. Anyone age ten or over knew that Egorgo was very provocative. At was not someone to provoke.

As the morning turned to high sun, people moved about. Many wondered where Whug had gone and when he'd return.

By early afternoon Whug, Oppermatu, Litmaq, and Lefa exited the forest far to the east and instantly the SealEaters saw them. All were curious. It would be bad manners to rush up to inquire where Litmaq and Lefa had been, but all were aflame with curiosity. Lefa stopped at Mongwire's hut, her home. Litmaq went to At's hut to put his spears into their place and unload his travel gear.

Whug found Amoroz gathering wood at the forest edge.

"Chief," Amoroz called, "I would like to speak with you."

"And I with you," Whug replied.

"You, first," Amoroz said with deference.

"In Reg's absence I think it time to correct some injustices we've been permitting. I think that men should take wives, and that the women should have the right of refusal restored. SealEaters should no longer require our approval to take wives."

Amoroz stared at Whug without showing any emotion at all. Bags under his eyes were prominent. They floated over dark shadows. He was thinking through what Whug proposed. Finally, he replied, "I agree."

"After we eat this evening?" Whug asked.

Amoroz nodded.

Whug went to At's hut. He told him the same thing, and At agreed. Whug obtained agreement from Forth as well. Reg and Mongwire were both on the voyage; there was never a substitute for an elder.

Not one elder nor Oppermatu, Litmaq, or Lefa divulged any of the information that would be given that evening. Yet, everyone knew there would be an important elders meeting after the evening meal, and all were fascinated because all the SealEaters had been invited to attend, not just the elders. Egorgo was devastated to have to remain in the family hut.

While Whug canvassed the elders, Litmaq and Lefa walked together from the Cove south to the big rocks that stood in deep water. Out of sight of the SealEaters, they embraced for a long time. They knew their lives and the lives of their people were about to make a significant change, thanks to an opportunity during a voyage in search of a new land.

Returning to the Cove from their walk, Litmaq asked, "Did you know that once women had the right of refusal?"

"No. I never heard of such a thing. The Chief made it sound like the terrible sickness made it possible for the elders to remove our rights. I wonder whether there were others they could restore."

"I wouldn't push for a lot of change immediately," Litmaq said quickly.

"Believe me, I'm quite content for the moment. Do you suppose somehow the elders blame us for the terrible sickness?"

"That would not make sense, Little Rabbit."

"When did making sense enter into what SealEaters do?" Lefa partly teased.

Litmaq laughed and swatted at Lefa as he'd swat at a bug. The two went toward the waterfall where they sometimes bathed. They wanted to bathe after being in the forest for so long. They also wanted to honor the meeting with cleanliness and clothing that gave a serious demeanor.

The evening meeting began with much solemnity. The people gathered quietly and sat waiting silently with great expectation.

Whug stood before them all. He cleared his throat. "SealEaters, for some time now, I think we have irritated, if not angered, the gods."

People looked from one to another with some fear. What could they have done to displease the gods? they wondered.

"Long ago, there was a time of a terrible sickness. No one knows what caused the terrible sickness. People coughed and became very hot. They ached awfully so that some had difficulty walking. Many had trouble keeping either food or water in their bellies. People coughed up ugly, bloody mucous. The SealEaters scattered. It was a sickness that one person could give to another. After much time, we came back together, and clearly the sickness had passed."

Whug looked around. There were so few people who knew of that time. He wondered how many heard this for the first time.

"Many of us lost a wife or a husband and children to the terrible sickness. It was a time to pull the SealEaters back together. Unfortunately, many who had lost a husband had no interest in continuing to live, especially if the terrible sickness took their children also. A man would seek a wife and she would use her right of refusal, because she still grieved for her lost husband. It made rebuilding the SealEaters almost impossible. So the elders withdrew the right of refusal for women. Women were furious, but, elders ruled, so it had to be. We were not thinking well at that time, and we set no limit on the time of the withdrawal of the right. Also, at that time we decided that men could take a wife only with the approval of all the elders. We did not anticipate the situation we've experienced with Reg. We just decided that to make a rule to permit a man to take a wife, all elders must concur. It seemed reasonable at the time. We could not have predicted Reg would become what he has become. For those of you who are young—Reg wasn't always like he is now."

Whug let that settle in. Clearly many people had never heard this history.

"I now ask the elders to restore the woman's right of refusal. Do all agree?"

Whug said, "Amoroz?"

Amoroz said, "Yes."

Whug said, "Forth?"

Forth said, "Yes."

Whug said, "At?"

At signed, "Yes."

"And I agree," Whug exclaimed.

The SealEaters were very quiet but looked meaningfully at each other as if in shock.

"Second," Whug continued, "It is so easy during times that are tough to take away the rights of our people. Another right that was removed is that of men taking a wife without approval of all elders. That is absurd and abnormal. Look at nature! Elders, I now ask whether you agree to remove elder approval from a man taking a wife?"

"Amoroz, what do you say?"

"I agree."

"Forth," Whug said, "What do you say?"

"I agree, a man should not require our approval to take a wife."

"At," Whug continued, "What do you say?"

"I agree, that requirement is absurd and abnormal. I readily agree to remove the need for approval by the elders for a man to take a wife."

"And so do I," Whug said.

By this time the SealEaters were still deadly silent but looking from person to person, as if they had not heard correctly. They were bewildered.

"Now, SealEaters, I plan to add some requirements. Before you ask a woman to be your wife, I want to see that you've built a hut and have set up some provisions. I want to talk to each pair, so that I am confident that the woman has been freely able to use her right of refusal."

"Finally, I want from the elders another change. We have used the rule of drowning to reduce strife and to control behaviors. I think we have gone beyond what is reasonable. I want the elders to have to approve without a single dissent any proposed drowning. I do not mean to be lax in our punishment of unacceptable behavior, but I do intend to keep people from being drowned by differences in the heat of the moment. This rule covers all SealEaters. Accepting this rule means no one can independently decide to drown another without the concurrence of all elders. There are many ways to punish those who behave badly. Ending one's life should be the last consideration, not the first."

"Amoroz, do you agree?"

"Yes."

"Forth, do you agree?"

"Yes."

"At, do you agree?"

"Yes."

"And so do I." Whug continued, "That is all. Do not ask a woman to be your wife until you have built your huts and provisioned them."

Left at home alone, Egorgo still could hear. She knew that Afte-ba's threat to drown her now was worthless. She felt emboldened.

As if he sensed what might happen, Afte-ba quickly went to the hut and stood over the girl. "Just in case you think the drowning rule sets you free, Egorgo, let me make this clear. Did you hear there are other methods of punishment that are useful before someone requests the right to drown someone? This I tell you: disobey me, and I will break your legs. Do you understand?"

Egorgo's emboldened spirit disappeared and she shrank back, fully cowered.

"I understand, Afte-ba. I will obey you, as if you were our father."

"You had better obey me better than that. You did not obey our father well."

"I will obey you." She pulled the sleeping skin up to her neck.

Afte-ba left the hut to gather and discuss the event with others, leaving Egorgo to seethe under her covers.

The Cove was alive with excited talk.

Contrary to what they'd been told, Momomu walked over to Belah, one of Reg's daughters, who was carrying water to Reg's hut. He offered to carry the water bladder and whispered to her, "I want you for my wife. I'll be a good husband. Will you be my wife?"

Belah, who genuinely liked Momomu, whispered back, "You're supposed to build the hut before you ask, but, yes. I want you for my husband. I'll refuse any other who asks. You will build the hut quickly?"

"As quickly as possible! I awaken early. I'll be searching for wood before the sun is totally risen."

Belah smiled. Momomu wasn't the best looking, the brightest, or even gifted with a great sense of humor, but he had what she wanted—a steadfastness and loyalty that she could count on for the rest of her days. He was truthful, gentle, and kind. He would consider her and her wishes.

Momomu carried the water bladder all the way to Reg's hut. There was a hole near the top of the water bladder. On a piece of wood from which the hut was constructed, Momomu found the protrusion that had been a tree limb. He hooked the hole at the top of the bladder over the protrusion.

He'd seen it hooked there when he had come to Reg's hut one day. Belah was surprised he'd noticed.

Emu, Amoroz and Fluga's son, and Tink, Reg's oldest daughter, at some distance from each other kept gazing at one another, smiling until they felt their unused smile muscles cry out in discomfort.

Whug climbed up on the large log from which Urch had spoken to all of them the day before. He watched the SealEaters experience their new freedom. He savored all of it. He had done what was right. As he looked to the sky, his chest raised in praise of the gods for showing him what needed to be done. The sun's warmth on his chest affirmed for him that Father Sky approved.

Within a few days twelve new huts stood where there had been nothing but land. One of them was in the forest at its edge. Why Momomu would choose the forest edge for a hut, Whug had no idea. The hut was good sized and Belah seemed delighted with it. The shape was different from the other SealEaters' huts where downfall wood was stood on end leaning into other pieces of approximately the same size. The top was vined or tied with leather strips to provide stability while shorter pieces were added to the exterior to fill the gaps. Mosses and grasses would be stuffed into the gaps and eventually the entire structure would be mudded inside and outside. Momomu built his structure using six trees that formed a four sided base for the structure. He and Belah took smaller fallen trees and tied them from tree to tree horizontally. They added vertical small trees once branches were removed to the horizontal pieces. They collected bundles of grasses from the lowlands beyond the first hills and tied them starting at the bottom of the crosspieces. There was no cover from above. Then, Momomu climbed up the structure and tied a crosspiece to the trees growing in the ground. The crosspiece was a good arm's length higher than all the other sides. The crosspiece was also larger. At one point he had to ask for assistance from Begalit to secure the crosspiece. Once the new crosspiece was well secured, he and Begalit stood on the crosspiece even jumping a bit to try to dislodge it. It was secure. Momomu began to lay smaller downfallen trees from the upper crosspieces to the top edge of the structure on the other side. Tree roots held the new pieces to the uppermost crosspiece. Eventually only the tallest side above the top part of the building remained open. The rest was closed with bundle after bundle of grasses.

Suddenly Whug could see what Momomu was building. The hut had one side taller than the others and there was a top covering that sloped so that rain and snow would slide off. The SealEaters had never conceived of a separate roof. They built cone shaped huts of logs. This building was amazing to all who watched the construction. What was also amazing is that the

SealEaters had considered Momomu slow of understanding, not clever at all. Yet, he had built a home for Belah and his family for the future that was spacious and had an opening for light. A good sized hunter could walk around in the home without hitting his head. A home unlike any that had ever been seen. For days on end, Belah carried skins of beach sand to establish the floor of the structure.

Whug walked over to Momomu and put his hand on the young man's shoulder. "You have done an amazing thing here, Momomu. How did you arrive at this unique plan?"

"I guess, Chief, you could say I dreamed it while I was awake."

"You what?" Whug asked.

"Sometimes, when I sit and stare off into the distance, I can relax my thoughts. When that happens, I see things that could be but aren't. It opens a world to me that is not here, but could be. Do you understand?"

"No," the chief answered honestly. "If anyone here would understand that explanation, it would be At. He talks with those who seemingly could be but aren't."

"Oh, I see what you mean," Momomu said with enthusiasm. "I had never thought of At's talking with the gods as having anything connected with my relaxed thinking place, but I can see now that there may be a link I hadn't recognized. I wonder whether At relaxes his thinking place as I do mine."

"You should ask him sometime," Whug suggested.

"Hi, Chief," Belah said with a great smile. "Have you been inside?"

"No, I haven't," Whug admitted.

"Come in, then," Belah invited, holding the skin that stretched from the top crosspiece to the ground between the middle of one side to the tree attachment.

Whug stepped inside and instead of the dark that met him in his hut, light entered into this one. The floor was even and filled with dry soft sand. He guessed there would be no need of evergreen branches on the floor. But what he saw struck him. There were wooden box-like structures arranged on the floor. One was large.

"Is that where you go black?" he asked incredulously.

"Yes. Try it. The skins Momomu prepared are so soft and comfortable. I've never gone black so well," Belah said showing how pleased she was.

Whug laid himself down on the sleeping place. Lying there he could see out of the opening where the roof began its slope. He could see the hill tops in the distance. The sleeping place was like none he had ever felt anywhere.

His entire thoughts of Momomu changed in an instant, though the change had been growing since he came to examine the structure.

Whug stood up and looked around him. Beside the head part of the sleeping place, there were projections from the tree where limbs had been. Those limb projections held Momomu's spears standing straight, ready to grasp if needed at night or anytime. There were other four-sided objects with seeming solid tops that held stacks of skins and other things, such as winter clothing and boots. Other things such as bladders had their places either stacked or hanging on projections from the trees. Everything was neatly placed in this spacious hut.

Of one thing Whug was certain and he told Momomu and Belah when he left, "There will soon be many of us living in huts like this in the forest. Do you think they'll call us the Forest People?" He laughed.

"No," Momomu said, and with Belah they chorused, "We are SealEaters!" They laughed as Whug turned with a grin to leave.

Chapter 2

Murke's Story

Murke fell and fractured his skull on a rock. Blood poured from the wound as he lay on the ground. Then, the blood stopped flowing. Not long afterwards a white, thin, almost invisible mist rose from Murke's unmoving chest. It rose up slowly, exuding from Murke's chest as if a non-palpable part of him were diffused to the air, manifested as living while leaving behind a cicada type non-viable shell. It should have moved, as the rising of mountain mist in the warmth of a morning sun to the sky above. Instead of rising it hovered over the tunic Murke wore. The white mist moved in the way of an oily substance on a pond, not separating from the water but not joining with it either, certainly not rising upward. The mist joined with nothing. It collected itself, moved from Murke's body to a rock ledge several body lengths away, and it rested on the rock ledge which overlooked a wide valley below with a lake where geese floated with their little ones following in a line behind.

While the white mist lodged on the rock ledge, two people buried the body. They lacked enough dirt to cover the left hand of the body, so it remained sticking out of the soil resting on a rock.

The formless white mist made no apparent acknowledgement of the burial. It simply rested, as if focused on the lake. One could conclude that the part of the mist that arrived at the rock ledge first was its actual front and had adequate vision and intent to arrive there when leaving Murke's chest. That front faced the lake.

'Every time I see a lake, I think of my name! Why did my father, Amoroz, have to name me Murke? I've wondered about that all my days. Murke! A water bird, but not a bird of the sea. A bird with strange feathers atop its head. A water bird of the lakes. SealEaters are not Lake People, but there is a lake downhill from me now. I can see it easily from here. I need to stand up. It's just so inappropriate for me to have such a name. Water bird of the lakes? Almost embarrassing. We are SealEaters. Water birds don't eat seals. But that's my name. Is anybody listening? Why doesn't anyone answer back? How I wish I could talk to my father! I must hear a human voice, even if it's my own. I'm confused, a little disoriented. Where am I?'

'My father. Oh, he was wise to send me instead of going himself on the voyage to find land for our people. My father is a man of great courage—on land. He hates the sea.'

'What in the name of all the gods is wrong with me? I'm confused. I'm so pale I can almost see through myself. Something's wrong. I'll stay calm. I have to stay calm. I'll talk it out, and maybe my memory will return to my thinking place.'

'The sea trip was terrible. I've never been so frightened. The day of the whale killer was enough for me. Oh, I'd seen whale killers, those black and white whales that seek the young of other whales. They surround the babies, separate them from their mother, and kill them for their food. It is the way of life of the sea. This time it was different. We had hauled out on some sea ice that was low and appeared flat on the top. All of us were tired. I wanted to rest. First, we hauled up the bundles which were all tied together on one long cord to keep them secure. Each boat had its own corded bundles. Then, we hauled all the boats up except Reg's giant boat. Rowers on Reg's boat had to tie that one up to a spear we secured in a crack in the ice. Seals began to haul out on the ice we were on, but at the time we didn't need any more seals to eat. We ignored them. They were on the other end of the ice. But the whale killer didn't ignore the seals. The whale killer swam through the water toward the ice we were on, its giant top fin cutting through the water like a new knife through boneless meat. It didn't care about us. It wanted the seals on the other end of the sea ice.'

'At first it tried to throw itself upon the ice far up enough to reach a seal, but it fast learned that wouldn't work. Then, it decided to try to tip the ice over to slide the seals off into the water. Of course, that would have slid us and our boats off into the water. Quickly, Blad and I tied ourselves to a spear in the ice and took our sturdiest spears to which we'd tied a recovery cord. We tried numbers of times to spear the whale killer. Once it realized we were after it, its attention turned to us. Blad with a terrible shout finally speared it in an eye. He lost his spear, but the whale killer left us. Later, the seals also departed. I'll never forget that as long as I live. The beast had huge teeth! It also had a very bad attitude.'

'One thing made us laugh. It was a rude laugh, because we laughed at Reg. We did try to conceal it, but that was difficult. When the seals departed, some of them decided to use Reg's boat for a resting spot. You know seals don't smell good. Reg was furious when he discovered their presence on his boat. He had to fight to remove them permanently from his boat. Then, when his back was turned, they'd hurl themselves back in the boat. Reg became furious because we laughed so loud, he could hear us. It was just something nobody ever expected to see. I will admit that they didn't smell as bad as the ones back home on the Seal Beach. That far out on the water, they probably didn't wallow in their own filth as they do at the Seal Beach.'

'As if that weren't enough, the sea ice is everywhere out there. To think of becoming lost at sea is a horror. Among us there were four boats. SealEaters had to stay together. We could move a little faster and easier through the ice than Reg's boat could. Often he snagged the arm of his boat on the sea ice that didn't show above the water. In our boat I could reckon our direction according to the sun during the day and at night by the star that never moves. That's only partly helpful when the sea ice is tall and along most of our route it was very tall. If we could've just gone in a straight line, it wouldn't have taken so long. As it was, we meandered in and out of the huge masses of ice seemingly forever.'

The mist rose a little and then settled back on the rock ledge.

'I guess I'm complaining a lot. It makes me and my family look bad. My complaints are not without reason, though that doesn't make it right. That trip was the fright of my life. In some ways I'm happy not to have had to make the trip home and back here again to re-locate our people. Or do I still have to do that? It's so strange that in some places my memory is terrible. I just cannot remember some things at all. In other ways, well, my memory is clear, and I miss the others. I don't see any of them anywhere and fear they may have abandoned me. Why would they abandon me? I just don't understand. Maybe they went to hunt? I seem to have no food.'

The white mist stretched itself taller and turned around stretching more and contracting as if in some great indecisive moment. It settled back on the ledge.

'The storms out there on the sea were the most frightening. The water rises in huge waves like nothing we'd ever seen. In the extremely tall waves of storms, there is the fright of the giant pieces of ice. During the storms we were able to see the size of some of those giants. Consider a person. The part of ice you see above the water is very large. Compare it to the top of a person's head. All the rest of the body lies under the water. In storms the wind pushes the huge ice around as if it were nothing. One of those huge pieces of sea ice could kill your boat and all in it. Once I saw a giant wave overturn one of the enormous chunks of ice. To see something that big roll about in water nearby—that is the worst thing I ever saw. Yet, what could we do? In a storm you just have to hope the gods are with you. Most of the time we held on and rode it out, trying to keep all our things in the boat. I was the oldest on my boat. I had to appear courageous and knowledgeable for the others. I was so scared. I wanted to hide my eyes from the storm like Torq and Wapa did. Torq was only seventeen and Wapa was twenty-one. At thirty-seven, I was supposed to be a seasoned mariner. I wonder whether there is such a thing as a seasoned mariner. I tried to assure their help to keep the front of the boat headed into the waves. All I know is that when the others went black from exhaustion I'd occasionally let myself cry silently. The rest of the time I'd pretend to be brave, shouting out to them to row. By the gods, some of those waves were tall! If there could be a pure torment, a storm at sea with sea ice—that's pure torment.'

On the rock ledge the white mist took a horizontal alignment though not perfectly flat. There were parts of the mist thicker than others, and there was constant motion though hard to detect as would be seen in clouds in an almost windless sky.

'In storms, the wind would blow small amounts of water from the peaks of the waves at the boat. If we hadn't had such good protection from our furs and gut coverings, we could have been stoned to death from liquid water. I know that makes no sense, but a small amount of water hurled by the fierce wind can feel just like a rock! A trick of the gods, making a liquid feel like a solid. I would have been quite content not to learn these things.'

'Sometimes we'd have a favorable wind and we'd put the sail up. That was my favorite time. It meant the sea ice was not tall and we could make good time moving through it—except for Reg in his big boat that kept hanging the arm up on smaller ice pieces. Reg is a terrible example of a mariner—or person for that matter. He's demanding of everyone but almost never goes out of his way for anyone else. We kept waiting for him to be abusive to Vaima, but he just seemed to want her to row while we were on the water.'

The mist arose again to a vertical plane almost appearing in a human form, but remained attached to the rock ledge.

'One thing Reg was good at was spearing seals while they swam in the sea. More than once he gave us seals he'd speared when we'd speared none. He seemed to enjoy spearing seals and was very good at it. Well, from his youth he did practice even when he wasn't hunting. He'd take armloads of grasses and build a heap. Then he'd put a small piece of skin on the heap and practice still spear thrusts, and then he'd practice running at the heap from all angles and thrusting as he moved. Some SealEater hunters would practice, but they never stayed with it as long as Reg did. Reg's spear tip hit the skin almost every time.'

'We became lazy when the seals hauled out on Seal Beach. Kills were simple. Very easy. Our harpoon skills for seals in water had deteriorated from lack of use. Not Reg's skills which were sharp as ever. On the boat when Reg offered one of the smaller boats a seal, he didn't even ask for anything to be given back to him. It was a side of Reg I'd never seen. He did, however, make us feel incompetent, but that didn't bother me. What concerned me was securing food when my belly was empty and we had none. Reg wanted to make us feel as lesser people all the time, so his castigation that accompanied the gift of a seal, when we had none, came as nothing new. I learned at a young age, and with help from my parents, to become used to it and not take it, as if it were our lack of worth—which it wasn't. It was his lack of real strength of character according to my father. Reg had to keep saying how wonderful he was, for it was certain nobody else would tell him that.'

The mist flattened out again on the rock ledge. It appeared to cling there, wrapping under the edges of the rocks.

'Unless we caught them on the ice, we had to clean the seals on the boats. We skinned them in the boats and cooked them on the slate flats we'd brought for making fires. We always shared the liver raw when we reached it. It was so good! And warm. What was critical was to keep our embers alive. We needed fire for cooking our meat and melting ice for water. Occasionally, someone would lose an ember and we'd have to bring our boats close together to start a fire from the fire on another boat. Oh, we could have done it the hard way, but that takes a long time and with the wind out there, it was next to impossible. Toward the end of the voyage, we had to start eating things raw because we didn't bring enough wood and charcoal for many fires. Mostly our meat remained in frozen strips.'

The mist rose up and began to move back and forth about the distance of two man-lengths. Had the mist been a person, it would have been pacing.

'And, why I keep wondering, am I reduced to talking to myself or the imaginary person I hope is listening? Are you out there listening to me? Are you? That was louder. Did you hear it? I remember falling. That's all I remember. Then, I opened my eyes in this empty world, or is it just the same empty world we explored, looking for a home? It's all so confusing. By the gods I'm lonely. I'd do just about anything to hear a human voice right now. This is painful. I don't remember ever being alone. I don't like it.'

The mist moved from the rock ledge to the body that had just been buried. A single hand was exposed. The mist, almost appearing in the form of a human, bent over the grave. It moved to take a better view of the hand that lay exposed.

'My hand lies there resting on a rock. How can that be? I cannot seem to make my fingers move. How can I see the back of my hand at ground level with no arm while I stand above looking down? I thought the sea crossing was frightening. This is worse, because it suspends and reshapes reality. I don't think I feel anything. Does my body have weight? I seem to be able to move, for I've been pacing, but it's not by walking? I don't even understand my own words. I must have gone black in the sun and have overheated. I'm just so terribly confused. Nothing makes sense. I'm beginning to fear this perhaps as much as I did the sea crossing.'

The mist returned to the rock ledge.

'I must pull myself together before I glide away as an eagle on the wind. When I was a little boy, I would sometimes dream of gliding down from the heights. My father told me to wake up when that happened, and he cautioned me not to linger on the thought. I don't know whether he thought I'd jump off a hill. I certainly had better sense than that! Maybe he thought I'd become confused as I am now. I'll go back in time memory and come forward. Perhaps that way I can remember what is hidden from my thinking place.'

'Mongwire and I were the same age, though he was an elder and I wasn't. He was an elder, because he and my father and Whug, Reg, Forth, and At all had the same father. Their father is dead now. Their father's name was Elunkatimal. I don't remember him. I was my father's first son. Mongwire and I used to play together. Akla joined us when he was old enough. We wanted to be great hunters. We threw pebbles at targets day after day. We were born just after the terrible sickness. There were very few children then. My father's father had many sons, but seven died from the terrible sickness. Their fathers also died from it. The SealEaters scattered for the time of the terrible sickness. During that time there were a few wars. Both sides of the wars were fighting the terrible sickness, so the wars weren't very long. At least that's what my father told me. We know that far to the east there are many wars. There have been some people who entered the valley beyond the tallest hill, but they never seem to stay long in my land. Climbing the hill from that direction isn't easy.'

The mist began to move back and forth again.

'I wonder where Mongwire is. He has to be on this new land somewhere. I feel as if someone is missing.'

'I still have a sense of awe that all the boats made it to land at the same time. We didn't lose a single boat or SealEater. When we turned southward after moving west for a long time, we came across endless coastline where the ice sheet lay so very tall against the sea. Our surprise was great when we saw the end of the ice sheet and the massive expanse of green grassland. My astonishment knew no bounds. It was wonderful. Of course, we still had to avoid the huge chunks of floating ice along the edge of the land, but we could see land, beautiful flat land as far as our eyes could see, it stretched out to the west before us. When we came to a river that emptied into the sea, we rowed up the river. It was a small river, but it gave us access to the land. We rowed for days. Occasionally we'd see mammoths. They moved across the grassland exactly as they did at home on the other side of the hills. They formed groups as they did back home. They would not go hungry in that grassland.'

'We rowed up the river to where the trees began. It was a strange thing to us that the large old trees were so far inland. Why, we wondered, was there so much flat land? Sometimes if you dug down into that flat land, you could find shells from the sea. It made no sense. It remains a mystery.'

The mist moved back to the body from the rock ledge. It almost took on human form as it approached the hand exposed on the rock. The mist bent over the hand. Then, it returned to what seemed to be its resting place. It was some time before the mist continued speaking.

'It was a welcome sight to see color back on the land. Oh, the sea ice crossing was not totally without color. Sometimes the water and sky were incredibly blue. Occasionally, the ice contained blue or greenish color. I've seen a mist from the giant hunks of ice show a rainbow, if the sun happened to be in the right place for us to see it. From time to time at night we'd see colors waving in the sky. But color didn't surround us all the time.'

'In the open grasslands, however, we'd see the brown of the mud and dirt, the various shades of green. The gray-brown of the mammoths was a thrill. The colors of the birds were amazing. There were some birds there that were red. Brilliant blood red. I was speechless when I saw the first one. Their heads are peaked.'

'While color returned, so did another pest. Bugs that bite were plentiful, more plentiful than at home. The bites of the flies leave different sized welts on the skin. We finally hauled the boats ashore near the line that began the trees. This land has large bugs that scream in the night from the trees where they live. It is a daunting experience to hear them. It was better when we found the source of the sound was a bug. If it had been an evil spirit trying to terrify us, it would have been very effective. I haven't been bitten in this land. It has been at least a day since a bug bit me. Is the land here too elevated for bugs? I wonder.'

'It took a while for my legs to become accustomed to land. Who would have guessed that would happen? At first I thought the earth was shaking, but then I realized the clues were missing and that nobody else was experiencing what I was. Then, later someone else would feel the shaking. We soon realized it was our own bodies adjusting to the land. We've learned that this new land is not a copy of our Cove—that is certain.'

The mist elongated itself vertically, continuing what appeared to be pacing.

'Akla, my brother, and I decided to take my boat to explore the area. We left at night to use the star that never moves as a guide. By high sun the next day, as we traveled back to the sea to go up another river, Akla discovered that Vaima was hiding under a furless skin. She was terrified to have been discovered. Akla cursed her, finally checking himself. I felt sorry for her. She had been ripped from all the security of her family, not even a woman yet, and she had to travel with us through the terror of the sea storms. Worse, she had to wonder what Reg would do. Akla and I decided to continue on with her. We would pretend to Reg that she just went black in our boat, which she had. We would assure him she meant no disrespect. She was not found until we were too far to turn back. Vaima wept with relief, took an oar, and helped to row.'

'We traveled south until we came to a river wider than the one we'd explored the first time. We turned west and passed through the same long flat land. Then the area became treed, just as we'd seen happen the first time. Suddenly, Vaima whispered to us. Initially we didn't hear her, but when we did it filled us with dread. There were people following us along the shore— on both sides.'

'We pretended not to notice, though we stayed to the center of the river. Occasionally, we'd see a watercraft they'd made, pulled up on shore. Their watercraft is tiny compared to ours. We wondered how stable those boats might be. We felt safe to talk among ourselves. In our land there were many different ways of speaking. There were commonalities, but you had to become used to them. With people this far from us, we guessed they'd not understand us. We expected to have to use hunter signs. It would be more than a day before we'd learn that our assumptions proved true.'

'I'm beginning to remember! The people came out to meet us in large numbers. They circled our boat and aimed weapons with small spear tips at us. We hadn't even raised a spear! They made it clear that they wanted us to follow them and we did. They took the three of us to their meeting place. All gathered. There were many of them. I guess it was their chief who spoke to us. He wanted to know where our land was. With hunter signals, some they seemed to understand, and using a stick to draw in the sand and rocks to mark things, they finally realized we'd come from across the sea where the morning sun arises. They were surprised. I wondered whether they were at war and thought we were the enemy. But they kept referring to our clothes, so I think they were ready to accept that we came from somewhere far away. We tried to explain what seals were, but they kept confusing seals with river otters which we'd just recently seen for the first time. We had to explain about fresh water and salt water, something they could understand. They also understood the difference between the river and the sea, and we told them we lived by the sea many moons to the east.'

'Once they learned we were the people of the morning sun and not from the west, they seemed to accept us. They made us understand that people from the west make war against them. From that time on we became People of the Morning Sun across the Sea, their interpretation of our word, SealEaters. They accepted us among them. We could have lived with them for the rest of time. We stayed there for many days, learning their language enough to communicate simple things. Vaima was delighted and became woman there. She learned the language quicker than we did. The elder women took good care of her. When we were ready to leave, Vaima wanted to remain behind. Akla and I didn't know what to do about that. Their Chief's son very much wanted Vaima. It was obviously a mutual desire.'

'We'd lived crazy for too long. This was how people should live. She'd been through so much fright. We hadn't chosen to bring her with us. Reg even saw us leave. She'd hidden on the boat. When we left we didn't know she was there. It seemed to Akla and me that we could let her remain. After all, she was not charged to us for safekeeping. It would make Reg furious if he knew, but how would he ever know she went with us, unless we told him? She could have wandered off along the river. An animal could have taken her to feed its young. It didn't have to be that she went with us. We let her stay. The Chief's son asked what we wanted for her. Vaima served as translator. We let him know we wanted him to be very good to her for all her days. When she translated for him, he put his arm around her protectively. We thought that was the best thing to do for Vaima. She was obviously happy. I could not return her to Reg. Her smile had come back. She was genuinely in the right place for her. As for me, it felt good to let her stay.'

The mist again appeared to take on human form. It sat on the rock ledge.

'How strange. I just remembered before I came to this unusual place, my back hurt. The pain's gone. That's wonderful! Talking it out must be bringing memory back to my thinking place.'

'Akla and I left to explore a few other rivers to the south. With Vaima gone, we could relax and not have to think about what we said. It gave us a freedom that we cherished. To explore a different land is a very exciting thing. You never know what you'll see. It was warm even though it was the cold time on earth. Often we could swim upriver. To be clean was so refreshing. Frankly, my skins from the trip stank. I'm sure my own skin stank.'

'It was easy to spear animals and catch fish or other food along the way. Knowing there were people in this land, we took caution, but we did not meet others until we came far to the south. That was the land of great lizards and many snakes. We stayed there for no more time than it took to turn about and retreat quickly to find the SealEaters. We saw a people in that large lizard infested land who threatened us from shore, pounding their spears into the ground while gesturing and grimacing. We've never turned a boat around that fast in our lives. They did not chase us by boat.'

'We loved the great grassland, but it was very time consuming to cross it to the land where the trees began. It was, we thought, not a place for the SealEaters to live. We needed to have the closeness of forest to make our huts, unless we built differently. Still, then, we would need forest, I think. In some ways the forests are protective, though we don't like to go deep into them. Spirits live in the deep, dense forests. They don't want us there.'

'We started upriver and were certain we had the right river. The turns were familiar. It certainly seemed the right river. Once we'd rowed for a long time, we found what appeared to be the place where we'd pulled to shore for the first time. We could see marks of numbers of people and we tried, as hunters, to learn what happened there. Too many footprints converged. Off to the side, they had obviously skinned a furred animal. More than one. They were careless to leave parts of the deer above ground just lying there. That wasn't very respectful to an animal that gave up life that the SealEaters might live. Understanding what happened was not easy. But we could see where the boats had pulled in and out. Certainly that long slide in the mud had been from Reg's big boat. The SealEaters had left. We then began to look for hunter signs. At last we found the sign that pointed back down the river towards the sea. They had carved it into the bark of several trees. We had to return to the sea to look for markers telling us where to go to meet them. Surely they hadn't gone south or we'd have seen them. We felt so fortunate that the people we met where Vaima now lived had supplied us with a large amount of jerky of various types and baskets of fruit. If they liked you, they could be very kind. I think, if you were their enemy, you'd better beware of their potential for ferocity.'

The mist arose definitely in the form of a human. It appeared to look out on the vastness of the valley below.

'Oh, Akla, where are you? I'm remembering in pieces! I don't remember separating from you anywhere. You should be here. Such a good brother. I enjoyed growing up with you. We had such great times when we were young. I remember the days when we spent all our time in the forest hunting for food to spear for dinner. I remember the first time we—just you and I—were permitted to stay in the forest land overnight on a hunt. We brought home a horse. Everyone was so proud of us. It was hard for us to carry home, but somehow we did it. I can remember the look on your face, Akla, when we knew we'd make the kill. We would contribute to the family's food supply. We were growing up. We had stayed out alone at night for two nights. I'd felt so very responsible for your safety, Akla, but you did well on your part. Only rarely did I need to caution you.'

The mist in human form began to pace again.

'I look around me and see nothing familiar anywhere. It seems a land where nothing lives. It is a lovely land, like much of what we've seen on this land exploration, but it still has a feel of unreality about it. I would think that At may be more familiar in settings like this than I am, as if this place has more to do with spirits than people. What an awful thought! I didn't really think through those words. Could this land be filled with spirits—not people. It makes me shudder. It's probably just my fear speaking. Fear? Yes, fear. Fear of being in this strange land—alone.'

'Akla! Oh, Akla! Akla, if you cannot answer in words, make a sound. By the gods, Akla, do not tease me! No, I will not cry. I'll continue to pace, think, and try to remember.'

'I remember one night at sea. All was very still. Torq and Wapa went black while I rowed alone. The sky was filled with crackling waving colors. The sea was black. Stars were everywhere. Oddly, I felt comforted on the sea that night. It was as if the gods were with me on the boat. I could feel the closeness of a spirit, and it was pleasant, not at all frightening. It was as if whatever that presence was gave to me an assurance that all would be well. That was the only time in my life I ever had that experience with a spirit. I'd like to experience that again.'

'Should I descend the hill? Maybe Akla is in the valley below. If not Akla, maybe another SealEater. I would even welcome seeing Reg! But, if I leave this place don't I also leave my hand that still lies on the rock there? I can see a faintness of my hand where it should be, but the hand on the ground is much clearer. Much clearer! This is definitely something I would like not to have learned. I shall leave this place and go below. Maybe my anxiety is just causing me to see strangely. If I leave, things might be better.'

'I see no path to below, so I'll just try to move downward by going on an angle down, not straight down. Then I can turn back the way I came and angle downward more. I'll keep doing that until I reach the bottom.'

The mist moved down the hill in alternating downward diagonals. Up by the buried man, a woman and man arrived carrying dirt and rocks. They put the dirt over the hand and covered it completely with rocks they'd brought. They left the way they came—on the other side of the hill. Meanwhile, the mist stood on a rock ledge further down the mountain on the side opposite from where the people came and left.

'Ah, what a lovely overlook this is! The rock is big and strong, and I can see so far away. It seems there are people below. I hope they are mine. If it turns out they are strangers, I won't really care. Strangers are better than nothing. Oh, that is contrary to the rules we have for hunting. Even alone, a wise hunter is cautious around strangers. I suppose I should conceal myself until I have studied to know who the people are—SealEaters or strangers. I have to have self-control here, not let my wants run away with my safety. I wouldn't want to die here all alone or in the presence of evil strangers.'

'While I continue on this approach, I find that my legs still work differently. When I was pacing, which is normal for me when I'm anxious, I felt as though I were gliding, a little like sliding on ice. I still feel that way. At least I move where I'd like to go.'

'I fear I don't know these people. They are as clear to see as my hand that I saw on the ground. They look nothing like SealEaters. I will observe from up here.'

'That one is very old. She reminds me a little of my mother, Fluga. My mother—how I love her. She is a quiet person. She thinks very little of herself. By that I mean, she doesn't have a lot of pride. My mother lives her life to see her family strong. She works constantly. Her teeth have little slits in them where the cord she makes starts life by sliding between her teeth, so she could separate out the fibers from what's attached to them for making cords. Mother said the substance attached to the fibers makes lumpy cords, so she chews it to clean the fibers. Her teeth are strong, but they do have slits in them from smoothing fibers by pulling them through her teeth. When we grew up, my mother's presence in the tent was like the dirt on the ground, or the moss that stuffs the holes between logs—her presence was taken for granted and not noticed. No one ever told her she did well, nor did she demand to know. Mother simply did what was required and a little beyond. She never offered her opinions; she listened. Mother never blamed; she simply supported her own. She never offended; she accepted. Mother watched to be sure our garments were mended, and she did not ask for skins to make something for herself. Unlike most of the SealEaters, her only concern for herself was cleanliness. She picked her teeth after eating. She bathed even when it was very cold. Her hair was always clean and combed. It was shiny. When I was injured, Mother would put her arm around me, wash the injured skin, put honey on it, and wrap it. She'd look into my eyes and tell me how many days to expect before it was healed. If it was very bad, she'd tell me to work hard on something that caused me to think. Working hard while thinking would decrease the pain. Although it made no sense, it worked. She is a good woman. Women praise my mother. Men have said they wished their wives were like my mother.'

'These people are leaving. To see people at last and now to see them leave. That is sad. They don't seem to know I'm here.'

The mist rose appearing human. It moved quickly toward a man at the edge of a creek, the closest man to the mist.

'I am Murke, of the SealEaters, I say to the man who just stood up from drinking water from the lake, introducing myself politely.'

'He stares in my direction, over my head, as if I do not exist. Does he intend to ignore me, or is he not able to see me? I do not understand. I see no clear intent that he might be devious. Is it that in this strange land, people cannot see SealEaters? I really don't want to learn any of this. I just want to find the rest of the SealEaters and be gone from this place. I want to be among my own where things are clear as to intent and the rules are well established and don't keep changing. This man clearly can see, but he acts as if I were not here. I see no malice or guile in him, just simply that he doesn't see me. As he leaves, I realize that I must be maturing. If that happened to me in my younger years, I'd have wept when alone. I have no desire to do so.'

The mist lost the human form and collapsed to the ground by the creek.

'Now that I'm down here in this valley, I have no knowledge of where on the hill above I was. In my excitement over finding people, I neglected to make sure of my return route. I can't believe I overlooked what is normal hunter behavior. Maybe that's the rock outcrop where I overlooked the valley. But there's another there and yet another in that place. I wonder whether I have a reason to return to there. I'll look to find a river leaving this lake. I could follow this creek to a river.'

The mist arose, exceptionally thin and pale, and began to follow the creek in the direction it flowed.

'When growing up, I remember Mongwire and I had voice change and we began to grow hair where it had not grown. We talked about girls who were changing to women. There was only one girl close to our age, and we both thought she was wonderful. Mongwire was an elder, so the girl, Guint, was his. As a result of the terrible sickness, girls of my age were just not available. The elders thought about traveling to find us wives, but with all the wars, it did not seem wise to do so. Sometimes, I thought about traveling across the tallest mountains to steal a wife. Then, the elders made the rule that they had to approve the taking a wife for all other than elders, and approval required a unanimous decision. Reg always disapproved the requests, so even when time passed and girls became available, it was impossible to take a wife. At that time, I secretly wished Reg would have an accident on a hunting trip and die. That was evil on my part, but he prevented things that are normal in nature from happening. He did it for no reason except that he could. I've never been able to understand it. I hated him for it.'

'There is something that keeps arising in my memory. When I try to understand it, it fades. I've followed this river for a long time now. There are snakes here. I don't like them but I don't fear them terribly. They don't bother me. I can walk right past them and they ignore me. That is good. I guess they don't see me as a threat to them. I'm not, of course, since I have no weapon. Where are my weapons? My thinking place must be terribly broken! I never go away from my place, wherever that is, without a weapon for defense, if not to bring home food. Have I received an injury to my head or become confused from old age too early in life? Something is just so wrong. My thinking is very bad.'

The mist collapsed to the ground, seemingly thinner and less cohesive.

'Do I hear singing? Far, far away, I think I hear voices singing. I'll keep following this tiny river. It appears to be heading to the east. The sun is setting. I had better find a place to go black. That's strange. I've been very actively doing something all day, but I neither hunger nor thirst. I'll go to the area just to the south, where those trees are. I can go black there.'

'I remember just before I was twenty years old, Mora, and I were in love. She was fourteen then. One day she and I ran off to the forest, the deep forest to the southeast. We made love all afternoon. Then, knowing I could not take her as wife, we returned home with bittersweet feelings. How I'd love to have had her as my wife. She was beautiful, still is. Her wide forehead and broadly spaced, lovely brown eyes attracted me. So, too, did the curls in her hair, curls like twisted cordage fibers. She is filled with thoughts. I could talk to her forever. Well, not now that she's someone else's wife. She said she wanted only me. It made me feel so special. To our utter fright, that time in the forest caused her to become pregnant. She could have been drowned for becoming pregnant and not a wife. I talked to Mongwire, because we had been so close in childhood, and remained close as adults. I asked him to take her as wife. He did. Twice, he took as wife women I wanted. That is how life is sometimes. I was very grateful that he made it so her life was spared. In some ways it was delightful for me to see Torq grow up, knowing he was really my son. He'll never know. It's enough that Mora, Mongwire, and I know.'

The mist moved to the tree and rested against the trunk.

'Ah, here, under this tree I will go black. It's warm enough that I need no fire. I will lie here. This is good.'

'I'm not drowsy. Usually when my head rests on the ground, I go black quickly.'

'The stars are fully clear, tonight.'

'There it is again, my memory is trying to intrude upon my thoughts.'

'Land gives way. Rocks cause it to crumble and my foot slides. So that's what I've been trying to remember. There was pain in my right foot at the ankle. I glided down—it was like my dreams of gliding when I was a child. Then what? It all goes blurry there. I must've twisted my ankle, but it couldn't have been very serious. I don't remember anything about gliding down except what just came in memory.'

'So, I must've fallen. Surely I was not alone?'

'How long have I stared at the stars? They have moved a lot since I began. Why do I not go black? I'm not tired, but darkness usually brings on black.'

'Vaima was there! She was there with her husband, a man whose name I cannot pronounce.'

'How did I come together with them?'

'I don't know where Akla was.'

'Did I fall to where they couldn't reach me, and they left me there? That doesn't sound like what SealEaters would do.'

'Oh, you gods! There's a large cat walking through the grass of this valley. It's close to me! Very close! I have no weapon. I must be calm, quiet, and totally still.'

'It sniffs. It coughed.'

'It looks around. It doesn't appear to see me. Maybe an old one?'

'Ah, it seems to hear something in the south.'

'Off it goes at a run. Thank you, gods!'

'I remember the hunt with Urch. He was teaching me some hunting skills. He was older. I was about eight years old. He was fifteen. We were in a forest that was becoming dense. He turned to find me looking behind us, and was about to caution me to be more attentive. Then, he saw my spear fly. My spear went straight through the heart of a cat that was leaping toward him. It certainly did surprise him. And me! What a great time we had that night! He told the story after we ate. Whug cautioned him, but Urch had already learned what he needed to learn, and I learned the rule then, too. Never forget your back! That's why I like to go black when I have a tree behind me. It protects my back.'

'The stars continue to move in the night's sky. Still I have no desire to go black.'

"I remember I felt something like bubbles popping from my fingers and toes. Is that why I'm so pale? The popping fascinated me. It was emptying something from me, I think. I know not what!'

'They dragged me up the hill. Vaima and her husband dragged me up the hill. I remember that I wondered that I didn't feel the rocks on my skin as they dragged me up there. I didn't feel anything.'

'There are some clouds gathering to the east. In this land, that seems to happen. In the morning, the clouds come overland from the east and then in the afternoon they go back often dropping rain. I suppose when it's colder than this, the clouds could drop snow. I never asked them about snow.'

'So, I fell on the hillside. Vaima and her husband pulled me back up the hill. What else?'

'Nothing. My memory is blank.'

'Akla! Akla! I can't shout any louder than that.'

'Akla! Vaima! Vaima! Was Akla with us then?'

'Silence. Not even the bugs make noise.'

'And, still, the stars continue their rotation. Will this night ever end?'

'Bats. They fly in their jerky way eating bugs in the night air. I wonder how they manage not to collide with other bats. There's a rosy glow to the east, so I suppose these bats are heading home wherever that might be. I wish I were heading home, even if it means a sea trip.'

The mist rose up in human form, having returned to its cohesiveness. It moved away from the tree heading along the creek toward the hill.

'The rays from the approaching sun show in the east. It's welcome. I rise again to follow the river. I'm eager to find Vaima. She was near here. I know that now. I wonder whether she is on the other side of the hill. Maybe I should climb the hill instead of following the river. My staring into the water is not helping me decide. I suppose if I climb the hill to the top I can gain a better view of the entire area. I will do that.'

'It was easier earlier when I came down the hill. There is more brush, and large trees grow here. I'll just keep pushing myself upwards. I won't worry about making the back and forth movement. I just saw an owl in that tree. It gave me a look and almost silently moved its large body to another place, where it won't be disturbed.'

'I'm glad I had a son. Torq, Mora's and my son, is a son to make a father happy. He knows the rules and follows them. He is careful to respect elders and holds his tongue, even when others might find it difficult. He will be suc- cessful in life as a SealEater. He was terribly frightened at sea, as was Wapa, but both of them did well on the voyage. Torq's patience is remarkable for one his age. He has learned to be patient with himself as well as with others.'

'Vaima! Vaima! Vaima! Can you not hear me cry out your name?'

'Let me secure a good footing here. I don't want to fall again. I'm coming close to the top. Oh, I remember! They pulled me up the hill. There was a small ledge there. They laid my body on the ledge. Vaima stayed with me. Her husband went somewhere. She cried quietly. She pressed my eyelids shut. She must not have wanted me to see her cry, but I could still see her. I guess she didn't know that my eyes were open again.'

'I'll try to make it to the top this time. Sometimes I expect there to be a swing back with these tree and bush limbs I move aside, but I must be dodging them well. Almost to the top. Finally! Well, I can see for a very long distance. There's a river. Now, I wonder, is that the river where Vaima lives now? North of here is another large river. One of them is likely the river we traveled where she decided to remain behind. But which one? I'll go south.'

'It has taken me such a long time to reach this river. I cannot look at the banks to determine whether it is the river for which I search. Vaima! Vaima! Vaima! Please hear me and respond, girl. Nothing. Ah, I feel so alone! In this vast land there are people here and there. They do not cover the land. Where is anyone?'

'I hear something. Coming downriver there are two tiny boats. I'll call to the rowers. I should move out where they can see me clearly."

The mist moved out into the river. Thinning itself and losing cohesiveness again.

"Hi! Hi! Hi! Rowers! I am Murke, one of the SealEaters! Hi! Hi! Hi! Stop here, please! They're going to go right past me, as if I weren't here making all this noise. By the gods, surely they saw me! They couldn't have passed me and not seen me, could they? Is that possible?'

'Here comes another. I'll go further out into the river. Hi! Hi! Hi! Rower, please stop. By the gods these people are rude! If I hadn't jumped aside, he'd have knocked me down. None of these people seem to know that I'm here. How can that be? I'll walk the shore upriver.'

'That black snake is so very large! I didn't know snakes could grow that large. It's huge! This land has many snakes.'

'As I walk along this trail, I do not see anything made by people. It's a lot easier to go by boat, but this gives me the experience of this waterway. It may be that it'll be beneficial in the future.'

'With the sun straight overhead, it's not warm here, neither is it cold. I suppose it's the trees that join overhead to shade the path. I'm almost enjoying this walk. I just wish I weren't alone. Oh, here's a small boat. I almost missed it, so well concealed it was in the grasses. Still I hear nothing. If this is where Vaima lives, there should be noise, noise that could be heard from here.'

'There's another small boat. I wonder why they conceal them so carefully. Do they fear someone might take one? That's why we conceal them. Is that the noise of human life I hear? I will quicken my step.'

'Finally, people! I will approach carefully. I hope these are Vaima's new people. The place looks familiar. The people dress themselves as the people we met. I do think that I have managed to find the very place I sought. Children. They're coming my way. Any closer and they'd have knocked me down. What's the matter with people that they don't seem to see me?'

'Vaima! Vaima! Vaima! I see her, but she gives no recognition that she hears my voice.'

"Spirit! I see you. She cannot. Come here!" The man with the bear head hat from which the skin trailed down his back clearly addressed him. "Come with me, before you frighten someone and cause panic."

'I will follow, I don't want to cause anyone to panic. This is your place?' I asked.

"Why would I take you into someone else's place?"

'I was just talking.'

"I hear you. The others out there cannot hear you."

'Why not?'

"Because you are spirit."

'Well, how do I go back to how I was before?'

"You cannot."

'What do you mean?'

"You're spirit."

'You said that. I don't understand.'

"Don't you know what happened to you?"

'I know I fell. Vaima and her husband pulled me back up the hill. I know nothing else. Oh, I know Vaima cried and tried to shut my eyes so I wouldn't see. I could still see her cry. I don't know any more. Oh, my hand was not attached to my body. It is attached to my body, but the hand—I saw it resting all alone on the rock. It was clearer than I am now, and it just lay there.'

"Vaima and Evito went back to the place and covered your hand."

'I don't understand. My hand is right here.'

"That's your spirit hand. The hand that goes with your earth body is back up the hill."

'How can that be? I haven't the slightest understanding of what you try to tell me. Are you mocking me?'

"I do not mock you. Do you not know why Vaima pressed your eyelids down or why she wept?"

'Not at all.'

"As a Spirit Talker, this is a first for me. I've met many spirits, heard many tales, and helped many. I've never met anyone who is spirit and lacked understanding of what that means."

'I don't even know why you call me spirit.'

"I call you spirit because you are no longer Murke. Murke fell on the hill and hit his head. He died on the hill. Vaima pressed your eyelids shut and wept because she was grieving your death. You are not supposed to be here, Spirit."

'How can I talk and you can hear me, but others act as if I am not there?'

"I am the one who talks to spirits here. I have that ability. The others truly don't know you're here. If they knew a spirit is among us, there would be panic. Some might die, for they greatly fear spirits."

'You're telling me I no longer breathe air? How can I not know that I died? I don't feel dead.'

"The head injury probably made your understanding die just before you died, so you didn't know what happened. The result, however, remains the same. Have you not had experiences that showed you that people don't seem to know you're present?"

'Yes.'

"That's because to them you aren't there. You're spirit and they cannot see or hear spirit. The physical part of you from your earth life is buried atop that hill under the dirt. When you die on earth, you die to that body but your spirit continues to live. You cannot return any more than you could climb back into your mother's womb."

'That's why people seem to look through or just beyond me. That's why the people rowing the boats past here a little time ago didn't acknowledge my presence?'

"What people rowing past here?"

'Three people. That's all I know.'

"How did the boats look?"

'They were small. They were like yours with a red circle showing on the front.'

"Was there anything you remember about the rowers?"

'They all three had short hair held in place with white headbands.'

"Stay here!" The man leapt to his feet and went outside his hut.

"Sound the alarm! Three Niktonkata just rowed downriver! Spread the knowledge and look out for more."

The man returned, sat, and continued, as if nothing had happened. "You saw our enemies, and no one here noticed. That is frightening. We must be more careful. Thank you for telling me about it. So, did it surprise you that the three rowers failed to see you?"

'Yes. Just as it did when the man by the lake far to the east of here on the north side of the hill failed to know I was a body length from him. I spoke to him and he looked just past me, as if he might have heard me, but didn't see anything.'

"Did you brush against him?"

'No, I was at least a body length away.'

"Then, he may have heard something. Some people have a sense of spirit presence, but they don't have enough knowledge to know what they sense or how to communicate."

'I could have set his people to panic?'

"Possibly, but he'd have had to acknowledge encountering you, and he'd probably not want to do that for fear others would mock him."

'Have you seen my brother Akla? I was with Akla. Then, I remember climbing the hill with Vaima and the man you call Evito.'

"Evito is his short name. His long name is complex and not necessary. You and your brother stopped here and Vaima remained with Evito. You and your brother traveled south. You both seemed impressed with the large lizards you saw. You went to where the group of SealEaters had been north of here, and they were gone, so you came back here. Apparently you liked it here from your former visit. I'm not certain why you came. The morning after your arrival, Akla was nowhere to be seen. You, Evito, and Vaima tracked him to the hill. Then, you fell, and that has been the end of it. Akla's tracks stopped at the top of the hill. We do not know whether he lives or not."

'The more I hear, the less sense I can make of it all. You say I no longer breathe air.'

"That's true. Your earth body is dead. Have you not found it baffling that you also have no hunger, no thirst, and no need to sleep?"

'You know about that?'

"I know spirits."

'This is all so sudden. I have lost my brother and my life, it seems.'

"Yes, Spirit, and you need to leave this place. You must go to the spirit world. You are out of place here."

'How do I go to the spirit world?'

"You have to turn loose of this one, acknowledging that you are dead."

'How?'

"What holds you here?"

'Well, at first, I didn't know I no longer breathed air. Not knowing what happened to Akla probably holds me here.'

"You were responsible for him earlier in life?"

'How'd you know? He was my younger brother. I looked out for him.'

"That's a habit you no longer need to continue. If alive, he's a man able to take care of himself. If dead, he's probably already in the spirit world."

'Spirit Talker, I was unable to understand your language when I arrived here. How is it that now I'm no longer breathing air, we can talk?'

"Because, Spirit, we both speak the language of the spirit."

'That's a different language to you and me?'

"You could say that. It's definitely your language now. I had to learn it."

'How do you know that it's my language now?'

"Because that's what you're speaking. You didn't speak it when you were here. What you think you're saying is perhaps what you intend to say. When it comes out of your mouth, though, it is the language of the spirit."

'Spirit Talker, your words are frightening.'

"There's no reason they should be. Each of us is born, lives, and dies. Death is not an end, it is simply passing through an entry to another part of life. It is no more fearful than moving from the belly of your mother to the world outside. It is no more fearful than moving from child to adult. It is fact. Nothing less. Nothing more."

'How did you learn all this, Spirit Talker?'

"By many years of talking to spirits such as you. I also learned from the Spirit Talker who was here before me. There is much I must learn. It keeps life interesting."

'Sometime, when it seems appropriate, will you let Vaima know that I am grateful for her tears and for shutting my eyes? It is good to know when you die, that someone cares. There are others who care, but they have no way to know. They have no reason to know that I no longer breathe air.'

"I will let her know. She was also responsible for making sure they went back to cover your hand. There is little soil up there at the top of the hill. She had to gather a bag full and Evito carried stones to put atop the dirt. They took good care of your body."

'That is very kind and I appreciate their effort. Will you tell them?'

"Yes. You will rest until I return. Then, I'll help you leave us to go where you belong. Just do not leave my hut."

'I will do as you say. I will pace in the Spirit Talker's absence though there is little room here. The Spirit Talker is an old man. He is wise. He has understanding beyond his physical body—that is certain. I'm glad I could contribute something to his people before I pass through the entry to my new life, even if it was simply to tell him three rowers passed by on the river. It is warming to know that although we are very different people, we can come together with respect one for the other. That is good.'

'I am about to leave this life. I leave early. I've only spent thirty-seven years on this earth. That is a short life. Maybe there is a reason, something I must do when I go through the entry to this next part of my life. I hope that the gods will approve what I have done in this part of life. It would be good to know that.'

'I'm pacing, and there is little room to do that here. I dare not go out of this place for fear of causing panic. Someone might realize a spirit is here. Even though the Spirit Talker tells me there is no reason to fear, I do feel anxiety. It gnaws on my thoughts. I just wish I knew what happened to Akla. He is my special brother. We were somehow separated. I don't understand what happened. Does he live? I feel no certainty that he does or does not live. It feels unfinished to me. I suppose when you reach the last thought, the gods are not obligated to permit me to know how things finish before I leave here. It's what I'd like to have, not what I need. Akla is no longer a child. He is adult. He knows all I know, maybe more. Even if he were still a child, it would not change my death. I can, however, feel relief, knowing he is adult. To me that matters.'

'I wonder what is keeping the Spirit Talker. In some ways I wish to linger, but in other ways, probably with greater strength now that I've heard the Spirit Talker's words, I yearn to go, to begin the next part of my life. And I don't know how to go there. He will guide me, I hope.'

'Things seem to have been good for Vaima. I was so worried for her when Reg demanded she go with him. I know At was undone back at the Cove that day when we left. But her life is good now. It seems she is well loved by Evito. For that I have a wonderful sense of relief. I wish At could know. Back at the Cove she would have lingered waiting to be wife to someone. It is not good back there the way we live with the elders making too many decisions. She is free among these people to live life fully. And what stories she has to tell about the sea. I wonder how many people living here know about the enormous chunks of ice that float down the place where the water meets the land. If they know, I wonder what they make of that. And yet, does it matter that I know? I hold onto so much that could keep me here for tiny fragments of time. It is time to leave. Where is the Spirit Talker?'

'Parents of mine, I cannot say it to your faces, so I will put the words in the air. It may be that someday you'll find those words in the air and be glad. You taught me well. I grew up loved. Both of you showed me how to be. I thank you for your love. I thank you for your lessons of how to be. I hope that you will find your way to this land beyond the ice, though the trip is frightening across the sea. This is a good land. You will find more to eat here than seals. You will like this land. I will not know what happens. But I know both of you. No matter where you are, you will be good to each other, and that is what life should be. You make it good for each other and for others who pass your way. I thank the gods you were my parents.'

There was a slight noise and the man with the bear headdress and skin entered.

"You are ready?"

'Yes. I am ready.'

"Then, lie down."

The mist flattened out on the Spirit Talker's sleeping place.

'I'm not going to die in your hut, am I?'

"Spirit of Murke, you are already dead. This time you simply make the entry to your new life where you belong. There will be nothing left of you here."

'I think I understand.'

"Now, here's what you're going to do. Shut your spirit eyes so you see nothing. Stop trying to use your senses that were for this earth. You won't need those where you go. Relax. Turn loose of anything that holds you here. Then, think of those you've loved who went before you. Just think of them. You can feel yourself drift toward them. When you meet them, go with them and don't try to look back. There is nothing here for you."

The mist began to rise.

'I can see you, my dear Aunt Gemu. I come.'

'Take my hand, Smiling One. Remember when I called you that?'

'Yes.'

'Let's go now.'

'I'm ready Aunt Gemu. I am ready.'

The mist rose through the smoke hole in the Spirit Talker's hut. It rose above the tops of the trees and beyond until it could no longer be seen by those living who see the almost invisible and talk to spirits.

Chapter 3

Emuka's Story

Emuka muttered, "I can't believe one of the Maiket people speared me from that great a distance. The thrust of that spear was a true wonder. It was all Reg's fault. He can be such a blundering fool! He assumes the whole world thinks as he thinks, and when they don't he makes no room for them to have a different view. It would be fine, if he limited it to himself, but Reg drags us into his bad dealings with others, because they associate us with him. I'd like to gag him when we meet new people in this land. Maybe tie his hands behind his back. I am just lying here. Reg and the others fled. I tried to run, but I was unable to make it to the boats fast enough. I ran through brush and hid, but the Maiket successfully tracked me and brought me down. I'm not old enough to die. I have but thirty years on this earth. Have not yet had a wife. After the sea voyage, I thought nothing else so filled with awe could happen. I was very wrong. Now, the Maiket carry me back to the village. I'm sure I'll die there. The Maiket will probably kill me, if I don't bleed to death first. I bleed profusely from the place on my leg where the spear hit. They just jerked it out. I appreciate saving good spear points. I suppose there's no gentle way to remove one."

He continued muttering as he observed the progress to the village, "It's not far to the village now. I can see the tiny little huts near a very large tree on the top of the side of the river where the bank is about twice the height of a man. Maiket hut construction is similar to the ones we make at home, but these are covered with pine branches and other branches that have a lot of moss hanging from them, but they don't seem to use the coverings to fill in the holes in their construction. The coverings just lay over the construction. Maiket huts are not as carefully made as ours. Some are just large enough to creep into, since they are so low to the ground. Whoever made those chose short tree trunks. I think the people inside would be uncomfortable. They seem to put them up quickly and have little worry about them. I'd think they would become wet if it rained. A few of the structures are larger than anything we make. I have never been inside the large structures."

The men carried Emuka into a comparatively large structure that was made of poles inserted in the ground and strengthened by crosspieces tied to the poles. A bent branch went from pole to pole so that the top of the structure was arched. Arched poles were also strengthened by crosspieces. The structure was covered with pine branches. Some skins were tied over the pine branches at the top. There was an opening in the top to let out smoke from the hearth underneath the opening. The warriors laid down the stretched skin on poles on which Emuka lay. The spear point had prevented him from walking despite the fact it had been pulled out. The pain was too great.

"You stay," one of the men said firmly in the language of the Maiket.

Emuka nodded, having learned that nodding was the sign of acknowledgement. He'd learned some basic words from being with the Maiket, but he would have stayed anyway.

An old woman crept crablike on bent legs to the place where Emuka lay. She noted the condition of the wound. The old woman left only to return shortly afterwards to bring a basket filled with many things. She knelt beside Emuka and began to clean the wound with a soft piece of leather.

Emuka looked at her face. She was very old. Her brownish skin hung in wrinkles on her arms, barely covering her tiny but prominent bones, and her face was scored by deep wrinkles seemingly with no end. She had few teeth. The old woman looked like a dried piece of fruit. He noticed her eyes were dark blue, clear as the eyes of a young person, which surprised him. The old woman had short eyelashes and her hairline came very near her eyebrows. Her hair was pulled back in a single braid, white hair more than black. The woman squatted on feet that were turned inward and she maintained that position as often as she could because rising up was clearly painful. Although the Maiket seemed to consider him an enemy, much to his surprise, the old woman was very gentle in her care of him. The SealEaters had been in this village for a half moon, but Emuka had never seen this old woman.

Emuka looked at her face, pointing to himself, "Emuka," he said.

She pointed to herself and said, "Nagangna," which meant old woman. It was not her name. It was what she was.

Emuka looked at her and said, "Nagangna is kind."

She smiled. He didn't have any understanding of whether she comprehended his message to her.

The old woman knew from his tone, he was saying something about her that was good. What he said specifically, she did not know. Knowing it was good was sufficient to her.

Emuka closed his eyes. The woman finished cleaning the wound and then covered it with some herbs and dripped honey over it. She bandaged it with soft skin and tied a longer strip of leather over the covered area. The wound lay between his hip and knee towards the back side of his left leg. It was terribly painful. The old woman patted his shoulder. Emuka turned to look at her. She smiled. She made the sign for breaking a stick or bone. She shook her head negatively. Emuka returned the smile. He also knew the bone was not broken, but understood it was not something that would let him walk, let alone let him run.

The old woman crabbed her way to the door and the carriers came to lift the stretcher, taking him outside. Their chief, Dai, sat under the raised door cover to the largest building. The stretcher bearers carried Emuka and lowered him to the ground about three body lengths in front of the chief. Dai responded by moving his eyes, not his head, to see Emuka.

"You want to die?" he asked.

Emuka clearly didn't understand. A young boy, realizing that Emuka didn't understand, acted out death.

Emuka looked at the chief and said, "No," in the Maiket language. He nodded with a smile to the boy.

The chief told the two stretcher bearers to take him to a piece of leather where a large basket lay. They carried Emuka there and made him sit so he could lean against a rock. Emuka looked at the contents of the basket. There were rocks for making spear points and stones for flaking, chipping, grinding, and some stones the purpose of which he had no idea.

"Am I to make spear points?" he asked as close to what he perceived their language to be.

The chief nodded, showing with his hands that he wanted the large spear points that Emuka's people had, not the small ones they used. Emuka reasoned that if he made spear points he would live. That seemed to him a good trade. He removed the stones and examined all of them closely. There was some excellent flint, obsidian, and chert there. He loved the feel of obsidian. He rubbed his finger over a smooth spot with his eyes half closed, taking care not to be cut by a sharp edge, enjoying the touch of it.

Emuka studied the large piece of obsidian, turning it over and over. Someone had already made the cores from the rocks. He was interested that they used the same technique used by the SealEaters. He put the other supplies beside the basket. He looked around for a piece of leather to cover his legs for protection. He looked up at the chief.

"Leather?" he asked.

The chief didn't understand.

Emuka picked up an edge of the piece of the leather on which he sat. He raised a corner of it and repeated, "Leather?" while he showed him the dimensions he wanted, a square the length from elbow to wrist and back again.

The chief told Emuka the word for leather and told the young boy to bring some. Emuka went back to studying the piece of obsidian. He looked at the chipped corners and began to gain the feel for how it would fracture. The boy returned with the piece of leather along with a few smaller pieces and one that was a little larger. Emuka nodded to him with a smile. The boy returned to the chief. The chief watched Emuka from the corner of his eyes, not to appear too interested. Finally, the young boy wandered off. Emuka had done little to work the stone. Instead he examined it from every possible angle.

He picked up the second largest piece of leather and laid the edge under the leather beside him. Meticulously, he slid all the extra flakes and chips from the fragmented pieces of obsidian onto the piece of leather. Then, he gathered the corners of the leather and placed the bag it formed along with all the tiny unusable obsidian bits inside the basket.

Emuka placed the largest skin across his legs. He could bend his right leg, but the left one had to stick out straight. He normally sat on a stone or log when working stones to spear points. He discovered that the chute he wanted to form from the leather across his legs was too low to work. He cleared his throat. Chief Dai looked at him. Emuka used every word he could of the chief's language and every sign he could imagine to explain that he needed an elevated seating. The chief finally understood. He spoke to a man nearby, who left and returned with a fairly good sized smooth rock. Two men noticed what he was doing and came to help. They moved Emuka so he could sit on the stone. Emuka nodded to each of the men and made the chute from the leather that lay as protection across his legs. It ran straight from his legs to the soft skin fragment keeper of the basket. The men were fascinated. As many points and tools as they'd made, never had they thought to make such a device to catch the little rock splinters that could lodge in a foot, even a foot that was covered. They left the tiny flakes where they fell, usually at a location away from where they lived. The men sat down to watch. They had already learned from this man. They wondered what else they might learn.

Emuka took the forms that were given him in basic core form, noticing they made the cores in the same way he did. Emuka began by preparing the basic form from the core. He would make a spear point that he knew the chief had seen. His spear point would be pointed at each end, a little more than twice as long as wide, and used to kill horse, mammoth, cave lion, woolly rhino, bears, and aurochs. Emuka was skilled at this task, but it was not an easy one. All the SealEater men could make these spear points, but Emuka was the best. He became one with the stone as he worked. He almost never broke a point while making it. Others often lost their spear points when they tried to create a crosswise flake and the tool broke in half. They'd have to re-purpose the point as a knife or another tool, perhaps a drill. Then, they had to do something else with the broken tool parts and start all over again to create a spear point.

Emuka worked on the basic form for a long time. He began slowly hitting the obsidian with the wide part of a single pointed antler. Emuka worked cautiously waiting to reach his connection with the skill and with the peculiarities of this specific rock. He began to feel familiar with the rock, knowing its strengths and weaknesses. Emuka began to envision the spear point within the rock. As he worked, he fell into his spear-point-making rhythm. Emuka did the initial thinning strikes forming a platform for a harder strike to take off a large flake from side to side; he'd strike to remove the piece he wanted, holding the rock just above the leather on his leg and with his fingers not touching the line on which he wanted the flake to travel; then, he'd strike. Afterwards, he'd take a piece of rock and rub it briskly against the place where the hit occurred. Emuka wanted to remove any small fractures that could become problems as he worked, and he wanted to dull the cutting edge to prevent injury to himself. He continued the process while forming the basic leaf shape pointed on both ends. Emuka was careful when the opportunity presented itself to take off the transverse large flakes.

The piece Emuka had was in length a measure of his longest finger past his wrist to mid forearm. It was about as thick as his longest finger. It would become SealEater size and would be thinner than most of the other SealEaters were capable of making. Being made of this stone, it would be beautiful as well as functional. The rhythm came to Emuka. After a short time he no longer felt pain or was much concerned with his environment. He and the stone had merged in a strange way and he was simply revealing the spear point which had been hidden in the rock so all could see it. It would then be useful. At the moment only he could see it.

The Maiket watched in utter silence as the small flakes slid from the stone down the leather and into the basket. No one came by to interrupt. This place was very quiet. Emuka continued tapping sometimes hard and at other times softly. He twisted the stone back and forth looking across the edges he'd made. He'd cease tapping and rub briskly a stone across the newly formed edge to dull it. The process repeated and repeated. Each of the men watching tried to guess what Emuka would do next. They anticipated while they learned. If they guessed wrong, they tried to watch to learn why they guessed wrong.

While he worked, Chief Dai was taking his measure of the man. So far he was impressed. The man was intelligent, made tools with care and precision, had good focus on work, asked for what he wanted, appeared to want to do well at his task. Clearly, the man could do these things while in pain. He also was considerate enough to let watchers see what he was doing.

Emuka never noticed the woman who came into view to his right with a tray of food. The chief waved her off. Emuka missed that also. The chief and the two men had noticed that as he worked, Emuka hummed to himself. They realized he was very deeply involved in his work.

After the basic form was successfully completed, Emuka began to tap lightly around the edge on first one side and then on the other. He made note of the ridges and low places on the basic form and began to determine the steps he'd take to continue thinning the stone to flatten it evenly on both sides. He studied the rock in his hand. He executed a few more taps and examined it again. He made a small platform on the edge and then took an antler with the thick end placed on the stone and the pointed edge braced against his right leg. Using a separate antler's thick end, he struck the antler that was braced against the stone. Off came a flake that travelled all the way across the width of the piece. Emuka smiled, unaware that he did so. He continued that process for a long time.

Those who watched had never seen anyone use the two antlers to strike a flake while making a tool. The chief had risen and squatted by Emuka to watch. Emuka was distracted for a moment but he was not focused on anything intricate, so it was not unsettling.

One of the men who had come to watch noticed that blood was beginning to drip from Emuka's leg. He pointed it out to the chief.

The chief said, "Emuka, stop."

Emuka looked up startled.

The chief called loudly, "Nagangna!"

The old woman crabbed out of the large structure and began to move toward the chief who stopped her before she'd gone far.

"The wound bleeds," he said to her.

The old woman returned to the large structure. She came back with a basket of items. She said something to one of the men. Emuka could not understand for she spoke it quickly. The man left right away.

The chief and the other observer lifted Emuka off the rock and laid him on the ground. They indicated a problem with his leg. He looked and saw blood coming from the wound. The old woman was wiping the wound. Some pus came out on the soft leather wipe.

Emuka groaned when he saw the observer return with a piece of wood on fire at the end. The old woman took the piece of wood and while the three men held Emuka down, she shoved it into the wound. Emuka shrieked.

She removed the wood from the wound and poured a mixture of honey and herbs into the wound. She took a bone needle and pulled the gaping wound together but with enough space between the ties that the wound could still drain. Emuka felt exhausted.

The old woman told him mostly by signs, "Stay flat. I'll return when it's okay for you to sit up. You'll be able to do more stone work later this day."

Emuka lay there, staring into the tree top. Such a huge tree it was. An oak that had branches that almost covered the huts, and what that one didn't cover the other two oaks in the area did. Such huge things.

Emuka shut his eyes and remembered. The sea voyage was truly amazing. I had a wonderful time riding the huge waves of the monster storm. As soon as I understood the way the boats took to the water, I lost my initial fear. We were given to see splendors of the sea that others cannot imagine. The tall waves and the great chunks of ice. What a sight to see! When the colored waves in the sky matched the turbulent sea—that was the peak of excitement for me. The waving colors in the sky that night seemed almost to pull me towards them in adoration. And then when we'd slide down a giant wave or rise up on one, you could feel the power of the sea as never before. The great unbound power of the sea. What exhilaration! How it made my blood flow through my body! It was as I'd expect it to be if we were able to visit the gods. Great power unleashed: visible, palpable, power almost having a scent of its own!

Emuka realized he needed to make water. He was embarrassed. To have needed help with something like that back at the Cove was one thing; in this place where he was captive, quite another. He looked at the chief and indicated his need. The chief half smiled.

"Nagangna!" he cried.

The old woman appeared at the entry to the large structure. She held up a red clay container taller than it was wide. The chief nodded. She brought the container and showed Emuka how to use it. He did. He smiled at her with gratitude. "Thank you," he said.

She nodded, having no idea what he said. She took the container and went off to the far edge of the village where she emptied it down the riverbank, beyond the point where the people gathered their clean water.

The chief called to a woman who brought food. The men ate. The women had prepared horse, turtle, greens, artichoke tubers, and fruit. Having been so deeply involved with his spear point making and then with the shock of having the blood stopped so painfully, Emuka didn't think he hungered. When he tasted the food, however, he found he was very hungry and the food was delicious.

A few men started a fire which provided Emuka even more light than he needed, though the sky had darkened and a few stars had appeared. Once the food and bowls had been removed, Emuka had help to sit again on the rock to continue the spear point making. He began to do the final overshot flaking to regularize the width of the spear point. When Emuka did this he was most cautious. Overshot flaking meant flaking from one side to the other side across the large stone. One wrong strike would likely shatter the point in the middle. Finally, Emuka began pressure flaking with the antler point along the edges to remove any remaining tiny fractures that might exist and to make a standard edge. He was well pleased with this spear point.

When Emuka finished, he turned, looking directly at Chief Dai. He pressed his finger against the edge of the spear point and brought blood. Emuka put his finger in his mouth and extended the spear point to the chief. More people had gathered to watch. Women had gathered their children and all were fascinated with the stranger who made the huge spear point. There was silence while the people watched.

The chief took the spear point and examined it. He pressed his finger against the edge of the spear point. His finger bled. He smiled a broad smile, stood, walked over to Emuka, took Emuka's hand, and pressed wound to wound.

"Good work!" the chief said.

Emuka nodded.

"You make spear points, while you cannot walk," Chief Dai told him, and Emuka understood. He motioned for the two men who had been stretcher bearers to take him back to the structure where Nagangna lived.

Emuka could not understand the people's acceptance of him. He fully expected to be killed, but instead he'd been disabled. He was treated well. It was confusing to him. Not that he wasn't grateful. He was. He just could not understand. He had tried to build himself up so he would die well, not fearfully—all for no apparent reason.

The stretcher bearers carried him to a different place in the large structure. There were several older women there and his place was far toward the back. Someone had placed pine branches on the ground and covered them over with a thick, furred skin, probably bear, Emuka speculated. There was a skin with fur removed. He used it to cover himself. He lay on the sleeping place and was grateful for the comfort. The old woman brought him a bowl of water and his relief container. She examined the wound and smiled, patted his shoulder, and crabbed off to her sleeping place.

Emuka lay there. He thought, These people have accepted me, though they ran off all of us SealEaters. I'm sure it was Reg's way of being that caused their animosity. I cannot understand that man, though I have lived near him all my life. He should never have been an elder. He has harmed our people in almost every way possible. People who are not SealEaters certainly are not impressed. Among the SealEaters he is seen to have much power. We probably contributed by failing to stand against him, but every time someone tried, they were beaten down. Reg knows how to make people suffer mightily. When he threatened the chief I was horrified. The chief is many things, no doubt, but weak and cowering is not one of them. Aside from that he has many warriors, far more than there were of us. Reg just thinks that all think as he does and what took place at home applies everywhere. He will discover his error someday, I expect. I've always heard that Reg has a terrible secret. I don't know whether it's true. If it is, I don't know what his secret could be.

Emuka moved a bit to avoid a branch that had an uncomfortable hardness to it. He continued reviewing, I was happy to be in Urch's boat. I was given a special brother in Urch. Plak was with us, and he was a great rower. He was distraught about his sister. Being on Reg's boat—not even as wife—put her in a dangerous position, if she became pregnant. He kept watching, but none of us ever saw Reg do anything to her, except insist she row. He kept her in constant panic. I don't know what became of her. I know she was terribly frightened the whole time. We all thought she ran off from the camp that night. When Murke and Akla left, we wondered whether they'd taken her, but when we met up with them, it was clear they had no idea what happened. I hope she wasn't eaten by a wild animal. Reg has a problem with women except for his wife, Waywap. He seems genuinely to love her. I've never seen him treat anyone that well. When he grabbed the woman in this place, one of the warriors speared his arm. Reg was ready to attack the man who speared him only to find six warriors with spears raised. Reg backed down quickly, bragging about how he could take them all, but didn't want to create a lot of injuries. I think based on what I've seen tonight, the woman he grabbed is the wife of the one who raised his spear first.

Emuka moved his head just slightly and went black until he awakened the next morning from Nagangna's wiping his wound. It no longer seemed to be so flaming red. He didn't see gobs of pus as he had seen the other day. He credited Nagangna with knowing what she was doing. He used the relief container she'd given him, and she left the place with it filled.

The stretcher bearers arrived. They put Emuka's arms over their shoulders and helped him walk to the place where the rock remained. They made it clear he was to put no weight on his left leg. He sat down on the rock ready to begin another spear point. The chief came out from the large structure. He had a pipe, though Emuka didn't know what it was. The pipe was made of clay and wood. There was something, Emuka noticed, burning in the bowl at the end of the pipe. The chief inhaled and blew smoke to the east. He repeated the process and blew smoke to the west. He repeated the process and blew smoke to the north. Finally, he did the same, blowing smoke to the south. Then he said a lot of words that Emuka never had heard. Emuka knew all this was very serious; he just had no idea what it was about. He thought it must have something to do with a ceremony honoring their gods. Emuka was fascinated. He noticed all stood while this event occurred. He couldn't stand without help, and no one came to help him, so he decided it was acceptable for him not to stand.

After the ceremony Emuka noticed a large basket had been placed next to the one where the rocks were stored. Someone had replaced the stones in their original basket. The leather liner with flakes and chips had been carefully placed to line the basket that had just appeared. The new one was well worn in comparison with the one he'd used the day before. He understood.

Food was served and all the people ate in the area where Emuka and Chief Dai were sitting. While they ate, they were quiet and remained seated. Emuka watched. It appeared as though children were not permitted to stand up until they had permission to do so. The children were well behaved, he noted. There was much fruit and some things that Emuka had never seen. He tasted them and they were very good. Never in his life had Emuka eaten so many greens, root vegetables, and fruit. He found the flavors sensational.

He began to work, but found the closeness of the two men from the day before a little disconcerting. Then, he realized he was not only expected to make spear points but also to teach these two men how to do it. That caused him to relax. He was glad to teach them. First, they would watch, and later they would try it themselves.

"Emuka," he said to them, pointing towards himself.

They repeated his name. Then one said, "Moah," and the other followed quickly with "Buph."

Emuka began making one of the points from the second piece of obsidian. He studied the piece for a long time. "Moah, Buph, I look first to see where to expect to begin flaking. I want to thin the depth of this large piece without causing too great a decrease in width." With his fingers, he tried to show what his words said. He knew they probably didn't understand but would remember a little of the ideas he was putting forth.

After his long study of the piece, Emuka began initial thinning and establishing the basic form. He went a little slower to let them see what he was doing. He'd point out how to establish a platform, how to strike it, and the flake that resulted from the strike. Emuka let them hold it before and after the strike. He let them remove and replace the flake that he'd struck off. Emuka would show them carefully how he wished to smooth the ridges at the edges of the flaked spear point. It was good to have them feel things. So much of spear making was feel.

At one point he told them, "There is a rhythm to making spear points. You need to know what you're doing. You don't want to think too much. Enter into the rhythm of thinning. This is how it looks." Emuka speeded up the work he was doing. They could see what he had been saying though they didn't catch every word. They understood the rhythm, for they made points themselves, but never had they done anything so complex or thin. The thinness of the large point he made yesterday awed the men. The Maiket were also drawn to the beauty of the point. They didn't doubt it was successful in killing. They wanted very much to be able to make spear points like Emuka was able to make, points with function and lovely form. Emuka stressed trying to see the finished product when first examining the stone they'd work.

The work on spear points went on for days. Emuka had to keep cautioning Buph that when he left the platform too thick, a flake from it would not travel far, too thin and the flake will not be large enough. After continuing to break basic forms or even almost completed spear points, Buph was gaining skill. Moah had a different problem. He kept forgetting to watch where he put his fingers to brace the rock for a tap. Consequently, he kept blocking the travel of his flakes. It made it tough to work the centers. It also caused him to narrow the width of the point.

"Oh, no, I've broken another point," Buph moaned.

Emuka waited.

Buph continued working on the beautiful piece now with a pointed end and a flat end. He noticed a bit of a point projecting at the bottom of the flat end. He set up and struck, aiming carefully at the projection, as if it were a platform. When he turned his hand to see what flaked off, he discovered the beautiful flute caused by the strike. He looked at Emuka, who was watching him intently.

Buph turned the stone and began with a pointed deer antler to construct a platform on the side where the flute was. When he struck that, a flute formed on the opposite side of the rock.

Buph, glowed. He said, "I will return fast." He went quickly to his hut. He returned with a broken spear shaft. He took his knife and shaped the end of the shaft into a dome. He carefully carved a notch into the end of the wide broken spear shaft that now would become a knife handle. He placed the wooden halves of the spear shaft to align with the fluted sections. The wood fit into the grooves as if it had been made for that purpose. Both Emuka and Moah came to see closer. Emuka grinned broadly. With the short handle, they were looking at a knife that would be extremely useful for separating the skin from a killed animal. This could also be a new style for spear points. They had to wait until the great fire at night when Buph could take the pine pitch glue sticks and sinew to merge the shaft and spear point. It was very clear that through a mistake they'd all learned something new. Everyone could see it.

Emuka worked hard to learn the language. He had gained a basic understanding of it when, after examining the wound, Nagangna told Emuka he should begin walking. He was delighted. He found his leg a little weaker than the other, but he was fully able to walk.

Chief Dai took a walk with him to the pond at the top of the hill.

"From here you can see for long distances everywhere," the chief said throwing wide his arms to take in all while he turned around. It is a good land."

"It is a good land, Chief."

"Do you want to find your people or would you rather remain here?"

"Chief," Emuka said with great temerity, "I came here with the hope of finding a place our people could live, for we are squeezed between the great wall of ice and mountains where my people now live. I also had another desire. I have wanted a wife since I was old enough to have needs. We had to have approval of each of our elders to take a wife. One elder would never give approval to anyone. I yearn for a wife. Is it possible that you have someone who would be my wife? If so, I would stay here and live my life. If not, then, I should soon move on."

The chief looked at Emuka. He was impressed by the man. He had all the good qualities he wanted to see in his people. "I will talk to two people. Then, I will let you know."

Emuka was overjoyed. For some undefinable reason, he felt certain the chief would find him someone who would be his wife. He was swimming in hope. The two walked back to the little village.

That evening, the chief found Emuka after dinner. He told him to follow. Emuka did as he was bidden. He saw a young woman standing by the tree to the east. The setting sun shown on her. She was beautiful. Emuka had not seen her before. She smiled.

The chief looked hard at Emuka. "She is my niece. She will be your wife. There were two of our young women who wanted to become your wife. I thought about you and what I know of you. Kik is the best woman for you. You will take her as wife tomorrow. Now, you may talk alone." Emuka and Kik walked up the hill where earlier Chief Dai had spoken with Emuka. From the pond they could see all three trees, the name of the village, Three Trees, she told him. They were wonderful spreading oaks, very old and graceful. She climbed them when she was a young child. Their time together, though short, showed that the chief had chosen well.

Kik knew Emuka's story. She made conversation easy and walked with him while they talked. She took his hand and placed it around her, resting his hand on her shoulder. Emuka was terribly excited. He had thought for many years that he'd never have a wife. This was bliss. Kik explained that he'd have to start making a hut early in the morning so all would be ready for that night. They stood arm-in-arm looking at the expansive sky with its dark reds, oranges, yellows. Kik had been dissatisfied to be wife to any of the men in their group. Her alternative was to go to her mother's people far away to find someone outside her group. If she had refused all men prior to age twenty-five, the chief would have to select one for her and she would be bound to him. That was the way of the Maiket. She had almost reached twenty-five.

Meanwhile, Turakia, talked with Adn. Adn was Turakia's older sister. Adn listened to her sister's disappointment at not having been chosen.

"He's my father. That should have counted for something."

"He had to choose the right person for the Stranger," Adn replied. "He cannot play favorites."

"But it's not fair!" Turakia wailed.

"Sister, you should have accepted Iviron. He loves you more than anyone. He still does."

"Iviron is boring."

"He is a fine hunter. He is a good man. And you wait for the last moment, just like Kik. Will our father have to find a husband for you, too?"

"But I wanted Emuka!"

"You are a whiner. Only a very few people here know anything at all about Emuka. You are creating your desires on baseless fantasies."

"Yeah. I guess you're right." Turakia replied credibly, but her thinking place festered. She was not satisfied.

Adn watched Turakia for days. She knew her sister very well. In some bad way, she expected Turakia to try to do something terrible to Kik or Emuka. She could resort to some very mean revengeful deeds, Adn knew first hand. On the third day after Emuka had taken Kik as his wife, Adn watched Turakia furtively steal down to the bog. Adn could not wait. She sought out her father.

"What is it daughter?" Chief Dai asked her, realizing something was very serious.

"I hope I'm wrong, Father. Turakia was outraged that you chose Kik for Emuka. I tried to reason with her to no avail. I have watched her because she can be vengeful."

"I know you have taken the brunt of her mean spiritedness for years."

"This morning she headed to the bog. I fear what she has in her thinking place. Knowing her, it is unlikely she'll rest until she has reeked her vengeance on either Kik or Emuka or both."

"You watch from the west end and I'll watch from the east. If you see her, find me. Either way, I will stop her and search her. If she carries anything poisonous, I'll do with her what I should have done long ago."

Adn nodded, having no idea what he meant and not wanting to know. She went to stand watch. There were only two ways to and from the bog.

As it was, Chief Dai was the first to see her return. Sure enough she came from the bog.

He hid himself behind one of the large tree trunks. She'd have to walk past him.

When she did, he stepped out in front of her, startling her.

"What's in your bag?" he asked.

"Something for dinner," she replied coolly.

"Good! I'll take that and because of your consideration, I'll ask Nagangna to cook it up for you now."

Turakia looked horrified, and she was unable to mask her horror as her father's words came too quickly.

"That displeases you?" he asked.

"Well," she replied.

He took her bag and dumped the contents on the ground. There were five different poisonous plants on the ground. She looked at him in terror.

"Pick up every single piece," he told her.

She did while he watched. Each piece went back into her bag. She'd spent a very long time making the bag. It was very special to her.

Chief Dai took the bag by the middle of the carrying strap and grabbed Turakia by the arm. He grasped her arm so tight that the circulation of blood was seriously impaired. She dared not make a sound.

They walked to the central hearth and he dropped the bag into the fire. Fire ate the bag and plants in moments.

She kept wondering how he'd known what she had been doing. She thought her wait had been long enough.

The chief took her to his large structure and called to one of the men for some leather strips. He began to tie Turakia's hands behind her. He gagged her. He tied her feet together. She wept. He ignored her.

Chief Dai looked at his daughter. She was a beautiful woman. If any man were to describe what he wanted a wife to look like, it would be Turakia. Her way of being was not something anyone should really want to live with. It had gone on too long. Once he had her tied, and gagged and assured himself that she could no longer move, he dropped her just inside his place.

He found Buph working with Emuka.

"Buph, I would speak with you."

"Yes, Chief?"

"Do you still hunger for Turakia?"

"I know it's weakness, Chief, but yes. We had wonderful times when we were children together."

"How much do you hunger for her?"

"I'd do anything for her."

"How about for your people? Would you ever put your people at risk?"

"Of course not!" he replied indignantly.

"I want Turakia gone. She picked poison today to try to do away with either Kik or Emuka or both. I burned the poison and that bag she loves. You still think you want her?"

"She was willing to kill two people?"

"Yes. She wanted me to let her be Emuka's wife. I chose Kik instead. She is filled with vengeance."

Buph was shocked terribly. He had always thought that Turakia was given the least in everything. She had been certain he believed that. It was an effective way to use him as she used many others. She was acutely aware of her manipulations. Buph had avoided the truth.

"Chief, how can I believe that?"

"If you take her and don't believe that, Buph, you'll be dead in a year. She's like a beautiful bag on the outside, but inside is a privy bubbling with sickness."

"Chief, I need to re-think this. Can I return to you after thinking?"

"Of course, but I need to act on this swiftly."

"It will not take me long. I want to talk to my brother, Moah."

In a short time, Buph returned. The chief stared at him, arms crossed, waiting.

"Chief, I have concluded that I need to rely on reason, not emotion. For someone to be willing to kill others because she failed to obtain what she wanted, that's too much for me. I am not equipped to live that way. I have to admit I didn't want to believe you, but I've never found you willing to lie. I have found Turakia in lies. You have finally shattered my dream."

"You're a good man, Buph. Go now, and do not ever ask about what I do."

"Yes, Chief," Buph replied emotionally spent.

The chief nodded to an older man, a huge man with a broken nose. He was older than the chief by ten years. He was his cousin. They had been the greatest of friends since childhood.

"Ot, take her. The boat is prepared. I want you to take her south. Take her to where you cannot go any further south without entering the sea. We went there once, remember?"

Ot nodded.

"Leave her there alone. Are you up to the task? Do you want anyone else to go with you?"

"I'm up to it, Cousin. It's past time to do this thing. I'd have pushed you harder had she not been your daughter."

The chief went over and embraced Ot. "Do you want anyone else to go with you?"

"No, this is best done by me alone."

"Then, my Cousin, go with good speed and return to us safely."

"I will return. I will return to let you know the deed is done."

"Very well. The boat is provisioned well."

"Of that I was certain."

Ot went to the chief's large hut and picked up Turakia. He gently placed her in the boat and covered her with a skin. He pushed the boat out into the river and departed for the sea.

After the morning ceremony, Moah showed Emuka the spears he'd made. Emuka was truly impressed and showed the spears to Chief Dai. The chief ran his fingers over the tools and raised them as if to throw. He smiled a broad smile at both men.

"Would you like to use these on a hunt today?" Moah asked Emuka.

"I thought this day would never come. Yes, of course."

Moah's wife brought a backpack which she held while Moah shrugged into it. She handed the water bags to Emuka. The two left the camp. They traveled far into the highland to the south. Emuka had found some fresh scat from a bear. Both men were alert, for they wanted to see any bear before it saw them, and bear scent filled the air. They were among the trees when they noticed the scat. Signs of the animal made it seem that it had moved out of the forest into the grassland. They both knew that these bears were carnivores and could move at speeds in excess of anything they could. They had three spears apiece, and if they encountered a bear it might take at least that many.

Moah elbowed Emuka. "There, down at the bottom by that pond."

Emuka saw the bear and dared to breathe a sigh of relief. He did not lay down any of his alertness. Both watched, unmoving.

Moah motioned for them to move back into the forest quietly. Emuka followed him with great care. No birds sang in the trees, and Moah was jittery. He wondered whether they missed something. In time, they relaxed a little, but the bear had definitely added a level of caution. They had been careless. It wouldn't happen again that day.

Emuka touched Moah's shoulder. He pointed, moving his arm slowly. There in the field to the north was a small camel, just the right size for them to transport back to the village. Both of the men chose a spear from what they carried. They laid down the others. They crept closer and closer to their target. At the signal from Moah, the two thrust with all their strength and both spear points hit the camel right near its left foreleg attachment. The camel went down. Emuka gathered their spears while Moah went to the camel to cut its throat. He joined Moah and the two began to attach the camel to a spear shaft they'd use to transport the animal home.

Moah taught Emuka their hunting success song and they sang it as they walked to the village. It was a song of thanks to the animal for its life-giving gift, to the Great Creator for making the animal, and to their hope that the food would impart strength and health to their people. When they reached Three Trees, they turned the spear carrier over to the younger men who'd take it to butcher.

Noticing the return of Emuka and Moah with the camel, Buph took the time to pick up his broken spear point at his hut, the spear point he'd turned into a knife, and he handed it to Yul, who was beginning to remove skin from the camel. He asked Yul to let him know how well it worked. He expected it would be seen as an improvement, but he kept that thought to himself.

Little ones were running about as the men returned to the gathering place. A small boy of about three to four years ran right into Emuka's legs. The boy looked up, startled. Running in the walking places at Three Trees was not done. The boy knew that, but he had tried without caution to catch up to the other boys he wanted to join.

Emuka stooped down, looking at the little one.

"What is your name?" he asked

"Boo," the boy replied head bowed.

"What does Boo mean?" Emuka asked.

The boy didn't understand.

Emuka smiled, "Slowly, Boo," he told the young boy.

Boo looked at him quizzically and then left to find the other children.

Kik learned Emuka was back and came to find him.

They embraced. Then Emuka said, "Kik, what does Boo mean?"

"It's an apology."

"I do need to work on learning this language! A little boy just ran into me and I asked his name. He said, 'Boo,' so I said, 'Slowly, Boo,' which clearly he didn't understand."

Kik laughed gently, "Well, no, that would be like saying 'Slowly, forgive me,' which would make no sense."

"I understand. Please help me, Kik. I learn too slowly to satisfy me. Can you teach me so I learn faster?"

"Certainly, I'll try, Emuka. Also, ask Chief Dai, Buph, and Moah to help."

The two of them walked to the water gourds. Emuka was very thirsty.

They rested against the huge trunk of one of the oak trees. Emuka thought he had never been so happy. Kik reached for his hand. He looked at her smiling face.

"Emuka, I think I grow life in my belly."

"You—don't—mean," he choked the words out.

"Yes, I do mean that if all goes well, you will be a father."

Emuka was overwhelmed. He put his hands to his face as tears fell from his eyes and he felt that wasn't manly.

"Are you sad?" she whispered.

"Of course not," he replied squeezing the words out. "I am the happiest man alive." He embraced her letting his tears find routes to the sea through her hair.

He thought of the tree. He remembered his parents, Whug and Gemu. They had children even as a branch has smaller branches. He would be a father. He never expected to have a wife let alone children. His branch would branch. He felt overwhelmingly blessed.

"It is custom not to talk about the baby I carry in my belly until it is obvious to all. Please, Emuka, do not share this information. Not only do you need to learn the language better but also you need to learn custom."

"I understand. My teaching is in your hands. Please provide information as fast as possible. I want to fit here. This is the best part of my life, and I would like to savor it as deeply as I can."

Two women arrived holding themselves back slightly. They carried grass bags that were lightly stained.

"Emuka, I must go now. We are going to look for foods for tonight's dinner."

Emuka nodded. His whole emotional component was so filled he feared it would burst if he spoke.

A boat came up the river quietly. Ot pulled the boat to shore concealing it carefully in the vegetation. He went directly to find Chief Dai. The two entered Chief Dai's hut without speaking.

"It's the right thing to have done, but it was painful," Ot said quietly.

"It had to be—for the Maiket's future. I will grieve behind my face," the chief replied also very quietly.

"I, too, will grieve behind my face," Ot said. "I will leave now to visit my mother's people upriver."

"Thank you, Ot. I understand. I wish there were a place where I could retreat."

Ot touched his shoulder. "I understand," he whispered.

Emuka decided to walk along the small river that passed by the place. He stood and gathered as much composure as he could. He left without looking about or making eye contact with others. He wanted to be alone. He followed the river beyond where he had been. Exploring had never been something which drew him. He needed to expend energy. He passed some women at the water's edge. They were washing something, but he didn't take time to see what it was they washed. In keeping with his hunter instinct, he kept lookout on his surroundings. The day was sunny, warm, quiet.

The river bank lowered nearer the water as he walked. He mused that the Maiket chose their site well. If floods came, they were well protected. They also had high enough ground to see the surrounding area so they were protected from any who might want to make war. This was a good land. A large brown bird flew by, followed or chased by another bird, not quite so large. He squinted to see the details of the birds. He realized he needed to learn the names of the animals and their habits, for not only did he need to fit in but also he would have a son to teach. The thought of a daughter never crossed his thinking place. Tonight he'd ask Kik to teach him the animals and their habits. He would practice until he learned them well.

Emuka passed a log by which he saw a snake with a triangular shaped head. He knew they were poisonous, and he took great care to keep his distance.

Far away, at the edge of a wooded area, Emuka saw either mammoths or mastodons. He was unsure which from that distance. He wondered whether the hunters sought them. He had his doubts, because most hunters who killed them wanted to display the tusks in some fashion at their living area. He had seen no evidence of bones or tusks of such animals. He would add that to his questions.

Emuka absent-mindedly touched the scar on his leg. It was a large rounded, somewhat rough area. He wondered whether Nagangna saved his life by burning it. He'd never know. He shuddered remembering. Emuka looked back towards Three Trees. The sky was darkening from the tall clouds of a storm. He decided it would be best to return home.

By the time he reached home, the storm had already begun to send rain to the ground. Lightning flashed and thunder roared. There was little wind. Emuka slipped into the hut he shared with Kik. When she had become his wife, he had gone to the forest to find the tallest lengths of wood he could find to construct their hut, so it was roomier than most. He had also filled the cracks with moss from the oaks and covered that with the muddy clay from the river side. They had a small hearth for warmth and they remained dry from rain. He had moated around the hut to prevent rain from running onto the floor of the hut. Kik scraped the rain from Emuka's skin, and he put on dry clothes. The hearth fire had warmed up the hut, casting a rosy glow over the hut interior. They sat on the bearskin and smiled at each other. Kik had brought a bowl of jerky and some freshly cooked edges of camel that were still roasting under the oak nearest them. She was very happy to know that Emuka was pleased with the idea of a child. Some of the men did not wish to have children enter their lives so quickly.

Emuka wore a hairless mid-thigh tunic and a knee-length loincloth. The tunic was made simply of a long piece of leather cut transversely for his head to slip through. It was sewn simply on either side. He tied a soft piece of leather around his waist more for carrying things than for any other reason. Kik wore a brown rabbit fur tunic made from skins most women spurned. It was designed to go over one shoulder. Her tunic was not belted. It fell to just below her knees. It was somewhat lumpy for it was made of many skins. She loved the softness of her tunic, even if it was lacking in longevity.

"Do you think our child will have your blue eyes and reddish hair?" she asked.

Emuka was surprised. He never thought of the color of his eyes or hair. Except for Nagangna, everyone at Three Trees had black hair and brown eyes.

"He will probably have brown eyes," I think, because all the Maiket have brown eyes.

"He?" she asked. "Why do you think our child will be a male?"

Emuka was brought up short. He looked into her eyes, startled. "I just assumed that's what our child would be." He paused considering. "Kik, if it's a girl that's fine. When I knew you carried a child, I just saw a boy."

"Well, I have no control over whether it's a boy or girl child, Emuka. We must be accepting and happy to receive whatever the Great Creator Spirit gives us."

"Of course, Kik." Emuka had to spend some time readjusting his thoughts. He had fantasies of teaching his son to hunt and catch fish. Somehow a girl hadn't fit this picture. Now it did.

"Among your customs, do girls hunt and fish?" he asked.

"We hunt some things," she assured him. We make snare traps and use the forest animal trails to place numbers of them at one time. We use bolas to catch geese and ducks."

"What's a bola?" Emuka asked. He well understood snares.

"Rock weights on cordage," she replied and rose to pull one from one of her bags that hung on a partial projection from the side of the hut. "Here you can see it. I made mine with three stones. You can use two or three or more. It can tangle an animal's legs so you can kill it; a direct hit will stun or kill animals, maybe break a bone; and for geese and ducks, it can entangle them in air and bring them down."

"How does it work?" he asked.

"You hold all the pouched stones in your left hand straight down while you hold the other end in your right hand, arm stretched to the right. Raise your left arm out straight following with the right. Turn loose of the stone pouches with your left hand, while swinging them around your right side with your right hand. Turn loose when your aim is right to hit your prey. If the prey is at a distance, sometimes you'll circle the stones about your head to make the bola fly farther."

Emuka held the bola, examining it carefully. "You would have to make five or seven holes in the leather pouches, so as to make the attachment come from the center while the tie that wraps the pouch comes from the outside?"

Kik was startled at his thoughts of construction after just having examined the bola. "You are right, Emuka. How'd you learn that?"

"It's my life to know tools and how to make them. Whoever designed this was very clever."

"These tools were in use before memory," she replied.

"Will you teach me to use one of these?" Emuka asked.

"Of course," she said, "the Maiket, however, see them as women's weapons."

"Women's weapons?" he laughed. "Any tool is valuable for anyone, if it works. You said this could entangle the legs of an animal. Could you catch a camel or horse with one of these?"

"Well, yes," she admitted, "if you could cause it to wrap around two legs or made a direct hit."

"Then, the Maiket may see it as a woman's tool, but I see it as one that would function well in the grassland, whatever the animal you hunted."

She smiled. She thought that she was very fortunate to have such a man as her husband.

For days she taught Emuka to use the bola. Some of the men and many of the women were fascinated that he'd spend so much time learning that weapon. As the days passed he became more and more proficient in its use.

Early one morning six of the best young hunters left before the morning ceremony. They all carried spears that bore tips made by Emuka. By early afternoon, Yul returned at a run. After catching his breath, he asked Chief Dai for help. They had killed a mammoth in the place Emuka had pointed out, and they needed butchers and people to transport the meat. Quickly, more young hunters, and a few who were not so young, went across the river and grassland. That night they would celebrate the kill and the effectiveness of Emuka's spear points.

The same day Kik and Emuka followed the river beginning early in the morning. He carried spears, and both of them took bolas. About high sun, they spotted a number of peccaries.

"Now, the test," Emuka whispered. "I take the one on the left; you, the one on the right."

Both laid down everything but their bolas. They prepared, looked at each other, aimed, and slung the bolas toward their peccaries. A loud thwock let them know a stone had connected directly with something. They gathered their things and jogged to the site. Sure enough there were two peccaries lying there. Emuka quickly killed them. They tied the legs of the animals together. Using two spears which they held on their shoulders, Kik walking ahead and Emuka behind, they carried the animals back home.

People were delighted with the feast that would come from their kill, and men took another look at bolas. It was a lightweight tool that could be carried on hunts with ease. All it would take is practice in making and using them. They found that learning the skill was not as easy as they had thought. Some men gave up in disgust claiming the tools were women's tools. But some men learned with practice just as Emuka had done.

Months passed. One day, Kik stood up and promptly put her hands on her belly. "I think the time nears," she said. I will talk to the baby bringer woman," she said with a smile. "Whether it comes as a boy or a girl, you'll teach our child to hunt using all tools," she said.

Emuka nodded.

It was not until high sun of the next day that the infant arrived—a girl. She had blue eyes. They named her Gemukik. By the time she was five-years-old, she could handle a small bola and spear. Her distance was short, but her accuracy was superb.

Emuka would live to the age of seventy. Kik died at the age of sixty. He and Kik had fifteen children. Three died before Emuka no longer breathed air. He taught every child how to hunt and fish. Even the girl children were required to attain mastery. They were also required to master the technique of making the large double-pointed spear points. His concern was that despite their place in life, they could survive well.

Chapter 4

Mongwire and Wen's Story

Having fled the Maiket, the SealEaters traveled north on the sea to a wide river. They built a cache for their sea traveling clothing and some of their winter garments for their return to the Cove. The group split into fragments, planning to gather at the headwater of the largest river below, where, at the solstice in two years, all together the SealEaters would set forth for home at the Cove. They hid their boats they were not using. They would decide after regrouping which place seemed best for all their people. Meanwhile they'd explore, each going in a different direction. Mongwire, of course, kept his youngest son, Wen, with him. He had two other sons, Morg and Torq. Morg remained at the Cove. Torq had come on the voyage in a different boat. He and Mongwire were not close. Torq had already matured into a strong, responsible man.

As he belonged to the water, Mongwire had chosen to take a small boat north as far up the river as possible. He and Wen rowed far into the land, going north until the river split. They took the northeast direction. They had rowed for days. Early one morning as they set out, Mongwire noticed what looked like a trail. They hid the boat well and climbed the hill only to discover that the trail led over a hill and up a mountain. Laden with heavy backpacks, skins, some food, and spears, Mongwire began his assault on the trail. He rarely did anything indifferently but rather drove himself as if powered by something others lacked. Wen followed, grateful that no branches remained to block his progress. His father removed them as he climbed.

Mongwire's thick heavy legs seemed never to tire. Wen was much more slender of build and had his mother's features. He was light-footed and had good stamina, but he always tired before the day went dark. SealEaters could go on the trail from sunup to sundown, pushing into dark, if needed. Wen gave out too soon. Mongwire wanted him to become more like himself and his other sons, in a word, manly. He wasn't ashamed of Wen. Quite the contrary, Wen was his favorite child. But he was still just that—a child. It was past time for him to grow out of his childish ways like drawing in the sand or feminine things like learning names and functions of plants. Mongwire wanted him to become a great mariner or hunter, if not both. Mongwire had taken Wen along to toughen him, to grow him into the man he thought Wen should become.

The forest was composed of some birch interspersed among countless evergreens as far as they could see. Mongwire's thought that a shape in the vegetation was a trail proved correct. The trail they took towards the west up the hill and mountain led to another trail clearly man-made that went from north to south. It seemed to Mongwire to be a trail used by humans as well as by animals, but he admitted that thought remained to be proven. It was too well used and too wide to be an animal route through the mountain forest, he reasoned. They came to a rock that jutted out over the valley. Mongwire turned off the path and walked out upon the rock. The valley below was green and treed as far as the eye could see. He couldn't see the dirt floor through any of the trees, so closely did they grow together. Mongwire was convinced they could go back now to begin to bring the people to this new land. He saw no need other than caution to wait for two years. But that was the agreement. Nowhere did he see heat waves from hearth fires, and if a SealEater could have seen it, he'd be the one. So keen was Mongwire's vision that SealEater hunters relied on it. He decided to wait that night to observe the valley below for human life. Wen was looking badly trail worn, but Mongwire credited him with keeping his fatigue to himself.

They shrugged off their backpacks and began immediately to build a hut for the night. They found enough dead wood lying about to create a very small hut into which they placed their things. They gathered evergreen boughs to keep themselves above the ground and on softness, piled them in the hut into rough rectangles, and laid their furred skins over the boughs. Each rolled his leather sleeping cover, and placed it on the sleeping skin.

Nearby was a small spring from which they could drink.

"Which way do you think we should explore this north-south trail?" Mongwire asked, setting Wen up to learn how to make good hunter decisions.

Wen knew his father was testing him. For a long time he did not reply. This was his silent, mysterious son, Mongwire reminded himself. Mongwire was patient.

Finally, Wen said, "We should go north, Father. We should find the limit of this land. We should know where the ice begins so we can assure ourselves we are well south of it, in case it grows. With so much ice in the sea, we cannot be far from where it should be on land, if it rests on the land. We should keep in our thinking places the value of the ice. The ice is like a huge wall keeping others from making war from the north. Any who live near it have protection from one side."

Mongwire was startled as usual. Rarely did he guess what Wen's thoughts might be. He had planned to steer his son to the south where conditions would be warmer and better for the SealEaters to begin a new life where varieties of food animals abounded. But Wen had thought it through and made good sense of his reply.

"Then, Son," Mongwire replied, "We'll follow your recommendation to see what we will see. It may be we can find this boundary." Mongwire grasped a handful of jerky, offering some to Wen. They ate silently. Mongwire was musing over the idea of limits of land. Certainly, he knew land had limits, but he'd never considered that as something to think on systematically. As was so often the case, he thought Wen had said something significant. How, he wondered, did a child of thirteen have such thoughts?

Mongwire looked at the jerky. He frowned. "You stay here. I'm going to hunt for some real meat," he told his son.

Wen raised his hand in acknowledgement. He also raised his left eyebrow. His eyes spotted a couple of plantains and other greens that he knew were edible by observing the local people they'd met.

Wen formed the hearth, surrounded it with stones, and laid the twigs and branches in the pattern that would encourage a fire to burn readily once a spark ignited their starter. He gathered the greens. Using the fire starter platform and the revolving hard straight fire starter stick, he began rubbing his hands in practiced motion to spark the dry moss that laid beside the platform. It did not take long. He had a perfect small hearth fire by the time Mongwire returned with a young deer from which he'd removed the guts. As evening turned dark, they ate very well.

The next morning Mongwire and Wen packed a few things, concealing the others except for the deer meat that hung out of the reach of scavengers. They began following the path to the north. They traveled it to the end of the mountain on the path. From the top of the mountain, which wasn't a very tall one, they saw the ice sheet, not expecting it would be so close. Both were astonished at the sight. Mongwire and Wen couldn't take their eyes from it. They'd never seen such a sight. The ice sheet was so much thicker than they had even begun to imagine. It looked one way as the sheet met the sea; quite another from where it met land as viewed from the mountain. Both were eager to reach the lowland to see the ice sheet closer. Others must have had similar thoughts, for the trail had a descending pathway not more than ten body lengths ahead. Mongwire and Wen began to descend the path. It was steep, but they could go down, even with their backpacks.

Hours later when they had reached the lowland, the two were astounded. The ice sheet looked different to them from the ground. Not only were they amazed at the size of the sheet which rose quite a way overhead, far beyond the heights where non-migratory birds flew, but also there was a palpable power there, so close to the ice. It was something they each could feel. It was as if the ice sheet pulsed with life. It raised hairs on the back of Mongwire's neck. He was not used to feeling things he couldn't explain.

"It's as if the ice were a living human, and we are ants," Mongwire said.

"Good comparison, Father," Wen said really meaning it.

Momentarily Mongwire forgot the ice sheets. The compliment from his son was a treasure to him. He glowed in it for a brief time.

Wen went straight up to the ice sheet and touched it. At a distance the ice groaned. Wen backed away quickly, as if the spirit of the ice had groaned at his touch.

"That was not wise," Mongwire said to admonish his son, all the while wishing he'd done the same thing, but for fear had not.

"It's really ice resting here on land!" Wen said, still clearly in awe. "I'm used to seeing it on the water, but on land it looks so out of place!"

A huge cracking sound rent the quiet. As if in slow motion, a piece of the ice sheet broke off in the sunshine and fell to the ground below to the west of them, smaller pieces shattered off flying through the air on the large chunk's impact with the ground. The impact shook the ground. Wen and Mongwire looked long and hard at each other. That was a caution from the gods, they both understood without exchanging a word.

There was a breeze blowing from the ice, and it chilled them. Mongwire and Wen sought refuge in the forested area across from the ice. As if frozen still themselves, they watched the ice. A little later, they heard the sound of trumpeting mammoths. The ground moved again. Mongwire and Wen were glad they'd retreated back into the forested area. They could see the grassland below, and when the mammoths drew near, they could observe the large beasts without being in the way. Each was startled to see the speed at which the mammoths could move. They'd only seen them walking slowly. The forest also provided another benefit. They were at a distance from falling chunks of ice.

"Could we remain here for a while to observe?" Wen asked. "All we know is that it's cold here and mammoths pass by. There might be more we should learn. If we stayed for a moon or more, we might gain information."

"I'm willing to stay until the full moon. More than that and we take the chance of too cold a winter. We are supposed to explore this area. I don't need to remind you that our winter clothing is cached back at the mouth of the river we followed. That winter clothing must last us for our return trip home, so we're not going back to take it. We'll have to go further south than our cache to be warm for the coldest part of the year. Either that or we must make winter clothing. I don't want to do that."

"I understand, Father." Wen was already looking for a cave or shelter.

"Let's go back up the hill. I may have spotted something earlier as we were leaving to come down here," Mongwire said, taking charge.

They climbed back up the hill. Mongwire found the dark area behind some bush. It was a small cave, ideal for a half moon's time. He and Wen gathered their things and put them in the cave. Wen climbed the tree and lowered the deer carcass they'd tied over a limb. Mongwire cut off pieces of meat from a back leg, and Wen raised the deer and re-tied the cordage around the tree. Mongwire was glad they had food from the day before. Instead of having to hunt this evening, they prepared a new hearth by the cave and set up the y-shaped holders for the tree branch they'd run through the meat for roasting it. Wen looked up at the bird above that was singing in the tree. Another bird answered not far away. He looked for a nest but couldn't see one.

Wen liked the land. It drew him with amazement and wonder, causing his thinking place to become more active than it had ever been. He felt alive as he had never felt. Until this point in his life, he'd lived in a small area walled in by mountains and hills on three sides and the sea on the other. He'd never met people from other places. In their land he knew they had just gone through a time of terrible sickness. According to their elders, the stories of their ancestors had been lost when the tellers died. The terrible sickness had eaten away many people in many places on the earth. In addition to the loss of land from the ice sheets that continued to move south, there were fights over who would live where after the terrible sickness. What the sickness didn't kill, wars did. Sometimes when people lost a war, the victors set fire to the huts of all the people. They thought it would purify the place for the victors to live there free of the terrible sickness. Some of those who made war called the terrible sickness the white death, because people became so pale when they had it. It was not a good place or time, Wen thought. In this place there was more land than he knew existed in the whole world, and it was covered with a wonderful forest of tall healthy evergreens mostly. Clearly people lived here, for they followed a path, too wide for a typical animal path. It was a wonderful location for SealEaters.

Stars began to appear. The hunks of meat they'd cut off and speared on the stick were well roasted. They took their pieces off the roasting rod and laid them on the greens Wen had gathered. Wen laid the roasting rod across the y-shaped holders. He speared his pieces of meat one at a time with a shorter stick he'd cut off from a dead branch from which he'd removed the outside bark. He had cut the end of his meat spear on a slant. Juice ran from the meat down the meat spear to his hand. Mongwire ate with his hands, while juice ran down his arms dripping to the ground from his elbows. Juice from their mouths would dribble to their chins. The meat was hot and very good, Mongwire thought. A whippoorwill cut the silence. Then, another. Wen wondered whether he heard more than just one. He could not determine well enough the source of the sound. He found the sound restful in some ways and at the same time it was a little bit unsettling. He mused over entertaining conflicting feelings about a single thing.

Mongwire was an explorer at his core. He wanted to be gone from this place, but he also wanted his son to grow. The moon rose. It was at the thinnest crescent, exactly as he thought. The moon was something to which Mongwire paid much attention. He had to wait for thirteen days. He decided to do as Wen suggested. He'd take the time to learn the way of the animals in this place. That could improve the hunting, he decided. He needed something to occupy him during this enforced rest. Oh, the things he did for this son! he thought.

At the spring Wen washed off the sticks they'd used to spear the meat to cook it over the hearth. Mongwire often teased him for doing that, but Wen didn't want pieces of old meat sticking to what he was about to eat. The women at the Cove were very careful about that. The spring was conveniently close by. Father and son entered the cave and laid down on their sleeping places, covering themselves with hairless skins. They went black immediately.

In the morning Mongwire arose first. He folded his cover and stretched. His thick graying beard was littered with particles of leaves and dirt, so he ran his fingers through it wondering where the debris came from, shaking it a bit. Wen opened his eyes. He raised himself up waiting until his father left the small cave before he stood up. He folded his sleeping skins and left the cave. Wen went to the tree to lower the deer carcass. Mongwire came immediately and cut off a hunk.

"That what you want?" he asked.

"That's a good portion," Wen replied.

Mongwire cut a piece for himself. He took the pieces to the cave entryway while Wen quickly tied the deer out of reach of bears and other animals. He snatched some greens and quickly placed them on the ground for Mongwire to put the meat on. Mongwire had become accustomed to the wait. He never bothered with things like that. A little dirt didn't hurt anyone, he always told Wen, but he realized it made a big difference to Wen, so he waited patiently for the food that he knew would be coming. Mongwire laid the meat on the greens and wiped his hands on his tunic.

The banked fire still had embers. Mongwire started the fire, and they cooked the meat over a blaze, hoping it would cook faster, which of course it did.

Mongwire and Wen set out, leaving their backpacks in the cave. They carried pouches of jerky knowing they'd return. Mongwire and Wen also put some of the morning's meat in their pouches, because it was decidedly better tasting.

They neared the bottom of the mountain and Mongwire was about to depart to study animal life until he spotted the most extraordinary looking animals he'd ever seen in the valley to the east, moving towards them. They were musk oxen. These animals had horns that appeared parted. From great lobes the horns wound down in a tapering curve pointing slightly forward at the end of the curve. Because they were shedding, they had brown shaggy coats that were ratty looking where strips of tangled lighter colored hair fell like thick cordage or in sheets like skin from their sides and back. They had faces a little like an aurochs. As they moved closer, Mongwire observed they had hooves that split in two parts. A few of them had black hooves that curled like his fingernails and toenails when they grew too long. Mongwire's nails curled under; the animal he observed had hooves that curled upwards. The animals were quiet, only slightly murmuring or exhaling with a noise.

Wen noticed movement to the far west. A single animal, fox or wolf, he wondered which, was heading towards the musk oxen. Wen exhaled and Mongwire looked at him. With his eyes, Wen showed him what he'd seen.

Mongwire watched as the wolf approached. It tried to reach the smallest in the herd, but the whole group of musk oxen began to circle and wound themselves around the curled hoofed animals and the young one, creating a circle from which their heads with formidable horns appeared on the outside. The wolf just remained, head lowered, waiting. Some of the male musk oxen left the group and began to gallop towards the single wolf. They chased the wolf a good way from their tight musk oxen circle of protection, still surrounding the seemingly old and definitely very young.

They followed the wolf until Mongwire and Wen could no longer see it. Then, they returned and the circle disbanded and grazing continued. Mongwire and Wen were amazed. Never had they seen such behavior. Mongwire thought momentarily that they'd have missed this display, if he and Wen had begun to travel south that morning. It had been well worth the wait.

It was after high sun when the musk oxen began to travel east. When they had followed the musk oxen a long distance, Mongwire left the forest soon followed by Wen. Mongwire wanted to examine the leavings of the musk oxen. He also wanted to see the shape of their prints in the soil. Those two clues were fundamental to hunters. They examined the signs and Wen gathered hunks of the fur that the animals had left behind. He was amazed at the softness of it. Wen gathered a lot of it, shoving it into his tunic above the belt until it gave him a very strange appearance and would take no more.

"Why are you bringing that?" Mongwire asked.

"I thought it might be good to line our boots this winter." Having stuffed his tunic from neck to waist, he hung the long lengths of the musk oxen shed around his neck.

They headed back to the cave. Mongwire and Wen both were very satisfied with the event of the day. For some reason, Wen was extremely hungry. He pulled a piece of jerky from the pouch. That was all that was left, since he had consumed the fresh meat earlier while watching the musk oxen.

Mongwire checked the area when he returned to the cave. It was something he always did. Nothing had bothered the carcass. There was no sign, human or animal. He relaxed and began to make a fire in the hearth.

An extremely loud grinding noise ripped through the quiet. It was accompanied by high pitched shrieks intermittently, then more grinding and more shrieks.

"That must be the ice sheet," Wen voiced his thoughts needlessly. The sounds could only have come from one source. The sounds lasted to the slow count of fifteen.

"That could be annoying," Mongwire said.

"Yes, Father, but now we know it happens. Do you wonder what else happens?"

Mongwire found it unsettling. His desire was to leave the place immediately, but he could see Wen's point of learning something. They had seen new and different animal behavior and heard an ice sheet make a lot of noise.

"I don't really wonder what else happens. We know the ice breaks off, and it makes noise. It's ice. On land it cannot turn over as it does in sea water. What else could there be to know?"

"I don't know. I do know it can melt, because it's ice. A lot of it melting at one time could create quite a lake."

"I suppose," Mongwire replied losing interest. He was not comfortable speculating in this manner.

Wen moved over to the area where the fewest trees were. The area was flooded with sun. He pulled his tunic over his head and lay down on it. His chest absorbed the sun's warmth. It felt wonderful.

Wen thought of the noise he'd just heard. He wondered whether ice had a spirit or whether the sounds were just a part of the environment—and ice was not really alive. He'd been carefully taught that all things were alive and filled with spirit, but he could not find a sense of life when he picked up a dead stick or a rock. If a stick had a spirit, did the spirit leave when the stick separated from the living tree as a human spirit did when the human died, or was it just cast off, spiritless, while the whole spirit stayed with the tree? Did a part of him have spirit when it died or did the spirit remain with him until his whole person died? He thought that loss of a fingernail did not reduce by some tiny amount the totality of his spirit. The separated fingernail, he was convinced was spiritless. Nor did a separated fingernail take part of him to the land of the dead. Some rocks had a feel of life to them, as if some force of life flowed through them, but as for a small rock, he compared that to a dead twig. He'd heard similar sounds in the ice on the water, well, not the grinding sounds, but certainly the high pitched ones. Was it just a sound that occurred in the natural world of ice? It was hard to question against what one had been taught, he thought.

He remembered the voyage past the ice. What an amazing chance to learn. He did not like the storms at sea. That frightened him terribly. He wanted to live. He wanted to learn everything there was to learn about this land they were going to explore. He'd never felt so alive. The fierce winds and the pelting with rain, hail, water, or ice during the crossing was not pleasant. Comparing his experience with others, he was dumbfounded that the gods could make water from the tops of waves feel like rocks when the wind threw it at you. What he expected to remain forever in his memory was the huge storm where they saw some of the enormous chunks of ice literally turn over and over in the water. The largest part of the ice chunk was so deep in the water it seemed impossible to believe that they could overturn. He had seen it happen more than once with his own eyes. Fact was established. He didn't really want to see that ever again. It made him aware how small and fragile he was.

Wen thought of Camun, daughter of Amoroz and Fluga. He and she had played together since they were young. He preferred her company to Sted, Whug and Gemu's son, who tried to emulate Reg, thinking that would make him powerful like Reg. Among the others in the age group, Megg, Camun, Egorgo, Pligo, Tob, Vaima, Pupe, and himself, nobody much wanted to be around Sted. Wen pitied him, but not enough to want to offer friendship. A person like that, he reasoned, would not return friendship, any more than Reg would.

Camun's beauty lay more inside than outside. She was a girl that one would see but not see, he reasoned. Until she blew into her flute. Camun played haunting music on her flute. It could raise the hairs on the back of his neck. It could cause him to see wonders in the ordinary things about him. It caused him to see and feel and almost smell or taste things in unique ways he'd never dreamed. When they talked, he'd found she was able to keep up with his thoughts and he could keep up with hers, which were reasoned in much the same way, except for the intuitive part of her reasoning, which left him breathless. She could reach conclusions quicker and, he wondered whether he shouldn't credit her as having more accuracy than he did. He wished he had that intuitive sense. But more than all that, Camun made him feel special on a personal level. It drew him to her as to no other.

He and Megg had talked about which girl they'd like as a wife. Megg was devoted to Egorgo who seemed to feel the same about Megg. Egorgo was stunningly beautiful everyone agreed. She had brown hair, not really remarkable, bright blue eyes that showed deeply into her spirit, dark long lashes, and eyebrows the color and shape of crow wings. Her lips were soft looking, very full, and startlingly, naturally red. Her body was beginning to take the shape of a woman's and promised to be curvy. She was just beginning to use her body to learn the effects it might have on the men and older boys. Megg looked the other way, not really grasping the importance of what she was doing. He thought she returned the devotion he felt. She let him believe that. Reg paid little attention to her. Had he known of Megg's interest in his daughter, he would have quashed that, but all who knew or suspected were careful not to let him become aware. Wen had loved Camun since they were young children. He could see no one but her as wife. Thoughts of her warmed him as the sun warmed him. He turned over on his tunic to let the sun warm his back. There in the sun he dreamed of her, almost hearing the tunes she played.

Mongwire had gone inside the cave to lie down on his sleeping place. He felt odd, as if something was wrong. He had a slight feeling of nausea. Perhaps, he thought, if I lie down for a while this odd feeling will pass. He lay there rubbing his left arm with his right hand.

Some time passed, and the sun moved off Wen's back and he felt a little chill. He picked up his tunic and put it back on. He was slightly surprised not to see his father anywhere. He stooped down and put his head into the small cave.

Mongwire looked at him. He was sweating.

"Father?" Wen asked, "Are you sick?"

"I just felt a little tired," Mongwire replied in the manner of SealEater men, minimizing anything physically aberrant.

"You don't look like you feel well," Wen persisted.

"Why don't you fix the meat? By the time I eat, I should be fine."

Quickly Wen went out and found that he needed to re-start the fire from a spark. He took the fire starter and quickly had a small fire going. He climbed up the tree, untied the deer carcass, scrambled down and tied the carcass lower. He went to the area where he harvested greens and picked a handful. They were smaller than the others had been. He noted that he'd need to find another location for the greens. He went to the spring and ran water over the greens to wash the dirt off. He laid them on the rocks he'd prepared beside the hearth. Then, Wen took the straight cooking rod and headed toward the deer. He cut off hunks the normal size for them and threaded them on the cooking stick. He laid the cooking stick in the holders and went to tie up the deer. He climbed the tree and tied it up high.

He looked in on his father when he returned. He had turned so his back was to the entryway. Wen tightened the corners of his mouth in consternation and returned to cooking the deer meat.

He heard Mongwire moan and went into the cave.

"Father, what is it?" he asked deeply concerned.

"I just need some help to stand up," Mongwire admitted.

Wen helped him rise to his feet to go out to the place where they sat to eat. Wen became more concerned as time passed. Ironically, Mongwire began to feel a little better. He was hungry.

When the meat had cooked, Wen took the meat for his father and placed it on his greens. Wen was becoming a bit more optimistic. His father began to eat.

Wen used his meat spear and began to eat also. He finished up quickly and went to the spring to wash the sticks. When he returned, he found his father clearly in extreme pain. Wen helped his father back into the cave where he lay back on the soft skin.

"It just has to wear off," Mongwire offered as an explanation to Wen. He actually had no concept of what was wrong, only that something rather serious was happening. He did not consider himself old enough for the problem to be extremely serious. He'd had no injury. It bothered him that he was having trouble breathing. He hadn't just exerted a great amount of energy.

Wen was deeply troubled. He tried to remain patient and trust that his father knew what was wrong, but it didn't look like anything he'd ever seen, and his father seemed too vague to give Wen confidence that he understood his condition.

Wen sat by the hearth. He kept his hearing focused on his father. He watched the fire's glow and the occasional flames. He wasn't sure that he would go black that night. Dark fell on the forest. Stars came out in amazing brilliance. The whippoorwill began its odd song. For the first time in his life, Wen felt alone and helpless. He wanted to cry, but he knew that at this time, his father would need him to be strong.

In the cave Mongwire arose. He no longer felt the horrible pain, just slightly disoriented. Oddly, there was a great light in the cave. He could hear far in the distance where the light was brightest his parents calling him. It was strangely compelling. He hurried to them. Suddenly he stopped. Wen, he remembered. Wen is only thirteen. He's alone. From the distance he heard his mother and father calling. They kept telling him all would be well. Mongwire realized that he no longer breathed air. He could see his body on the sleeping place below him. He was surprised to notice he lacked feelings of emotion he thought he should have had, but the thought passed like a vapor. He went to his parents irresistibly drawn, his thoughts of Wen evaporating the closer he came to his parents. They reached out to him and he was pleased to see them. He felt at home. The new place he'd been seeking across the sea was right before his eyes. He'd found his new home.

Wen listened and waited. At one point during the night he nearly fell over, having momentarily gone black. He jerked himself awake and listened. He heard nothing from his father. He wanted desperately to know how his father was doing, but he didn't want to take the chance of wakening him, if he had gone black. He crept to the cave entrance and listened. All was quiet, so he returned to his place and resumed watching the fire. Morning came as it does slowly in the mountains. Wen waited, giving his father plenty of time to awaken. Finally he could stand it no longer. He went to the cave entrance and looked inside. He was utterly and completely shocked. His father lay on his back, mouth hanging weirdly and eyes askew. Wen knew instantly what had happened. He did not understand why.

He went immediately to close his father's eyes, for the visual effect was something he couldn't bear to see. Then the reality fully hit him. His father had died. He loved him so much. He collapsed to the ground in tears. As the initial grief began to subside, the one thing he had not thought to consider came like a hit to a boat from a hidden, underwater log. He was utterly alone in a strange land where he was not due to meet other SealEaters for two years. In some ways Wen was mature way beyond his years; in others, he was what he was, a thirteen-year-old boy. He sat at his eating place, put his elbows on his knees, put his hands on his head and wept again. A bird landed on a tree branch where the deer was tied. The bird scolded him very loudly. Wen didn't hear it.

Finally, when Wen's tears were emptied, he stood up woodenly and looked for a place in the land where he could dig a suitable grave. Morning had turned to evening. He was hollow inside, flat emotionally. He had something to do. It was distasteful. He would have a thousand times preferred not to do it. He had no choice. Wen decided to use the place under the hanging deer. Somehow, though he didn't understand why, it seemed appropriate.

Wen dug with the scapula of the deer for hours. There were rocks in the soil. Wen was in no hurry. He simply dug. By night he had a suitable hole in the ground. He took his father's body and laid it carefully in the grave on his side with his knees bent and raised to his chest. He had no ochre and there were no nearby flowers. He sat at the edge of the grave staring at his father's body. More tears fell. Wen wondered where they came from. He had shed so many tears that day. He stood and slowly began to fill the grave back. When he finished, he placed rocks atop the mounded earth.

Having eaten nothing that day, he entered the cave and went black. He had already decided to leave the place the following morning after eating some of the deer meat. He'd travel south hoping to find other humans. He was desperately lonely and frightened. He was not the hunter his father was. He would find his way to the path down the mountain and over the hill to the boat. He would head to the confluence of the two rivers. That was a typical place for people to live. He hoped to find people there.

Wen dreamed that night of a great monster chasing him. He ran and ran as fast as he could run, but the monster kept gaining on him. He remembered the dream when he waked up. He looked all around, but the area was as calm and quiet as it had ever been.

Wen sat up on his sleeping place. He looked at the things he had to decide to take from the cave. He wanted all the spears. His father was an expert point maker. He was far from good. His father's backpack was larger. Maybe, he thought, he could take both backpacks. His father's furred skin was bigger and of greater warmth. He wanted that one. He decided to try to carry both furred and hairless skins. He'd take all the jerky. Unlike his father, what he ate was not of great significance. He did not tire of eating the same thing meal after meal.

Wen forgot about eating. He gathered all the things together that he chose to take and left. Carrying the smaller backpack filled entirely with jerky was something he could manage. His backpack had the unfurred skins, his and his father's bowls, a few stones his father carried, the fire starter, cordage, and his musk oxen discarded shed. Carrying all the spears was hard, so he tied most of them upright to his father's backpack. It also carried the two furred skins, rolled tight and tied on top of the backpack. The backpack fully loaded and with additions was extremely heavy. He was glad he didn't have terribly far to go to the canoe.

Going down the mountain and across the hill took the whole day. Spears kept coming loose from the tied cordage, and he feared breaking a point. He battled to make it to the water, not eating at all but pushing onward. Night was coming on when he reached the boat. The boat was tied. He carefully placed his treasures in the boat and tied them to the edges. He climbed into the boat, laying a furred skin in the bottom of the boat since there was no water inside. He opened his backpack and took out a few strips of jerky. He chewed it while his thinking place remained silent.

The vague sense of his dream washed over him. It was disturbing. He looked all around and listened carefully to the noises. Nothing was the least unusual. A great groaning noise split through the area, but Wen knew well what made that sound. The ice sheet was moving. That's all. No monstrous thing of the dream time. He wondered whether the dream he had was from hearing a noise from the ice sheet while he had gone black. He didn't think that was it. Something gnawed at him. Each time he felt he was coming close to understanding, it slipped away.

After watching the stars for a while, Wen pulled the furred skin over him and went black in the boat.

As the sun rose over the hilltop to the east, two men in a dugout rowed upriver. They noticed the boat in which Wen slept. It looked like the boat they sought. They'd never seen a boat quite like it. It was different from and larger than theirs. It was made of a frame covered with a skin unlike any skin they'd seen. They saw the boy in the boat and wondered whether he was alive. They pulled their boat to shore and quietly approached the boat with the boy. Wen woke up and was frightened when he saw the two men. He tried to separate himself from the furred skin, but the exit was in the direction of the two men. It was awkward. Being frightened made him reflect back to the dream. In it the more he feared the closer the monster came. Wen stood up in the boat and yelled at the men.

The men were surprised and halted. Wen continued his bombastic rhetoric, ordering them to leave. He said just about anything he could imagine to appear strong.

The men were seasoned warriors. They realized the boy was young. They credited him with bravery, but they caught him and held him by his arms.

They calmed him down and the three of them walked to a flat place where they could sit.

The older of the two men began to ask questions. Wen didn't understand their language, but he seemed to know they wanted to know who he was and how he came to be there.

He said, "I am Wen." He pointed to his chest and said, "Wen." Then he pointed back once at each of the men.

The older one said, "Akti," while pointing to his chest.

The other man said, "Doho."

Wen repeated their names carefully. He felt a sense of relief, because the men had not shown any violence towards him. Wen listened to every word the men spoke. He knew that he could only communicate by learning their language.

Akti said, "How old are you?" He pointed to the sun and then stood by a tree, pointing. He pulled off leaves. Then he acted out cold by shivering and appearing to pull a skin over his shoulders. Then he stopped pretending to shiver and pointed to the tree again.

Wen understood. He took a stick and made thirteen marks in the sand.

Doho counted the marks and said, "Thirteen. Wen, thirteen years,"

Wen repeated nodding to show he understood, "Wen, thirteen years." He added, "Akti? Doho?"

Akti drew twenty-eight lines in the sand, and said "twenty-eight." Doho used the same process to tell that he was twenty-seven.

Wen was struggling to keep track of all the words.

Through the use of sign language and acting, Akti asked Wen where his father was. Wen burst into tears. It took him a while to control his emotion. Even with the two strangers, Wen felt terribly alone. He tried to explain what happened to Mongwire. He acted out pain in his chest and rubbing his left arm. He really didn't understand what other pain Mongwire might have had. He acted out digging while tears flowed.

The two men could understand enough to know that Wen was grieving and also frightened at being alone. They asked carefully where he came from, because the boy did not look like any of the people they knew in the area. Clearly he spoke in a way with which they were unfamiliar.

Akti made it clear that he was to come with them. They tied his boat to theirs and told him to step into their boat in the center. Wen did as told. He knew he was out of options. The men seemed good to him.

As they rowed Wen practiced the words until he felt certain he wouldn't forget what he learned. Then he put his hand in the water and in his own language said, "What's this?"

Doho told him, "River." Doho turned to face Wen. He picked up a handful of water. Pointing to it he said, "Water." He pointed sweepingly to the river and said, "River."

Wen practiced the words first in his thinking place and then aloud, so he could hear himself say them, to see whether they sounded right.

While practicing "river" Doho turned around and smiled.

When Wen began to practice "water," Doho turned around and said, "Water," emphasizing the t. Wen had reduced the t sound to a d sound, the SealEater word for water was wudah, close but not the same.

Wen was careful to make the t sound and Doho nodded with a smile.

The men and Wen traveled for four days. Wen wondered why the men were there, because once they found him, they seemed to have no other reason to be on the river. They told him they were returning to their home. The answer didn't tell him anything.

Wen was doing well enough with the language that by the time they reached the men's home, he was able to converse in very basic language. What he had discovered is that the languages had differences, they were not that different from his own. He had been able to adjust easily. The thinking pattern behind the language was the same.

They arrived at evening in time for their evening meal. All three of them were very hungry. The people were surprised to see a boy in the boat. The two men had gone upriver because there had been two children who said they'd seen two men row upriver in a strange boat. The two children came forth and identified the boat the men towed home as the one they'd seen going upriver. On the front of the boat was a carving of a strange animal's head, one they'd never seen, so they could not tell anyone what it was. It was a carving of a seal's head. None of them had ever seen a seal. Just before entering the water, but above enough that dragging the boat to shore wouldn't remove them, there were either the two front legs of the seal or fins like fish have. The people could not determine what the projections were. In the back of the boat there were two very odd looking carved things that were not feet. They looked like double fish fins. The people who observed the boat wondered at the animal that appeared to be a land animal with fish fins. Sinehaught walked down to the river's edge where they'd pulled up the strange boat and looked at it carefully. Never in his sixty-five years had he seen anything like it.

The people gathered to eat, but they were eager to hear about this new boy who had come to their home. The gentle hum of normal eating conversation was silent as all ate as fast as possible.

Wen looked up and noticed a girl who appeared about his age staring at him. She was bold, he thought, for the girl didn't look away when he noticed her. Instead without expression she looked right into his eyes. He blushed.

Tapti was confused when she saw Wen blush. She was curious. She didn't mean to cause him discomfort. He was just different and those differences inflamed her desire to know more. She looked away.

People gathered around a small hearth fire. The Chief asked Akti to tell what happened.

Akti spoke slowly, "We found the boat five days upriver from here. It was well concealed in the watergrass. The reason we found it is that Wen—that's the boy's name—had fallen asleep in the boat and was covered with a fur. We saw the fur above the watergrass. We have asked Wen many questions. He learns our language fast; his use of signs is commendable. His people are spread out in this land looking for a place where they can come. They live across the salt sea where the sun rises. They used boats to cross the sea, eating seals, like the animal carved on the boat, along the way. The ice has caused seals to come to the beach where they live by the sea. The number of seals is decreasing so they need to find a new land. There are wars beyond the mountains that surround them on land. There's nowhere for them to go."

Akti continued. "Doho and I asked him how he was there with no father. He broke down in grief and wept. His father died from chest and arm pain. He buried him. He was frightened, for he'd seen no people, and he was alone in this big land. He'd never been alone. At solstice in two years, all his people plan to gather at the place where our river enters the sea. From there they'll decide whether to bring their people here. This is something to consider for us. Do we wish to see others move to our land? I hope I've understood correctly."

Doho broke in, "There is room in this land for all, Akti. Would you try to stop them?"

The conversation was moving a little fast for Wen. He had the feeling that some of these people might not welcome his people to this land, though he could not understand why.

"I'm just mentioning it because we have great hunting. With more people, the hunting will be affected.

"Akti," Kalu spoke up, "The next people to us are a five-day boat trip or a seven-day hike over the mountain trails to the west. There is food for all here."

Akti continued, "I like Wen. His people may be very good people. Just think how it would be if many, many people decided to come here. It could be a bad thing for us. I just feel something pressing me to say these words. Their arrival could mean war someday for us."

Doho replied, "Akti, our Creator, the Great Spirit who guides us, has made it clear for us to be especially kind to those who travel, to those in need, to those who struggle. You would go against the few stories we have remaining from the old times?"

Akti was feeling pressed into a place where he was not comfortable at all. It was as though some spirit had put the ideas he spoke into his thoughts and he just said the words. He genuinely liked Wen, and personally he had no problem with his people moving to this place. He was wrapped in confusion.

"Sinehaught, will you help me?" Doho asked quietly.

Sinehaught looked down. He took a stick he'd been poking hearth surround rocks with and began to make parallel wavy lines in the sand. All eyes were on their medicine man.

Finally, looking up with sad eyes, the old man began to speak. "Akti, you speak a truth out of time."

Everyone looked at Sinehaught as if he misspoke.

Sinehaught continued staring at the sand, as if he could see the future in it, "At some time far from now, boats will come with white wings, as birds on the water. When they come the ice will be gone from the sea. No great pieces of ice will flow past the shore. The ice that rests on the land north from here will have melted. Those who come in the bird boats will come here pretending peace. We will go to war against them as they flow over the land as clouds flow over the sky, and we will lose the war. The people of the bird boats will do unspeakable things, thinking they do what's right. They will not understand that the land on which they walk is sacred to the Creator. They will waste and ruin. They will not, however, kill all of us. We will preserve the truth. We are given the truth and we are told to preserve it. That is so far into the future. By the time it occurs, Wen and all his people who come here will be part of us. You speak the truth but not of this time. You speak the truth for us and Wen's people, if they choose to come. Do not try to apply what you've seen to our time. Welcome Wen's people. Their boats have no white wings. No bird boats. Sinehaught laid down the stick.

"Thank you, Sinehaught," Doho said.

"That's quite alright," Sinehaught replied. "When the spirits push you to speak," he looked into Doho's and then Akti's eyes, "it's important that you do. Just remember to do what you did. Ask for someone who understands to make sense of what you said."

"I will do as you say, Sinehaught," Doho replied. Akti still struggled with his having spoken a truth out of time, a truth that chilled him to the bone after Sinehaught made sense of it.

"Wen's people made a dangerous voyage," Ohmut said, looking at Wen. He assessed Wen as having done something that took enormous courage.

People murmured assent all around. A few of them had actually seen the sea. None had been on its waters.

Sinehaught looked at Wen. He knew he must guide and protect the boy. "You will share my hut," he said. "Do you have sleeping skins?"

Wen understood the old man.

"Yes," he replied quietly.

"Bring them here," Sinehaught told him.

Wen stood up, walked to the boat, and pulled out both backpacks. He carried them to Sinehaught, who stood up and led him to his hut. His hut was very large compared to the others. A pile of evergreen branches were cast by the opening.

"It seems someone or more than one person has brought you some soft material for your sleeping place. Put the evergreens over there," he said, pointing to a place along the hut wall.

Wen did as he was told. He laid his furry skin on the boughs with the fur side up. He laid Mongwire's skin with the fur on the down side, so he'd be between two layers of fur when he went black. He folded the hairless skins on top of the sleeping place. He put the backpacks against the wall after removing the spears from the cordage that attached them to the backpack.

Sinehaught stepped over and took one of the spears in his hand. He examined it carefully.

"Did you do this?" he asked.

"I wish I could say I did it, but no, my father fully mastered the crafting of tools. He made them."

Sinehaught did not understand all of Wen's words because he mixed words he knew with the ones he'd just learned. But Sinehaught learned that Wen's father made the points.

"Do you know how it's done?" he asked.

"Yes. My hands are just not skilled," he said.

"Will you let me take one of these to our expert spear point maker?" Sinehaught asked.

Wen hated to part with any of them, but he handed the spear that was his least favorite to Sinehaught.

Sinehaught returned the one he examined and took the one Wen offered. He understood.

A whippoorwill began its nightly call. Wen huddled on his sleeping skins and began to shake, tears falling from his eyes.

"What's upset you?" Sinehaught asked, concerned.

After some time, Wen replied, "My father died. I heard a bird (he made the sound of a whippoorwill). I was alone. You are like a father. I hear same bird." Tears fell down his face.

Sinehaught leaned the spear against the wall and squatted down beside Wen. "You are now my son. The whippoorwill is not a sign of death, Wen. It is a bird of the evening and night—nothing more, nothing less. Do not let fear grasp you. The Great Spirit created you. You have already found that when you were alone and in need, that same spirit brought you here to us. You have us as your people. There is no cause to fear. Whatever life brings you, the Great Spirit will not forsake you. He provides." Sinehaught was slow and deliberate, signing often.

Wen looked Sinehaught eye to eye. He understood. He wanted to believe. "The bird does not tell of the approach of death?"

"No, Wen. It's just a bird."

Wen smiled. "Thank you, Sinehaught. Thank you." Wen understood he had a new father. That father was not about to die.

The old man touched Wen's shoulder. He stood. "I will return. I go to share this amazing point with our best spear tip maker."

Sinehaught left the hut with the spear. Wen was tired, not so much from rowing which he had done, but from the stress level he'd been experiencing. He laid down on the sleeping skins and went black.

When Sinehaught returned, he took the folded hairless skin and covered the boy.

The next day, Kalu asked Wen to talk to him. He had the spear point and was examining it. He wanted to know about the overshot flaking. Wen composed himself. He struggled to remember all the details of what his father had taught him.

He explained about determining the size of the spear point by looking at the fragment of stone he'd be using to make it. He explained that a good point maker would see the point in the hunk of stone and then work to release it. He was unsure whether they understood, even though he used every sign he could imagine. He talked about examining the larger piece until he could see the stone that lay within. He admitted that he found that part confusing. His speculation, he told Kalu, was that you had to have a certain level of skill before that made sense.

Kalu understood. The boy was right.

Wen explained that you flaked to thin from side to side, being careful not to let the piece become too thin in the process. You did one side, flipped the piece over and worked the other side. Then, you rotated the pointed ends and repeated the process.

Kalu was fascinated.

Then, Wen explained, you had your basic form for the spear point. Because Kalu was their expert, he understood Wen.

Then, Wen said, "From there it's just flake with the wide end of the antler horn, dull down the flaked edge with a stone to remove little fractures that might collapse a platform from which you'll strike. Dulling it also keeps you from cutting your hand. Then you strike off a flake causing flakes to go across the stone from side to side. It's important to keep your fingers out of the direction you want the flake to travel. Fingers can stop travel of a flake. Each flake at this point can serve as a guide for the next. Watch the platform you set up to strike. Too thick and the flake won't travel far. Too thin and the flake will be tiny."

"I would think, Wen, it would be difficult to do this when the point becomes thin."

Wen laughed, having experienced that too often. "Well, when one breaks between the center and the tip, it makes a good knife," he replied.

Kalu laughed a good laugh and Wen joined him, pulling out a knife from the sheath tied to his belt. "This was forming so well," he said still laughing, holding up the knife and turning it to show both faces of the object.

Kalu took the knife. "You made this?"

"Yes. Good knife—ruined spear point. It removes the flesh from a kill with great speed."

Others were fascinated to know what the two were laughing about, but even those who heard did not understand.

Sinehaught was well pleased. He'd connected two people who needed to connect.

Wen knew he had to find a way to fit into this small group of people. There were only twenty-five of them. Only one child was an infant. Wen noted it, but did not try to understand. He understood that the pairs were Akti and Uloma, Doho and Nomelt, Kalu and Ga, Ohmut and Talus, and Chief Os and Ain. Wen liked them and was impressed that they interacted well with each other, far better than SealEaters did with other SealEaters. He wondered how they maintained the peace so well.

One day as he walked along the river's edge with Bagaguha, Ohmut's daughter of his same age, he asked her how it was that the people were so peaceful with each other.

She tossed back her long unfettered hair and laughed gently. "We know when it's time to break apart," she replied.

"What?" Wen asked. Clearly he did not understand.

"We learned that when too many live too closely, it's a good place for unwanted strife to grow."

"How many is too many?" Wen asked fascinated.

"Forty to fifty," she said without hesitation.

"In our land we have no peace among our people. There is always some irritant. We have about a hundred people living together at the Cove. How do you find wives or husbands not too closely related?" he asked.

"Once a year, when the leaves turn color, we gather in a single large group. There are about twenty of us small groups. Then those of us willing can choose to pair with another. If the group's not too large, we can choose whichever group to join we would prefer. If the group size is approaching forty to fifty, we have to choose a different group."

"That's interesting," Wen said. "Bagaguha, I need to fit into this group, but I don't know how. My age is a problem, I think. That, and my father is not here."

"Wen, what is it that interests you, if you were free to do anything at all you wanted?"

"What I loved doing was learning to become a healer. I wanted to know what causes sickness and what plants to use to cure it. I also wanted to know whether there were sicknesses that could not be cured. My father felt that was not manly. He wanted me to be a mariner or a hunter."

"How interesting. Have you talked to Sinehaught about it?"

"No. Why would I do that?"

"That's what Sinehaught does. He's our connection with things that are spirit, and also he knows how to keep healthy and how to cure sickness with the plants that grow here."

"Thank you so much! I may yet have a chance to become what I want so much to become." In Wen the seed of hope sprouted again. The seed was precious to him.

"Well, I'd think Sinehaught would be delighted to teach you. You're quick to learn, Wen. You have a great ability to reason things."

Wen blushed. He didn't understand blushing, and he wished he'd stop doing that.

"Would you like to gather greens with me for our evening meal?" she asked.

"That would be good," he replied, "Will you tell me the names of the plants?"

"I'll share the names of all I know. Some I'm afraid I know are good to eat, but I don't know their names. Sinehaught knows them all. Wen, you're going to need clothing for winter. I see you have an extra fur and a hairless skin. If you give me those, I can make you some clothes for winter. You ask how you can fit in. That's how I fit in."

"You'd do that for me?" he asked amazed.

"Well, of course, I'm almost finished what I was making for Omm. I can start yours as soon as I finish his. Helping to keep us clothed is what I do."

"I am very grateful, Bagaguha. How can I return the favor?"

"Someday I may be sick and you will cure me or at least make me comfortable. Just bring me the skins as soon as possible."

"I will," he promised.

They began to pick the plants that Ain and Talus would add to the boil bag for dinner. They found a good supply.

After the evening meal, Wen asked Sinehaught whether he might teach him to become a healer. He admitted that his father wanted him to become a mariner, but he really wanted to become a healer from the time he was very young.

Sinehaught looked down at the ground. He thought for some time. Then, he asked, "Are you asking because you bear ill will to your father for dying?"

Wen looked at him as if he asked a question that was unthinkable.

Sinehaught laughed, "Don't bother to answer, Wen. I can see the answer. I just wanted to verify my own thoughts."

"I would never wish to offend my father alive or dead," Wen said.

"Good. Yes, Wen, I've been eager to find someone who could learn what I know. You have the ability to do it. Your thinking is the kind of thinking a healer needs to have. I will teach you. We start tomorrow."

Wen smiled. He could not believe that finally he'd have an opportunity to learn what he'd always wanted to learn.

When Sinehaught wasn't teaching him, Wen often walked the river's edge. Often Bagaguha would join him and they'd walk and then gather greens for the evening meal. It wasn't that it was planned but both looked forward to the meetings when they occurred.

One day Bagaguha asked, "Wen, do you find me attractive?"

"Well, of course, who wouldn't? You are beautiful."

It was Bagaguha's turn to blush. Nobody had ever said that to her.

"I think you are growing into a very good looking man. In fact I sometimes dream of you."

Wen's mouth fell open. He was shocked. Somehow he hadn't thought of girls in a long time. He thought that Camun was the only girl in the world for him. As a result he hadn't looked at girls as someone to be approached—as girls.

"Have I offended you?" Bagaguha asked horrified.

"No, not at all. Bagaguha, back at the Cove I grew up with Camun. We expected to try to pair, but we were too young. Even if we'd been of age, all the elders had to agree that we could join and one of the elders flatly refused any time anyone tried."

"That's really strange. Why would he do that?"

"He had power and he chose to use it in a bad way. I don't know what caused him to do that, but though Camun and I wanted eventually to be husband and wife, we knew Reg would say no."

"That's against all nature, Wen," she said shocked.

"It is. I have uncles who are in their thirties and forties who have never been able to take a wife."

She looked at him dumbfounded.

"Why haven't you all together risen up to overtake him?"

"Because he's an elder."

"There's somewhere, Wen, I think, where respect for elders ends when they go contrary to nature."

"He is a strong powerful man."

"A strong powerful man can be subdued by many who are not as strong."

"That may be true, Bagaguha. Somehow, though, either no one ever thought of it or no group ever tried."

"That's as sad as the other is unreasonable." Bagaguha didn't hesitate to voice her opinion.

Wen nodded. He'd never thought of many weak against one strong. It was so simple, he wondered why the SealEaters hadn't thought to use it against Reg.

"Are you going to want a hat for the gathering this year?" she asked.

"I don't understand," he replied.

"When you go to gatherings, people who want to find a person with whom to pair don't wear anything covering their heads. If you're not interested this year, you wear a hat or some kind of head covering. Since you mentioned Camun, I thought you might want a head covering."

"Well, I'd like a head covering. I am not interested in pairing with anyone right now. I have much to think on, and I have much to learn from Sinehaught. Also, my body is not ready yet. I may meet my people two years from now, but I don't know that I have the courage to cross the sea again. If I lack courage, then I'll go without a hat."

Bagaguha listened. She was happy that he wanted a head covering. She actually would like very much to pair with him, but she was aware that there was someone named Camun who had occupied his thoughts.

"Promise me something," she said.

"What's that, Bagaguha?" he asked stopping to look into her eyes.

She kept the eye contact while she said, "If you ever conclude that you can take a wife other than Camun, please let it be me."

Wen was startled.

"Bagaguha, I promise you, if it's not likely Camun and I will pair, I will ask you. That is a solid promise. I think you are wonderful, and I'm sure you would make a very special wife."

It was Bagaguha's turn to be startled. Still locked eye to eye, both smiled. Wen walked to where she stood and they embraced. The promise was sealed.

Instead of going to the gathering, Wen and Sinehaught along with Kalu and Ga whose children were very young, Akti and Uloma and their son, and Ain and her young ones remained at home. Bagaguha wanted to remain at home, but was not permitted.

Winter came and it was cold, but Wen realized it was no colder than where he lived at the Cove, maybe a little warmer. The clothing Bagaguha made was wonderful. He had to admit it was better made than his clothes that were cached. He had provided the musk oxen material to Bagaguha and she used it in his boots. His feet had never been so warm in winter. She had put it as a layer between the boot and the boot liner. The mittens and hat she made for him were like nothing he'd ever seen. The hats had extensions that went out from the neck all the way around the neck and back so that snow melt and rain didn't run through onto his shoulders. He could be outside for long times and still be fully warm without fear of frostbite or becoming damp within his winter clothing.

The seasons passed, each with much to learn. Finally, the second year solstice drew near. Wen felt compelled to go to the cache site. He was in conflict over whether to return or to stay in the new land. He was thoroughly attached to Bagaguha. But then there was Camun. He felt guilty somehow that he couldn't quite pull an image of Camun to his thinking place.

It was decided that Akti and Doho would accompany him to the cache site. By now, Bagaguha had become of an age that she decided to accompany him to the site, and she did not ask for permission from anyone. She simply would go. They would take the seal boat.

The four left early in the morning. One of Wen's backpacks was stuffed with jerky and the other was filled with Bagaguha's pemmican made from bison, fat, and blueberries. All four rowed for a while. Then Akti and Doho stopped rowing, leaving the effort to Wen and Bagaguha. After a time, Akti and Doho relieved the other two. It went that way through the days until they reached the cache.

Wen looked at the site. It did not appear that anyone had been there. They set up camp in the forest just beyond the cache. They were far back enough that they were not visible to any people—not SealEaters—who might pass by. Bagaguha was hurting but gave forth nothing but a brave face. She knew Wen was conflicted, but she didn't allow herself to believe that he would return home with her. She went to be with him until the last possible moment.

The four of them finally pulled over for the evening. They had reached the cache. Wen and Bagaguha went off into the forest to a glade they could see just beyond the forest's edge. In the glade they picked greens and mushrooms for the evening meal. They'd warm them in a bag of water with heated rocks. Wen ate a few bites raw. He liked the greens either way.

That evening, just after they finished eating, they heard some noise apparently on the sea shore. All four of them walked cautiously to the edge of the forest hiding themselves behind trees to watch.

Suddenly, Wen exploded, "Urch!" he shouted, bursting from the forest and running to the river's edge. Entering the river was a boat with Urch and Wapa. Wen called out, "Wapa!"

"Is that Wen?" Urch shouted over the sound of the waves.

Wen jumped up and down from the joy of seeing them again. The men rowed hard and made it to land where Wen, Akti, and Doho pulled the boat onto land.

"Wen, I hardly recognize you. You've grown so tall. And look at the muscles!" Urch looked for Mongwire.

"My father died just after we reached the headwater of this river," Wen explained. "He had terrible pain in his chest and arm."

Urch pulled Wen to him and embraced him. "I'm sorry Wen. We all thought you were too young. It looks like you proved us wrong."

Wen introduced Urch and Wapa to Akti, Doho, and Bagaguha.

The men gathered their things from the boat and brought them to the campsite.

"No others have arrived?" Urch voiced the obvious.

"I've seen no others," Wen replied.

"Are you planning to make the crossing?" Urch asked.

"I have conflict about it, Cousin," Wen replied truthfully.

The men sat and Bagaguha brought them each food on a slab of wood.

Both looked quizzically at her, and thanked her. They were very hungry and the food was delicious, even still warm.

They ate while Akti and Doho began to prepare their skins for sleeping.

"Wen," Urch said quietly, "We need to oil our boat skin before we leave. Do you have any seal oil available?"

"No seal oil, but we do have sheep oil. You are welcome to it. That's why I brought it here. There's enough for a use here and twice at least while at sea."

Wen stood and went to the boat. He turned it water side up to prepare for oiling when the sun returned. He remembered that every half moon on the sea, they had to haul up to oil the small boat skins, to keep them from letting water through. It was a tedious but necessary process.

Bagaguha went into the lean-to that she and Wen had prepared. It was enclosed to some extent on three sides, but the roof was very well done and had it rained torrents, it would not have passed through. Bagaguha knew how to make a rainproof roof.

Urch and Wapa finished eating and quickly threaded cordage through a skin and tied it between two trees. They took the end pieces and tied them to trees at a distance so that the skin angled. They tossed their rolled skins into the space and unrolled them. They were ready to go black.

Soon all slept except for Wen. He lay beside Bagaguha, with his arm across her. Her regular breathing told him she had gone black. He looked at the stars and thought about the sea voyage. He really didn't want to take that trip again.

He had come to love Bagaguha. What if he drowned at sea? He would be of no use to Camun or Bagaguha. How likely was it that someone could make three sea voyages as the sea was with all that ice? He gave himself a long list of reasons not to make the trip and then fell back to guilt. What was the likelihood, if he went back, that he could take Camun as wife? he wondered.

It had been so long since he thought about Camun. He truly loved Bagaguha. How would he feel without her? How would she feel if he traveled across the sea and drowned?

His thinking place could think no more, and he went black.

In the morning, Urch arose and went to the cache. It was a huge cache. He began to remove the rocks. The winter clothing had held up well, the gut outers to protect them from water weathered better than the furry skins to protect them from the cold.

There were some spear points.

"Do you think we need these?" Urch asked Wapa.

Wapa shook his head. He had no use for more. He'd made a good supply. They were in his backpack.

Urch noticed that the two men had double pointed spear tips. "Did you teach them to make the spear tips?" Urch asked, knowing that making them was very hard for Wen.

"Yes. I knew what my father told me over and over. The people here have more experienced hands than I do. They learned fast. I'm a little better now than I was."

"I see," Urch said, examining the closest spear tip that Wen had actually made.

"Come with me," Urch said.

They walked along the edge of the river.

"You love her?" he asked.

"Yes."

"Can you take her as wife?" he asked.

"Yes."

"I want to tell you something. Listen well. Reg prevented me from taking Kol as wife. Life is short, Wen. Do not take the voyage. It's dangerous as you well know. We may not even make it home. Bagaguha seems to be a wonderful person for you as wife. Don't take a trip because you feel a sense of obligation to someone you knew long ago and is now far away. Not one this dangerous. Much changes at your age in two years. Much! Live your life as it is now. You didn't choose to come here. That choice was made for you. Make the best of that choice. I know you and Camun were close. Much has happened in both your lives since then. She could already be the wife of someone else. She could be dead. Don't make a mistake this time, since it's your choice. Take a certainty over a hope. It's wise. Three crossings. That is not wise. I do it because I have no one else I want but Kol. If I died trying, I'm old. To me dying would not matter so much. I've had a good life. Your life has just begun. You know that. I'd rather die than miss seeing Kol again. We have shared much over our lifetime. Your life is different. Take Bagaguha as wife and love her with all the love you have to give. Live life as fully as you can. We leave just after high sun."

Wen was silent. He had to think and that's all he'd done for days. He didn't want to make a mistake. He knew his cousin was wise.

As high sun approached, Wen, with a somewhat heavy feeling, carried the backpack filled with pemmican over to Urch's boat.

"I think, Uncle, you'll have more need for this than I will," Wen said quietly.

Wordlessly, Urch embraced his very young cousin. "I'm proud of you, Wen. Your father would also be proud. You've grown into a fine man. Stay strong. Have many children. Be happy. Treat your wife well."

Wen looked up at Urch's face. He smiled looking eye to eye with his cousin. He turned and walked back to the others. Urch and Wapa had gathered and stowed all the things they would take on the voyage. They began to push off. The three men on shore ran out and pushed the boat into the water while Urch and Wapa climbed in.

"Do you mind, if we stay here until they disappear from sight?" Wen asked.

"We agree that is the only way it would be right," Akti said and Doho nodded.

Wen turned Bagaguha toward him and kissed her.

Bagaguha was filled with joy. She turned to watch with the others until they could no longer see the boat.

Wen and Bagaguha had eight children. Wen lived to the age of fifty-five when he was killed in a hunting accident by the bison he was attempting to spear. Bagaguha lived to the age of seventy-three adored by her children and grandchildren. In his lifetime Wen never saw another SealEater, though a few times he heard that some people from the land where the sun arose had migrated to the west. Wen's contribution to his children and grandchildren was to teach them to study their environment. He insisted they learn the names of all plants, animals, and people with whom they came in contact. He questioned them frequently regarding the data connected to those names. With them he established an intellectual curiosity that lasted for many generations.

121

Chapter 5

Plak's Story

Plak sat on the bluff overlooking the wide river expanse that separated him from the land that continued on to the west. He had just parted from Torq, his friend from childhood who had been with him all the way to the river. Torq had no intention of going further. He wanted to be sure to return to the cache to meet the other SealEaters in time for their return to the Cove. Plak had just made it clear to Torq that his interest lay beyond the river to see the breadth of this land, the features it had, and the people and animals living there. What he'd seen so far had filled his thinking place with delight, feeding his desire to explore further. Plak was adamantly not content to stop his search. Both were young and very determined. He and Torq had argued terribly through the entire night, as Torq tried to convince Plak that they had a singular responsibility to return to bring others to this land. Plak was equally determined that he had no such responsibility. The argument had erupted again about the time the night watch should have changed, had they chosen to go black that night.

"Torq," Plak said calmly, "I have no intention whatever in turning around. You keep saying the same thing over and over."

"You have a sacred duty to Father Sky and Mother Earth to return to the Cove!" Torq stood as tall as his stretch allowed.

"I took no oath, did not swear, made no obligatory promise to the gods or our people. I have no duty. I was forced to make this trip. I did not volunteer. Do not tell me what my sacred duty is." Plak spoke gently as if in a light conversation.

"Plak, have you no love for the SealEaters?" Torq was pacing furiously. Plak's seeming comfort in his decision disturbed Torq greatly. Plak's calm voice poured oil on the flames of Torq's anger. He was reaching the end of his patience and available points to make. He was convinced that something had happened to the thinking place of his friend.

"I love them as much as you do, my friend. I just have no desire nor intention to cross the sea again. There are plenty of others who will do it. Without me there are twelve people who can make the return and guide people here. One of them stands here before me."

"Love involves purposeful doing, not self-absorbed intentionless pursuing as a child, whatever notion passes your thinking place."

Plak turned around where he sat to face the pacing Torq. "You tell me I have no love? I have no sense of sacred duty? I do nothing? I am a child? Torq, I've made it clear. I have acquired a desire to explore. I didn't start that way. I knew no other way but the way of the SealEaters, a people who live—because of Reg—an unnatural, even sick, existence. I know what love is. I love a girl at the Cove. Reg blocks every attempt for anyone but elders to take a wife. That's a sickness the SealEaters permit. Here I have found a promising new land filled with food and people who are not like us. There are women here who would make wonderful wives. Women who are accessible. I want to learn, to know what this land has to show. There is nothing wrong with my desire or determination to carry it out. You are making something of nothing."

"Do you hear yourself? You make excuses to do as you choose rather than consider the good of the people we left behind. I wish I had the thinking place of Whug! Maybe then I could reach you."

Plak laughed. "Torq, my friend, if you had the thinking place of Whug, you'd be an old man indeed!"

Torq stopped his pacing and kicked Plak hard in the leg.

"Ow!" Plak exclaimed.

"You deserve more than that, you coward!" Torq blurted out, anger rising. "Fear of the sea crossing has made you weak in your thinking place!"

"By your punishing kick, you act as if you think you could substitute for my father, the go-between. Don't you know, my friend, that I have taken all your pointed words through my thinking place—examined them before you spoke them? Don't you think I've compared them with the obligations taught me by my father? Don't you consider that I have a desire to see my parents again? All these things are true. I also have considered that I have another life to live that is separate from our small number of SealEaters. I am a SealEater. Nothing can change that. I am also now, having been made one against my wishes, an explorer. I have no more fear of the sea crossing than you do."

"You are no SealEater!" Torq leaned against a tree, slid down it, and sat on the ground leaning against the tree. He glared at Plak. His anger continued to smolder.

At dawn Torq stood up wordlessly, put on his backpack, picked up his spears, turned on his heels, his dark brown hair blowing in the wind from the west, and his husky body fairly stomping as he left his friend on the bluff. Plak sat cross-legged overlooking the river contemplating how to cross it. Torq hadn't considered the wind, and the hair that blew into his face was bothersome, but in his anger he kept walking towards the forest, deciding to tie his hair back once he was well into the forest. Just in case Plak looked after him, he didn't want Plak to see him stop. Plak might think he was reconsidering. Torq didn't look back. He considered Plak selfish and mean-spirited, a deviant from being a good SealEater for not following the plan. He knew now Plak had no intention of meeting at the cache at the assigned time. Torq's whole view of his friend had changed following the argument of the previous night. He no longer considered Plak a friend. Torq stormed off into the forest heading east.

Plak rested his chin on his hands. His light brown hair needed a good cleaning, but it blew in the wind despite the weight added by the oil and dirt. His gray eyes were intent on the river and the western horizon. He had a heaviness in his spirit at the separation from Torq, but, he knew, it would have been heavier had he given up and returned with Torq. Friends were friends for as long as they chose. He knew he couldn't hang onto another person against their will—for any reason. He would continue, however, to love his friend, because Plak had never learned to put an end to love. He wished the gods would go with Torq to keep him safe and to speed him to the Cove and back unharmed. For hours Plak watched the powerful river. It was not a clear blue but rather a turbid brownish mixture swirling and moving quickly. Plak guessed the river simply reflected the recent storm that had covered the land with much rain. How, he wondered, could he cross it?

After a long time of unproductive contemplation, Plak gathered his backpack and spears and climbed down the river bank to the sand along the river's edge. Fatigue from lack of sleep the night before weighed upon him but not enough to cause him to go black. The river noise was louder here than where he had sat above it. He felt the temperature of the water. It was tepid in the shallows. At the bank it didn't move as quickly as it did towards the center. Plak decided to immerse himself in the river to clean the sweat and dirt from his skin and hair. Using sand, he rubbed himself with it and spent a long time rinsing, enjoying the water. He submerged, rubbing his back against the sand. The river water left no residue on his skin like sea water did. He faced the south, so he did not see the dugout that was heading toward him. In it were three indigenous people, clothed as scantily as he had been before entering the water. They had short black hair they kept cut above their shoulders and across the upper part of the face. Each wore a blue colored band across the forehead and tied in back to keep their hair in place and out of the face. Three stony sets of black eyes stared at the stranger.

Feeling watched, Plak turned around in the water and jumped. He was startled by the presence of three men he hadn't even heard approach. His loincloth lay on the ground, and his spears were beyond by his backpack. Knowing he could be speared before he could return the effort, he leisurely walked to his loincloth and dressed. He noticed the natives were moving their dugout to land. He went to his backpack and shrugged into it. He lifted his spears. By then the men were upon him.

Plak stood in a resting stance. He had been taught well, because of the local wars in his land. The information was reinforced by Urch on the voyage over the sea. He would not give indication that he harbored any fear. The natives approached. They were not threatening, but their faces were hard set.

"Who are you?" one asked, and Plak didn't understand.

They asked other questions, but it was clear that Plak didn't understand.

The tallest man slapped his own chest, "Arangawee!" he said loudly, as if the man were hard of hearing.

Arangawee slapped Plak's chest.

"Plak," Plak said, shocked that anyone would touch him without permission, while trying to act as if this happened all the time. Urch had reminded them on the boat to use a no-fear response to natives, if they encountered any. So far it had worked well for him.

"Shingamoana," the second native said, and repeated "Plak," while pointing to Plak.

Plak, repeated "Arangawee," and pointed to that man and "Shingamoana," pointing to the second man. He pointed to the third man.

"Pelamutazona," the third man replied. Arangawee realized that Plak had just taken control of the introductions. It concerned him. Clearly, Plak gave no hint of fear of them. Arangawee didn't want to lose control of the events.

Arangawee said in a demanding manner, "How did you arrive here?" Plak looked at him blankly.

Arangawee took the end of his spear and drew into the sand. He drew first the big river that would one day be named the Mississippi. Then he drew mountains off to the west. Big pointy mountains. Then to the east he drew the eastern sea marked with wavy lines with little mountains between the eastern sea and the river. The little mountains ran roughly northeast to southwest. Arangawee drew the coast line of what is now Florida with more water south and west of the peninsula. It was an amazingly accurate map for the time.

Arangawee looked at Plak. He pointed to the river and showed the alignment of the river to where they were. He showed the direction of flow. He took a small rock to show where they were on the map.

Suddenly Plak understood. He retraced his journey back through the forest, over the smooth mountains, back to the tidewater area and onto the eastern sea. He drew a boat and made a spaced line to show the voyage through the eastern sea. He drew an arc in the sand with his spear end. He acted out water as liquid and then shivered pointing to the water, trying to cause them to understand ice. Then Plak showed more land with little mountains around a small area of land. He took a small twig from the sand and put it on the place where the Cove should be. All the while, Plak was memorizing the map.

Arangawee was shocked. The man was believable. There appeared no guile at all. Yet, this man said he crossed the salt sea where there was ice. Arangawee knew about the ice sheet on land. It never occurred to him that it extended into the sea. Yet, he could imagine it.

Arangawee pointed to the ice and to his mouth and belly. He wanted to know how the man ate while on the sea.

Plak understood. He moved further down the sandy shore. With his spear end, he drew a seal the best he could, then carried sand to the drawing to give a three dimensional appearance to the seal. He tried to explain that the seal was in the sea and would climb out on the ice. Plak lay down on his belly, spear at his side, and crept up on the sand figure of the seal. He speared the seal, demonstrating with his spear thrust into the sand seal he'd created.

Arangawee, Shingamoana, and Pelamutazona cheered when he speared the sand seal. They understood. Their mouths gaped. Arangawee quickly recovered and told Plak to climb in their boat. He was more inviting than threatening. Plak, without a lot of alternatives, climbed in the boat. Shingamoana and Pelamutazona pushed the dugout into the river and they headed south. As they traveled, the men would sometimes point to something and say a word. Plak tried hard to learn the words he heard. By the time they arrived at their destination, he had learned enough to communicate on a basic level.

At their main village, they introduced Plak to their chief, Piatne. They sat at a large fire and talked. Arangawee told of their meeting, where Plak was from, and how he lived crossing the eastern sea. Plak understood nothing of what was said.

Chief Piatne told Arangawee to take Plak to the men's house for a moon to teach him their language, so he could question him. Arangawee seemed a little reluctant, but he did as he was told. Days passed quickly while Arangawee neglected all normal duties to focus on Plak's learning the language. Fortunately for both of them, Plak wanted to learn as much as Arangawee needed him to learn. While learning Plak began to ask many questions. Frequently his questions were geographical.

Plak had learned that these natives knew of four bodies of salt water: the eastern sea, the southern sea, the western sea, and, from their description, the fourth body of salt water seemed to be a lake. It made no sense to him that a lake could be a sea.

Plak learned well. After two moons, Arangawee brought him to Chief Piatne. The chief didn't bother to put him at ease, but rather he began asking questions.

Piatne asked, "Where were you going when our people found you?"

"I am a SealEater. Some of us came here to explore to find a new land. Our people are squeezed between advancing ice sheets, mountains, and warring people. I was to return to my land across the eastern sea to bring others here. I chose to explore this land. It is an amazing land and I want to see all of it." Plak's use of language was good, but occasionally he had to supplement with signs.

"You do not feel responsible for your people?" Piatne asked.

"I am one of thirteen people who came here. Others can make the crossing and bring our people to this land. It was clear as soon as we found land this would be a good land. We should have returned then. Now I've seen this land. I want to see more. I starve for exploration. Here I'd be fed well for the rest of my life—both for my belly and for my thinking place."

The chief looked at him for a long time. Then he asked, "Why do you have so little concern about your people?"

Plak was deflated. He thought about what the chief was saying. Finally, he replied, "I love my people. There are problems. We have six elders. Unless they all agree, no one can take a wife. Elders have multiple wives, and no one else has been able to take a wife. One elder named Reg refuses all requests. We have some men in their fortieth year who have not been approved to take a wife. I am but seventeen. I don't want to wait that long. I want to explore and take a wife, when I find someone who wants to be my wife."

The natives who listened to Plak were dumbfounded. The chief had a much wrinkled brow. Finally, the chief said, "That is utterly unnatural. Why haven't the people killed this man, Reg?"

Plak looked at the chief, shocked. The question had been asked numbers of times, and it always made the SealEaters look weak in his mind.

"Chief," Plak said, "Reg is very large. He has the strength of two or more men. Men among the SealEaters fear him."

"Many men can overcome one strong man," the chief said. "It sounds as if your people are cowards. At your age, there is no way you could be effective at making change. I can now understand why you were not feeling a strong sense of responsibility for your people. If I were you, I would not wish to return to that. What is SealEaters?"

Plak was momentarily thrown off balance. He replied, "SealEaters are my people. Seal is the animal that we ate in our eastern sea crossing. They also come to rest on our beaches. We have little land. Our land is enclosed by mountains and ice. Beyond the mountains people are constantly at war. They fight over land. They fight over who can hunt on certain lands. The seals are reduced in number because they have become our primary food."

"We don't know seals. Your land is the source of our rising sun. We shall call you Plak of the Rising Sun. You are welcome here as long as you desire. Should you choose to leave, talk to us. At this time you are too thin. We will put fat on your bones. We can help you go where you might wish in the future."

"I must speak," Danumite, another native at the meeting, said briskly. "I was with Toa in our boat two moons ago. We had been visiting the Red Band people to the north with Arangawee and the others. We left to return home earlier than Arangawee who visited there at the same time. I saw this man at dawn with another man upon the eastern bluff. There seemed to be bad between them. The other man was much larger than this one. What has become of the other man?"

The chief looked surprised and then looked at Plak carefully.

Plak said, "The other man is a SealEater. We were both on the exploration together. We were childhood friends. His name is Torq. Torq was ready to return to the place where SealEaters are supposed to meet to return for the people to bring them here. I didn't want to return there. He tried to make me feel guilty, telling me I had a responsibility to the SealEaters. I made no promises, and I certainly didn't—oh, what's the word? Arangawee?"

Arangawee smiled. "The word you keep forgetting is *volunteer*."

"Thank you, Arangawee."

Plak turned his face to the chief. "What I wanted to say is I didn't volunteer for the trip. No oaths were required. I was forced to make the crossing. After we explored more, I wanted to continue. I wanted to learn how to cross the big river to continue my exploration. There were thirteen people who came here to explore. There will be plenty of SealEaters to return to the Cove. They will bring people to this land. I saw no need for me to return. I lost a friend, because I did what he didn't want me to do."

"Plak," the chief said, "Do you feel badly that you lost a friend?"

"Yes, of course. It hurts. I do believe he has a right to end our friendship. I would not cut off a friend because he believed something different, but a man is free to choose his friends and to terminate a friendship. He has done so."

"Plak," the chief said, "He was not your friend. A friend does not insist you do what they want to remain your friend. Friendship is a free commitment for life. Otherwise it's not friendship, it's acquaintanceship. They are very different. Your friend chose not to be your friend. That was his choice, but it shows where his things of first importance lay. It lay in his control over you. Plak, do not let others control you, when you have any possibility of avoiding it. Your people have a problem with control. This man Reg has been allowed to control others for too long. Perhaps your friend learned wrong things from this man, this man who seems strong but is really a coward."

"Thank you," Plak said to the chief. "I have to work this through my thinking place."

"I understand," the chief replied. "Now, we eat," he said.

After they ate, Plak walked to the edge of the hill where the village bordered the river. The boats were neatly pulled up on the shore. The rosy glow of the now disappearing sun was making great rays through the clouds. Plak desired to cross that river and continue on. There was so much to see. He was sure there were wonders yet that would surpass anything he could dream. He heard what sounded like a small bird. He looked down over the ledge and saw Arangawee motioning to him and signing to be quiet. Plak was curious and followed the man. They walked to the river and waded into the water walking to a place that could not be seen from the village.

"You wonder why I motioned for you to come?" Arangawee asked.

"Yes," Plak stated flatly.

"Danumite, Toa, Shingamoana, Pelamutazona, and I went to visit the Red Band. There is unrest among our people. Atematemano, who is the Chief of the Red Band and also head of all the bands, whispered to us that Fusledge, Chief of the Green Band, has gathered the Yellow Band to try to overtake the authority of Atematemano. Then he plans to go after Piatne of the Blue Band. He wants to gather all of the bands into one, move them to the smooth mountains, and rule over all. It's a bad plan."

"Can you not fight him?"

"We can fight but some of the young men are drawn to Fusledge. He speaks big of himself, he tells how wonderful all will be when he is the One Leader. He never talks specifically, just in hints of how great life might be. Some of the older men also find him fascinating."

"How awful."

"Plak, it is a battle we will have soon. Pelamutazona shared this information with our chief. Piatne will not be pleased. Pelamutazona is loyal to our chief. I think the loyalty of Danumite and Toa has been lured by Fusledge. I want your help."

"What can I do?" Plak asked with interest.

"Sometime in the next few days, mention your desire to see the great split land to the west. I will avoid you carefully until I hear you have asked. Then, I will propose that my two sons, my daughter, and my wife accompany you. My wife knows the way. I am certain that there will be no problem. The land is far to the west. My wife came from there. My children have always wished to see it. I want them gone, for we will have a war, and it will be soon. Only a few men know of the coming war, and I think a small number of our Blue Band will fight against us when the time comes. The great split land is far from here, way beyond our land and our control. You and they will be safe there. If Fusledge is successful in overtaking our village, I will escape to find you there. If there is no war, I will come for them in the season of the changing leaves. If my life is taken, her family will provide. My wife knows how to make the signs to lead me. My wife knows I ask this of you. The children do not. Speak of this to no one. Trust no one."

Plak looked at his feet. It was a great responsibility, but he liked Arangawee. "I'll do it at the fire before we eat tomorrow. Until then, I'll avoid you."

"Thank you, Plak. I now consider you a friend."

"I consider you a friend, Arangawee."

"Return the way you came. I'll go back a different way."

Plak nodded and headed back to the village.

On his way back Plak saw Pelamutazona. "Nice clear night, Pelamutazona," he said.

"Yes. I've seen some lights streak across the sky. I wonder if they are dying stars or spirits who have gone before us to the great land of death."

"My people wonder the same. One person long ago told my father that the lights are made from stones, and they have bubbly holes in them as if they'd boiled."

Pelamutazona laughed. "That's a good one, Plak!" he laughed.

"Supposedly he followed the light to a place where the grass was on fire, near where one landed. He showed my father the rock."

Pelamutazona was quiet. Then he laughed and turned away toward his home.

Plak wondered at all he'd heard since he arrived there. The initial meeting with the chief was a good one. The Blue Band had seemed ideal, when he compared them to his people. Amazing, he thought, how things can appear one way while underneath they were so very different. It made him think of trees that appeared healthy outside, but inside there was open space where there was no life. Plak felt he had much to learn. He was not very good at being deceptive, but now the safety of four people depended on his being able to be convincing.

The next night at the fire, Plak said, "Chief, I have thought. I have appreciated your welcome. The Blue Band is a good People. I must go on. I have heard that to the west there is a great land that is split and a river runs through it. I very much want to see this land. I have to cross the river to go there. Will you help me?"

"This is a fortunate thing," Arangawee spoke up before the chief could reply. "For many summers my wife has wanted me to take her to visit her people with the children. Not only could she lead Plak there, but also he could protect her and my children from harm during the travel. I have responsibilities here each year and have been unable to grant her wish. When the leaves turn, I will be able to join her for a visit and to accompany her and the children home."

The chief looked up, his eyes examining Arangawee's face and body. The man appeared guileless. "This meets fully with your approval, Arangawee?" he asked.

With full eye to eye gaze, Arangawee nodded.

"Let it be as you say," the chief replied. "Plak, you have your answer. You will take full responsibility for their safety?"

"Yes, Chief," he said solemnly.

"Arangawee, gather some rowers, take the large boat to make the crossing, and try to make the crossings in less than a day."

Arangawee nodded and with much relief turned to make the preparations needed for the river crossing and for his family and Plak to have provisions for the trip. Plak gathered his backpack and spears.

Pelamutazona ran over to Plak. "You are leaving, yet you just arrived. I wanted to learn to make spear points like yours. It appears I have waited too long."

Plak smiled at the man. "I'm not very good at it. I have a broken one that I planned to turn into a knife. Take this," he said, pulling the point from his backpack. "Make the other end just like this. The point broke in the center as I was finishing it. It happens."

"Thank you," Pelamutazona said looking at the half point in his hand. "I am very grateful."

"Be patient," Plak said smiling, turning to walk to the shore with his things.

Plak saw Arangawee beside a very large boat. He'd never seen that boat. Plak had already met Verra, Arangawee's wife. Verra took his backpack and placed it securely in the boat. Plak went to Arangawee who introduced his second son, Snat. Snat was twelve. He was clearly excited at the thought of the visit to the split land. Arangawee introduced his first son, Grobulit. He was a little standoffish, but greeted Plak with due respect. Grobulit was fourteen. The girl who had been arranging things in the boat looked up. Arangawee introduced his daughter, Tanturto. Plak tried hard not to display his reaction. Tanturto was fifteen, beautiful, and appeared very kind. He wanted to wrap his arms around the girl and never let go. In his thinking place, he controlled himself to show no more interest in the girl than he had in Arangawee's sons. The only one who noticed the signs of Plak's attraction was Verra. She would stay alert.

In addition to Arangawee, Pelamutazona, Shingamoana, Danumite, and Toa came to row. Plak would also row. Plak remembered that Arangawee had made it clear he had no trust in Danumite and Toa. He was careful to keep his silence. The men pushed the dugout into the river and the crossing began. The river was swift and powerful. Rowing against it was difficult. The strain of the rowers showed early into the crossing. There was little talking during the crossing. Keen concentration was required and all rowers knew that. At one point a huge tree trunk nearly rammed the dugout. Quick use of oars to push themselves away kept them from a collision and free of injury.

Plak smiled to himself. Tanturto noticed the smile and wondered at it. Plak was thinking that having crossed the eastern sea made this crossing seem far easier than he'd thought possible. As he thought his muscles worked the oar in rhythm with the other rowers. Plak mused that the spirit of the river was not even near as strong as the spirit of the sea. He felt in some ways that the spirit of this big river could be reached by people for help and comfort in their needs, where the spirit of the great eastern sea remained utterly aloof in light of the needs and fears of humans. Plak asked the river spirit to use his spirit hand to block any collision that might occur on the river. At that moment the sun broke free of the cloud cover and shone on the boat. Plak felt he had an answer from the river spirit.

After a relatively quick river crossing, the travelers said their farewells and gathered their burdens and spears to begin the trek to the split land. The rowers returned to the dugout and began the crossing back to their home. Arangawee hoped that the war had not begun in their absence, but he felt an enormous sense of relief that whatever happened, his family would be safe. He waved to his wife who stood still watching him row away.

"Let's go," Plak urged.

Verra turned reluctantly from her river view to the western land.

"See those trees in the far distance. They're all grouped together. We go there," Verra directed.

Plak nodded to her. He certainly didn't know where the great split land lay. They walked, moving swiftly. Verra led and Plak followed at the end. They reached the group of trees very quickly. They stopped to drink water at the creek.

Plak had walked a bit downstream and was returning when Tanturto blocked his path. "I saw you smiling on the river crossing as if something amused you, Plak. What was it?"

Plak tried to remember and finally he recalled, "I was thinking that the spirit of the river was not nearly as strong as the spirit of the eastern sea."

"Was the eastern sea crossing fear filling?" she asked.

"Yes," he replied. "The great wall of ice was horrible and great chunks would break off and begin to float in the sea. Only a tiny part of the ice is above water. If you were a great chunk of ice, your head might be above water and the rest would be under the water. It makes sailing very difficult. One boat kept snagging on the underwater ice. We had to beware of ice breaking off those great chunks. It was hard to steer among them. The worst was in storms when the wind blew making water feel like rocks hitting us, and the waves were so high you wouldn't believe me if I told you how high. We feared the great ice chunks for they had no stability. They could crush us in an eye blink. The waves tossed the great chunks of ice about as if they were tiny pebbles. It was something I don't want to repeat, but I'm glad I had the experience—now that it's over. I admit that during the first big storm, I curled myself into a little ball and cried like a baby. I learned that fear and crying only wasted time, and they kept me from watching that we didn't lose things to the storm or let the boat become so filled with water that we might sink."

While Plak told the story, Tanturto listened to each word, trying to imagine. Grobulit came near enough to hear.

"Surely, Plak, you exaggerate," he said standing with his arms crossed in front of his chest.

"No, Grobulit," Plak said quietly. "I don't exaggerate at all. Someday you may see for yourself."

"I don't want to go to sea."

"Then, Grobulit, you'll have to take my word for it," Plak said and walked past the boy.

The group began to move again. They passed a lake where the trees that edged one shore were filled with great egrets. The sight startled Plak.

"What are they?" he asked Grobulit. Plak thought the birds were amazingly large to be standing in trees.

"Egrets," was the one-word reply.

"Plak?" Verra called.

He caught up and walked with her.

"There are many snakes in this land. You need to be very alert, for they look much like the land on which they rest. See the pile of rocks over there?"

"The ones where there is a dark rock atop the heap?"

"Yes. There is a snake under the lowest rock. Can you see it?"

"Yes. But I hadn't noticed it until you showed me."

"Look at that log. Can you see the snake there?"

Plak looked and he could not find a snake. He shook his head.

"Snat," she called to her youngest son, "show Plak the snake by that log."

Snat had not paid attention, so he had to look at the log. "It's under the branch that sticks out on the right side. Can you see it, Plak?"

Plak couldn't see the snake. He walked a little closer and there blending perfectly with its surroundings was a snake. He realized in that moment he was critically in need of learning to see in this environment, and was determined to use his eyes more.

"Thank you, Snat. Your eyes are much better than mine. My eyes need to learn to see this land."

Plak, Verra, Tanturto, and Snat continued on as sunset began to color the sky brilliant reds, oranges, yellows, and violets. They built a fire and ate jerky that they carried in their backpacks.

Plak looked at the river they'd have to cross.

"Do you think it wise to stop here for the night? We can make the crossing in light tomorrow."

"Yes," Verra replied more tired than she had realized.

The boys searched for firewood. Tanturto noticed her mother was overly fatigued.

"Mother, is something wrong?"

"I don't think so. I've just been feeling a little dizzy. Rest should help. Will you tend to the food?"

"Of course, but first let me make you more comfortable." Tanturto took her mother's sleeping skins, laid one on the ground carefully placing grasses under the skin at the place for her mother's head. She helped her mother to the place she'd prepared. She laid the sleeping skin over her mother. She swiftly began food preparation of jerky and dried berries. Verra slept immediately.

She dreamed. In her dream she could see the face of Arangawee. He was in terrible pain, but made no noise. Blood covered the left side of his face. He held out his left arm to her, but when she reached back, she lost sight of him. She stirred. She opened her eyes, and breathed out, "No!" in a whisper of terror. Surely, they had not had the war and Arangawee had been mortally wounded. "No!" she whispered again. Fear overwhelmed her.

After all of the children slept, she walked with Plak to the edge of the creek.

"I fear it is not well with my husband," she admitted.

"Why do you say that?" he asked.

"I had a dream. His face on the left was covered with blood. The war must have begun. I reached for him and he'd disappear," she whispered as if speaking it quietly would remove some of the certainty she felt.

"Verra, he may be safe. You knew there was a chance of war. Maybe missing him has just made you worry too much. Do you think that could be the reason for the dream?"

"I don't know, Plak. I just don't know. I know my whole being aches and I feel as if he may no longer be alive on the earth. I feel that I should not speak his name."

"Why not?" Plak asked very curious.

"Because if a spirit of a dead man hears his name, it tends to call him back instead of letting him go freely to where he should go after death."

Plak held her to try to comfort her. She let loose her tears, as if she grieved for one already gone. He knew there was a possibility that her dream had merit, so he comforted her as if it had. When her tears were gone, she thanked Plak and returned to her sleeping place. She expected to remain awake all night, but instead she fell to sleep immediately.

Day followed day. Full moon followed full moon. Plak was amazed at the size of the land and that Verra seemed to know the route as clearly as if she were a bird in migration. Finally, she told him, "We will see the split land tomorrow." She was placing the rocks in a certain way that would communicate to Arangawee exactly which way to go to follow her.

She always chose flat land for the signs. Arangawee would put the side of his head to the ground to locate her signs. He could see them elevated above the flat ground.

When they awoke the next morning, they headed quickly to the path that traversed the small mountain before them. When they reached the top of the hill, what stretched before them was astonishing.

"This is the split land. It goes for a long distance both that way and this way," Verra explained. "No one knows what split the land, but you can see that it is real with your own eyes. I was born near here. My parents and all those who lived before them have been here always. They lived down at the bottom of this place, where green things grow. It is a good place. I will lead you there. When we start to go down, be very careful. None of this land is stable. You could slide or fall. Follow me and walk where I walk."

Everyone listened to her, but their eyes remained on the land. The colors of the land were warmly inviting. It was a place like none other. Floating puffy clouds drifted by seeming to change the color of the scene for a moment.

Suddenly Snat screamed. He stood on one foot and held the other in the air. A triangular-headed pinkish-colored snake slithered away from him.

Instantly, Plak bounded to the boy's side. He sat the boy on the ground, pulled his knife, and located the bite on the side of Snat's leg. Snat wept while Tanturto comforted him and Verra watched carefully to see what Plak was doing. Plak cut into the first puncture in an X shape. He cut away the flesh as deeply as he dared under each flap formed by the X and removed it, laying it on the ground. Then he did the same with the other puncture mark. Snat had two gaping, bleeding wounds and was in extreme pain.

Verra gave Snat a dried leaf and told him to chew it for pain. Plak told her to sew the skin flaps together, leaving the wounds so they could drain.

From a distance Grobulit and Tanturto watched. Grobulit had looked after his brother since he was born. He loved him very much. He felt utterly helpless while a stranger stepped in to take over. He watched every move Plak made, his emotions torn in concern for his brother.

Verra watched carefully. She'd never seen anyone do what Plak had done. She wondered whether the loss of skin would affect her son's ability to walk. Tanturto had already formed in her mind a picture of Plak in which he ranked at near-hero level in her esteem, because of the eastern sea crossing. If Plak helped her brother, her esteem for him would grow.

"How far to your people?" Plak asked.

"We have to go down to the river level and walk upriver less than a quarter of a day," she explained.

"I'll leave my backpack here and carry him," Plak said. I should be able to find it again. "Lead us quickly," he said a bit sharply.

Grobulit reached down for Plak's backpack.

"Young man," Plak said, seeing the attempt. "That's too heavy for you. It's okay to leave it here."

Undaunted, Grobulit replied, "Is there anything in there that you would hate to lose?"

Plak looked at the boy. He realized some of the resentment had subsided. "Look inside and you'll find a small package wrapped in the softest hide. It contains a leather strip that passes through a drilled piece of mammoth tusk carved like an animal. It would mean much to me if you brought it with us."

Grobulit quickly found the necklace. He kept it wrapped in the same soft leather in which he found it. He instantly stepped into the line moving down into the deep valley. As he walked, he was amazed remembering the weight of Plak's backpack. He was unable to lift if off the ground.

It was evening when they could smell the camp of Verra's people. They were about to serve the evening meal when the travelers arrived. All the food preparation came to an abrupt halt as relatives embraced and introductions were made. Verra explained the immediate need for Nogathat. The bent over woman was very old, but she knew her medicine. Plak carried Snat to the old woman. She asked for boiling water and began to clean the wound. She felt the boy and realized he was not as hot as she expected. Warmer than normal, but not hot. She noticed the odd way of handling the punctures, but while she worked she kept her own counsel, only occasionally peeking from the folds of skin about her ancient eyes to examine Plak.

Grobulit remained like a shaded stone against the wall of stone that surrounded Nogathat's home. He did not put himself in the way of busy people. He simply wanted to be near his brother and know how he was doing.

"Come, Grobulit," Plak said. "I'd like to have my little carved mammoth tusk now."

Dutifully, Grobulit stood up. The carved tusk was in his backpack. He showed Plak where he'd put it just outside the stone house. Inside he found the wrapped necklace and handed it to Plak.

"Thank you for doing what you could to save my brother. I love him. I want him to be well."

"I only did the little I know. I think now he's in Nogathat's hands, he'll have a better chance."

"Plak, do not make little of my words. I've seen grown men die from such a snake bite in less time than it took us to arrive here. If my brother lives, it's because of you. I have treated you shamefully. I resented your coming with us when I wanted my father to make this trip. There was some reason he wanted us out of there, and I don't know what that reason was. Do you?"

"Yes. I know."

"Will you tell me?"

"Your father loves your mother and all of his children with a great passion. He wanted you safe."

"Safe? Safe from what? I know there was a reason, but it had to be more than just wanting us safe."

"It was all about safety. Among your people, Grobulit, there was treachery. It moved like the snake that bit your brother. It hid looking as if all were well, but when the time was right, it struck with venom. That is how treachery works. If I told you that Danumite and Toa were plotting with the Green Band chief to overthrow Chief Piatne, would you believe it? That's what your father told me to encourage me to accompany you here. I hope I explain this right. Fusledge of the Green Band wants to gather all bands together to rule over them, eliminating the chiefs of today. He has promised the people who admire him that they will have wonderful lives with more freedom after this is accomplished. Your father suspected war was coming soon. This knowledge was shared among the men only. Arangawee told Verra so that she would be willing to take you far away to keep you safe."

"I should be with my father." He dropped to his knees groaning.

"No, Grobulit. You are nearing the man years, but you're not there yet. War is a horrible thing. Your father knows that. He knows your love. He decided that you were not ready, and he wanted a long life for you. That is the measure of his love. You must respect your father's decision. Try not to assume you know better than he does."

Looking at the sky, the words poured out, "O, Creator, how could you separate us from our father in his time of need?" The boy stood there hurting.

Plak went to him and embraced him. "Grobulit, neither the Creator nor your father is to blame for the separation. It's the rumor of war that has done it. Knowing that you're safe, your father's thoughts will not be divided when war comes. He will likely survive because he is not divided. He can keep all his attention focused on what is happening. Do you understand?" Plak stepped back.

"Yes, Plak, I think I do. I also heard my mother when she dreamed. Did she dream my father died?"

"That's a tough question, Grobulit. Your mother knew of the treachery and coming war. She might have had so much anxiety about the separation that she carried her fears into her dream, or she may have had a sense of your father's being injured. She did not dream of his death but rather of an injury to the left side of his head. Until you know for certain, don't let the suspicion eat at you the way the snake spit eats at your brother. Ask yourself whether you could do anything about your father."

"I know I could not."

Plak put his open hand under Grobulit's chin. He lifted the boy's face to see his eyes. "Could you make it home alone from here?"

"No," came the answer with a sob.

"Then, do not trouble yourself with fears and grim imaginings. Stay in this time and place. The rest will take care of itself."

Grobulit stared at the ground.

"What does your Creator tell you happens after you die?" Plak asked quietly.

"We go to the sky to live among the stars. There is no hunger there. No time of too cold. Hunting is good."

"It is a good place, then?"

"Yes. Of course."

"Then do not continue to worry about your father. You are in a good place here. If all goes well there, your father will come to take you back home. If not, he will either come here to live, or he will be in a good place. You need to learn that what you cannot control, you must release. Trust the Creator in whom you believe."

"What I cannot control, I must release?"

"Yes. If you do not, it can make your thinking place fail to work properly. You become an unreasonable man."

"What must I do?"

Plak thought a bit and then very slowly said, "Leave your father to the Creator. Leave your brother to Nogathat. Enter into this people and find where you can fit. Take time to see the beauty that is around you. Take time to laugh. Take time to come to know people. Be useful. Learn everything you can learn. Trust only when you know someone well. Make a friend for life, but if they turn away from you, give them their freedom. Do not cling to the past. Live life in the present day by day. That, my young friend is all I know."

"That is a lot," he admitted. "At first I didn't want to like you at all. I like you, Plak, and I respect you."

"That means a lot to me, Grobulit. More than you can imagine."

Plak put the necklace around his neck. The smooth polished bone was carved into the shape of a seal. It had been polished until it had the shine of a wet rock. It was his treasure. Grobulit looked at it. He reached out to touch it. The smoothness surprised him.

"It's a carved seal, Grobulit. Once when I learned to make spear points I did so poorly that I went to our pile of supplies and took a piece of mammoth tusk and carved it. I made this seal. My people are called SealEaters. The seal is a sign of my people. I was a better carver than spear point maker, but we each had to master spear point making. I asked my uncle, Amaroz, to drill the seal so I wouldn't break it. He did. I treasure it. Thank you for bringing it along. Tomorrow I'll go to retrieve my backpack."

"Plak, what's in your backpack? It's the heaviest one I ever tried to lift."

"Mostly spear points and tools."

"That explains it," the boy laughed.

The next day Plak retrieved his backpack.

Winter came and then spring. During that time, Plak and Tanturto had come closer and closer together. They sat on a large stone near their home after sunset in their valley. Long ago before people, the stone on which they sat had fallen from far above them leaving its home in the high wall above. It was smooth and afforded a good view of the river. A slight wind increased the sense of a light chill. Plak put his arm around Tanturto, pulling her to him. She complied, comfortable in the movement she'd experienced so often lately.

"So much has happened since we arrived here," Tanturto said eyes fixed on the stars above.

"It has," he agreed, his gray eyes looking down into hers, swimming to her spirit through them.

"I will never be able to thank you enough for saving Snat. What an odd way of taking care of snakebite."

"I only did the best I could. I know you need to eliminate as much snake spit as possible. That was all I could think to do." He pulled her tighter to him.

"Well, Nogathat was impressed."

"Tanturto, you have no need to continue to thank me. Let this be the last we speak of it. Snat is well. That is all that matters."

"I'll try. Sometimes it just comes over me as I remember."

"Let's start new memories, sweet Tanturto."

"What are you thinking?" she asked totally unprepared for his reply.

"I think you should be my wife, and I, your husband."

Tanturto began to laugh. She laughed quietly, but the laughter once started did not wish to cease.

"Why are you laughing?" Plak asked with some consternation.

Finally, the laughter subsided. "You surprised me. I think your idea is wonderful. Plak, what's that?"

Plak listened to the quiet of the night.

"I hear nothing."

"There it is again," she said.

Plak strained to hear what she heard.

"I hear it," he said. "It seems to come from . . . . Is that a man at the top of the split land wall?"

"Yes, I think it is. Want me to call the hunters?"

Plak nodded, keeping his eyes on the man and heading towards the split land wall ascent.

Hunters came running from the larger stone structure. They ran past Plak and up the path of the split land wall far faster than he could have done. Plak returned to Tanturto. They along with many others watched the ascent to the man at the top. Slowly they reached him and began to help him down.

The man was emaciated. He seemed not to understand much. Nogathat told them to bring him water and to make him drink it very slowly.

Verra ran into the room and knelt beside the stranger. She lay across him despite the dirt that clung to him. She sobbed and sobbed.

"Arangawee, Arangawee, you're safe now. You've found us. It is I, Verra." Verra repeated the words and later Arangawee moved, turning to her, recognizing her, losing tears from his eyes. He was too tired to speak, but he squeezed her hand.

Nogathat cleaned his wounded body and the hunters put Arangawee on soft skins in the far corner of the stone building. He slept and awakened only briefly for days while Verra kept feeding him soup broth and spooning water into his mouth.

Finally, able to speak, he offered the explanation all had awaited, "The war broke out the day after you left. Danumite and Toa set fire to our homes and then from the woods the Yellow and Green Bands came. They killed everyone they could find. Men. Women. Children. We had that tunnel under our place. It gave me a place to hide to escape the slaughter, for already I was blooded and sick. For many days I could hear them and finally, one day, there was no human noise. I came from the tunnel very slowly but needn't have been so careful. They were gone. They might have gone to the Red Band. Their talk about how good things would be was a lie. Danumite and Toa were dead. I have no understanding why they killed everyone. We could have stood against them, but instead, they destroyed us all. I'll never return."

"Arangawee, as sick and injured as you were, how did you cross the big river?"

"I took a small boat and knew you were on the other side of the river."

Verra embraced him.

Back outside by the river, Plak and Tanturto sat on the big smooth rock.

"I ask again, Tanturto, will you be my wife?"

"My dear Plak," she replied, "What of your adventuring?"

"What are you asking?"

"Plak, what if I awake one morning and you tell me you're leaving to adventure? If I have children, I could not go with you. I could not fight you about it anymore than Torq could fight you long ago."

"Tanturto, I no longer need to adventure. I adventured to find. I've found what I sought. I found you. This split land has many opportunities to adventure close to what is now my home. I would not leave you. You are my home."

Tanturto gazed unblinking into Plak's gray eyes as he spoke. She was silent, still gazing. Finally, she said, "Then, yes, Plak, I would be pleased to be your wife."

"I love you Tanturto. I have loved you since I first saw you at the boat for the river crossing. You are beautiful, kind, smart, and unique."

They embraced.

The coming together of Tanturto and Plak was cause for great celebration. The men hunted and women gathered greens. There was great music and dancing all through the night. They had built their house of stone back from the water's edge. They slipped away for a while and then returned to the festivities. Fishers had brought fish from the river, large razorback suckers and humpback chub; hunters supplied a bighorn sheep; women supplied available greens, nuts, and berries. Before dawn people returned to their homes to have a little sleep before the day began.

The next morning Tanturto and Plak emerged from their stone house early to watch the sunlight enter the deep valley.

"We begin a new life," Tanturto said.

"Yes, we do," Plak said putting his arm across her back with his hand on her shoulder..

"That's not what I mean, Husband," she replied.

Plak looked into her face. "What do you mean?"

"I'm certain I carry new life."

"From last night?" he asked surprised.

"Yes, my Husband. I'm certain. If not last night, when would it have been?"

He lifted her off the ground and hugged her tight. As it turned out, she was right.

Plak and Tanturto lived together for fifty years. They had ten children and many grandchildren. In the seventieth year of Plak's life, a great rain from far away mountains became a flood. It swept through their lowland, arriving at their home and removing any trace of the people who lived at the river's edge. All people who were in the river area at that time were swept away. The remains of the bodies of Plak and Tanturto lie near the black rocks near the volcanoes in the split land.

Chapter 6

Torq's Story

Torq left the open land by the river and entered the forest in a state of anger unlike any he'd ever experienced. A large blood vessel in his forehead had engorged and seemed to pulsate against his headband. He couldn't understand why he was unable to cause Plak to see reason. The two of them had grown up together. They spent their childhood playing together. They were taught together. Both had shared their personal views of things and always, they were together. Torq followed the path as fast as he could move. He wondered whether there might be something caused by a spirit in the new land, something that made people from across the sea do things they otherwise might not do.

By evening, the forest had become darker than he remembered. He slowed to find a place to go black for the night. Lack of sleep from the night before had left his energy level lower than normal. He laid his backpack and spears on the ground. He barely heard the scream of the cat that flew at him from an overhead tree limb. The cat was as tall at its shoulder as Torq's arm was from shoulder to the tip of his middle finger. The cat had black tufts on its ears. It landed on his back with a thud, holding on with sharp claws, while aiming to place its mouth around Torq's neck. It knocked him to the ground where he rolled over to fight with all his strength. Finally, Torq punched the lynx in the side of the face with the full force of his right arm, causing it to run frantically deep into the forest.

Torq managed to stand up, bleeding from his neck, back, and arms from the cat's claws and teeth. Plak was momentarily forgotten as Torq tried to remember where he last saw a source of water. He couldn't remember, so he went to the small bladder where he transported enough water to take care of urgencies. Torq dabbed with a skin at the places that had stopped bleeding. Then he put pressure on those that still bled. It was turning dark fast. He needed to prepare for the night. Continuing to bleed, Torq found some deadfall logs and set up a lean-to for the night. He covered it with limbs, leaves, bark, grasses—anything he could find nearby quickly. Torq put his sleeping skins on the ground under the lean-to. Then he carefully scraped the forest floor to the dirt. He gathered some dry material from the forest floor and set about creating a tiny hearth. Torq definitely wanted fire protection in case the cat returned.

One spot on his neck was still bleeding profusely and he had begun to feel a little dizzy. Torq grabbed a handful of jerky from his backpack and sat down. He ate jerky while he kept pressure on the wound on his neck. He looked at his skin in the light of the hearth fire. He was a mess. He carried nothing to prevent the wound from going bad—all that was in Plak's backpack, he reminded himself. Plak carried spear points and honey and herbs and something else wrapped in soft leather. Torq carried the food and little bladders of water. Plak had made the spear points. Torq just realized he had no spares except for two that he'd broken but still carried in his backpack.

Torq knew he could have asked Plak for spares, and knowing Plak, he knew his friend would have given him spares. He hadn't even thought to ask. The jerky was food for the hunger in his belly, but it didn't taste particularly good. It was sufficient for the night. Torq tried hard to remain awake, fearing a return of the cat. His fatigue overcame him and he went black, as soon as he covered himself with the sleeping skin.

When morning came, he opened his eyes, disoriented. His neck and back hurt terribly. He ate some more jerky, drank a little water, and gathered up his skins. He would continue his trek to the place where SealEaters were to meet to return to the Cove. He knew it would be many moons before he reached his goal. Late in the evening, Torq reached a small river. There he could clean the blood from his skin and loincloth to refresh himself. He felt not only dirty but also contaminated by things he didn't understand but knew could cause wounds to become hot and filled with pus. Some wounds already had a bad feeling.

He walked for days, trying to keep himself oriented. He did not feel at all well. He knew he was fortunate not to have had any serious encounters with predators. He had managed several times to spear deer to fill him not only with food warm from the hearth but also food that tasted good. Those times he enjoyed the trek. Other times he felt dispirited, still mulling over the treachery of his once friend. It mystified him that anyone could choose not to return to bring the SealEaters at the Cove to this place. Just thinking about it angered him anew.

Torq felt sick. He had been walking for how long he could not remember. He was struggling to see. He knew there were places on his back that had never healed. Torq was filled with a single minded purpose to reach the cache. Nothing else mattered. He slipped crossing a creek when he was startled by the sight of human foot prints in the mud. Torq went black as soon as he hit the ground.

At high sun some young girls found the body of the man and ran to tell their people. Hunters followed them and found Torq with a high fever, emaciated, and covered in stinking sores. They carried him to their village. Man-who-knows-herbs looked at the wounds and wrinkled his face. He doubted seriously that he could do anything at all for the sick man. He began by cleaning the body to see better what damage was done. The wounds made Man-who-knows-herbs' stomach turn. He began to clean the dead flesh off the wounds on the man's back and neck, expecting him to wake up from the pain. He didn't. Then Man-who-knows-herbs took firebrands while hunters held the man down, and he burned the wounds deeply.

Through it all the man slept. Man-who-knows-herbs couldn't believe the burning didn't awaken the man. When they turned the man over, they found the wound on his arm and claw marks on his chest, but they were not terribly infected. They rolled him to his belly and placed herbs and honey on his back wounds. Man-who-knows-herbs laid a skin over the man's back. He was concerned about the neck wound. He had burnt it deeply, and he hoped he hadn't done more damage than the infection had. At least the massive stench was gone from the man.

For days women tended Torq. They fed him broth and cleaned his wounds. He occasionally mumbled "SealEaters," but they didn't understand his words.

"Will he live?" Hammer asked Man-who-knows-herbs.

"It has been a long time now. I expect him to live, but what his condition of life will be, I do not know. He has been moving a little this day. He may awaken soon. When he is awake, hunters must be nearby, for we cannot predict what he will do."

"I will arrange for several of us to stand by the man," Hammer said.

"Good. I think it's time."

"His eyes are open," Mat, an old woman who had been helping Man-who-knows-herbs, said.

Hammer went outside and brought two other men into the little structure. They sat at the far edges. Man-who-knows-herbs went to the stranger.

"Who are you?" he asked Torq.

Torq lay there on his side trying to reason where he was and who the people were. He was at a loss.

Man-who-knows-herbs put his hand on his own chest and said, "Man-who-knows-herbs."

Torq put his right hand on his own chest and said, "Torq."

There was a murmur in the little structure as men wondered what Torq meant. Each of them had a name that meant something.

Torq laid back down on the sleeping skins and went black.

Oak Nut came in with food and spooned it into the man's mouth. He let it go down without waking up.

The next day Torq awakened and was hungry. They fed him soup.

Torq looked at his body and was horrified at how much fat he'd lost. The SealEaters prided themselves in having plenty of fat to show that they were healthy. His hip bones protruded from his belly. It was embarrassing to him. Looking at the people around him, he noticed that none carried much fat on their bodies. Torq's concern was crossing the sea. He needed fat for warmth and energy.

Torq tried to communicate, but the natives were not ones who talked much. He waited trying to be patient.

Man-who-knows-herbs came in and sat near Torq.

He pointed at Torq, saying, "Torq."

Torq nodded, pointing back, wanting to know the name of the man.

"Man-who-knows-herbs," the man said. He showed Torq several herbs, saying the word herb. Then he'd point to himself indicating he was Man-who-knows-herbs. Finally, Torq understood.

Time passed and Torq gained strength. He put strong effort into learning the language of the people. Outside at last, he tried desperately to learn where he was. All Torq knew is that he was in the mountains. His wounds were recovering, but there were deep wounds in his back, wounds he couldn't reach. The one on his neck was deep. It itched. There were a few pus pockets that the women at night would place hot compresses on to make them drain. They covered the one on his neck with herbs and honey over which they tied a skin that went around the neck and under his arm. He didn't like it, but they insisted he wear it.

Torq worried about time. He had to go back to the cache. He had learned the language enough for basic communication. He tried to gain a sense of where he was.

"Hammer, do you know how far we are from the eastern sea?"

"What's sea?" Hammer asked.

"It's salty water."

"Water isn't salty," Hammer replied seriously.

"Sea water is salty," Torq explained.

"I don't know sea water," Hammer said. "I'll ask Blue Jay when I see him. He is the most likely to know because he travels to our friends to trade."

"What's trade?"

"If you make good spear points, and you obviously do, and you want winter skins, some people will trade you skins for spear points. They take your spear points, and you obtain skins."

"That's a clever idea," Torq said, barely following the words.

"We have done it forever," Hammer replied.

"I was following a trail that led from the west where the sun goes down to the east where the sun arises. Can you tell me where that trail is?"

"I know the trail. It is back down this hill and part way up the next hill to the north. Is that where you were?"

"I think so. I remember being dizzy. I was having trouble seeing. I kept falling."

"That makes sense. When we found you, we thought you'd die. Oh, what's SealEaters? You kept saying SealEaters."

"My people are the SealEaters. We live across the eastern sea. Our land is being overtaken by ice. We have the sea to the west. We have ice to the north, and mountains to the east and south. The land past the mountains is filled with people constantly at war. They fight for land for villages and for hunting. Many die. We search for land where we can live without war and with food to put fat on our bellies. When ice came the seals came to our land. We learned to eat them. We are called SealEaters."

"We chose to explore to find a new land. We followed the sea by the tall mountains of ice from our land to this one. As we crossed the sea, we caught seals and ate them, because they live in the sea and come to rest on sea ice."

"I was trying to return to those of us who will travel by boat back to the land of the SealEaters to bring them to this wonderful land."

"How many SealEaters are you?"

"Oh, I don't know. Definitely less than a hundred."

"That many people travel in a boat?"

"Oh, no, Hammer. We have many small boats."

"What is the size of the sea?"

Torq was surprised at the question. "It's huge. It takes moons and moons to cross."

Hammer thought he was joking. "You lie?" he laughed.

"Not at all, Hammer. It is frightening to cross the sea. Huge chunks of ice float in the sea. They break off from the enormous ice sheets that lay across the sea as they do on land. When storms come up, waves throw chunks of ice around. Little boats out there have people in them who are praying to the gods for protection. If you are hit by an ice chunk, you'd die out there. If the ice didn't hit you and your boat overturned or filled with water, you'd freeze to death in the water."

"You'd have to be disturbed in thought to go on such water," Hammer muttered.

"It was not disturbed thought," Torq said defensively, "We're desperate. When you're about to run out of land and food, desperation sets it. It's survival."

Torq stretched his body out on the rock, absorbing the warmth from the sun, and he thought back to the crossing. He was in the boat with Murke and Wapa. He thought it odd that he and Murke always had a special something. Murke seemed to approve of him. He never said it—it just showed in his face. Torq always thought he looked a little like Murke, but his father was Mongwire. But then, all Torq knew of his own appearance was what he saw in water, and that could make people look very different from how they really looked.

Torq shut his eyes. Hammer used the time to go back to the structure where Man-who-knows-herbs was. He told the old man about the progress of Torq and related the questions he'd asked.

Torq thought of the night of the worst storm at sea. How terrified he'd been. He and Plak both admitted to each other after they were on land that they cried like babies during that storm. They were in different boats, but it was a night never to forget. He remembered the huge ice chunks rolling and pieces falling off from them as they rolled. He thought back to the visions that remained in his thinking place of the ice chunks lifted on waves that rose far above the boats. He remembered the howling of the winds, like nothing he'd ever heard, so loud that it hurt his ears. And the pelting water that felt like rocks. That was horrible. It was awful to remember. For a brief moment

Torq wondered whether that was the reason Plak didn't want to return to the Cove. Then he realized that regardless of what he thought of his friend, Plak was not a coward. Torq knew there was more than cowardice in Plak's decision. Plak would have, he knew, been no more afraid to return than he was.

Torq remembered the whale killers hunting the seals. The time they were on the ice with the seals and the whales came by was terrifying to him. Worse was the time the whale killers swam past their little boats chasing a seal. They caught it and tossed it in the air near them. Torq was terrified that they might toss it into the boat and then crash the boat to retrieve it. The whale killer that swam right by the edge of his boat looking him in the eyes was the most terrifying of all. It was as if the enormous animal could look right down to the secret part of his spirit where his fear lay, pull it up, examine it, and toss it away as not being worth the while. He had felt dismissed.

Torq walked back into the place where he'd been cared for so well. He saw Man-who-knows-herbs.

He sat on the sleeping place the man had provided for him.

"Man-who-knows-herbs," Torq said, "I have learned where to find the path to the east. I need to leave this place to reach the cache where we meet to return to my land."

Man-who knows-herbs turned, looking at Torq for what seemed a long time. "You're not going anywhere, Torq."

Torq was shocked that the man planned to detain him.

"You're unfit. You'd not make two days before you'd become faint and need more assistance."

"I must reach the cache in time."

"It's better not to reach it at all than to die trying, young man. You are not thinking clearly."

"You don't understand. I need to help save my people. I must reach the cache site."

"Are your people sicker than you?"

"No, that's not what I mean." Torq was becoming agitated. "It's just that we are scheduled to meet there for the return trip."

"Young man, you need to calm down. I understand what you see as a problem. What you fail to see is that you are in no condition to make a journey of any length. Are you interested in bringing on your own death? That's how it sounds to me."

"I am not suicidal; I am loyal!"

Man-who-knows-herbs sat down facing Torq. "Loyalty never required one's death. You have your priorities upside down. First, you have to be fit.

What help could you be rowing if you almost die reaching this cache site? You'd require care, not be able to contribute. The truth is, however, that if the cache site is more distant than one day, you would not make it. That's fact, young man."

"If my people choose not to migrate, I could be left here alone. I just have to reach them."

"You are still thinking poorly. If you miss your chance to go back there, it's not like there are no people in this land. You will not be alone no matter where you go here. If you don't like one group you can travel to another you might like better. But to give up your life for your people, which is what you'll be doing—they won't even know! I do not give you permission to leave. It would be suicidal."

"I'm not suicidal. I'm loyal, determined . . . ."

"Stupid! Lie down now and be quiet. Calm yourself. You speak nonsense. Besides, you owe us."

Torq had begun to lie down when the words "owe us" hit him hard.

"What's *owe us?*" he asked.

"I have cured you and am trying to put some fat on your body. You are obligated to me at this time—not to people far away—people who don't know you should have died. You would have died, if you hadn't been brought to me. Then, your loyalty, your determination would be of no value to your people or anyone else, for you'd be dead. You're good to no one dead. You owe me ten days of hauling rocks from the top of our mountain to here. Ten full days. When you have done that, you're free to leave. Until then you have a debt to me and my people."

Man-who-knows-herbs could not look at the woman who was his wife. He feared that one glance at her would make him laugh and destroy the scene he had set for Torq. Torq was in no condition to make a journey, of that he was certain, and his people did not put others in debt to them for healing. But Man-who-knows-herbs also knew people. He had to find a way to reach this man to prevent him from suicide.

"Today I learned about trade and about debt," Torq said. "Trade sounds interesting, debt does not."

"You cannot trade unless you have something to trade. You have nothing. Your debt is like a trade—your work will be your part of the trade. You have begun to grow your health. You have to trade work for your regained health. Both are the same."

"I can begin to see that, but in trade two people agree. I didn't agree to the debt."

Slowly, Man-who-knows-herbs rose to his feet. He picked up Torq's spear. He held the spear as if to use it on Torq. "Would you then prefer I kill you? Then you'd be dead as you would have been if I hadn't helped. You want to die?" He stood there poised with the spear, far more athletic than Torq thought the old man could be.

"No, don't kill me. I didn't agree to the debt, but if it means my life or doing what you said, I will do as you tell me."

Man-who-knows-herbs held out his hand to his wife. "Let us go now to gather some plants that I need."

She stood up and walked outside with him. They walked to the edge of the woods where Torq could not possibly hear.

"Old Man," she chided, "You should prepare me for these things. I had to bite my lip to keep from laughing. We have no debt for curing others."

"Well, of course not, but how else could I stop him? The young man is hard headed. I expect he will try to escape. If he does, he won't go far."

"Will you have him tracked?"

"I haven't decided yet. I do plan to tell the hunters what I've told him. They need to know what I've said, so they don't give away my trade."

"You are clever, Old Man."

"That's why you love me."

"That is NOT why I love you, but it contributes," she laughed.

Man-who-knows-herbs stopped a moment to talk to Hammer. He agreed to let others know what he'd told Torq about ten days of rock transport.

Man-who-knows-herbs and Woman-who-brings-babies, his wife, entered the woods while he sought some plants that should be ready to pick. When they returned, some of the people laughed when they saw him, while they made the sign that they would not speak of what they knew. Clearly they cheered the man's cleverness.

Late that night, Man-who-knows-herbs heard Torq moving about very quietly. He knew instantly that the young man was ready to escape. He let him go. In the morning at breakfast, the others realized he was missing.

Pathfinder asked whether they should track the young man. All felt worried that he would not survive well.

Man-who-knows-herbs said, "I would not track him today. I would wait until tomorrow. If you find him today he will easily recover. He needs to learn that healers know more about healing than he does. He will not learn if you find him too fast. Let him have a night with no food, for he's in no condition to hunt. Let him struggle to learn he can't make it. Then he will be easier to heal."

"I'll go with you tomorrow, Pathfinder," Hammer said.

In the dark it was difficult for Torq to find the trail. It was too dark. He was short of breath. It was colder out than he thought it would be. His backpack was cutting into his sores. His legs were weak. He thought about returning, but he knew he needed to make it to the cache. He felt obligated to continue on but would sit and lean against the tree until daylight. After a while, Torq began to shiver. He reached into his backpack and pulled out his soft skin jacket. He put it on and after a while it seemed to help warm him, but not enough. He unrolled his sleeping skin and wrapped it around him. Torq set his spear by his side and waited for light.

When light finally came, Torq was still cold. He was able to find the path and move eastward. Finally, he was comfortable that he was fulfilling his obligation. He couldn't help but think that if Plak had accompanied him, the cat wouldn't have wounded him and they'd almost be at the cache site. That it was the time of leaves turning color, not the time of new leaves did not seem to enter his thinking place. Torq was way ahead of himself. He warmed somewhat by moving along the trail. It had widened a lot and was much easier to travel than he remembered.

Torq did not think of food or drink. He had jerky in the backpack and the little water bladders. He walked on. By high sun, Torq had been struggling for some time. He was still short of breath and had to lean against trees from time to time, for he became dizzy. Torq refused to take the signs as anything serious. He thought of the dizziness and the shortness of breath as symptoms of not having been active. He continued on.

Torq almost stepped on a brown snake in a pile of leaves. It shook its tail which made a noise. The realization that the snake had a triangular head made Torq force an alertness he didn't have. The carelessness could have cost him a lot of pain and death, he realized. He thought back to Man-who-knows-herbs talking to him. He would not have changed what he did, he realized.

Shortly after high sun, Torq was exhausted. He wrapped in his skins and leaned against a tree. He went black. When he awakened, it was dark. He knew he could not continue on in the darkness, so he wrapped in his skins and returned to black.

By morning Torq was awakened by two squirrels chattering as if scolding him for sleeping after the day had begun. He rolled up his sleeping skins and prepared to go again. He had neither food nor water. Those things hadn't appeared in his thinking place. Torq simply knew he needed to reach the cache.

He didn't go very far on the trail before his dizziness caused him to fall.

Already on the trail, Hammer and Pathfinder were gaining on him. They could follow his trail with ease. They had brought a stretcher, for Man-who-knows-herbs made it clear that the man would give out. It didn't take them long to find Torq lying on the path, worn out.

"Well, look who this is," Hammer said with heightened volume.

Torq turned to face the men who came to take him back. He groaned.

Hammer went to him and looked at his arms, pinching the skin. "He's dehydrated," Hammer said.

Pathfinder pulled out a skin filled with fresh water and dipped a gourd into it. He handed the gourd to Torq.

Torq drank the water gratefully. He hadn't realized he had failed to drink water. What, he wondered, had he been thinking?

Pathfinder and Hammer laid out the stretcher. They lifted Torq to the stretcher, put the water bladder away, placed Torq's backpack on the stretcher, covered him with his sleeping skins, and began the trek back home.

They took Torq straight to Man-who-knows-herbs' place. When they arrived, they carried him in, laid the stretcher beside his sleeping place, rolled him over onto it, put his sleeping skins folded by his feet, his backpack and spears against the wall. They left without a word. The old woman who was inside said nothing. Torq lay there struggling to breathe. He also said nothing.

Man-who-knows-herbs came into the place some time after Torq arrived. He said to both his wife and to Torq, "The evening meal is about to be served." To Torq alone, he added, "Stand up Torq; you need to eat."

Torq stood up, and felt aches and pains, but he ignored them and walked outside to the gathering place. He was dirty and tired, but the food smelled wonderful and he definitely was hungry.

Women dished up the food, occasionally asking the person they were about to serve whether they wanted one thing or another. Torq took his food with gratitude and ate it quietly. He was shocked that no one mentioned his escape.

After he ate, he put his bowl where it was supposed to be placed, and he returned to Man-who-knows-herbs' place. He felt defeated. He knew now to what extent Man-who-knows-herbs was a healer. He felt foolish.

When Man-who-knows-herbs came in, Torq asked, "Why is there no punishment, no verbal attack for my escape? My people would not ignore something like this."

"You are not ignorant, Torq. You knew what the dangers were. I told you. For some reason that I cannot understand, you chose to think that you know more than I do. You tried and failed. You have the opportunity to learn, or you can repeat the same nonsense. Be advised that the next time, if there is one, the hunters may have better things to do than track down a young man who refuses to learn. You understand duty. You have a duty to me that is not fulfilled. You will now add two extra days to your rock moving."

Torq groaned. Twelve days of moving rocks from the top of the hill to the bottom. As he relaxed, he finally understood. Moving rocks would put him in shape for the trek to the cache. The old man was doing his best to plan what was good for him. He realized he needed to attend to the man's words and do as he was told. The old man was right. Man-who-knows-herbs knows more than herbs. For the first time he was truly grateful to the old man.

"I am grateful, Man-who-knows-herbs. I was a fool. It will not happen again."

Man-who-knows-herbs nodded to him and added, "If you want to put fat on your body, eat twice what you normally eat."

Torq would do as he said.

A few days later Torq began to take purposeful walks. Each day he extended the walk, adding carrying things. He brought up water from the creek and did other work that helped the people with whom he stayed. Finally, when the leaves had mostly been blown off the trees, he went to the top of the hill. There were stones there, large ones. Surely, he thought, Man-who-knows-herbs didn't mean for me to carry these large stones down the hill? He looked around for other stones and found none. Torq lifted a stone. It was very heavy, but he was capable of carrying it. He walked down the path carrying the stone. He had to stop to put the stone down. He sat down and rested a bit. Then he stood up and began to carry the rock downhill. It took him five stops with the one rock to reach the village. When he arrived there, he put the rock down and went to find Man-who-knows-herbs.

Man-who-knows-herbs was gathering wind fallen logs for firewood. Torq picked up a few pieces and followed Man-who-knows-herbs to the place he was stacking the wood. When he reached the place, he said, "I brought one rock down from the hill. Where do you want them?"

Man-who-knows-herbs looked up at him and started walking to the cleared edge of the village gathering area. "Here," he pointed, "I want to see the rocks stacked side by side, tight. The dirt is eroding here, and these rocks can stop it. The wall should go from here to there with an opening for the path. I expect the wall to be at least two rocks high and possibly two rocks thick. Do you understand?"

"Yes. You want them packed together very tightly?"

"Yes. The wall must be strong to hold back the dirt."

"I understand," Torq said. He left to climb up the hill again.

By the sixth day, Torq was close to finishing. He carried down the last rock that made the double thick, double high rock wall. He went to find Man-who-knows-herbs. He found him sitting on a log talking to two other old men. Torq went over and as taught in his culture, he waited to be recognized before he spoke.

"Let's hear what Torq has to say," Man-who-knows-herbs said.

"I have only two rocks to bring down and the rock wall is finished. What would you have me do when that is finished?"

Man-who-knows-herbs stood up. "Come with me," he said.

Torq and the other old men followed.

Man-who-knows-herbs reached the opening in the wall. "From this point here, I want to see rock steps from here to the creek," he said. "You may see if any of the others will help you dig out the steps so they are level."

Torq was shocked to know what the man had in mind. The rock wall was one thing. Stairs. That was something else. Nevertheless, he talked to Hammer and then went back up the hill to gather the remaining rocks for the wall.

As he climbed the hill, he realized his breathing had improved. He also realized that he was going downhill without having to stop to rest. Torq stood still for a moment as the realization sank in. Man-who-knows-herbs had planned this work as a way for Torq to build up strength for the trek. It shattered Torq to realize what the man had done for him from his cure to the strength building. Torq esteemed the man greatly. He knew that Man-who-knows-herbs was not only knowledgeable, but also he was wise. He'd let his own thinking place see the man as mean-spirited, when in fact he was very kind. Torq was undone momentarily as he faced his own error.

Torq brought the last two rocks down and the rock wall was complete. It looked good. Torq was proud of the work he'd done.

Apt, Hammer's younger sister, walked over to Torq as he laid down the last stone for the wall. "Do you not like me?" she asked.

Torq was shocked, and answered truthfully, "I don't know you very well, Apt."

"I have tried everything I know to attract your attention since you began building the wall. You ignore every attempt I make."

Torq felt as if he'd hurt the girl somehow. He tried to choose his words carefully. "Apt, I have appreciated your bringing me food while I work on the wall. I have looked only at my goal. My goal is to reach the place I'm supposed to be to meet others. We will travel back to my land to help the others there to move to this good land."

"And you see nothing but your goal? The cache?"

"If I become distracted, I could be tempted to lose sight of the goal and miss it."

"I've never known any man to ignore a woman, unless he is a man who feels he's in the wrong body. In my experience that's the only time a man ignores a woman—regardless of his goal. Are you a man who believes he's a woman?"

Torq was shocked. "I don't know about what you speak. I've never known a man who thinks he's a woman. I just know I have a responsibility and I cannot lose sight of it."

"So you ignore what is natural so you won't lose sight of a future goal?"

"Yes," he said flatly.

"Do you find me attractive?"

"Yes." He did find her attractive, though he hadn't really noticed until she called attention to herself.

"Then, what's wrong with spending a little time with me?" she asked as seductively as she felt comfortable displaying to this strange young man.

"I'll ask you, Apt, the same question only differently. What's *right* with spending a little time with you?"

"What's right is that it might lead to pleasure," she said quickly as if the question were simple.

"You have only carried the question a little way. Suppose that pleasure were something that I would find very tempting to make me want to forget the future goal that is my responsibility? What then?"

"Well, then, you'd need to weigh which you'd prefer."

"To me that isn't a proper choice. To choose pleasure with you over my own responsibility to my people is wrong. It goes against all I believe."

"Could you not have both?"

Torq stood there looking at the girl. "I do not know how you reason in that manner."

"Suppose you found pleasure with me. Could you not then take me with you to the cache? Could you not take me with you to cross the sea?"

"Before I find pleasure with a woman, it is required of me to build a home for us. To build a home means I intend to remain in the place. I do not have time for anything now but to complete becoming well and to leave to travel quickly to the cache."

"You have an answer for everything, Torq."

"I have to know my thinking place. I have to know what I believe. Otherwise my thinking place is like a leaf blowing in the wind."

Apt had been sitting on the wall. She slipped down from the wall and walked away. Torq was an enigma to her.

Torq noticed that Hammer and Pathfinder had gathered the boys and had them working to level out steps. They guided the boys and the boys did the work. They began to level it out at the bottom first. Torq went up and sought stones that were fairly flat. There were many of them. He began to carry them down. When he reached the bottom, the first step was ready for the stones. It would take about six stones per step, Torq thought. He kept going up and carrying stones back down. By the second step, it was clear that the steps would be a great contribution, and that they looked very nice. He was happy to have work that he needed to trade for his healing. The work would remain with the people and look nice; his healing would stay with him the rest of his life. Torq went back up the hill.

By the eleventh day, the steps were finished. He wondered what Man-who-knows-herbs would have him do. He found the man and asked.

Man-who-knows-herbs went to the wall. He examined it. He went to the steps and examined them. Finally, he said, "I think that it would be good where the steps meet the creek to put stones there so the water goes over stones, not pebbles and dirt. Then on top of the rocks add stepping stones to the other side so when water runs high, we can walk across without wading through water."

When Torq returned with the first stone, he noticed to his amazement that the boys who dug out the steps were digging out the creek bed so it would be level for the stones. It took Torq through the twelfth day to finish the creek crossing. It was good, he could tell.

That night at the evening meal, they all gathered to say farewell to Torq who would leave the next day. He hoped he'd make it to the cache in time. All was set. Women had packed him good jerky, nuts, and dried berries. His water bladders were filled and ready. That night he went black well. He had put on some fat and muscle. He felt better than he had felt in a long time. Man-who-knows-herbs is a good healer, he admitted.

After the morning meal, Torq set out again. He had learned not to allow himself to become too tired, not to put off attending to wounds, and to listen to elders. He also had learned that when someone gives to you, it should be automatic to see if there is something you can give back in return.

That night Torq sat with Pathfinder. Pathfinder asked him to explain the location of the cache. Torq told him what he remembered. Pathfinder had a good sense of the general location of the place. He drew in the dirt the land from his village to the sea. He showed the remaining mountains and rivers that Torq would encounter. He drew the path that went from their location to the east and west. He showed how to travel on that path until it met the second north to south path. Then, Torq should turn north. He would make it over the rivers easier that way. He warned Torq of the places where bears and large cats were known to be problems to travelers. He pointed out some good hunting places for meat along the way. He showed where to expect to encounter people. He reminded Torq that he could encounter people on any trail. The common courtesy on the trail was to ignore others. Occasionally, someone on the trail would take advantage of others they met there. Torq was putting the information in his thinking place. Pathfinder warned him about the swamp he'd find between the path and the cache. He urged him to go around the swamp, not try to go through it, because it was filled with terrible biting bugs, large poisonous snakes, large lizards that kept to the water but could crawl out on land, and some strange people who lived there. After Pathfinder finished, Torq asked him to let him retell the route. He asked Pathfinder to correct him if he made a mistake. It took Torq three times to go through the information before he mastered it. Pathfinder was amazed at the care Torq took.

Torq left after the morning meal the next day. He thanked the natives for their help. He left on the path he'd made down to and across the creek. He walked up the hill across from the village until he reached the path. He turned east on the path and began his trek to the cache.

Torq was more single-mindedly intent on reaching the cache point than he had been earlier. He was concerned about the time it took to recover from the cat attack, so he was far more observant than he had been. He was also in much better condition than when he'd left Plak.

The path was different from the ones he and Plak had taken that took them to the big river. This path was wider and he made good progress on it. There were convenient places to stop in the evening, and he took advantage of them and made sure that he was well rested.

As Torq went along, he noticed something small moving on the path. He stooped to see what it was and discovered a young flying squirrel that was missing its back left foot. He picked up the tiny gray creature and talked to it. It looked at him with large black unafraid eyes. He stroked its head. Torq was fascinated. He wore his jacket and without much thought, he put the animal into the chest pocket on the left side of his jacket. The animal quieted. He continued walking until evening and then he found a good stopping place and set up his shelter and sleeping skins. He opened his backpack to take some jerky and remembered the flying squirrel, which he pulled from his jacket pocket. He talked to the squirrel while he ate a few sticks of jerky. He gave the squirrel some broken nut meat and a dried berry. The squirrel ate the food quickly enough that Torq gave it more of the nuts. The squirrel climbed up Torq's jacket and entered his pocket. After checking carefully around his shelter, Torq went black. While he was deep in black, the flying squirrel came out and examined the shelter. It could smell the food in the backpack, but it could not find an entry into the container. It found a few bugs and ate those. There was water in a gourd Torq had set aside by the backpack. The flying squirrel helped himself. Finally, he climbed back into Torq's pocket and curled up.

When Torq emerged from black, he noticed the little creature was still in his pocket. He looked inside and two very dark eyes stared back at him. He stroked the squirrel's head.

"May you have a good day, little squirrel," he said. "We will travel far today. I feel well rested and we have a long way to go."

Torq ate quickly, dropping some nuts, seeds, and dried fruit into his pocket. He packed his things ready for the day's trek. Torq pulled on his backpack.

"Well, here we go, little one," he said to the squirrel.

Torq liked having the squirrel along. It gave him something to talk to. He didn't feel so alone. Feeling lighter of spirit, Torq cautioned himself to keep his acute level of environmental awareness. He hummed a tune, keeping his volume extremely low. He felt happier than he had at any time since the incident with Plak.

Far out on an open meadow, Torq noticed a short faced bear. This was the area where Pathfinder warned him of bears. Torq moved through the area as fast as he could. Fortunately, the wind blew the bear's smell to him, not the other way around. It took him two days to clear the area where the bears predominated. He was more comfortable once he'd passed it, but he didn't let his caution decrease.

Torq came to a river where he'd have to swim to cross—either that or make a raft. He opted for the swim, but realized he had a flying squirrel in his pocket to protect. Torq took the small squirrel from his pocket and placed the squirrel in a pouch on the backpack. He placed his clothes atop the backpack where he tied them with a small cord. He entered the water with his backpack secured to a two-log raft he'd made to transport his things that needed to remain dry. The cordage he used to tie the logs together left pieces long enough to attach to his body. Torq tied the ends of the cords together and laid the cordage in front of the log raft forming a great U shape. He stood in front of the cord and pulled it up. Facing the direction of the river, he placed the cord over his head so it rested on the back of his neck. The cord went under his arms. He entered the water. The log raft dragged across the dirt behind him to the water's edge. The cordage pulled on his shoulders. When the raft began to float on the water, the tug on his shoulders decreased significantly. Torq began to swim across the river, pleased that the raft was following so well behind him. He reached the other side and pulled up the raft, dressed, replaced the squirrel in his pocket. He gathered the cordage and tied it to the outside of his backpack. He resumed the trek, his hair and beard still dripping.

When the sun began to descend behind him, Torq looked for a place to go black. He saw little but flat land with a few trees in the distance. He headed for the trees, hoping to find some deadfall limbs to make a lean-to. By the time he reached the trees, he found little deadfall, but enough wood for a small fire. Torq thought it odd that since most leaves had changed, this one still retained green leaves. He wondered whether some trees that appeared to be ones that lose their leaves might sometimes keep the green leaves through the winter. He gave up the thought of a fire, because it would signal his location to humans and perhaps animals from a wide range and long distance. Fortunately, the oak tree grouping had two trees that had grown together and made an arc at the base. Torq used the deepest part of the arc to protect his back. He put his sleeping skins in that place and sat down. He pulled his backpack close. By then, the flying squirrel had learned the routine, and he crawled from the pocket to the space beside Torq where he waited on the skin. Torq laid nuts, seeds, and a few dried berries on the skin for the squirrel. He watched, amused, as the squirrel went to the gourd where his own water waited him. The squirrel drank its fill from Torq's gourd and returned to the food on the sleeping skin. Torq didn't mind sharing his gourd.

Torq listened to the night noises. He heard nothing that caused him alarm. He looked up through the branches and saw the night sky, twinkling with stars on the clear night. He felt a presence near him and without moving at all, he looked in every direction his eyes would move. He felt as if his father, Mongwire, were there. It was a strange sensation.

"Father?" he said aloud.

He had a strange sense that he could see Murke. Why would he see Murke? Torq wondered.

"Murke? Is that you?" Torq was confused.

As clearly as if he stood next to Murke, he heard Murke's voice say, "I'm proud of you, my son." Torq had once thought he looked like Murke, but he didn't take it seriously that the man could be his father. Was Murke his father? The image of Murke disappeared.

Torq lay back, musing. It didn't really matter whether Murke was his father or whether Mongwire was. Both men had contributed to his life in various ways. He hadn't really been close to his father. He hadn't been close to Murke either. He shut his teeth tight together. He'd been close to Plak. The community at the Cove did not limit their interaction to their own hearths. Murke felt his beard. Certainly, his thick beard was more like Murke's thick one than Mongwire's very thin beard. He turned the thought aside. It didn't really matter, he told himself again.

Torq pulled his sleeping skin over himself and went black.

When he awakened, he ate quickly, fed the squirrel, and rolled his sleeping skins to tie onto the top of his backpack. He reached for the spears and began to head the short distance to the path he'd been following. Torq reached the path only to realize there was a brightly colored small snake on the path. He saw the colors of warning on the snake, red and yellow and black. The snake moved away with some speed. He watched where it went. He was careful to avoid it. Torq listened to the morning sounds. Trumpeting off to the south he heard either a mastodon or mammoth, he wasn't sure which, but guessed at mastodon, since he thought it was in the woodland.

By high sun the open area was gone and Torq was back in forest. He reached the path where Pathfinder had told him to turn left. He turned onto the wider path and continued on. In the evening Torq came to a river and decided to cross it before setting up his night's camp. He had to make another raft for his backpack. Carefully, Torq placed the little squirrel in the pouch on the backpack. He laid his clothes and the backpack on the raft and secured them with cordage. Torq didn't feel it necessary to free both his arms, so he held onto the cordage and walked across the river. It was slippery where algae grew to the rocks, but he managed to stay upright and pull the raft. He swam a very short way and then climbed the bank on the other side. He dressed and untied the backpack. He folded the cordage and tied it to the backpack.

A short walk found him a rock shelter for the night. Torq was delighted. He decided to make a small hearth fire for warmth and he set up quickly. His ember had become extinguished, so he had to make the fire using his fire starting tools. Torq knew that would help to warm him. He found some dry wind fallen wood and quickly made his hearth fire. He ate some jerky and a few nuts and berries. Torq shared with the squirrel. It took little time before he went black.

Torq was in deep black when he felt something poke him in the side. He jerked himself awake and started to stand but was prevented by the spear in his side.

The spear holder asked, "Who are you?"

Torq had no idea what the man said.

He touched his chest and said, "Torq."

The man looked at the three other men. He laughed and so did the other men. The laugh sent chills through Torq. They used his cordage to tie his feet and hands together. They took a spear and pushed it through so that he would be carried like an animal carcass. They shoved his backpack onto his belly. They lifted the spear and began to transport him north on the trail. One of the men covered the hearth fire.

Torq was frightened. He had met some indigenous people in this land, but he had never been treated in this manner. When they arrived at their village, there was much light from firebrands. They dumped him on the ground in front of a man who was bent over and had many wrinkles on his face and loose old-looking skin on his arms, legs, and belly. Torq wondered whether he'd ever seen anyone that old.

It was obvious that the natives held the old man in high esteem. They acted like wolves when greeting the chief wolf. Torq had not seen that in any of his meetings. He wondered where this would lead.

He tried to pull himself together so that he would not show fear. It was extremely difficult in these circumstances.

The old man prodded Torq with his foot. Torq turned his head to look at the man.

"Who are you?" the old man asked.

Torq replied, "Torq is my name." Then, in the language of the people he'd just left, he said the same thing in their language. At that a woman said, "I understand." She had been of a related group and knew the language.

The old man called her to interpret.

"Ask him why he is here on the path that goes past our village," the old man told her.

"Why are you on the path that passes this village?" she asked.

"I am headed to the north, to meet my people to return home across the eastern sea," he replied. Then, he wondered whether he should have volunteered as much information as he had.

The old man looked at him following the woman's translation.

"How far north does he plan to travel?" the old man told her to ask. She did.

"I plan to travel almost as far north as the ice sheet."

She translated.

"What business do you have at the ice sheet?" he asked.

The woman dutifully translated.

"I plan to go there to meet the others who explore this land. Then, we return home," he said carefully avoiding any mention of bringing other people to the land.

"Why did you come here?" the old man asked.

To the translated words, Torq replied, "We wanted to know what was across the sea."

"You come from across the sea?" the old man's face was blank. Torq could not tell what his thoughts were.

"Yes."

"How am I to believe such a lie?"

Torq tried hard not to give any sense of consternation. "I do not lie," he said with strength, though stretched out on the ground tied up gave not a lot of visual support to his words. "I know the sea well. I know it when it's calm and when it is stormy. I know the great chunks of ice and the expanses of water free of ice. I know what it is like to meet the whales, the largest animals of the sea. I know what it is to spear seals for food and to make water from ice."

The old man looked at him. He looked at the four men who brought him. "Untie him," he ordered. They complied immediately.

"He speaks the truth," the old man said.

The woman translated.

Torq sat cross-legged. He was quiet and tried to be acquiescent without being subservient.

The old man said, "Tomorrow, we will help this man leave. Prepare travel food for him," he told the women. "No one will follow him when he leaves. He is free to continue his trek."

The old man motioned Torq to his hut. He showed Torq where to put his sleeping skins. They returned outside and women brought the evening meal. After eating, they retired to their huts and to sleep.

Torq fed his squirrel by putting a little of the food in his pocket while they ate. He did it so it was not a noticeable thing. The squirrel did not come out. Torq pulled his sleeping cover over him and went black.

The old man slipped out of the hut and met the man who had put the spear against Torq's side. He returned to his hut with a smile on his face.

In the morning the people shared their morning meal with Torq and then they brought food to add to his backpack. He was grateful and thanked them and their chief. He turned and walked to the path.

Once away from the village, Torq lifted the squirrel from his pocket. He talked to the squirrel briefly and then put the animal back in the pocket.

Torq tried to remember to keep his alertness heightened. He had been completely unprepared for the people who found him and carried him like an animal to their chief.

The day was warm and it became warmer as he went on. Most all the leaves were gone and they crunched on the path under his feet. The path went on into small mountains, and he traveled up and down with ease, his body having become accustomed to the trek again.

Torq had a sense of accomplishment. He finally recognized the area into which he had trekked. The cache was not far from him.

Suddenly from what seemed like nowhere, Torq heard strangled yells coming from several directions. Swift spears struck him from arms he could not see well. He fell to the ground, knowing that two of the wounds would likely prove fatal. What, he wondered, caused this attack? Then, he saw the face of one of the attackers. It was the man who had put his spear against his side. The men came from their concealed places and pulled their spears from Torq's body. They grabbed his hands and feet and threw his body off the path. They turned and left in silence.

Torq lay there in agony. He was bleeding profusely. The squirrel climbed out of his pocket. It sat on his chest looking at Torq's face. The animal went to the place on Torq's side where the blood was pumping out. He returned to look at Torq's face. It chittered and then jumped off the man and climbed rapidly up a tree where he would watch the man below.

"What treachery!" Torq shouted. "What evil treachery!"

Torq became dizzy, he felt nauseated. He envisioned the cache. He thought of the people at the Cove. He'd not make it to the cache. In a short time, Torq no longer breathed air.

Chapter 7

Akla's Story

Akla had decided to explore the area. He climbed the hill to the east and surveyed the land. Suddenly someone gagged Akla and carried him off to the east, far from the place where moments before he'd stood to survey the lowland on either side of the rise. As he dangled from his own spear pole held over the shoulders of two of the four men, Akla could hear Murke's plaintive calls far away. He was desperate to answer, but could make no noise. He did not understand why these stealthy people wanted him. He did not realize that the men were stepping carefully from rock to rock at the top of the ridge blocked from view by great trees, so they left no tracks. Akla noticed all of the men had hair shorter than shoulder length, and they had white headbands to keep the hair from their faces.

After a half day's walk on the ridge, slipping in and out of forests, the people began their descent to the river on the south side of the ridge. They dumped him into the boat and quickly climbed in and began to row. His spear lay in the boat, but not where he could make use of it. They went with the current, but rowed rapidly, as if chased. Akla was surely out of hearing distance, but the men did not remove the gag. They eventually reached the sea, and they turned to the north. Akla was surprised to see great chunks of ice drifting down the coast. He knew the ice chunks came this far to the south, but the number of them surprised him. They rowed hard, moving north. Eventually they came to a river that Akla remembered. They rowed up that river. Akla recognized the placement of the cache left for the SealEaters' return to the Cove on the second summer. It was either not evident to the rowers or they did not consider it something to examine, for it appeared untouched. The rowers moved quietly up the river further and further to the north.

The natives removed his gag when it was time for him to eat. He tried to converse, but they ignored him. As soon as he finished eating, they'd replace his gag. They would not let him sit in the boat. He remained tied up and lying down. Akla's attempts to converse were rebuffed. He wondered what could possibly cause them to act the way they did. He had concluded that the four men who captured him did not have authority to kill him. Apparently there was a reason for his capture, but he could not conceive of anything that made sense with respect to the treatment he was given.

Day after day the river they followed narrowed and became shallow. They reached a place where travel was no longer possible by their boat. The four men and Akla stepped out of the boat. The tall one made it clear that Akla would continue to wear the gag, but he would walk between two of the men. They left his hands tied behind him. Akla had tried his best to learn words or make some sense of their speech, but he had been unable to learn it. It was unlike the words of the natives whose languages he'd tried to speak. He was frustrated. Akla also worried about Murke. He knew Murke would be concerned about him and would do everything he could to find him. Akla was fairly certain there would be no way Murke could find him.

The men walked over some hills and when they reached the top, the huge ice sheet lay before them. The vastness of it startled Akla. From above, the whiteness of it in the sun virtually blinded him. Akla had seen the ice on the sea up close. This was different—endless as far as he could see. One of the men pushed him. They were moving. Akla responded, finding it hard to keep from staring at the ice, despite the pain it caused his eyes. As they walked they could hear the ice make cracking noises and groans from time to time. Akla concluded that the ice had a spirit that spoke. It did not sound happy. Not happy at all.

Akla hoped that the walk would be a brief one, so that he could find out finally what the abduction was all about. That was not to be. The men did remove the gag finally. Akla looked at it, wondering what evil it nurtured after having been in his mouth for so long. He hadn't even been able to pick his teeth. His mouth felt unclean.

He had anxiety where the huge ice sheet was concerned. He wondered, if it became wet below from melting, and the ice slid forward, would they be able to move out of the way fast enough? The huge ice frightened him as it had on the water. He knew what ice floating on water could do. What this might do, he did not know. As they walked, seemingly in response to his concerns, a large chunk of ice split with a thunderous crack. It fell off to the land below, shattering into splinters. Akla jumped at the ear shattering cracking sound. The other men, he noticed, were not the least bit alarmed. He found that puzzling, unless, he reasoned, they were accustomed to the event.

They entered yet another forest and continued their trek. This time the path was almost invisible. He had counted the days since they left the river. There had been seventeen days of trekking. He was tired of the walk and the uncertainty. Disgusted with the silence, Akla wanted to be able to talk to another person. He noted that these four men talked less than any men he'd ever known. He was beyond caring why.

One day he looked ahead and there was a human-made place at the top of a small hill. He'd seen villages, but this was no village. It was huge. There were stones on stones making a wall. Inside the wall there were stone structures. There were many people there. Akla was dumbfounded. The hill top at the north end was very close to the ice. It was like nothing he had ever imagined or could imagine. His interest grew. These four men had abducted him to bring him to this place? He could not make sense of any of it. Still they continued on in silence. It took the largest part of the day to reach the place.

They had to pass through a narrow opening to enter the walled area. One of the four men spoke to the person who seemed responsible for who might enter. They were waved through quickly. Akla tried to absorb in his thinking place as much of the place as he possibly could as the men moved quickly into the center of the area. There was a structure that was taller and much bigger than anything in the walled area. They went to that structure. There were three steps that were larger than most men could easily climb. Akla wondered at that. They climbed with difficulty to the place where the lowest terrace leveled off. The structure had three terraces.

A man walked up to the leader of their group and told the tall man to go up one additional level. They climbed three more too large steps. At the second level they were led to a room inside the center. All five men stood, waiting. The wait was a long one. A man entered and told them to follow. They went through corridors and entered a large room where a man occupied a seating place carved of wood. The arms of the seating place looked like mastodons, each mastodon in a different pose. The seated man rested his arms on the backs of the mastodons. The carving was the best representation of an animal Akla had ever seen, looking so life-like he could almost imagined it moved. The carving was of brown wood, not the light wood he'd seen in the villages he'd visited. The four men lowered themselves to their knees on the floor. Akla continued standing until a man pushed him roughly, pointing to the other men. Akla adopted the kneeling pose they took. He was not comfortable.

The man who led them into this large room spoke to the man in the mastodon seating place. The seated man said, "Dom?"

Akla assumed the man on the mastodon seating place was the chief, and the tall man, the apparent leader of the four men who captured him, appeared to be named Dom. Akla could follow none of the rest of what was said, as Dom spoke many words fast.

Akla noticed that the man he thought of as chief seemed sometimes pleased; sometimes not pleased. The chief asked a few more questions. The man called Dom answered. To Akla it all seemed unreal. He wondered whether he'd gone black and dreamed. Surely, that was not the case, his knees reported.

The man on the mastodon seating place called for Huthang. The man told Huthang to take Akla. He wanted Huthang to teach him the language and to learn why the man was there, from where he had come, what he wanted there, how many people came with him. Once he found out those things and could speak their language, Tai Oh, the seated man, wanted to speak to him.

Huthang signed for Akla to follow him, and he understood and followed. Akla noticed that his spear lay on the floor by Dom. Akla stopped following Huthang and reached for his spear. All four of his captors began to rise to prevent him from taking his spear. Huthang turned and signed to Akla to follow. Reluctantly, Akla left his spear in the custody of his captors.

Huthang led Akla below the building accessed by steps of ordinary size. Akla estimated that the rooms he saw were underground, though they were lined with stones. Huthang showed him a seating place and signed for him to sit there. Huthang sat on a seating place exactly like his across from Akla. Akla was surprised that the seating place was comfortable.

Huthang began the lessons in their language. He started as most people do with names. He introduced himself and asked Akla's name. Akla learned quickly, which pleased Huthang very much. Akla felt a great sense of relief just to be able to begin communicating. He had been starved for it.

As the lessons progressed day by day, Akla learned that the walled city was a place for learning. It was the place where the Niktonkata power lay. The

Niktonkata were an ancient people in the land. They had much knowledge of the stars; the land on which Akla had travelled; and the ice that lay on the land. They made it their goal to know what happened all across the land east of the great north-south river. They had some knowledge of the land west of the great river, but it was not the same as east of the river.

Akla learned that Tai Oh sent men he called spies out over the land to report on what they saw. His supply of spies was vast. Spies were identified by their white headbands. All the natives in the land knew about Tai Oh. They stood in great fear of the man and his spies. Most of the time the spies did not contact the natives but rather stealthily observed them from a distance, reporting their finds on the development of the villages. The spies in some cases had learned the languages of the natives. Sometimes they abducted a person from a village to learn from them at the walled place, which Akla learned was called Uhurkamakono, or land beside the great ice. Uhurkamakono had another name, Niktonkata North, which made no sense to Akla.

When Akla shared that he found the presence of the ice frightening as if it held a menace, Huthang laughed. He explained that every cycle of seasons for many, many numbers of years, the ice had been advancing. It moved south at the rate of one to ten arm lengths a cycle of seasons. To Akla that seemed very slow. Huthang explained that at that rate in the lifetime of one born at the present, the ice would reach their wall. He said in that case, the place would be evacuated. A new place would be prepared. He also explained that someday, the ice would melt and go away.

Akla wondered how the man knew so much. How could he know the ice would go away? He asked. Huthang told him that the men had been living there forever. The Niktonkata had kept information forever. That let them know what to expect and how to live to survive. They measured many things, Huthang told him. Measuring ice movement was only one.

Huthang had gathered the information Tai Oh wanted from the man. He also had found Akla to be among the brightest of people they'd captured, and he wanted the man as an assistant. For that he would have to convince Tai Oh. Huthang asked for an opportunity to speak with Tai Oh. He had to wait several days, but finally, his chance arose.

Tai Oh motioned for Huthang to approach.

"I have learned what you wish to know and have also come to ask a favor," Huthang said obsequiously.

"Tell me what I wish to know," Tai Oh said, running his finger over the carved mastodon's head.

"Akla is from the land beyond the eastern sea. His people are called SealEaters. They live by the sea where seals haul out on land near their village called the Cove. Opportunistically, they began to eat seals and have a marine diet. He and twelve men traveled by boat, eating seals along the way and melting ice for water, to this land. Remarkably, the explorers managed to stay together and all arrived safely here. They seek a new land for their people, because they are losing their land to the advance of ice and to mountain barriers which wall them in from warring people."

"Do you see them as a threat?"

"No. Even if their people come, they number less than a hundred. Some would be lost at sea. Some may refuse to migrate. They are not a warring people."

"Our people have examined the spear point he brought. There is a real desire to learn this new method of making such points. Talk to Uti. You said you wish to ask a favor. What is it you would have?"

"I would like to make Akla an assistant."

"You already have many assistants, Huthang," Tai Oh said flatly.

"Akla has a special gift when it comes to reasoning. He solves problems and could be a valuable addition to our pursuit of knowledge, perhaps even our wisdom."

"You jest!"

"No, I do not," Huthang said, holding his viewpoint as strongly as was politically wise.

Tai Oh stared at him for some time. Huthang remained calm, waiting.

"Then take him. You know well what we need to know. Just be certain, Huthang, that he doesn't best you."

"I shall keep him under my knee," Huthang promised.

"See that you do!" Tai Oh said.

"Do you wish to see him?" Huthang asked.

"No. Just keep him available in case I have a future desire to meet with him. That's all Huthang."

Huthang bowed and left the room quietly. He was delighted to be able to keep Akla. Otherwise he'd have been sent to manual labor maintaining the walled place or, perhaps, destroyed. They never freed abductees.

Outside Tai Oh's meeting room, Huthang headed for Uti. He found him sitting on a smooth rock under trees by the common well.

"I understand you wish to see Akla, my new assistant," Huthang said without greeting.

"I do," Uti replied.

"How about high sun tomorrow, here at the common well?" Huthang asked.

"That would be good. So, you were permitted to keep the man?" Uti asked.

"Yes, he is worth keeping. You'll see."

"I don't doubt your assessment, Huthang."

"Have a good day, my brother," Huthang said, turning.

"You, also," Uti replied.

Huthang went to his meeting room and had Akla brought to him. He told Akla to sit on the seating place. Akla complied.

"You must listen well, for your safety," Huthang said seriously.

Akla nodded.

"I met with Tai Oh and gave him the information you shared with me. It was information he told me to gather, and he was pleased with what he heard. This place lives for information. What I want you to understand is this. Tai Oh and those who came before him have an interest in what occurs on all the land east of the great north-south river, and Tai Oh sends spies out to gather information. Tai Oh knows more about what goes on than any other on this land. He is like a god to us, his knowledge is so vast."

"The four captors in my case, they were spies?"

"Yes." Huthang leaned against a wall and continued, "Tai Oh has other learning: he knows the workings of the stars, the sun, and the moon. He can predict the change of seasons, and he does way more than count with numbers. He assures peace in this land."

"He rules with a very strong hand, Akla. You have been abducted. Normally, when one has arrived here resulting from an abductrion, one of three things happens to him. He may be asked to be an assistant to someone, he may be sent to labor for this place, or he may be destroyed."

"What do you mean destroyed?" Akla asked.

"Killed," Huthang said without any emotion whatever.

"Well, now that Tai Oh has the information he wanted from me, what will become of me? Will I be killed?"

"Not so fast, Akla. First of all, Tai Oh lacks some information he wants from you. It seems the master of weapons wants to learn to make spear points like the one your spear has. He is very interested in it."

"So, I live until he learns to make spear points like mine?"

"Akla, you thinking from fear not reason. You will not be killed or put to hard labor. You are now one of my assistants. I already asked for and received permission from Tai Oh. Now, I realize you will want to return to your people. For your life to continue, Akla, listen carefully. If you leave the walled place, you will die. People will be sent to find you and kill you, bringing only your head to prove you are dead. Your body would be left to the beasts to eat. Like it or not you cannot leave here."

"You mean ever. There is no way I can earn freedom?" Akla was becoming claustrophobic at the thought of being a prisoner for the rest of his life.

"That is what happened when you were abducted. You now belong to Tai Oh or me, depending on how you view it. That is simply how your life changed at the moment of capture. The good part is that you will be given more and more freedom here as you show that it is warranted. I warn you, however, not to consider escape. Escape will bring on certain death. You saw how far from the rest of life in this land you are. Do not for a moment think that you can fool people who've lived here their entire lives. You would be found, and your death would be so horrible you don't want to think of it."

"What do you mean?"

Huthang sighed. "Returned escapees are beaten and their arms and legs are broken. They are staked to the ground. People may do to them whatever they like. When they die, they are fed to the dogs. We have some women who think it quite the thing to peel the skin from these people while they live. Believe me, it's terribly painful. They do it for many days. Bugs find peeled skin attractive. Eventually, the escapee's body stinks horribly, yet the body remains for all to see—as a warning. You'll probably see some of these during your life here. I tell you these things to warn you. Do not try to be heroic for your SealEaters. Others stronger than you have tried. You have no chance of having any success if you try. Just don't. Accept what has happened to you and make the best of it. You'll find that you can spend the rest of your life trying to learn what there is to learn here, and never reach all the information. There is much here to keep someone like you with good ability to reason busy for a lifetime or two. Give yourself over to learning. You'll find answers to questions here that you've thought could not be answered. You'll find answers to questions you've never known to ask. Learn everything you can learn. It's something you can do to make the best of what has happened to you."

Huthang decided not to drag out the information. "It's now time for you to go back to your place to continue your memory work. Have you ever taught anyone to make spear points like yours?"

"Yes," Akla replied.

"Then prepare yourself for tomorrow. Be certain your thoughts are in order. People here come prepared to learn. They learn quickly. They will expect you to keep up with them."

Akla followed the man into the descending stairway in the big structure. It was there, under the ground, where the people who were Huthang's assistants lived and learned. Akla took a brief look over the wall at the forests beyond before entering the stone building. He sighed. He descended the steps with a heaviness of spirit. He sighed again. "At least," he murmured, "I will not be destroyed."

A moon after Akla had taught the spear point technique to the weapons makers, Huthang called him after the morning meal. They went outside to the lower part of the hill.

"I want you to see the construction down there," Huthang said, pointing to a place at some distance from them inside the wall. Much dirt had been moved to a pile. From the second level of the large building, it was easy to see.

"What are they building?" Akla asked.

"A well."

"What's a well?" Akla replied.

"It's a like a tunnel that goes straight down to water. It keeps us from having to walk to the river. We can lower containers to the bottom to fill them with water. It's a great convenience. I want you to see how it's made and to hear your thoughts."

Akla began to move toward the large steps.

"No, not there, Akla," Huthang said with a wisp of a smile. "Follow me."

They descended the narrow steps to the interior of the great stone structure. Huthang led Akla through a corridor that somehow he'd never noticed because of the construction. They followed the tunnel from which other tunnels branched. Akla was confused. Suddenly, Akla could see a slash of light, and then it widened. They were on the ground level. Akla was startled, but he realized there was purpose in the great stairs, but for those familiar with the maze of tunnels, the effort required by the great steps was not necessary. Akla quickly reasoned that the great steps must be designed to intimidate, to raise the inaccessibility of Tai Oh. Akla began to realize these people thought in ways he never imagined. He looked back. The tunnel exited to a place where no one would normally go. It was close to the wall and well designed to look like a solid wall, designed as were moths to look like tree bark. Akla knew these people were filled with knowledge his people had never known. The difference was becoming more and more evident, and it was far wider than he would have guessed from the early days at Uhurkamakono.

"Now, Akla, they have been digging far down. Once they are down to a certain level, they can no longer throw the dirt to the ground, so they transport it out in buckets. Eventually, the collection of water from the well reverses that process. People will lower buckets to the water and let the bucket drop to fill with water. Then they haul it up."

Akla was amazed at the wonder of making water available. He knew they had water available inside the great stone building all the time, but he had not thought of its source.

"You can see they have just reached water, for the earth is very wet at the bottom. Notice over here they have rectangle forms. What do you think the rectangle forms' use will be?"

"I have no idea, Huthang."

"They will mix this dirt with cut grasses to make a mud-grass mixture. Then they will put the mud-grass mixture into these forms. The mud in the forms will dry in the sun until finally, the rectangular shapes can be removed from the forms where they retain the shape of the rectangle. Can you imagine what use they might have?"

"I should think you could use them to build things," Akla replied.

"That's right. Build what?"

"I don't know. Homes, maybe?"

"Akla, this is a well, focus on the well."

Akla studied the well. He thought for a long time. He considered it for its purpose. Then he began to consider other things such as the environment of the well. Water needed to be clean. An open dig like this would make it possible for things to fall into the water and contaminate it. Rain or snow could carry dirt inside the well. Suddenly, Akla realized that the rectangular shapes could be used to hold the earth back so as to keep the dirt from contaminating the water.

"I think I finally have it," he said quietly.

"What then is the purpose of the rectangular structures made of mud?"

"I think they will make a wall within the well to keep dirt on the sides from contaminating the water."

"Is that all?"

"Well, I think the rectangular structures should go higher than the ground, so that dirt from the ground doesn't go into the well. What I cannot imagine is how to keep the water clean from things falling in a walled well."

"You have not observed while spending your time out here. Look over there by that big tree."

"Am I supposed to see the stone wall with the lean-to built over it?"

"Yes. And what might that be?"

"Is that another well?"

"Yes. You haven't observed anyone using it?"

"Huthang, I have only rarely been outside the huge stone building. When I entered Uhurkamakono, I was frightened and angry, and I didn't look around to learn from what I could see."

"That is something you should learn. Despite fright and anger, it is always wise to examine your surroundings very carefully to make note of anything you do not understand."

"I shall heed your words."

"Good. Now, go to the well under the tree and pull me up some water to drink."

Akla did as he was told. He carried a small gourd to Huthang, who drank it dry.

"Have some yourself, if you're thirsty," he told Akla, who was and did.

"Now, let's go measure the ice encroachment," he said and turned. It wasn't an option.

Akla followed him through the narrow place where the lower tunnel entryway was to the huge building. They went up a ramp between the wall and the huge structure. The ramp was steep and there was a rope laid on it so that a climber could use it to assist in the climb up or let themselves down with greater ease. Some men walked up with their feet parallel to the top and bottom, but most used the rope to assist with ascent and descent.

At the top there was a horizontal plane, a little like the terraces, about two by six man-lengths. Huthang walked over to the center of the flat terrace and looked down.

"That is completely unpredicted!" he exclaimed. "This will have to be reported. Let's go down quickly."

"Huthang, can you at least tell me what you've seen?" Akla had never seen Huthang become excited about anything. He was curious what had set off the response.

"Come here quickly. Look straight over the wall. Look down. What do you see?"

"The ice has pushed in a few of the stones below this wall."

"Yes. At the rate of the current advance, it'll be into the building in a matter of moons. Follow me."

Instead of going down the way they'd come up, Huthang went around an oddly shaped rock and behind it there was another tunnel. He followed Huthang who was moving quickly. They went to the big room where Tai Oh spent the day in the mammoth seating place. Huthang went to the far right of the entryway and lowered himself to his knees. He folded his hands. Akla did the same thing. They waited.

Tai Oh said, "Huthang and Akla, forward." They moved forward, and Tai Oh said, "Huthang, speak."

Still standing, Huthang said, "The ice has advanced more rapidly than predicted. It has moved stones in the wall." Huthang bowed. Akla didn't know what to do, so he made a slight bow.

"All leave but Huthang and Akla," Tai Oh ordered.

The few people who remained in the room left. When Tai Oh felt the area sufficiently cleared, he said in a quiet voice, "Be seated on the pillows." Both Huthang and Akla sat. Tai Oh asked with a sense of urgency, "How well are things going in the south?"

"The main building is completely ready. The wall remains to be finished. By the time we could reach it, all should be finished."

"Then, I will order that we move out in three days. We will go to our river, following it to the great river and from there to the sea. From the sea we can reach the old land. How I hate the heat down there, but it must be."

"Is there anything special you want me to oversee or provide for you or your harem?" Huthang asked.

Akla observed that with all the others gone, Tai Oh and Huthang acted like good friends. He was fascinated.

"No, that is all arranged. I had hoped that the glacier would retreat, but it seems it has to grow more yet. When we set up this place, it was so far from the great ice. My hope is now dashed. It is probably past time to make this long trip. I do so hate the heat down there, but we will have no fear of ice sheets invading, only bugs and snakes."

Akla observed that Tai Oh was not nearly as old as he thought the old man to be. He was exceedingly thin and his skin hung on him loosely. His face gave Akla an estimated age of somewhere between thirty and forty years.

"Do you wish to leave a remnant here?" Huthang asked.

"There is no need. From time to time, I'll send spies here to check. Perhaps in my lifetime the ice will turn, but if it melts, can you imagine the swamp this land will be until it is absorbed? Horrible even to consider. Akla," Tai Oh said.

Akla jumped. He hadn't expected to be addressed by Tai Oh. He felt out of place even being there. He had been wishing he could make himself invisible.

"Akla, I have good reports from all who have met you. I think you can see that Huthang is not only a well trusted member of my council, but also he is and has been a special friend. I charge you, as one of his assistants, to look after him well, for I should be undone if anything happened to Huthang."

"I shall do my best," Akla said quietly with sincerity.

"That is all I can ask," Tai Oh replied.

Akla had no knowledge of what was expected of anyone who met with Tai Oh, so he continued to try to be as invisible as possible.

"Thank you for your report, Huthang. Three days. Let the word go out."

Huthang stood and Akla, seeing the movement, also stood.

"I go to prepare."

Tai Oh said, "Three days."

"Three days," Huthang repeated.

They left the great room. When they were well outside the room, men with spears who stood at the entrance returned to their posts.

Huthang said nothing until they were descending the narrow steps to the lower level.

"Tell the other assistants that we leave in three days. Akla give them no more information than that. Tell them to make themselves ready to leave when I call for them."

"I will," Akla said. He went quickly to carry out Huthang's order.

Akla wondered about the message. He knew they were to go south, but he did not know what was involved. Akla just learned two rivers would take them to the sea. He realized that Huthang and Tai Oh knew of another place to locate, a place he'd never known existed. Akla learned that the place might have been used long ago and they had prepared it for the present as an alternative to where they lived. Akla never ceased to be amazed at these people and their knowledge and planning. One day they were building a well and the next they were leaving a place where many hundreds of people lived, all because ice had moved faster than expected, moving some rocks in the wall. Akla knew there was more to it than that, but he didn't have the information that would have made sense of it all. Suddenly, Akla heard loud cracks and groans from the ice sheet. He tried to ignore it and carry out Huthang's orders. He was determined to do what he'd been told, but it was hard. Gut came racing through the tunnel and stopped when he saw Akla.

"What is the noise?" he asked, obviously frightened.

Akla tried to remain calm. "It's the ice sheet. It may be preparing to drop a chunk of ice."

Gut turned to go back to the room where they practiced their memory work.

"Wait, Gut," Akla called out. "Huthang told me to tell you to be prepared to leave here when he calls you three days from now."

"Where are we going? Will it be for a long time?" he asked.

"I know no more than I've told you," Akla said convincingly.

"Very well," Gut said and turned into the room.

Akla followed him into the room where the remaining assistants were busily engaged in their memory work. He delivered the message to the others as a group. The same questions were raised, and then there was acceptance and quiet as they resumed their work. Another crack from the ice sheet and then all remained quiet.

Three days passed faster than Akla could have imagined. The third day Akla was astonished to see Tai Oh not actually walking but rather being transported on a platform made on two spear shafts that four men carried. He was at the forefront of the procession to the river. Behind him were women in a large group. Tai Oh's council members and their assistants came next. Then men many of whom Akla had never seen. Then more women with children. Then more men and women and children. Along the line were the men Huthang called spies. These were well trained people who had hunter and warrior skills that were superior to any Akla could imagine. They had after all captured him. Some of the spies led the line, and a number of them were positioned at the end of the line.

Despite the huge number of people, it was very quiet along the way. From time to time a child would make a noise, but it was quickly silenced. They walked for quite a long time, but they reached the river and Akla was astonished. The boats were like nothing he'd ever seen. They had rooms built atop them. Tai Oh made a speedy entry onto the largest of the boats. His carrying device was placed on the boat and tied to it. The boats were made in a manner that Akla could not determine from a quick glance. They were not rafts, nor dugouts. He would have to study them as they traveled. Apparently there were places for rowers to sit on either side of these boats. There were places for people to sleep. There was even a special place for Tai Oh. They had supplies and many, many people.

Huthang came over to Akla. "You must go on this boat," he told Akla. "That small room is for you and the rest of my assistants. My place is at the very front of that space. See that our things are placed in there and tell the others." Akla quickly found the other assistants and told them what Huthang had said. He carried his backpack and spear and Huthang's possessions for the trip and placed them on the sleeping skins already provided in the room. Once all boarded, they began the river trip. People were hungry and it was time for the evening meal. Each boat was provisioned, so the evening meal was distributed. Most of the food was jerky, but some dried fruit was shared among some of the travelers.

Rowers rowed hard though they went with the current. It was clear they wanted to reach their destination as soon as possible. Akla realized he was gaining an amazing understanding of the earth on which they lived. One of Huthang's assistants spoke of the earth's being a sphere, something Akla wondered whether he'd discover on the trip. He had covered a lot of the surface of the earth, but whether the whole earth was a sphere, he did not know. He had to admit that his first thought at capture and not being free to leave was unbearable, and he had chafed at the very thought. Having been placed as an assistant to Huthang put him in a place where he could learn more than he ever guessed about things he didn't know, and it opened a part of his thinking place that yearned to learn. It didn't so much matter what he was learning, he found learning fascinating in itself. The trip was another adventure but also it was a chance to learn. Akla was losing his sense of being a captive and considering himself more a part of this strange group of people. He no longer disliked it. He felt in many ways at home. He did miss his brother, and he hoped all went well with Murke.

It took three moons to travel from the beginning past the falls to the confluence of the great river. It was becoming cold, but the travelers knew the further south they went the warmer it would become. The little rooms that were placed on the boats were a help. Inside a bowl was placed in a pit of sand in which rendered fat supported a wick that gave light and warmth. Not all people had access to the little rooms, but for them extra warm skins were provided.

Akla discovered that the boats were made from logs going from the front to back covered by logs that went from side to side. All that was covered by sand to give a somewhat level place to walk. Each boat was fenced off by logs. The rowers sat outside the log barrier. Akla discovered that the boat had a flat piece of log that could be inserted into the center of the boat to keep the boat straight in the water.

Once they reached the great river, they moved faster downriver. It took another two moons plus additional days to reach the southern sea. By the time they reached that place, the people on the boats were becoming very warm. The entry into the sea was rather abrupt and it took some time for the boats to line up for their travel south with the land on their west.

Already they had been on the water for over six moons, when they began to feel the effect of the heat. To them this was not just warmth, it was terrible heat, more than they felt they could tolerate. Huthang tried to explain that they'd adjust to this change. It took bodies some time to adjust to it, but in time, they'd be comfortable. When Tai Oh was not observed and heard his friend, he rolled his eyes. He never became used to the heat.

Finally, a noise arose from the boats in the very front. These were the navigator boats, those rowed by people who knew the routes between the two living places of the Niktonkata. The Niktonkata had reached their destination. They began to beach their boats, and then the navigators helped with the beaching of the remaining boats. People arranged themselves on the shore in the same manner they were for the walk to the river when they left the north.

The carrier for Tai Oh was untied from the boat and Tai Oh walked to the carrier where he arranged himself on it. The carrier was lifted and the column of people began their walk. It wasn't far. They had to climb a hill, and there on the crest of the hill was another place similar to the one they'd left. More trees covered the hill, but from one place you could see the entire Niktonkata South. It was larger than the place they'd left. People were busily working.

On the walk to the place, people found themselves sweating profusely. It was very hot, hotter than most had ever felt.

Huthang walked beside Akla for a while.

"This is Niktonkata South. What are your thoughts?"

"Aside from being horribly hot, it looks very much like what we left. Was the other place called—Niktonkata North or Uhurkamakono?"

"It was both. We used the north-south designations among ourselves. Most people did not know there were two places. The northern place was modeled after this place. There have been two places for a very long time. When Niktonkata North was built no one could see an ice sheet, and no one knew it was there until Uhurkamakono had been occupied for a very long time. Spies out on missions found it. It has moved a long way since it came to our knowledge. I expect the ice will eat the northern place. That's sad. It's a great place."

"Will spies go to check on the northern place?"

"They will, just as they have checked on this place."

"A long way to travel."

"Yes. But that is part of our strength. We travel to know what happens in this land. We know the land. If we stop, we lose what we've gained."

"I see," Akla replied, becoming even more aware of the nature of this people.

The column entered the narrow gate. They went to their locations which were arranged in very similar manner to the place in the north. Tai Oh was glad to have arrived at his place to move out of the sun. Inside it was stifling, but at least the sun didn't beat down on his skin.

Huthang showed each of his assistants where they would have a room to themselves. He left them to arrange their things while he went to join the other council members to provide administrative support for the settling in. The place where they stayed underground was far cooler than anywhere they'd been since their arrival at the southern location. Outside the area within the wall the place was bustling with activity. Those who carried things from the north were directed where to put them. The mastodons from Tai Oh's seating place were wrapped in skins and carefully carried through the tunnel walls to the room where Tai Oh met with others. The mastodon carvings were placed beside the seating place and porters removed the skins. They used the edges of the skins to polish the mastodons. Nothing had broken in the move. In a short time many of the objects of the north location had been added so that, forgetting the heat, one might have thought they had not just traveled so far away.

In the new place in time, Huthang gave Akla freedom to roam the walled area at his own discretion. Akla enjoyed it, having as Huthang had predicted become accustomed to the heat. In fact he liked it. The sun beating on his skin felt good. Akla wandered over to the well and lowered the bucket made of birch they'd brought from the north. He let it fill, drew it up, and dipped a gourd into it. He drank the cool water. He thought briefly about the turns his life had taken. He was grateful to Father Sky for his good fortune. Akla had been gazing to the west and turned. He almost knocked down a girl. He was struck with the beauty of her.

"I'm sorry," she said in apology.

"No need for you to be sorry. It was I who bumped into you. Please forgive me," Akla said.

The girl hung her head. "Of course," she almost whispered.

Akla was disturbed that the girl didn't look him eye to eye. How, he wondered, do people communicate without looking eye to eye?

"I am Akla, assistant to the Councilor Huthang. Who are you?"

"I am nobody; I only come here to bring water to the cooking fire."

"What is your name?" he asked

"I'm called Po," she said with her face downturned.

"Po, look at me," Akla said.

Po looked at Akla's face, hers turning very red.

"What's the matter, Po?" he asked.

"We are not permitted to disturb people of your level."

Akla noticed that the girl was beautiful. "You have not disturbed me."

"We are told that to speak to someone of your level is worthy of beating. May I go now?"

"You will come with me."

Po was terrified. She followed behind Akla as she was told, but she was certain of a terrible beating to follow, and she trembled.

Alka found Huthang also outside, and went directly to him.

Huthang noticed immediately the girl and realized that there was a problem.

"What is it?" he asked Akla.

"I spoke to Po," he gestured towards the trembling girl. "She tells me she will be beaten for speaking to me. What custom is this?"

"It's true. The workers are not permitted to bother us."

"She wasn't bothering me."

"Her people might see it differently."

"How do I protect her from being beaten?" he asked.

"I should have warned you. I'm sorry, Akla, short of taking her as wife, there is no way to protect her."

"What?"

"Well, Akla, my friend, they won't kill her."

"What must I do to take her as wife?" he asked seriously.

Huthang laughed. "I should have known. You are serious?"

"Of course, I'm serious. It's time I took a wife. She's beautiful. I don't want her beaten."

"Not good reasoning for taking a wife, but then taking a wife is a strange and sometimes wonderful or dreadful thing. It's rarely tied to logic."

"Po," Huthang said, "How many years are you?"

"Seventeen," she whispered.

"Do you burn for any man?"

She shook her head to express a negative.

"Are you willing to be the wife to this man, Akla?"

"I don't know what to say," she whispered so they could barely hear her.

"What do you mean? Do you not know your own mind?" Huthang was losing patience.

"Sir," Po said with a little more volume, "I cannot consider someone at his level."

"Akla, are you seriously wanting this girl for wife?" Huthang asked.

By this time Akla was more and more aware of the girl and he was drawn to her for no reason that he could reasonably explain. He wanted her to be happy and clearly she was not happy. "Yes. I would take her as wife."

The girl blushed again. She could feel an intensity in Akla's gaze that drew her and she fought against it while at the same time continuing to feel drawn to it.

Huthang said, "Po, Akla wants you as wife. Will you accept?"

Throwing caution away, Po replied, "Yes."

Huthang took her by the wrist and said to Akla, "Follow me."

They went to the room where Tai Oh was on the mastodon seating place. Po began to tremble again. She'd never been inside the building. She had seen Tai Oh when he arrived and all the people kneel to him. Huthang led them to the far right inside the entryway to the waiting area. As soon as they entered, Tai Oh said, "Come forward." He gestured for Huthang to speak.

"Akla would take this girl, Po, for his wife. Will you approve?"

"Do you approve?" Tai Oh asked Huthang.

"With enthusiasm," Huthang replied.

"Very well! Akla, Po is your wife. Po, Akla is your husband. Huthang, is there anything else?"

"That is all," Huthang said in the obsequious manner he used when there were numbers of people in the room.

"Very well. See that her people are notified."

"I will see to it."

"You may go."

The three left quietly. Once outside the room, he took Po's wrist which he still held and handed it to Akla. "She is now your wife. Take her to Mumu, the harem mistress. Have her bathed and dressed suitably. You wait there while it is done and stay hand in hand in her company for a moon. She has the same rights as you, but it will take some time for her people to accept what has happened. Akla, teach her how to live at your level, for she has been a virtual slave. Do you understand?"

"Yes," he replied, reality beginning to enter his thinking place.

"A larger sleeping place and more skins will be added to your room. I go to attend to these things. This will be good for you, I predict," Huthang said with a sense of assurance. "Keep her by your side."

"I will," Akla promised.

He put his arm around Po. She didn't shrink or respond. She remained in a state of fear.

"Come," he said, "You are to be taken care of by Mumu. She is kind," he added.

Akla took the girl to Mumu.

"You must be frightened," Mumu said gently. "Come with me girl, your life is changing much for the better. Akla is a good man."

Po followed Mumu. The harem attendants would bathe her, rub oil into her skin, and dress her in animal skins that fit her level. When Akla saw her next, he would be surprised at the change.

After what seemed a long time, Mumu came with Po walking behind her.

"Your wife," Mumu said, stepping away to expose the beautiful girl who would be his wife. "She's lovely."

Akla was stunned. The girl had long straight hair that shone with a blue hue. She wore a hairless skin tunic that had been made white. It went from her shoulders to just below her knees. Akla had seen white tunics, but only rarely. The girl's skin was tanned; her black hair, black eyes, tan skin that glowed, and the white tunic made an image that caused Akla to stare. The girl was truly beautiful. Akla tried to control himself quickly, while many thoughts raced through his thinking place. He reached out his hand, and Po stepped forward to take his hand. Before she reached Akla, Po turned and went to Mumu.

"Thank you, Mumu," she said hugging the woman.

"You're welcome," Mumu replied.

Po then went to Akla and gave him her hand.

Akla led her from the room to the small steps that went to his room. By the time they reached his room, they discovered that a larger sleeping place had been placed in the room. The skins on it were luxurious. Akla was touched. The girl was amazed. Mumu had given her a comb. Po carefully placed the comb on a ledge on the wall designed for holding things. Mumu had told her to keep her hair combed well. She was determined to do all she was told and to do it well.

Feeling awkward, Akla took Po in his arms and held her.

"Are you still frightened?" he asked.

"No," she admitted. "Mumu told me what I must do and how. She explained the differences expected of me now. She told me I must look you eye to eye. It's awkward, but I will do it. She told me good things about you. I have no fear."

"I have wanted a wife for a terribly long time. I could not have expected a wife so beautiful."

"I don't think of myself as beautiful," she said flatly.

"I have never seen anyone with such beauty," he admitted. "If you could do anything you want, what would you do now?"

"I would walk outside while you tell me of your life to this point."

Akla took her hand and led her outside through the tunnel that went under the large structure. Po was as surprised as he was when he first learned of the tunnels.

Outside the day was still hot. They were in a space where few ever went. Trees gave shade and a sweet scent. There was a stone place where they sat. Akla took the afternoon telling her about his life at the Cove, the trip across the sea, the capture by the Niktonkata, and his life since then. Without intent he made her life easier by her knowledge that he'd been abducted. He too had been made to live a life he would not have chosen, but one which turned out for the better.

Akla was delighted with his new wife, and she loved him. They had ten children who lived. They remained at Niktonkata South for the rest of their lives. Akla worked for Huthang and when Huthang died of a fever, it was Akla who took his place. Po raised their children in the harem area in the structure where she lived. Occasionally, in the company of guards, women and children were treated to days in the forest where they learned about their environment. Po learned as the children learned, for she'd not been taught as a child. The children had some free time for play, but most of their time was spent learning. Akla lived to an old age of eighty, an age almost unheard of. Po died ten years before he did. Their life was a good one, envied by many.

When Tai Oh died in Akla's seventy-eighth year, there was great mourning, for he was a good and fair leader. The Council met to vote in a new leader. Their choice was unanimous on the first vote. They chose Murke, Akla's first child, a boy named for his brother. Murke became the leader of the Niktonkata for the next thirty years.

Chapter 8

Maber's Story

Maber had crossed the sea with his father, Reg, his brother, Blad, and the girl his father had taken along, Vaima. Maber's thoughts were on his father. His thoughts were dark ones. They traveled by boat having been chased by the Maiket from their village in the new land. The Maiket invited the SealEaters to stay with them until Reg approached a woman against her wishes. He didn't know she was wife of a warrior. It was a typical Reg blunder. The Maiket came after them, spears aimed to thrust.

The SealEaters fled from the village in their boats heading to the sea and then rowing north. In their flight, Reg and his sons used the big boat, rowing together to the cache point. Also fleeing in other boats were Urch and Wapa in one and Mongwire and Wen in another. Neither Maber nor Blad wanted to be part of their father's exploratory group. They had no choice. Reg had chosen for them. Reg expected his two sons to accompany him on his exploration of the new land. Neither of the boys wanted to do that, but they had difficulty determining how to break away. Reg was huge compared to other men. His strength was more than two other men combined. Everyone, including his children, feared him.

Maber, however, had a plan. At seventeen he was a little timid about his plan, but he could see no other way, and he was ready to try it rather than continue with his father who made all the natives they met angry not to mention his life miserable. Maber had been treated abusively, just as his brothers were, by their father. A broken arm or leg or a dislocated jaw was something that occurred routinely in their young years. Each of his sons knew Reg wouldn't hesitate to continue his punishing blows, anytime they failed to do his bidding. That they were fully grown didn't seem to matter. Maber reasoned that he'd rather die than put up with any more. So he waited.

He knew that once Reg snored at night, it was hard to awaken him. He was waiting for that opportunity. They ate that night a small horse that Reg had speared. Reg decided the next day they'd follow the smallest river using one of the other boats that had been cached. Reg had no intention of walking when he could take a boat.

Maber had carefully assessed the landscape. He looked for places where Reg would least likely want to go. In the distance he'd seen a small hill that looked rock rough. Little vegetation grew on it, and it appeared difficult to climb. It rose from a thick forest.

Maber knew Reg disliked dense forests and hated to climb, especially when it was rock rough. He decided to head for the rock rough hill and to go to the south side most distant from the river to climb as high as he felt safe climbing. He would watch the river in the morning for the boat to pass.

It didn't take long for his father and brother to go black and snore. Maber grabbed his backpack and quietly headed for the river. He crossed it to the center and walked downriver instead of upriver. That way it would seem less likely that his entry to the forest would be spotted, for they'd expect him to go upriver since only the sea lay downriver.

Maber walked as carefully as possible. He'd put on his boots to keep from stepping on a stick or something that might injure his feet. He walked rapidly in the little light afforded by the moon in the forest, which was, as he thought, dense. Before dawn he reached the small hill and began the climb on the far side from the river. The climb was hard. The sharp rocks removed skin from his knees and legs. By dawn Maber reached the top where he had a great view of the area. Because there were edges that jutted up on the river side, edges with spaces through which one could view the river without being seen, Maber felt safe from Reg for the first time in his life. He watched the river and rested for a long time. It was not until evening when Reg and Blad rowed upriver past the little rock rough hill. They didn't stop nearby, but Maber was certain that they wouldn't go far. They did have food from the previous night, for the horse would feed them for a few days, though Maber had apportioned some of the meat before leaving. He knew Reg and Blad wouldn't travel the river in the dark. He assumed correctly that they were late passing the rock rough hill because they'd been looking for him. Maber lay on his sleeping skins at the top of the rock rough hill and gazed into the starry sky. His life was about to change for the better, he was convinced. He went black.

In the morning, Maber awakened to see two men standing over him holding spears. He raised up on an elbow only to find a spear point pressing against his chest.

Despite the spear, Maber carefully rose to a seated position. He didn't want to give them reason to kill him. He'd just found freedom. He ignored the spear and touched his chest, saying "Maber."

The man with the spear removed it from his side. The two young men each introduced themselves by name, "Ghee" and "Akrumtry." They made it clear they wanted Maber to follow them. He felt he had no alternative nor desire to be alone. They showed him a pathway that led down the rock rough hill. It was on the west side of the hill. In the night, Maber smiled to himself, he hadn't gone far enough.

They walked through the forest. By evening one of them speared a young camel in a glen. When they made camp, they roasted the camel. The savor was great. Busily they made lean-tos for the night. A hearth fire separated the lean-to for Ghee and Akrumtry from the lean-to Maber made. Maber realized that would make it less likely that predators would bother them as they slept. No one had made any signs to set up a night watch. Maber was able go black lightly, and he did.

In the morning they ate more of the camel. Maber was learning their words as quickly as he could. He wondered how far their village was, but he didn't have the vocabulary or the signing ability to ask. They walked on for days. Little by little, Maber learned more of the language, though doing this while trekking was difficult. Maber learned that Ghee was twenty years of age and Akrumtry was two years older. He couldn't understand why they were in the forest. After a moon of traveling through the forest, Ghee made him understand they were headed to their relatives who lived in the far west. There they expected to find wives. They had arrived at a wide swift river and had to cross it. They searched for what Maber finally understood was a boat. They expected to find boats on the shore nearby. They walked a good day both north and south searching for boats, and found none. They were confused. Ghee and Akrumtry finally decided to construct a raft to transport their back-packs and spears across the river. They'd simply hold onto it and kick hard to make it go across the river. Maber understood and was eager to help.

By the time they had successfully crossed the wide river, it was clear that Ghee and Akrumtry had fully accepted Maber. The three were enjoying the adventure. One night, at another river, the three young men had climbed a hill to check for others in the vicinity. From the forest to the southwest, they could see that a good sized fire was sending up its sign. All three of them watched and listened.

"Are these the people you seek?" Maber asked.

"No," Ghee replied. "The people we seek are across the very high mountains."

"Not mountains like any we've seen?"

"No," Akrumtry laughed. "You haven't seen real mountains."

"I haven't?" he replied.

"Not at all," Ghee agreed. "All you've seen are hills. Little hills."

Maber was surprised. He was eager to see what these men called mountains.

"It is best that we are careful not to be seen by the people with the fire. We will not make a fire until we are out of range of their vision."

"Why? Are they fierce?"

"We don't know who they are. There are some people we do fear—the Niktonkata, and they have people everywhere. Sometimes they abduct one of us. We never hear from that person again. It's as if the earth swallows them up. Because we don't know who those people are, it is wise to be extremely cautious. Niktonkata do not travel in small numbers. For a fire that large, the numbers must be large."

"I understand," Maber replied in a low voice.

"Why are you here alone?" Akrumtry asked, settling himself to sit on a fallen log while Ghee began to set up their lean-to.

"I am a SealEater, a people from across the sea. We are being squeezed by ice and mountains, so we set out a group of explorers to come here to find a new place for our people. I did not want to make this trip. My father, a man of great stature and very determined to have his way, insisted my brother and I come. He is a violent man and has severely beaten my brother and me all of our lives. Coming here he has been careless in his treatment of the people who live here. We were run out from one group of natives. We rowed boats north, set up a cache for our return to our home in the east, and began to explore. I waited until my father and brother snored to depart. I saw them rowing up the river near the rock where you found me."

"Ho!" Ghee called out from the lean-to. "They row right into the Alu territory. They'll wish they hadn't."

"What do you mean?" Maber asked, turning from his lean-to preparation.

"The Alu do not permit anyone to enter their territory. Who knows what they'll do with strangers. I do not wish to be them!"

"I feel sorry for my brother."

"Why did you not ask him to join you?"

Maber looked down at his feet. "I just couldn't trust him. He could have told my father. Oh, I'm sure he'd have wanted to come with me. I think, though, that he'd have been frightened to take the risk. Angering my father and being caught, you could lose your life."

"Are you sure you do not exaggerate?" Akrumtry asked.

Maber stood before them slowly circling. He removed his jacket. "Look at the scars on my body. They were made by my father, not accidental misfortune. He is a brutal, mean spitited man."

"Eeeee, by the Creator Spirit, I wonder whether you were ever loved."

"Yes, my mother loved us all. She was powerless to do anything. She was the only person my father treated well. I don't know why."

"I understand well how you would wish to leave. It is better to die well than to live in misery."

"Sadly, not all would agree with you," Maber said.

"It's a matter of courage," Akrumtry added. "You have shown courage, Maber."

"Thank you," he replied quietly. He hadn't thought of courage or anything except escape.

"Let's rest. Tomorrow we have another big river to cross." Akrumtry entered the lean-to and stretched out on his sleeping skins.

A terrible howl split the night's quiet. The three young men grabbed their spears and crouched in their lean-tos. Apparently the people with the fire had been tracking a bear and had succeeded in spearing him in the forest at night. The noise from the bear was terrifying. Maber, Ghee, and Akrumtry listened. The noise was coming no closer, and the bear sounds ceased. The three listened carefully as the noise grew lower and lower. Finally, after a long time, the noise ceased altogether. None wanted to return to sleep. Quietly they packed their things, disassembled the lean-tos so as not to give away their recent use of the place.

Akrumtry whispered, "Follow me, Maber. We know the way, and in the dark it'll be hard for you. Try to remain silent."

The three left the place and moved through the quiet forest. They reached the river just before the sun had arisen, but there was adequate light to see.

"Let's make a raft for our things and cross this river now, before any early risers come to make sure the river's clear."

They used the cordage Maber carried and tied a few logs together with the backpacks on the top. They headed out into the water. It was cold and Maber was not prepared for it. He sucked in his breath.

"Silence," Ghee hissed.

They waded into the river and soon were kicking with all their energy to push the logs and themselves across the water. Once on the other side, they pulled the logs to the trees, untied the logs and backpacks, and vanished into the forest.

It was evening before Akrumtry felt free. "I think we can consider we made a good escape," he said with a sigh. He'd felt responsibility for the two younger men.

Ghee looked at Akrumtry, "Niktonkata?"

"Probably. I can think of none other skilled enough to chase a short faced bear at night into the forest to spear it."

"Is this land filled with many people?" Maber asked.

Ghee said, "In this area, north of here there are the Alu. We've already spoken of the Alu. We're careful not to tread on their land or even come close to it. There is much land that is not used, but where people claim territory, even if they are few in number, they will defend the land that they claim. They will defend it fiercely."

"I appreciate your letting me join you. I would not have known how to travel this land."

"We are not all knowing, Maber," Akrumtry added. "There are changes all the time. What you most want to know is where the people like the Alu are to avoid them. Most others will treat you well enough, if you treat them well. You may have to prove yourself."

"What do you mean by prove myself?"

"Show them you mean no harm."

"How do you do that?"

"You listen to what they ask of you and do it. You do it without cowardice or showing pain."

"Are you talking about fighting contests?"

"Possibly. Some of the people have unusual ways of asking you to show your good will. Some will only ask that you take your sleeping place with one of the women."

"That wouldn't be too bad," Maber laughed and the others joined him in the laugh.

"Some will ask you to inflict pain on yourself."

"I don't think I'd care for that."

"It's better than dying."

"Some have you go without food or water. There are a variety of ways."

"I have learned why it's best to be prudent and not be caught."

"You have learned." Ghee grinned.

The lean-tos were assembled and the three slept well.

It was moons before they ascended a hill and Akrumtry announced, "Those are mountains!"

Maber had seen many mountains, but none quite as astonishing as the large mountains that lay before him in the distance. They were intimidating. Clearly they were far in the distance, but the natives had made it clear they would cross the mountains.

As the evening came on, it began to rain. The land they passed through was not as dense a forest as they'd been through. Making lean-tos was not as easy. They did eventually find enough materials to keep the sleeping places dry. They ate some remains of a deer kill they cooked on sticks over the fire. Tired, they went to rest early.

In the middle of the night the wind rose. A terrible storm was in the making. The wind blew the logs off the lean-to shared by Akrumtry and Ghee. They grabbed their sleeping skins, backpacks, and spears, and huddled next to Maber in his lean-to.

Suddenly, Akrumtry stood up and said, "Grab all your things. We must move to high ground. I almost forgot."

In the drenching rain the three ran toward a rise in the land. In the distance there was a small hill. Akrumtry waved them on. He moved faster than Ghee knew he could. There was nothing for shelter, so they took their sleeping skins and wrapped in them.

"Why did we come here?" Ghee asked.

"The rain. I'd forgotten that on land such as this, the rain has to go somewhere. It gathers and runs fast in the lower levels sometimes making river-like floods. We don't want to be swept away in a flood."

"I'm glad you remembered," Maber said.

The three huddled together, watching the storm release its water and lightning. They were soaked by the time the storm ended. Dawn was breaking.

They decided to cook the remains of the camel meat before beginning the day's trek. Ghee set up a hearth with some dry wood he brought from the night's lean-to. To that he added some wood that Maber found inside a hollow log. It wasn't a great fire, but it served their purpose.

"I have come to love the forests," Maber said. "My people fear dense forests. I kept away from forests as a child."

"Why would anyone fear forests?" Akrumtry asked.

"I don't know. It was taught and I learned it. When I broke from my father, I found comfort in the forest. It is still a place I don't understand as I understand the sea coast, but it saved me."

"Unlike you," Ghee said, "the forest has always been our home. All our life is tied to the forest. It provides our food, water, shelter, clothing—all our needs."

"It also gives space to people you fear and short faced bears." Maber was still shaken from the bear spearing event.

"That too," Akrumtry said.

"Our next destination," Akrumtry said, "is that hill over there that appears to be split in two."

"That's not what I think best," Ghee spoke up.

"I don't want to go the other way, since we're aware there could be Niktonkata in the forest."

"Why do you think we'd run into them going my way instead of yours? We're long past them."

"Experience."

"Akrumtry, sometimes you're a pile of bison dung on a hot day!"

"Let's settle this our way," Akrumtry said.

They shed their clothes. Each laid a sleeping skin on the ground side by side. Each had a small knife.

Akrumtry looked at Maber. "Stay out of this. The object is to shed blood of the other while on the skin and then throw him off the skins. Once you blood the other and remove him from the skin, you both have to lay down your knives. Whoever succeeds first in both efforts chooses the route we take."

Maber stepped back. He did not for any reason wish to have his blood shed, but he watched as the men began to circle for advantage. Akrumtry's knife almost made contact with Ghee's arm. Ghee's knife missed Akrumtry's leg. They worked back and forth each having and losing the advantage. Much time passed for they were evenly matched. Ghee blocked a thrust of Akrumtry's and lost his knife. Akrumtry had the advantage and rushed Ghee. Ghee tripped Akrumtry who went outside the skins long enough for Ghee to retrieve his knife. When Akrumtry returned to the skins, he came determined. He succeeded in blooding Ghee's arm, but Ghee swiped his side. Both tossed their knives outside the skin area and wrestled, each trying to force the other off the mat. The wrestling went on for a very long time. Maber finally became bored, because they were so evenly matched that when one made a move the other knew how to counter.

Ghee suddenly shouted, "Brother, you're bleeding." At which time he managed to force Akrumtry outside the skins.

Akrumtry looked at his side and found that he was indeed bleeding profusely. The wound didn't particularly hurt, but he was losing a lot of blood.

"Will you let me look at it?" Maber asked.

Akrumtry walked over to Maber and showed him the wound. It wasn't deep. Just a dangling skin flap.

"I can sew it back together to try to stop the bleeding, if you like."

"You have the tools and knowledge?" Akrumtry asked astonished.

"Of course. We don't travel without what's needed to handle small emergencies. Ghee, will you please bring some water?"

Ghee had seen a small creek they passed over. He took the gourd and ran to the creek.

"You'll need to lie down, Akrumtry. This will hurt."

Akrumtry stretched out on his sleeping skin. Drops of his blood kept falling on the skin. Maber hunted around in his backpack until he found his bundle of herbs and honey. He gathered a few small pieces of leather.

Ghee was back with water by the time Maber had his supplies.

Carefully, Maber washed the wound. He took the bone needle and the twist of hair he'd taken from Ipsalu, his father Reg's second wife, whose clean long hair he treasured for his emergency kit. Because of Reg's cruelty to her, Ipsalu's thinking place appeared to be separate from her body, but she secretively communicated with Maber. He took a strand of hair and threaded the bone needle and warned Akrumtry about the pain and began to sew the wound shut. He didn't sew it so tight as to prevent it from draining. Then, he covered the wound area with a pinch of herbs and honey squeezed from a small bladder. Maber took some of Akrumtry's skins that Ghee brought him, made a cover for the wound, and tied a belt around it to keep it clean.

"Do you want me to look after that wound on your arm, Ghee?" he asked.

"No, it's just a little thing," Ghee replied.

"It's gaping open," Akrumtry interjected.

"So, we take my route," Ghee said without gloating, ignoring the comment about the gaping wound.

"We do," Akrumtry said, "but it is not the wise choice."

"It's days shorter," Ghee said.

Akrumtry did not reply.

They gathered up the skins that remained on the ground and began to trek to the spot on the horizon that Ghee had selected.

The day was cloudy and there were intermittent rain squalls.

In some places it was difficult to follow the trail. The land was open and the rains had washed out some of the lower levels.

"I hate this route," Akrumtry said, annoyed. "It leaves us so open. Any observer from the forests in the distance could spot us with ease."

"We've never met anyone on this trail," Ghee said.

"We're about to," Maber said.

"I told you," Akrumtry said, looking at the man running towards them from the northwest.

"Well, there's no place to hide out here," Ghee said.

The three men stood there—waiting.

After some time the runner approached, carrying a single spear. He arrived and spent a very brief time regulating his breathing. Then, he said, "Our village is sick. You must turn away."

"We plan to cross the mountains at the bald one," Akrumtry said, pointing to a tall mountain straight ahead with a treeless feature on the top. "There's a pass there where we can go through without climbing to a high level.

"I know the one. Then, I will lead you until you are across. There is much sickness here."

"Very well," Ghee said with a sense of relief.

The man began a slow jog and the others followed. This pace was much faster than they had used at any time on the trek. It took Maber a little time before he could regulate his breathing to something other than gulps of air. Maber's mouth was extremely dry from hard breathing.

The route definitely took a different turn from what Ghee had in mind when he began. They went through brushy areas and into rocky soil were they noticed numbers of snakes. The leader kept his pace throughout the jog. He seemed tireless. Akrumtry began to wonder whether the man was leading them into an ambush, but he pushed the idea from his mind. There was nothing they could do about that now.

In an area where there were some trees by a small stream, they rested briefly under a tree that provided welcome shade.

"I am Lag of the Ipeicuptet," the jogger told them. "My people have great sores on their skin and they die. I was leaving my people to find a healthier place. I don't want to be sick like they are."

"How do you know that you aren't already sick?" Ghee asked.

"I don't think I could have done all this running if I were sick."

"Probably not," Akrumtry said.

The men gathered their things and resumed the jog. They had reached the bottom of the bald mountain. Lag started up still at a jog. There were trees at the lower levels.

Akrumtry said, "Lag, please slow to a walk. I've been injured and this jogging is making my wound bleed."

Immediately, Lag slowed to a walk. Maber wished that Akrumtry had said something earlier. The walk uphill was much easier. Ghee also was relieved.

They were about a third of the way up the mountain when they decided to stop for the evening. They were in forest and Akrumtry and Ghee felt more at home. Ghee, Maber, and Lag set up lean-tos encircling the hearth fire. Akrumtry built a fire. Lag went off into the forest and returned with a small horse.

"Are there others in this area?" Ghee asked Lag.

"No. Not until we cross the mountain. Why are you crossing the mountains?"

"We go to the gathering. It is at the gathering where we can find wives and avoid close relatives. I'd have thought you'd know about the gathering, since you live out here."

"I never heard about it. Is it far across the mountain?"

"At least a moon," Akrumtry said.

"We don't normally travel that far to the west—to the east, yes, but to the west, no."

The men ate and then banked the hearth fire and crawled into their lean-tos for the night. Far away wolves howled to each other. The sound was a bit sad, but for some reason Maber smiled, contented, as if the sound belonged uniquely to this place. He went black.

In the morning they didn't eat but rather reached the summit and began to follow Lag down the mountain.

"We're going down, Lag," Akrumtry shouted.

"Well, of course," he replied. "You said you wanted to cross at the pass. We slept at the pass last night."

"Oh," Akrumtry replied, dumfounded. This was not the route he remembered, though they were heading west and clearly had crossed the mountain.

One half moon passed. At the head of the line traveling west, Lag spotted a camel. He signed for the others to wait in quiet. He crept up on the camel and in two spear throws, Lag had managed to kill the animal. They would eat well.

They stopped to bleed the camel and tend to the butchering process. Ghee made a fire and they ate camel cooked on sticks.

Ghee thought camel had never tasted so good. He asked Lag, "Do you know the land of the Maikumata people?"

"I do. It lies to the northwest. We can reach their territory in four suns."

Akrumtry was heartened at the distance they covered by jogging. It was so much faster, and he felt that once he became accustomed to it, it was no more tiring than walking. He realized that whole populations could not do it. Children and the old or injured would not be able to keep the pace, but for the young, it was wonderful.

"While we are stopped here, let me look at that wound, Akrumtry," Maber said.

Akrumtry opened the belted skin and Maber examined the wound carefully. "It's doing better than I expected," he said with a tinge of wonder.

"It must be the run," Akrumtry said with a chuckle.

"Maybe so," Maber said and began to think of all that Akrumtry had opened as possibilities by the casual comment. "Let me take a look at the wound on your arm, Ghee," Maber added as a precaution.

Unlike the wound on Akrumtry's side, the wound on Ghee's arm was ugly looking. Pus drooled from it.

"You should have let me take care of this when it happened," Maber muttered.

"What do you mean?" Ghee asked. He couldn't see it well, since it was on the back of his arm.

"It's gone bad," Akrumtry told him.

"Then, can you go ahead and clean it and burn it while we're here," Ghee asked feeling his stomach turn as he said it. He did know what could happen if the wound were not treated quickly, once it had gone bad.

Akrumtry and Lag had set up the cooking sticks over the fire. The meat had just begun to put its savor in the air. Maber put a stick of just the right size at the edge of the fire after having used his small knife to clean the wound. Maber would never understand why anyone would put off tending to something like that. He took the firebrand he'd prepared and touched Ghee's wound with it, holding it there for a brief time. Ghee had the knowledge not to move while the burning took place, but he had to cover his mouth to reduce the volume of his scream.

"I think that should make it heal now, Ghee," Maber told him.

"Thank you." Ghee wanted to jump around and scream and shout at the pain, but he knew that was childish and he had to leave childish things behind in his life. He just bore the pain as quietly as he could.

Akrumtry and Lag passed around the cooking sticks with meat sizzling on them. They ate the meat after a short cooling period. The juice ran down their faces. Maber was the only one with a real beard. His beard caught a lot of the meat juice. They each thoroughly enjoyed the meat. Maber washed off his face and beard after eating.

The men quickly continued the trek. They were not really following a trail, but they were heading northwest. Akrumtry had a sense that Lag could be something he wasn't, but he knew no way to prove it one way or another except to follow. He remained irritated that Ghee had won the contest, for he knew the other route well.

They reached an easily fordable part of a small river. Before they crossed, Lag said, "Across this little river is the territory of the Maikumata. I hope you know them well, for they do not like others to enter their lands."

"We are their people who migrated east. We speak the same language. They will know us."

"Will they accept me?" Lag asked.

"Yes. You are with us," Ghee assured him. "The same is true for Maber."

The men continued. After they had gone a way, Akrumtry said, "I know where we are now. Follow me." Leading now, he felt badly about his evil thoughts regarding Lag. He had been taught to be cautious, though. He dismissed all those thoughts and began to grow excitement at seeing his western relatives.

After a couple of days, they had their first encounter with the Maikumata. Instead of rushing forward or trying to find a strategic place to hide, Akrumtry told them all to set up a place to sit and to remain silent and let the Maikumata speak first. He knew his western family members were aware that they had been seen, since they made themselves very obvious. They had a protocol and Akrumtry was following it. The Maikumata approached directly. Akrumtry noticed they were led by Tu. He and Tu were friends.

"Oh, I can't believe it. Akrumtry, my friend!" Tu said as they approached. To the other western Maikumata he said, "These are our people. Relax." To Akrumtry he said, "Is that Ghee?" Akrumtry nodded affirmatively. "And who are these?"

Akrumtry introduced the others and very briefly told the story of each. He explained they were there for the gathering to find wives. That brought off a great amount of laughter from the western Maikumata.

"Why do you laugh?" Akrumtry asked.

"Why else would four men as bedraggled as you are be wandering this expanse of nothingness?" he asked. "Rise up and come with us. You'll be home before the dark comes this day."

The men were filled with hope and joy to know that their long trek was about to end. They followed the men who did not jog but rather walked in a brisk manner.

Before the men reached the village, they could smell it. The population had swollen easily to four times its normal size. The smells were varied, some good; some not so good.

Two of the Maikumata ran ahead to announce the approach of the Tua from the eastern sea. The reception of the news was enthusiastic. People ran from the village to see the arrival of their relatives.

Akrumtry noticed that many of the people did not look like Maikumata at all. He was curious. But the welcome was chaotic and soon all four of the men were separated from each other as the western people began to ask question after question. Until a large voice rang out, "Stop the noise," Chief Trajamuranta shouted above the din. "What have we become? Remember your manners. We will all hear the new arrivals at the fire tonight. Until then, leave them alone so they may rest from their travel. Merang? Where's Merang? Oh, there you are. Take them to the shelter where they can be together."

The four men separated themselves from the people who circled them and followed Merang, glad for the opportunity to be free of the sur-round of people.

"There are four spaces right here along this wall," Merang told them. "Put your possessions beside your sleeping places. There is a guard in this structure. Keturnatey," he called out. The guard stepped away from the side of the opening and showed himself. "Guard the things of these people well," he ordered. Keturnatey nodded, acknowledging the order.

The men set up their sleeping places and propped their spears against the wall. Keturnatey came over and quietly suggested they lay their spears beside the sleeping places wrapped in a turn or two of one of their sleeping skins, not prop them against the wall for all to see. They did. When they had nearly fin-ished, Murantanmo came into the structure and told the men to follow him.

He led them to a place where many were seated near the fire that had just been lit. They were to sit near the chief. No one needed to explain that this was an honor, but then these people were their people.

Hunters had brought their early morning kills and the meat had been cooking for a long time. The women and girls had been scouring the area for greens and nuts and berries and had added greatly to their choice of foods.

The foods had been arranged atop a long log. There were wooden planks set upright on the ground where people could lay their food choices.

Aimettual, a young woman of fourteen years, had noticed Maber. She was fascinated with his thick beard. He was quite stocky, which her people were not. He had brown hair, not black, and his hair had a bit of a curl to it. She thought him utterly appealing, finding it hard to wait until the fire that night to hear his story. Her friend, Garalumuta, thought Akrumtry was appealing. They watched the men from a distance, giggling about what they thought they'd learn about them.

"You have found no other men attractive, Aimettual?" Garalumuta asked her.

"No. I don't care for any I've met so far. One pursues me, and he fails to listen to what I tell him. The chief will speak to that tonight."

"You talked to Trajamuranta about that?"

"Yes. It's a problem for me and a few other women I've talked to."

"We have rules," Garalumuta said.

"Some people from strange places don't know our rules. We have one more moon for this gathering. I'm not willing to put up with that man for one more day."

"I understand."

"And you, you find the man with the wound on his side appealing?" Aimettual asked.

"You think that's what that is?" Garalumuta asked.

"What else could it be? If you look to the bottom of the belted area, you can see what may be a bit of drainage. It's hardly noticeable, but the man must have been injured."

"To travel from the eastern sea to here and not be injured would be an amazing accomplishment."

"I agree. But you have the skills to see to his wound, if that is one." Aimettual laughed quietly.

"Yes, I do find the man interesting. I'd like to know how he acquired his injury and why it is he seems so confident. I'd like to hear his voice. There are many things I wish to discover about that man."

The girls were fortunate, for their parents and consequently they were seated near the chief on the opposite side from the four new arrivals. They were face to face though unintended. There was a seating array that depended on the chief's designation. That designation was not to be breached.

The people ate and after all was cleaned away, the chief rose. All became silent as he stood.

"We have had quite a large number of guests at the gathering this year. We have to thank Wisdom for guiding all the people here." He paused a moment staring at the sky. "We have this gathering to join men and women from distant places to keep the people strong. We do have some rules here, and we expect the rules to be obeyed. Any disobedience to the rules will cause immediate banishment from this land. Any one banished who refuses to leave will die." He paused. "Are there any questions?"

There was silence.

"The first rule is that women can say NO to any advance by a man. If a woman says NO and the man continues to advance, he will be banished. No woman is forced to accept a man. That is a rule we will not change. There have been some attempts to pursue women here who have said NO. I know who these people are. Any further effort in those pursuits will result in immediate banishment. You know who you are. Do not try my patience, for I have none on this issue."

"The second rule is that any two who wish to join must come to me. Not someone else—me. I will either give permission or not, based on what I know. Once I agree, consider the two joined for the rest of their lives. No further pursuit is permitted."

"The third rule is that where they live is to be decided by the two who join. No one else. If they are having difference of opinion and cannot resolve it, they are obliged to come to me and I will solve it."

"The fourth rule, and it should be the first, is respect Wisdom, respect me, and respect all others. I do not wish to entertain violations of this rule. I deal very harshly with any infringement of this rule. Any questions."

There was dead quiet.

"In this place we do not offend Wisdom. Wisdom is the old name for the spirit many now call Creator. We still use the term Wisdom. Joining is a sacred event. It is two who come together to make a life for themselves and their children as long as they live. It is not something to enter into lightly. Some of you will enter into it lightly. Some of you will mistake lust for love. Some of you will place high value on appearance rather than the person. Do that at your peril. I urge you to think as well as to feel. Go with Wisdom." The chief sat down.

Slowly those seated began to rise. Aimettual wasted no time. She walked boldly to Maber and told him she wanted to come to know him. She also said that her friend was shy but wanted to know Akrumtry. Maber was astonished but touched Akrumtry and told him what he'd heard. The three walked to where Garalumuta stood. The pairs met and then the pairs went their separate ways to wander under the starry sky.

"Why me?" Maber asked, amazed that anyone so lovely would want to know him.

"Because you are different, but you don't appear arrogant. I want to sit with you and have you tell me your story. Come with me and I'll show you my special place for talking."

Aimettual led him to a place above the small river that bordered the village. They climbed up a hill by the river to a large, smooth rock.

"How old are you, Maber?"

"How'd you know my name?" he asked surprised.

"It is an easy thing to learn the names of four new people to arrive at your village. It is harder for the four to learn the names of the village people. Maber, I want to hear your story. I want to know who your people are and how you came to be here."

Maber began, "I come from the far side of the eastern sea."

She laughed. "That's not possible."

"It is possible," he said affronted. "I have lived it. Do you want to know about me or not?"

She quieted. "You are serious about having lived on the far side of the eastern sea?"

"Of course. I am a SealEater, a people who are being forced to find a new land. We are called SealEaters because the ice keeps moving towards us. Seals began to use our beach for their haul out place. They are easy to kill there, and with little else to eat, we began long ago as a people to depend on them for food. Their meat is good. We ate food from the sea, most of which was seal."

"What's seal?"

"It's an animal that grows about as long as I'm tall. They swim in the sea, eating fish and other food from the sea. They look a little like a dog in the face. They look a bit like this." He drew in the sand and in the moonlight she could see the image. "Do you want me to continue?"

"Oh, yes," she said.

Maber continued. "My land has strange rules. We had six elders. No one could take a wife without approval of every single elder. One elder refused all requests."

"Why?"

"No one knows. The elder who refuses is my father. He is a man with a thinking place that is mean spirited. Growing up, I was beaten, some bones were broken, my jaw was dislocated, and I was forced to join the explorers who came to this land to seek a new place for us to live."

"I'm so sorry to hear that. You had an awful life."

"Don't feel sorry for me. I'm fine now. When we arrived here after the sea voyage that frightened me out of my wits, my father kept angering one native group after another. One village threw us out threatening to take our lives. We fled to a river to the north where we were supposed to spread out to explore this land. My father decided to take both us brothers with him. That night, I waited until he and my brother snored. I slipped away into the forest and climbed a hill that had rough rocks all over it. I scratched myself, but I managed to keep my place on that little hill so my father could not find me. The next morning I was awakened by Ghee and Akrumtry, and now I am here. I have never been so happy as I am to be free from my father's mean ways. Now I am ready to live a good life."

Aimettual's concern for this young man was sincere and deep. She hurt when hearing of the abuse he suffered as a child, and silently cheered as she heard of his escape from his father. "I've never heard of anyone having gone through so much as a child," she said truthfully.

"It's in the past now," he assured her. "I am finally free from my father and can live a good life now," he assured her. "I see no value in looking back at what was. I'm not going to return to bring my people here. Others can do that."

"I understand," she said quietly.

"Now, tell me your story," he asked.

"Oh, Maber, my story is shallow. I was born to the brother of the chief and have been bound to obedience, but otherwise, I was free to do what I chose. Garalumuta is a wonderful friend. We grew up together. It is my hope that when we have husbands, we will not have to live far, far apart. We both hope our children will grow up together as we have."

"You have been blessed by Wisdom," he said.

"Did you grow up knowing about Wisdom?" she asked.

"No. We know there's a Creator we call Father Sky, but that's about all we know. There was a terrible sickness that raged through our land nearly a hundred years ago. It killed our storytellers and those who knew the sacred things. My uncle, At, is the one between the living people and the spirit beings. He does the best he can, but he cannot bring back the storytellers."

"Your people have had a very hard time," she said. "We also lost our storyteller. He died in the western sea farther back than any ancestors can say. They just knew there was one. No one knows the stories. We are in a new land, so the stories begin again."

"Our people have had a hard time, and they handled it poorly. I hope to do better with my life, since I've had the chance to observe how easy it is to go wrong, and how wrong doing affects people."

"How old are you, Maber?"

"Seventeen, and you?"

"I'm fourteen," she replied. "We are close in age. You, though, have had a lifetime of experience in your years, while I've had not much."

Maber put his arm around Aimettual. She was so soft. He enjoyed her presence.

Aimettual reached out and took his other hand in hers. She looked into his eyes. "I noticed you the first time I saw you and couldn't take my eyes off you. I wanted to know you right away. You are so far more than I ever could have expected."

Maber felt himself going weak. What an effect this girl had on him! He struggled to make sense of it, but it made no sense.

"You've never been with a woman, have you?" she asked.

"I've been in a home with a mother and sisters. Is that what you mean?"

"No," Aimettual said, trying not to laugh. "I mean, you've never made love to a woman. Have you?"

"No." He said it straightforwardly, not with shame or with arrogance.

"Maybe, while you're here, I can teach you."

Maber was shocked. He let go of her and leaned back a little so he could see her face. "You can see us doing that?" he asked.

"Of course. Why else would I have come to talk to you?"

Maber didn't know how to respond.

"For now, dear Maber, we need to return to the village to sleep. Tomorrow I'll come for you early."

Maber stood. She took his hand and put it on her farthest shoulder so his arm rested on her back, and they walked back to the village. Maber felt a sense of warmth inside he'd never known. He liked it.

Back at the village, Aimettual and Garalumuta slid into their sleeping skins and began to whisper as they did almost nightly.

Aimettual asked Garalumuta, "What did you think of Akrumtry?"

"I like him very much. He is able to make me feel comfortable, not demanding, but making me feel wanted. He listens to what I say. He treats me as an equal. That amazes me. And you with Maber?"

"He has had such an awful life, but instead of making him weak and mean, it has made him wise and gentle. I have already decided he will be my husband."

"How could you have decided that fast? Are you letting your feelings run away with your thoughts?"

"Not at all. I think you'd have had to be there. He is very different. He grew up on the other side of the eastern sea. Can you imagine crossing the sea? I cannot. But he did it."

"Heed the words of the chief. Keep your reason."

"I have not lost his command, Garalumuta. I did tell him that when I have a husband I want to live near you so our children can grow up together."

"You didn't," she giggled.

"Oh, but I did. It's important to me."

"It's important to me, too, but it would never occur to me to make such a request."

"Listen here, Garalumuta, you'd better make your wants known now. If he fails to heed your wants now, what would he do later? Don't stand back shyly. Make your wants clear."

"I understand, my friend. You are thinking, aren't you?"

"Yes, and I don't plan to quit."

"I'll learn from what you have told me."

"Good."

In another part of the village, Maber pulled his sleeping skin over his shoulder just as Akrumtry and Ghee walked into the shelter.

"How'd it go?" Ghee asked Maber.

"I met a lovely young woman. I like her a lot."

"So, did I," Ghee said. "Her name is Copatua and she has wonderful long black hair and long black eyelashes. She makes me melt inside when we touch. I am so happy to be here."

"How about you?" Maber asked Akrumtry.

"Garalumuta is lovely. She is shy, so I had to pull at her to start her to talk. Once she started, she seemed more comfortable. I like her a lot. She has been an obedient person all her life. She wants to be a wife and have children. She says I have to ask others how well she cooks."

"That sounds wise," Maber laughed.

"I can see her as my wife," Akrumtry said.

"This soon, you can decide that?" Maber asked.

"Yes. She would be someone very easy to live with. Her greatest goal is to be a good wife and mother. What else could you want?"

"I would want someone who stirs my passion," Lag said entering and joining the conversation. He laid down his spear and slipped into his sleeping place.

"Did you find one tonight?"

"No. I met a young woman named Lamelatua. She couldn't stop talking. She did not stir my passion, instead she made me want to gag her."

"So, you won't meet her tomorrow?" Ghee asked.

"You are right, Ghee. I have no desire to hear her again."

The men chatted only briefly. Maber turned over on his side and went black. He had had a wonderful, never anticipated day.

In the morning Aimettual was true to her word, she met Maber near the structure where he stayed. She was as lovely as he remembered. She took his hand and placed it on her shoulder. They walked back to the same place where they'd been the night before.

"Why did you want to return here?" Maber asked.

"I wanted to see if in daylight the delight was still there," she replied.

Maber could no longer restrain himself. He leaned down, encircled her in his arms and kissed her.

"Is it?" he asked.

"Oh, yes," she said with a wide grin.

"You make me feel like a melting glacier," Maber told her.

"You make me want you," she said.

"How is that?"

"I find you like a very warm spring that I'm drawn to. I want to touch and be touched by the warmth," she tried to explain.

"I can understand your words," he told her.

"Come," she said, standing and holding out her hand.

They walked hand in hand to the valley in a place he thought very secluded.

"Not very many people know of this place," she said. "This is the warm spring. Come, let's enter it to see what may happen." She began to remove her clothing.

Maber was unsure what to do, so he followed her lead. They stepped into the water together.

"It's hot!" Maber exclaimed.

"Isn't it wonderful!" she called back swimming through the water, her hair following behind on the water.

Maber immersed himself in the warm water. It had a not great odor, but the warmth made him forget the odor quickly. The water was clear, and he could see his toes from neck deep in the water. He swam to where Aimettual was on the far side of the pool. He was surprised to find her sitting on a rock edge. She stretched out her arms to him and pulled him to the rock edge between her legs. They embraced in the hot water, steam rising all around them. They came to know each other differently from the night before. They spoke little, each hungering for and finding in the other something they had both missed. Aimettual led him to another rock ledge, very smooth, about two by three man-lengths and a little less than two feet from the water's surface. There they consummated the love that had grown so fast.

"In the bright light of day," Maber laughed. "What a joy you are," he said, sparkles dancing in his eyes.

"As are you! I want you, Maber, for my husband. I never want to be without you."

"And I, you," he said.

"We will have to return to the village to ask the chief," she said.

"Now?" he asked.

"Of course, now," she said with a girlish giggle.

They swam to the other side of the pool, climbed out, and dressed. They skipped and jogged back to the village.

Back at the village, Maber saw the chief first. He led her to the chief and they waited for him to respond.

The chief nodded.

"Chief Trajamuranta," Maber said, "Aimettual has stolen something from me."

The chief's jaw dropped. Aimettual was shocked and stepped to the side.

"She has stolen my love, Chief. I must ask for your permission to take her as my wife."

"And, Chief," Aimettual said following along, "Maber has likewise stolen my love. This is a very special man and I ask your permission to take him as my husband."

"You have my permission," the chief said, his eyes dancing in mirth. Permission had been requested in many ways, but this one was definitely unique. The chief realized as soon as he saw them where they'd been. It was too cool to go in water anywhere but the hot pool. He could envision the day's events.

"There are three temporary shelters for this purpose. Gather your things from where they lie and choose whichever of the three huts you want for yours."

"I know which one to choose," Aimettual said, grinning.

"Then let us stop to gather our things, and when we have them, you lead the way," Maber said. He couldn't help but think quickly that if he hadn't been forced to make this voyage, he might never have had a wife. And such a wife he had.

They laid their sleeping skins and personal items inside the hut Aimettual had chosen. It was atop a slight rise. Of the three huts, it was the largest. They set up the hearth in the forefront near the entryway. That gave them a lot of space for their sleeping place.

Aimettual was delighted to see the furred skin Maber had for a sleeping skin. It was soft. She quickly realized it was made from many pelts.

"It's seal skin," he told her. I am SealEater. That is the skin of seals I eat."

Aimettual stretched out on the seal skin.

"Wait," Maber told her. "Come here."

She came to him. He pulled her soft leather dress over her head and laid it on the sleeping skin pile. Maber laid her down on the seal skin sleeping skin. Aimettual's body, he realized, was beautiful. He sat beside her and ran his fingers over her soft skin. She murmured. She touched him noticing the immediate change. They lost themselves in each other for a long time. Finally, satiated for the moment, they dressed and left their new temporary hut.

Maber and Aimettual went to Akrumtry and Garalumuta.

"I want to introduce you to someone, Akrumtry," Maber said in an utterly serious tone.

"To whom?" Akrumtry asked.

"To my wife." Maber grinned.

"You did it that fast?" Akrumtry asked stupefied.

"When you know, you know," Maber said.

Akrumtry and Garalumuta looked at the couple. Clearly there was a huge difference in the two. Suddenly, Akrumtry understood. They had done something, probably repeatedly, that he had not done this day. And they glowed.

"Garalumuta, remember the hot pool I showed you once?" Aimettual asked.

"Yes, of course."

"I suggest the two of you go there for a swim," the young woman said.

"If Akrumtry agrees," Garalumuta said smiling.

"Akrumtry agrees," Akrumtry said with force. The two left. Before evening, that couple would also be husband and wife.

That night, in the men's place, Ghee and Lag wondered how the others had managed so quickly to find wives. Ghee genuinely liked Copatua, but he was not as at ease as the other men had been, nor was Copatua seasoned in the search for a husband.

It was late in the day when Lag met Muhurandu. They were a good match, but very little of the evening remained. They planned to meet first thing the next morning. He entered the men's place uplifted in hope of finding a wife.

The man who had been pursuing Aimettual was greatly angered when he discovered she'd taken a husband. He was threatening loudly and was overheard. He was arrested by guards and taken to the chief. The chief, watching the man's inability to control himself, ordered the guards to escort him out of the territory immediately, while he signaled to the guards, that the escort was not to send the man on his way but to kill him. As far as the chief was concerned, Aimettual was unsafe as long as this man had such irresponsible ideas that somehow she belonged to him or that he had every right to her. The guards left with the man. He was gone and buried before dawn. The guards were at the morning meal even before it was served.

At the end of three days, Lag and Ghee had wives and both could not be happier. They had a goal coming to the Maikumatu, and they were successful.

In their hut, Maber and Aimettual had long discussions as to where they would live. Aimettual wanted to remain where she was. Maber on the other hand wanted to continue to the west. He wanted to see this land from sea to sea.

They went for a walk to calm things down before resuming the discussion. They joined Akrumtry and Garalumuta who were sitting on a rock overlooking the small river.

"How are you two?" Akrumtry asked, his arm around Garalumuta.

"Not the greatest. I want to travel to the western sea, and Aimettual wants to remain here. We have been in disagreement all afternoon."

"The chief can solve that for you," Akrumtry said, almost without thinking. "If you go to the western sea, I'd like to do that also. I've heard that the land there is wonderful. What do you think, Garalumuta?"

"I'd like to see the western sea. I've never seen a sea. It would be easier to travel to a place such as the sea before we have children."

Aimettual said, "I feel outnumbered. What's wrong with staying here?"

"Once you've traveled, it makes you more curious about what's over the next hill or around that bend. You want to know where rivers lead. You know there'll come a time when the traveling has to end, but when you can do it, it's wonderful." Akrumtry felt he had expressed what he wanted to convey so that someone who'd never traveled might have an idea of what called to them.

"You would be going with us, if we went there?" Aimettual asked.

"If Maber will have us along, yes, we will," Akrumtry said.

"Of course, I'd be glad to have you accompany us." Maber smiled. "Do you still refuse?" Maber looked right at Aimettual.

"No. I'll agree to travel there. It frightens me to think of such a trip, but, yes, I'll go."

Maber looked at Akrumtry. "Will you check with Ghee and Lag. They may want to join."

"Of course," Akrumtry replied.

Maber and Aimettual returned to their temporary hut.

Three couples made the trip from the west side of the mountains to the western sea. Lag chose to remain with the Maikumata.

The three couples lived in the low hills of the mountains on the southwest side of what is now Mt. Rainier. They had occasional encounters with others in the area. The meetings involved trade and were pleasant. Maber and Aimettual had thirteen children, only three of whom lived to adulthood. Maber lived to the age of seventy-five. Aimettual lived two years after his death. Their bodies now lie under lahars on the mountain.

Chapter 9

Reg and Blad's Story

Reg was forty-nine years of age. He was a very large man, towering over the other SealEaters, and his strength was legendary. He was unaware that his hair was graying. Appearance mattered not at all to him; what mattered to him was that he was in control. He and Blad were rowing upstream to learn where the best place for the SealEaters to migrate might be. Reg, seated in the back of the small boat they had taken, rowed with fury at least two strokes to Blad's one. His voice filled the landscape.

"I'll kill you, Maber, when I find you. You disloyal, slinking, sea slug snot frozen to Father Sky's upper lip in the cold! How dare you leave us? How dare you! Have you no sense of responsibility. I will find you. You'll wish you'd never been born, Pus Bag! Didn't I take care of you: seeing that you ate and had shelter all your seventeen years? Didn't I teach you how to hunt? How to live at sea? And this is how you treat me?"

Reg pinched his finger on the last swipe through the water with the oar. He gave no appearance of noticing any pain.

"You're the provider, Mother Earth! What a lousy effort you've shown! My son deserts and you fail to stop him! You let him go! Curses upon you and your daughter, the Pale-Faced Moon. Curses upon you forever. You let him leave with the love and devotion he should have had to me. Me, I tell you! For all I've done for him! You are a pretend god! Not real. Not doing what you're supposed to do—provide for me and Blad."

"And you, Father Sky. You went black while Maber left. You keep us warm? Not so! Ice advances to the Cove! You the supposed giver of life— you went black while my son stole away into the forest or up the river—I know not where. You went black! Curses also upon you, Father Sky. I do well without you. Curses upon your son, the Water that always moves, not because Water failed—he did not. Curses upon Water because he is your son. May you lose him as I lost my son."

"Hearth Fire, the source of family ties, cursed may you be also! You failed here. My family is untied. I curse you!"

"Maber, if you can hear me, know that you are a dead man! I have cursed those gods without whose help you could never have escaped. They cannot help you now that I've cursed them. Maber, may you rot. May you never have sons. May you meet with a great bear and have him claw you to pieces!"

Reg stopped his rant and reached for his water bladder. He took a great swig and then another. His rant had caused him to have a dry mouth. The water helped.

Despite Reg's inhuman energy rowing, Blad continued rowing with great strength, while his mind remained tied to his father's words. Horrible words! Words that froze his thinking place with fear. He knew better than to blaspheme the gods. Everyone knew that. How could his father do it? He wondered why his father didn't understand Maber's need to flee. Blad wished he could have been with his brother in the escape, but he knew his brother had reason not to trust him. Many times when they were children, he'd blamed Maber for his own wrongdoing so that punishment fell to Maber when it was due him. He wished the best for Maber. He had taken a great risk. Blad wished his brother well.

Blad then began to think of his father's cursing. Suddenly, it occurred to him that such behavior was something only humans did. Not all humans did it. Birds don't curse or blaspheme; four-legged hairy animals don't do it; fish and animals of the sea don't do it; birds don't blaspheme or curse. Why, then, do some humans do it? Blad had never seen that it had any effect whatsoever when his father did it. Why participate in such a non-effective rant? Blad rowed, unable to answer his own questions.

"Birds of the air and beasts of the land, I call to you," Reg continued, "Find my son and punish him for his treachery! Peck at his eyes, scratch him with your claws and bite him with your teeth. Remove all sources of food from him that he may starve. Let his wounds fester and fill with pus, stink, and rot."

Blad rowed and remembered that Maber had their supplies for emergency wound care. He hoped they had no need for those supplies.

Reg continued on with his rant until the day darkened and they had to stop for the night. His throat hurt. He stopped to refill the water bladders. He kicked a small rock, then looked at Blad.

"What's the matter with you? You rowed like a girl today! I don't suppose you have energy to find us real meat for tonight! Toss me my spear. I'll be back." Reg stormed off into the forest. He instantly switched to the silence and stealth for which he was well known. He went deeper and deeper into the forest, still carrying the sense that forests were not places for SealEaters, but driven for desire to eat some fresh meat.

Blad carefully started a fire. Then for the night he built a shelter made of windfall logs laid together in a circular arrangement. In between the logs he stuffed mosses, leaves, and branches, anything he could find to make it waterproof. The clouds above made him think of rain, and Blad was certain he could smell it. He placed their backpacks in the shelter and laid out the sleeping skins. Blad gathered and peeled as many sticks as he could find to cook meat his father was certain to bring. Then, Blad waited. Suddenly, he jumped up and went to the boat and tilted it, so all the water that had collected in the bottom could drain out. Blad returned to put some large logs near the fire where they'd sit to cook their meat.

It was not long before Blad heard crashing through the forest and knew his father was approaching. The man had a way of heavy breathing after a hunt that was unmistakable. Blad was glad to have meat but wished he'd had a little more time without his father.

They bled the beaver and butchered it. After cleaning it, Reg removed the beaver's head, sliced the beaver along the spine, and then each one skewered his half. They cooked and ate in silence. Reg entered the shelter to go black, while Blad finished eating. He took his time carrying the animal parts to the center of the river, where he'd dump them since they couldn't use all the parts at that time. He banked the fire and entered the shelter to go black, where he could hear Reg's snore. Blad wished he had the courage of Maber to gather his own things and go into the forest to disappear from Reg forever. He didn't.

Overnight a huge storm passed over. Neither awakened, but in the dawn's light it was clear there'd been a downpour. They wasted no time. Each wolfed down some jerky, loaded the boat, killed the fire, knocked down their shelter, and left. Reg was silent for most of the morning.

Reg kicked Blad. Blad turned to see what Reg wanted. Reg pointed ahead to a bend in the river where a large deer was standing. He pointed to shore. Both rowed as quietly as possible to shore. Reg exited the boat silent as a cat and headed toward the forested edge. He slipped up on the deer without being detected and threw his first spear, hitting the deer behind the front leg. The deer was stunned, and Reg threw the second spear. It hit the deer behind the ear and the deer fell to the ground. Quickly, Blad joined him and they took care of the deer and prepared it for transportation in the boat. They wouldn't have to be concerned about food for some time.

They resumed their rowing upriver. Reg, who had been fairly quiet all day, decided to make the shelter for the night. He used two trees at the edge of the forest. Between them he attached a single log and then laid windfall logs against the one that spanned the two trees. It gave him a wider interior to their shelter. He raised up the lower level logs by placing another wind fallen log under the ends. Reg set up the sleeping skins and put the backpacks inside.

Blad had a larger than normal fire going to roast the deer. He had buried two Y-shaped poles in the ground and put the deer meat on a horizontal bar resting in the Ys of the poles. The deer would roast over the fire for a good part of the day. By evening, it would be ready for them to eat. Blad gathered some greens and laid them aside for the evening meal. He noticed that his father had walked downstream a bit and was standing at the forest's edge.

Suddenly, Reg let out a loud noise. He was dancing from one foot to another.

"Blad, come help me. I've have things crawling all over me."

Blad went to his father quickly. Reg had been standing in a bug nest and was covered with amazingly tiny little eight-legged, gray-brown bugs. They were crawling up both his legs.

"Remove them from me!" he bellowed at full volume, as if he were terrified of the tiny bugs.

Blad pulled his father towards the river hoping to guide him away from the source of the bugs. He began to pull them off and rinse them off his hands in the river water. He was appalled at the number of them. Blad tried to wipe them off, but numbers of them had attached themselves to Reg's skin, and they had to be removed one at a time.

Reg stood there, completely horrified at the bugs crawling on him and angry that it happened. He tried to remain calm while Blad wiped and pulled at the bugs. It took a very long time.

"Oh, by the gods, there are some on my butt," Reg yelled.

"You'll have to uncover yourself, if I'm to reach them," Blad replied.

Reg removed his clothing with his back to Blad, covering his private parts with his hands. Blad found that somewhat amusing for the SealEaters were not shy about their bodies, but he would never have admitted his thoughts to his father.

Eventually, Reg seemed comfortable that nothing else was crawling on him. He pulled his clothing back on.

Time passed and one day Reg noticed two gray things he thought were growths on his groin. They were gray. They had appeared very fast, he thought. He asked Blad to look at them. Blad said they looked to him like two of the bugs that had crawled on him. He suggested to Reg they might be sucking his blood from the looks of them. Reg told him to remove them. After dislocating the first one, Blad squeezed it between his fingernails. Sure enough, the bug was filled with blood.

"Take the other one off!" Reg screamed.

Blad removed the other one. He didn't see any more.

For days Reg itched terribly at the places where the bugs had attached. He was totally disgusted with the effects of the bugs.

After several more days of rowing, they finally reached the place where the boat could no longer travel upstream. They hid the boat by the small lake, and Reg and Blad began to walk.

"What exactly are we looking for?" Blad asked.

"A place for our people," Reg replied not understanding why Blad asked such an obvious question.

"What I want to know is what makes a good place for our people." Blad was looking for the criteria for discovery.

"Then you should ask what you want to know," Reg replied, ignoring Blad's request for information.

Blad thought for a while and then said, "What are the things that make a good place for our people?"

Reg replied, "An open place, plenty open. Water nearby. Other people at a long distance. Food animals to hunt. Forests for wood. Good weather."

While they talked, two men on a rocky outcrop spotted the two men walking.

"No more than two?" Ga asked.

"No more than two," Cu replied.

"It would be wise to gather a few more warriors," Ga said.

"I'll go."

Within a brief time, two more men arrived with Cu.

"I see," Ja said.

"Let's go down. We must stop them."

The four men silently descended the great hill so they would arrive at a specific, well chosen place for their apprehension of the two who walked below.

Below, Blad was wondering why they continued on their course. He could not work out a way to ask his father what he wanted to know, for Reg could take his question as criticism, something he did not tolerate. Blad wanted to know why they were in a region that was cold compared to other places they'd been. There were no open places along this river. Why, he wondered, were they pursuing this place? He kept silent.

"By Mother Earth, I do not understand the disappearance of Maber. He could not have just walked off! I wonder whether he was abducted. But if abducted, why, Mother Earth, would you neglect your duties to protect us? What were you thinking? Were you even there?"

Blad groaned silently. His father was at it again. His face was red and stormy looking. Blad hated to be in these strange surroundings with a man who was one person one moment and another in a heartbeat. He hoped this would not continue for the remainder of the day.

"Father Sky, you who are supposed to have created all that is. Where were you when my son disappeared? Were you off fornicating with Mother Earth? You sopping wet bear turd of a god! I spit on your name! I bet your maleness is skinny and short! Skinny, short, pus-filled slug! I hate you! Hear me? I hate you. Worship you? Never again!"

Blad was becoming alarmed. His father might bring all the gods down on them. They began to walk through a narrow passage at the river bend, where they had to walk through one at a time. No sooner had Reg passed through than four men jumped him. They knocked him down, tied his hands together behind his back, almost cutting off the circulation of blood, and hobbled him so he could not take more than a single small step at a time. They did the same to Blad, but he was a lot easier to subdue.

They issued the standard interrogatories trying hard to obtain answers, and then gave up. Language was a problem. They signed for the strangers to follow Ga, releasing the tie of one hobble rope's end for walking. It took three days to reach their village. A capture of this nature, however, caused them to have to go to the Alu main village, Alu-a. That took seven days.

The Alu did not want to listen to the angry man whose voice they heard so much before capture, so they kept him gagged. It didn't stop Reg from railing, just kept it so they couldn't hear him. Blad was grateful.

Any time the strangers walked too slowly, the Alu prodded them with Reg's and Blad's spear points, points they admired. The prodding was effective.

Finally, they arrived at Alu-a. People came to greet them, awed by the size of one of the captives. They took them to the center of the village to meet Chief Xeno.

"Treat them as usual, but use double cordage on that big one," the chief told them. He turned and took his seat on the bench in front of his place to watch.

There were three trees in the village center. They took Reg to the first two trees. A few men tied one strand of cordage to his left wrist and one to his right. Then they tied another to each wrist. Reg had to stand while they tied one of his arms to one tree and another to another tree. They pulled the cordage very tight. His arms were slightly raised above his shoulders while he stood. Then, they did the same with his ankles. Then, to Reg's horror, they took sharp knives and cut his clothing off. He stood there like a bleeding kill—nude. Suddenly Ye, an old woman, began to laugh. Then more people saw what she noticed and they laughed. Reg's face turned blood red. His secret had been uncovered. Now, his son would know.

"We shall call him One Nut," the chief said. All the people who were in the area began to laugh.

Blad suddenly realized why they were laughing. It took a moment for the information to settle in his thoughts. He had always known that his father could not ever be elected chief, but he didn't understand why. Now, he knew Reg's awful secret. He was not by the SealEaters considered fully male. Blad had a quick flash in his thinking place that caused him to wonder whether his father was the monster he was because the other elders considered him less than fully male. It was a revelation.

Reg remained tied up. Women and men went up and touched One Nut. Some cut him with women's knives. They cackled as they did it. Reg wanted to become invisible. He hated every second of this torture.

Then, the men who'd secured Reg came for Blad. They tied him up and removed his clothing as was done to his father.

As the men circled Blad, they saw the scars that clearly denoted beatings. They realized this one had endured much pain.

The chief spoke, "We will call him Endured Pain." The chief looked at the men who had secured the prisoners. "Cut him down, Pi. I want him taught our language quickly. Will you do it, Pi?"

"Yes, Chief. Do you want him tied once he's freed?"

"Yes, until he learns to talk to us, and we are assured he will not cut the other man down."

"Very well."

Pi took Blad down from the trees and led him to his home, where the language lessons began immediately. Blad could still hear the natives taunting his father and laughing. Blad's jacket was ruined, so Pi's wife sewed it together at the place the men had cut the shoulders loose to remove it. Blad had so many mixed feelings that he was confused. He also was very tired. Having to sit to learn a new language was not something he would have wanted to do, but he gave it every effort he could.

For days whether it rained or the sun shone, Reg was tied. He was a very strong willed man, but pain and lack of sleep had broken him down. His arms were sending exquisite pain signals that frightened him. He feared his arms would soon dislocate. He hated his son's having learned the secret he'd kept all his life. He definitely was undone to be tied up like a helpless girl. They fed him food not fit to eat, such as animal gut, stomach of a beaver, dry grasses. They gave him water, but it was never enough. Reg had concluded they meant to kill him slowly.

His arms dislocated in a horrible wrenching one night. Reg didn't know whether he was pulled by many hands or just dreamed it. After some time, he was convinced that even if cut down, he'd never have the use of his arms again. He was certain they wanted to kill him slowly.

Pi told the chief that Blad learned enough of their language to be able to answer any questions he might have. Chief Xeno told him to bring Blad to him.

When Blad reached the chief's place, one look at his father caused him to wretch.

"Sit here," the chief told Blad. Blad sat on the rock provided.

"Where are your people?"

"They are across the eastern sea. We are the SealEaters."

"Why are you here?"

"The ice moves to our land and mountains hold us in." He showed ice with one hand and mountains with the other. "We run out of land. Some of us came here to look for a new land."

"How many of you came here?"

"Counting me, there are thirteen."

"Isn't that more than you needed?"

"We thought some of us would perish at sea," Blad replied.

"How did you acquire the scars on your back?"

Blad looked terribly sad. He nodded towards his father.

"Did you do terrible things?"

Blad shook his head negatively.

"He is an angry man?" the chief asked.

Blad nodded.

"For a long time?"

"As long as I've known him."

"Why didn't some people stop him?"

Blad shrugged.

"You know why! Why?"

"They feared him," Blad admitted.

"I thought as much."

"You cannot leave here. If you try, it's the last thing you'll do. Do you want to live here?"

"I would rather live here than die," Blad admitted.

"You know that we will not let your father live."

"That's what I thought. What I don't understand is why kill him and not me?"

"It's your name, Endured Pain. For anyone to have endured that pain and not be as your father is, you may be worth keeping."

"May I ask something of you?" Blad said timidly.

"Ask."

"Will you please go ahead and kill my father? I do not like my father because of what he's done to me. I cannot say I hate him, for I've been taught it's wrong to hate. I have great conflict in my thinking place. I hear him cry out, and it hurts me. What happens here may be justified, but it adds additional pain to me. Will you please end his life now?"

"You seem to have some manner of forgiveness for him, one who hurt you so badly. What a strange thing."

At that point Reg cried out pitifully. He was not fully conscious, but Blad winced as if the pain were his own.

"Ja and Di," the chief called out. Both came quickly.

"End the prisoner's life," the chief said.

The men left, spears in hand.

"Thank you, Chief Xeno," Blad said, tears in his eyes.

"Ye," the chief said to his wife, "remove the ropes from this man."

"Pi," the chief called, "see to the building of a hut for this man. Have him rest for three days. Then, test him for how well he hunts."

"As you say, Chief."

"Chief?" Cu spoke up.

"Before he is tested for hunting, could we use him to teach us how to make the spear points he has? We cannot look at them and learn how he does it."

"Of course. Pi, wait to test him until he has taught those who want to learn his spear making technique."

Pi nodded and went to secure help to construct a place for Endured Pain.

A few days after his new place had been built, Blad came rushing out of his home. He almost ran into Pi.

"What is that noise?" he asked.

Pi laughed a good natured laugh. "It's a sloth calling to others of its kind."

"What's a sloth?"

"It's an animal that eats plants. It's as tall as two men one standing atop the other."

Blad laughed, "Surely you are teasing me?"

"Not at all. Bring your spears and come with me," Pi told him.

Blad reached inside the entry to his home and grabbed his spears.

"This way," Pi said.

They jogged down a path and around a bend in the river. There standing incredibly tall was the oddest creature Blad had ever seen. It was eating leaves on a tree that grew out of the river bank. The creature was a little over two times the height of a man. It called again and Blad could feel the vibration in his chest. He was horrified at the claws on the animal.

"Do you want to take it, Pi?" Blad asked.

"No. Sloth is extremely tough meat, Endured Pain. It's not very tasty even when you add flavor to it. We just leave them alone and they don't bother us. How much longer do you think the spear making will take?"

"Probably two more days."

"I want to see how well you hunt. Two more days is fine."

"I guess I'd better return, so I can eat something before we start again."

"Let's go."

"What's the meat in this stew?" Blad asked. "We've had it for two days now, and I don't know what it is."

Ub looked at him over the food serving log. "It's tough bird," she replied smoothly with a crooked smile embracing her oddly overlapped teeth. "Just tough, old bird. We've almost finished it."

"Thank you," Blad replied. He took his bowl of stew and stood against a tree to eat it. He looked at Hei and said with a shudder of discomfort, "I don't think I ever ate meat like this."

"Having just come to this place, I'm sure you haven't," Hei replied. "You become used to it over time."

"I'm sure I will."

Above the din of the Alu's eating and finishing their evening meal, there was life—unobserved life, if you could call it that—above. It had hovered over Alu-a for three days.

A mist hung over the tree against which Blad leaned. The mist, being thin and intermingled among the branches of the tree, remained unseen by the people below. The mist held thoughts that were painful, labored, regretful, tied to place for want of a finishing.

'I was born Reg; I died as One Nut. In an instant after death, my eyes were open to truth. I could not stop truth from flooding me. The pain of that was worse than the pain I endured at the hands of the Alu. What a horrible mess I made of life for myself and my family, even my people. I let my own personal lack lead me, blind me to all that's important, change me into a person without compassion—all for the singular reason that I could never become chief, not being fully male. What a fool I was! I can blame no one but myself. Ah, the pain I caused others! I ache for the pain I caused others. I can offer no apology now. It's too late. I cannot tell my son how great is my gratitude that he caused the end of my pain at the hands of these people. He gave me good for all the bad I gave him.'

'These Alu are not right in their thinking places. They are cursed. They curse. Not with words—but rather with deeds. Even now my son, Blad, eats tough bird. Little does he know what he is doing. Little does Blad know that not one of these people is to be trusted. Oh, Blad! All have lost their sense of what is humanly acceptable. Alu are empty shells, trying all day every day to fill what's empty inside and, being unable, they become emptier the more they eat. On the outside, they appear normal, but they are not! I have been as they are, but not for the same cause. I do not pity them, but I pity Blad among them. To him these people must look like a relief from me. He seems happy enough to be where he is. I know he'd rather be back at the Cove with some girl. I never knew which one he found appealing.'

'How can I show him that he needs to be exceptionally canny to escape these wretched people? People? I am too kind. Alu are worse than snakes. They deserve to be eradicated from the earth. But while I do all this condemnation of them, I must include myself with them.'

'Maber. Maber. Blad, my son, you need to acquire the courage of your brother, Maber. You need to break free of these people even as he broke free from me. You must learn this, my son. You are not like these people. You must learn to see the truth about these people. I cannot reach you in this world where I find myself. I must let go of this place and leave. I've tried everything I know to reach you.'

'Mother Earth, Father Sky, I cursed you. I blasphemed you. You have no reason to listen to me. I call to you at this time, not for me, but for my son, Blad. Let him see soon the true nature of these people, so that he may know the need to break away. Then, Mother Earth and Father Sky, please show him the way. I deserve whatever you have planned to do with me, but he is a good man. Please protect him. Remove him from here, and let him find joy in this life while he lives. Is he not deserving?'

'Aunt Gemu? Is that you? I hear your call.'

'Come, Reg, it's past time,' his aunt called to him. 'Turn loose the hold this world has on you. It's time.'

'Aunt Gemu—is it really you?'

'Yes, my boy, come now.'

Reg could see her, not as mist but as she used to look before she became sick. Mist rose like a lightning bolt from the tree and flew upward, not to return.

The Alu and Blad never knew of the presence of the mist that had just been hovering above them.

Pi, Ga, Cu, and Endured Pain left one morning early to test Endured Pain's hunting skills. They traveled south to what Endured Pain thought to be the way he had come from the trail as prisoners. He was certain it was the same way, but they took a different trail about half way to the place. They went farther to the west.

In an open space they saw several white tailed deer. The four of them became very still. They watched the animals who were upwind and hadn't detected the presence of danger. Pi told Endured Pain to lead. Endured Pain signed to each where to move. He moved to the place he expected the deer to run once they detected danger. All the men were soon in place. Endured Pain from the cover of an old tree tossed a rock behind the deer. The deer began to leap away in the path Endured Pain expected. His was the first kill, then Cu and Pi each speared one. Ga's was trying to escape, so Pi had to spear that one.

"Excellent!" Pi told Endured Pain. "We likely need do no more testing."

The men removed the entrails and then returned home.

There was a great feast when they returned. Endured Pain was thanked and congratulated in excess. It made him slightly uncomfortable. Hunting for meat was something expected of his people.

The feast continued for a few days and then it was time to hunt again. There was a feast–hunt cycle. No one seemed to pre-plan by making jerky. Endured Pain did not understand. He began to hunt more and to set up a smoke hut to make jerky. He made it, but as soon as he made it, the people consumed it. Clearly, he did not understand their ways.

Endured Pain was not accustomed to sharing his thoughts with anyone. He simply observed and kept his own counsel.

After living among the Alu through two full changes of seasons, Endured Pain became restless. He felt a sense of flatness among these people. Pi called for him to join the hunt and he gathered his spears and joined Pi and Ga. They headed this time towards the exact place where he had been captured. He understood that they were to hunt humans, not animals for meat. He remembered the time he had been on the other side. He had mixed feelings, though he knew how important to the Alu it was that others not enter their lands. Endured Pain prepared to join the others. He worked his senses to their best keenness. He became one with the environment. He would help these Alu protect their land against entry from strangers.

They positioned themselves just inside the narrow passage along the path the men followed. They remained still and quiet. The first man passed through and was hit in the back of the head with the end of a spear shaft. The second one, was wrestled to the ground and bound, just as he had been. They tied up the first one and waited for him to regain consciousness. Both were gagged. As soon as the older man became conscious, they began the walk to the main village some seven days away. When they reached the village, the two men were tied to the trees and stripped of all clothing. There were no questions asked, Endured Pain noted. This was what he observed numbers of times when men were brought to the village.

Returning from a hunt a few days later, Endured Pain realized the men had been killed. That night, Endured Pain ate tough bird stew. After his evening meal, he walked to a high point overlooking the low land. As clear as the night sky became, Endured Pain realized that the tough bird stew followed the deaths of the captives. He *knew* with a clarity that only comes with considerable certainty—he'd just eaten human flesh. Tough bird stew must be made of the bodies of those who were captured and killed. Endured Pain rose and ran to the forest where he vomited up the contents of his stomach. He returned to the rock and sat there dazed. How could he have missed it for so long? he wondered. He also realized he had eaten his father's flesh. He began to shiver. Endured Pain wanted to scream and shout obscenities in the acknowledement of his understanding. That would, however, avail nothing but bring the Alu people to add him to those killed and eaten. Sitting alone on the hillside, he realized he had to escape or he might become an Alu. No longer would he think of himself as Endured Pain. It was time to return to Blad and do what his younger brother had done, take the courage to leave this place.

Blad lay on the rock which still retained some warmth of the day. He remembered hunting one day to the west. Far in the distance he saw a river. He wondered how he could reach a river. That river or any other swift moving river would become his goal. As he lay there he heard steps. He sat up.

"Endured Pain, I wondered where you were."

"I came up here to look at the stars this night," Blad said, trying to sound normal. "The rock stays warm for a while after sunset, and I enjoy the warmth of it."

Pi sat next to Endured Pain.

"Aren't they spectacular tonight?" Blad asked.

"I just see stars," Pi replied.

Blad didn't pursue it.

"I came up here to ask whether you want to join a hunting group. We leave for the west tomorrow at sunrise."

"That sounds interesting," Blad replied.

"Then you better have some rest," Pi said, standing. He was glad Endured Pain would join them. The man was a skilled hunter.

Blad stood and walked down the hill to his place. He went black well that night, for he was convinced that he'd never return to this place. He'd find a way out.

The hunters, Pi, Ja, Di, and Endured Pain left at sunrise. They walked briskly to a path Blad had never seen. They had to walk one behind the other, for the path was narrow. They walked for days, camping overnight and on the go the next morning. At the end of ten days they reached a lake. The grayish turquoise-colored lake was fed by melt water from glaciers in the mountains. In the distance there was a roaring noise.

"What's that noise?" Blad asked Pi. He noticed Pi was growing a lot of gray hair.

"There's a waterfall down there," he said pointing.

"I want to see it!" Blad said with partially feigned enthusiasm. He knew Pi thought his joy in seeing beautiful things in nature was strange, but it gave him a freedom. He'd use it.

"If you go there now, you'll be putting your shelter together in the dark."

"I'll run there and run back," Blad said, leaving.

"Be careful," Pi warned, not the least surprised that Endured Pain wanted to see the waterfall. Turning to the others, he said, "Sometimes I think beauty feeds him more than meat."

"What's this beauty? He sees things I don't see," Ja said.

"Me too," Pi replied.

"I agree with you. This beauty thing is strange," Di said to assure his part in the group's comments.

Blad ran with every bit of energy he had. It was, he was convinced, now or never. Never had he been given such an opportunity. He reached the falls. It was in fact beautiful. It was also impossible to descend to the river. And it was a big river. A swift river. Just the river he hoped for. The sides were steep and that steepness went on for as far as he could see. There was no easy way to reach the river—except jump.

"Mother Earth, Father Sky, help me," he shouted and jumped. The descent was faster than trying to climb, but it also took a lot of time to reach the bottom The water was very cold. At least Blad felt it took a long time. At the bottom, he fell into a deep water hole from which he ascended to the surface. Blad gulped air while the pressure of the falling water pushed him under again. He swam underwater as far from where the water entered as he could. Suddenly the rushing current of freed water caught him and began to carry him downstream. He had no time to think. Blad just followed along with the current, trying to keep his head above water. At one point he saw a small log and he grabbed it. He rested atop the log after several attempts at climbing up on it. He didn't care where he went as long as he could evade the Alu.

Through the night he rode the log. Blad was cold, but he did not want to leave the water until he was well clear of the Alu. At sunrise, he thought he might be free of them, but he was uncertain. He knew he needed to warm up, for he was shivering. He had no weapons, tools, or backpack. He did, however, have himself. For the first time in his life, he felt truly free.

The log snagged on the side of the riverbank and Blad pulled it to shore and headed to the few trees that grew along the river bank. He had to create a fire starter, make a fire, dry himself and his clothing, and decide what to do. The walls that rose on either side of the river remained steep. The little group of trees gave him hope. He examined them. They were flexible trees that would bend easily. Blad was hungry, but he knew he should start a fire first.

Blad made a friction fire starter and the fire he made encouraged him. He took off his clothing and hung the things on poles he tore from the trees and drilled into the sandy soil. Blad set his mind to food. He looked around the place and saw little that would do for food. There were buds on some of the bushes that grew in the area, so he began to eat the buds. He ate some greens unfamiliar to him, hoping he was safe from poisonous plants. Finally his hunger was satiated. He drank some water.

While looking at the plants, Blad decided to make a boat like a basket. The flexible trees should work well that way, he thought. How to make the boat float was a problem. There were no animal skins for covering the basket boat. A couple of dead trees gave him an idea. He'd use the bark on the trees to line the boat, tying them to the frame he'd make with fibers from just under the bark of the flexible limbs of the trees. Then he'd use grass and clay from the river bank to seal the tree bark to the boat. It was the best Blad could think with the lack of resources available. He felt he needed to work fast in case the Alu were looking for him.

The Alu were uncertain when Endured Pain failed to return. It was too dark to look for him, so they waited until morning to search for him. They followed his trail to the falls. Then they looked everywhere they could. His tracks ended at the falls.

Pi said, "It looks like he was so interested in the falls that he fell into it. Let's walk a little way down the wall here. His body may lie there somewhere."

"How awful," Ja said.

They walked a long way along the upper edge of the river and found nothing.

"His body may be stuck under the falls," Di suggested.

"I hadn't thought of that," Pi said.

The men returned to the campsite. They took their spears and headed south to the area they planned to hunt.

Blad finished the frame for the boat, weaving it just as he'd weave a basket. He went to the logs where he hoped to gather bark to line the boat. The bark still retained some flexibility. Blad harvested the bark and brought it to the basket boat he'd constructed. He then took limbs from the tree and began to peel the bark off to reach the fibers just under the green bark. He pulled them out, gathering as many of the fibers as possible. Blad put the fibers in a hollowed out part of the river bank which quickly filled with water. He didn't want the fibers to dry out.

That night he made some drillers to make tiny holes in the bark so they could be tied to the frame. Normally, he'd have made cordage from the fibers, but he wanted to start moving down the river so he chose to use the fibers for ties without turning it first into cordage. It took three days for Blad to complete the basket boat.

"My father would have said, 'Pretty pathetic girl's work,' or something equally as deprecating," he said out loud. Looking at his boat, he said, "Now I'm going to put you over the embers of the fire to dry out. All I need you to do is take me down the river and out of this land safely."

Blad placed the basket boat over the fire embers and lay down. He was hungry and tired. He went black. When he awakened, Blad turned the basket boat over and felt the clay where he'd coated the inside of the boat. It was dry. He turned the boat back over, thinking to keep the clear night's dew from moistening what he'd carefully dried. He'd wait until morning to use the boat.

When morning came, Blad ate as many buds of the plants he'd already eaten as possible. Then, he put the boat in the water and it seemed to hold off water's entry. He didn't fool himself; a hit against a rock could easily break his bark and clay liner—probably the boat itself.

Blad began his float down the river. He went faster, he thought, than he had on the log. He also turned in circles because the boat was, after all, a basket. He had a pole to push the boat along or away from rocks.

He thought he had made much progress the first day. As night approached, he poled his boat to the side of the river and stepped out. Blad noticed a few small cracks in the clay and some water in the bottom of the boat. He took his fire starter and then turned the boat upside down to dry out.

Blad noticed he was obviously losing weight. He needed real food. The walls of the river were still high but they had reduced in size. Blad studied the walls near him. He looked for a way to reach the top. He couldn't see anything that appeared promising. Blad hoped another day on the river would bring the walls lower down or at least give him a way to climb out. He looked carefully for anything to eat. There was nothing available. Finally, he ran his hands through the river wondering whether there were fish in the water, though he'd certainly seen no evidence of fish and found nothing. Blad took a deep drink of water and curled up under the boat to go black.

He continued down the river. The river walls, he noticed, were decreasing rapidly in height. Blad was delighted. He gained hope once the sun reached the water for more than a very brief time. The boat too was taking on water. By high sun, the walls were low enough that Blad poled the boat over to the shore and pulled it out of the water. He felt terribly tired.

Blad walked to the wall and examined it well. By chance he looked to his left and noticed just beyond him was a great tree. He ran to the tree, jumped to catch a branch, and swung himself into the limbs of the tree. After a bit of a climb, Blad had a view of the land surrounding the river. It was flat with hills in the distance. Using the tree, he could climb to the land above.

Best of all, there were grazing animals just above the river. Blad climbed back down the tree. He knew what he needed to do. First, he needed to make a few snares to catch some small animals to eat. Then, he needed to create a very basic tool kit. Blad felt that he'd made a successful escape and would ultimately find people—people he hoped were normal people, if such a thing existed.

Blad made some cordage, not his best ever, but serviceable. He climbed the wall using the tree as a brace along one part of the climb. He looked carefully for anything that resembled an animal trail. Finding one, he looked for a likely place to tie the snare. He found several. Blad went a different direction and found a few more places to set his shares. In all he set six snares.

By nightfall, Blad found he had two successful rabbit snares. He carried them back downhill and eventually had them cooking over a good sized fire. He could smell the delightful savor and his stomach grumbled in anticipation. When they were ready, Blad ate slowly. At one point he said aloud, "Mother Earth, Father Sky, Pale-Faced Moon, Water, Hearth Fire—thank you from the farthest reaches of my spirit. You saved my life."

He sank down on the sand and looked up at the sky. It was a clear night with countless stars. Blad had a sense of expectation that all would be well. He sat up, pulled the boat to him, and lifted it over his head. He did not wish to awaken damp with the morning's dew.

Blad awakened as someone lifted his boat over him and laid it to the side.

"Who are you?" the man with long braids asked.

Blad placed his hand on his chest and said, "Blad." Then he pointed at the other man.

"Moc," the man said, placing his hand on his chest.

Neither understood any words from the other. Blad knew he had the need to learn the language of the other man. By hand signs and endless questions, Blad finally after some days could communicate in the most basic language of the Luphac. He felt a sense of relief.

Moc was greatly concerned for Blad when he first found him. The man was starving. He learned that Blad was from somewhere called across-the-eastern-sea. He didn't understand that. He learned that Blad had been captured by the Alu. Moc knew the Alu were fierce people who didn't want anyone on their territory. He was surprised that Blad escaped, until he heard how Blad had done it.

Surely the Alu would have known that likelihood of survival in that canyon would have been impossible. That Blad survived at all impressed Moc.

Moc wanted to take Blad to his village, but he knew the man needed some food before he could travel. Moc spent time supplying food and comfort to the man. He also taught him how to do basic communication in his language.

Within a moon of Moc's intended return home, Initu and Ampers had tracked down Moc, happy to know he was well. They were astounded that Blad had escaped the Alu, gone over the falls, and made a boat to carry himself down the river. They were appalled that the man had no fat on his bones. Considering the situation, however, the fact that the man was alive was awe inspiring.

Sitting around the fire that night, Ampers asked Blad, "How long were you with the Alu?"

Blad replied, "Two sets of full seasons."

Ampers didn't understand, so Moc translated.

"What are the Alu like?" Initu asked.

"They are unstable in all their thoughts," Blad replied, signing the word unstable. "They find people and eat them. Alu don't know right or wrong. They are a people waiting to die. They are empty people, incapable of thinking, incapable of reason. They are utterly without caring for others."

"How did you survive?"

"They tie captives to trees—arms up, legs down. They strip off all clothing. When their chief saw my scars, he asked how I received them. I told him my father. My father was tied next to me. The chief told them to cut me down. He made me part of them. He gave me a horrible name, Endured Pain. I had to live with that name for eight seasons. But, I was permitted to live. If at any point I had done anything they disapproved, they'd have killed me. They are utterly unmoved by the piteous cries of captives. When people die, they make food called tough bird stew. It is human flesh. Everyone eats it. It's despicable! I survived. I waited to reach a river to take me away from them. When I saw the waterfall upriver, I leaped over the falls."

"You are lucky," Initu said with stress on the last word.

"Mother Earth and Father Sky protected me, I think," Blad said, "But I'd rather have died than continue a prisoner of the Alu."

Moc said, "Tonight we must rest. Tomorrow we leave for home."

The four men stretched out to sleep. Ampers had a spare sleeping skin which he gave to Blad. Blad thanked him. Moc had given him an extra skin to use, but it didn't fully cover him. He scooped up some sand and made an elevated shape that he could cover with the sleeping skin and lay his head upon. Blad pulled the skin over his shoulder and went black.

The next morning they began their trek to the home of the Luphac people. On the trek, Blad felt at home for the first time in his life. He felt relaxed among these people, not having a felt need to guard every word, every facial expression. His facility with the language grew rapidly. At night they'd share stories, Blad about the SealEaters and their trip across the sea and learning the new land, the Luphac people about their customs and events.

When they reached the Luphac main village, there was a huge welcome. People came from all over to greet them. Blad had never felt so welcome, so accepted. There were the usual welcomes, the feast, the sharing of stories. This time, however, Moc asked if he could tell the story for Blad, since he'd had to tell it so often already. He told Blad if he said something wrong to let him know and he'd fix it.

Blad was delighted, since he was new to the language. Moc told the story, every once in a while looking into his sister, Ammatoshi's, eyes as if speaking without words. He wanted her to know that he spoke of a man of whom he approved with great esteem.

Ammatoshi understood the message from her brother. He had urged her to find a husband, and she had declined every possibility he put forth. This new man did capture her interest.

When he finished, Moc told Ammatoshi to prepare a place for Blad in their home. She raised an eyebrow, stood, turned, and went to carry out his request.

Blad was exhausted from the trek. He asked to lie down. He needed to go black badly. Moc led him to his place, and by the time they arrived, his place inside was set. The girl had put out a bottom sleeping skin of soft fur and a soft hide for a top sleeping skin.

The next day, Ammatoshi asked Blad, "Will you go with me to gather some greens. I know that's not what you would think manly, but I would like to hear more of your story from you, not my brother."

"Of course," Blad agreed. "I have no spear. I need to make some."

"What kind of points do you prefer?" she asked.

"I love beautiful flint."

"I will take you to our best flint source, then," she said, "We can do both. We will take two baskets. And here are my two spears."

Blad enjoyed her gentle sense of arranging the day. He was shocked that her spear was the same as a man's spear. He wasn't impressed with the spear point.

They left and he felt the freedom again of not having to check for permission with the Alu to go where he wanted and with whom. He breathed deeply and enjoyed the sense of liberty.

"We do have to go through this narrow opening to reach the flint source, Blad. Give me your hand, it's slippery." Blad started to assure her he was just fine, but he gave her his hand instead, because he wanted to touch hers. It was good that he did, for he slipped, and she helped him avoid falling into the water. The algae on the rocks in the spring that exited from the opening they had to pass through was indeed slippery.

"It's beautiful," Blad observed as they entered the area where the flint was. There was a natural wall through which they passed and a lovely grassy area beyond the supply of flint. Ammatoshi went to sit on the grass to enjoy the sun while Blad gathered flint. His enjoyment of beauty was a significant thing to her. So many of the people she knew never saw beauty.

Blad gathered numbers of rock nodules. He sought fairly large ones. The bag would be heavy and he had no idea how far he would have to transport it. For the moment, however, he was overjoyed to be able to find materials to make his spear points. He gathered as much as he thought the bag could safely hold.

Ammatoshi watched him. He was so strong, so intent on what he did. He had great appeal to her. His scent sent thrills through her, something she'd never experienced. She enjoyed being close to him. She liked watching him select the right rocks.

After Blad finished filling the basket, he joined her in the sun. They locked eyes for a moment, neither wishing to break the hold.

"What was that?" Ammatoshi asked before thinking whether she should ask.

"Beauty," Blad replied and kissed her. She was utterly compelling in his thinking place.

They lay together on the grass, locked in embrace. Neither taking it farther, but neither wanting to end the simple embrace.

"I think I'm falling in love with you, Ammatoshi, and I don't even know you," Blad said, shocked at his own behavior.

"I'm having exactly the same feeling, Blad. I've been seeking you ever since I became a woman, not knowing you were so far away."

"Your words pierce my spirit, for I too have dared to dream of you."

Ammatoshi held him tight to her chest. He had had a terrible life. "I am so sorry to have asked you such a thoughtless question, Blad."

"When you speak words to me from your mouth, dear Ammatoshi, I am blessed. Your words are not thoughtless. I receive each as a genuine gift."

"Your special way of speaking draws me, Blad. It draws me as a moth to a flame at night."

"I hope, dear Ammatoshi, that if you carry out that image, it won't happen."

They both laughed. So many moths were found in the morning dead by the oil lamp.

"I certainly didn't think that one through." They laughed more.

"Come now, you wanted to gather some greens. I'll help."

They stood up and walked through the opening in the rock by the spring. They held hands and no one slipped. They went to a lower level on the hill where there were many greens of various types. They filled the basket quickly.

"When we return, since we have accomplished the task so quickly, I'll take you the long way home. Look down here and you can see the way we wound through the forest to reach this place."

"I see it."

"Now, Blad, look to our right. You can see the path through the separation in the tops of trees if you look carefully. We'll pass a lovely lake and there are views of the hills that are beautiful." Ammatoshi grinned at her use of the word beautiful.

"I do see it. It's quite a bit longer, and I suspect quite a bit different on the ground than trying to imagine it through the tree tops."

Ammatoshi smiled. They walked toward the longer path.

When they reached the lake, both knew they'd swim. Neither said a word, but both removed their skin clothing and entered the water. The water was warm and refreshing. They swam about and then towards each other. For a brief time the two were lost in each other. Time and place were irrelevant. Then the spell was broken and they left the water to put their clothes back on and return to the village. Neither had said a word, but they both knew in their own ways that destiny had brought them together forever.

Moc came to meet them when they arrived back at the village. One look at Ammatoshi's face, and he knew. Ammatoshi glanced at him, and she knew he knew. Both smiled a slow happy smile.

"What are you planning to make with the stones?" Moc asked Blad.

"Spear points. Then, I'll have to make shafts. I left all my tools with the Alu so as to escape."

"Of course. I have about six shafts already made, Blad. Help yourself to them."

"Where are they?" Blad asked, delighted, for he didn't care for shaft making.

"Follow me. I'll show you and you can take two of them now."

Blad followed and Moc let him choose the two shafts he wanted. One at a time Blad lifted them, weighed them, stood as if to use them, and carefully positioned his hand around them. He chose two. Moc found his choice interesting, for he did not choose the ones Moc preferred. He seemed to be communicating with something in the feel of the shaft Moc didn't understand. He didn't ask.

Blad was delighted with the stones. Ammatoshi gave him some leather pieces he wanted. Blad lined the basket after removing the stones. He put a piece of leather in his lap that would catch the little flakes to send them down the chute to collect in the basket. Flint knappers were interested in what Blad was doing. The chute for collecting flaked off pieces in the basket would save many feet from cuts. A few watched surreptitiously to avoid impolitely staring.

Blad worked the first stone so that he could begin to see the point within. He began to hammer it with a small stone he'd picked up at the flint site. Ammatoshi stopped by and he asked whether there were any antler horns available. She brought him three. He chose two of them.

"Thank you. This will make it so much easier," he told her.

He worked the stone. Suddenly, flint knappers realized he was making something they'd never seen. It was huge. A few overcame their natural polite distance and asked if they could watch. Blad told them he'd be happy for them to watch. He kept his rhythm going, removing flake after flake, the large thin point beginning to make its appearance. He tapped the stone and tapped it. The more he worked the more fascinated the villagers became.

"When you have your spear points made, will you teach me to do that?" Initu asked.

"Me too," Ampers asked.

"I'd also like to learn," Moc said.

"I'd be delighted to share this technique with you," he told them.

Silence again surrounded the tapping of the antler on the beautiful brownish colored flint. The observers were shocked at the thinness of the stone.

"It would be easy to break one of them at this point, hey?" Initu asked.

Blad looked up and nodded, "Very," he replied.

He continued working and the questions ceased. No one wanted to ask a question and cause a spear point break. Finally, as the sun began to sink, the spear point was finished. The Luphac people had held the evening meal until the spear point was finished. Blad looked up from his work. He hadn't realized the passage of time.

"Have you held the evening meal until now because of me?" he asked, shocked.

"Yes, of course," Womna assured him. "It has been a long time since something so interesting has captured our attention. Come, let's eat."

"May I examine it?" Moc asked.

"Of course," Blad told him. He handed the spear point to Moc and went to have something to eat.

Moc was fascinated with the point. It had a sense of strength that the shape belied. He was eager to see it used.

Ampers and Initu both came to examine the spear point. Both were awed by the size, shape, and beauty of the point. They placed it carefully beside Blad where he sat near Ammatoshi. Blad noticed it.

An old woman came over to Blad. He looked up into blue eyes.

"I have sinew and glue. Any time you want, you call for me. I am Ana. I bring you what you need to finish."

Blad was touched. "Thank you Ana. How about first thing after the morning meal?"

"I will have it ready for you," she said and smiled showing many missing teeth and a lovely full spirit.

That evening, Blad asked Ammatoshi what was required for him to take her as wife.

"First, you have to ask me."

They both laughed.

"I said yes. Then you have to ask Moc."

"Moc? Not the chief?"

"No, it's a family thing. My father died, so Moc is where you must go to ask permission."

"If he agrees, then what?"

"Then, he'll announce it to the people here. We share a sleeping place that night."

"It's that easy?"

"Or hard."

The two burst out laughing.

"When should I ask?"

"How about now?"

"Will you come with me?"

"Of course."

He gave her a hand to help her up.

They approached Moc. "Oh, what a surprise! This soon, huh? Well, you have a positive answer," he said with a smile. Then, he made the announcement.

Blad and Ammatoshi lived for forty-four more years in more happiness than either knew was possible. They had twelve children who all lived past childhood. Their grandchildren were many. Blad and Ammatoshi were both killed by a rockslide at the lake where they had gone to recreate their first day together. Blad was seventy-one and Ammatoshi was sixty-five.

Chapter 10

Urch and Wapa's Story

The SealEaters arrived back at the place where they first touched land after their initial travel across the sea. Indigenous people from the warmer mid-Atlantic region, where they'd once been welcomed, had chased them from their native land after Reg had terribly offended them. The SealEaters who gathered there had no idea where Vaima, Emuka, Murke, Plak, Torq, and Akla were.

When they would leave the cache point this time, Urch decided to go south—only farther south this time. Since that's the direction from which they had just come, some thought his decision odd, but said nothing. Urch sought warmth for the SealEaters. He'd seen enough of the north and middle part of this land. It was an improvement over the Cove, but it was cold. Torq and Plak had already gone west. Mongwire and Wen in one group and Reg, Blad, and Maber in another group planned to explore the more northern ice-free zone. The remnant of the explorers still remained at the cache site, preparing for their last exploration before crossing back to the Cove. Urch felt it was too cold at the cache site northern location. He thought the SealEaters would appreciate more warmth. Urch definitely wanted warmth. Wapa decided to go with Urch when the older man announced his decision to go south. He didn't want Urch to go alone and he didn't want to be part of either of the other groups. Warmth sounded good to him.

They still had some seal oil, and since he'd turned the boat over the night before to dry it out, Urch began to apply seal oil to his boat skin. He knew that to keep the boat waterproof, it was necessary. It also kept the boat skin soft, not to mention that it was wonderful for his hands.

Mongwire and Wen had already left as evening came. Reg, Blad, and Maber had a deer to finish preparing for their trek. Urch and Wapa decided to leave even though it was becoming dark. They knew the water way, and the sky was free of clouds. Both were glad to leave Reg and his empty prideful mouth behind.

It took a while to row out to the sea. In the quiet of the sea Urch thought of Kol. He had trouble bringing her face to his thinking place. He remembered the lovely black hair, but his memory of the image of her face had faded. Urch was shocked. He remembered the last day they spent together in the forest. He remembered so much, but her face had disappeared. Urch rowed harder, as if by extra effort he might compensate in one area for what he felt he'd lost in another.

They had wonderful weather. A few great chunks of ice were floating in the sea water just east of them, towering mountainous islands in the water. It reminded Urch of the two sea crossings they'd have to make to bring their people to this land. At least it was not yet. Urch and Wapa could reach land in a very quick time traveling as they did now.

After many days they passed the mouth of the river that led to the place where they'd been chased away. Wapa turned around in the boat and looked at Urch.

He said, "I don't suppose you want to go up that one?"

Both laughed, remembering how they'd been chased away from that river.

"I can begin to feel the warmth," Urch replied. "I want more warmth than this."

"The sun does feel good on my skin," Wapa agreed.

Off to their right the marsh was already busy. In the distance they could see a small number of mammoths in the grasses shared by shore birds. Great white birds and other great ones, gray in color, stood on long legs. Little ones flew about, sometimes overflying them as if curious. There were two horses and some other animals too far away to identify clearly, but they were noticeable.

For days more they continued to travel. The increased warmth was becoming more obvious, evidenced by their sweat. They rowed into the mouth of a large river that seemed to head to the northwest, and they went slightly upriver to find a sandy spot they agreed would be a good place for the night. A large wide spreading tree grew at the place casting shade in an area devoid of other trees. Wapa took some of the cordage and tied the boat by the carved seal head to the tree. It would not be good to lose the boat as they went black, something both thought out carefully every time they stopped.

Urch had created sleeping places in the lowest branches against the trunk of the massive tree. For comfort, he placed the sleeping skins across the thick branches, which were fully wide enough for going black. He was convinced that with tidal changes, in the tree was preferable to below the tree.

"This is the last of the jerky," Wapa said, bringing two pieces to Urch and keeping two for himself. "We're going to have to do some hunting. We need to replenish our supply."

"Let's go upriver tomorrow to see whether this place seems good," Urch said. He was sufficiently older that he could have ordered it, but there was no need for that. Wapa did as much of the work as he did. Urch did not consider himself superior in any way.

"Good," Wapa replied, scooping water from the river. "Oh, awful! It still has too much salt in it."

Urch laughed. "It takes traveling a lot farther upriver before water is fit to drink in this place," he said with a smile. "We still have plenty don't we?"

"Of course. I was just trying to take the easy way."

Urch pulled himself up into the tree. They'd left the singularly evergreen forests long ago. There were pines here, but the trees that lost leaves in winter were beginning more and more to mingle among the evergreens. The night noises were becoming greater the further south they traveled.

Urch and Wapa had decided as they traveled to try to notice where changes occurred. They'd validate their findings as they traveled back north to meet the others for their return.

The next morning they gathered their sleeping skins and untied the boat. They were ready to row upriver to see what they might find in this place. For days and days they rowed through marsh land. That was no surprise. It had been the way this land was all along the coast. It was flat for a long way before anything like hills arose. Day after day they traveled on. They stayed with the main river instead of going into the branches off to the sides. After a moon of travel, they came to a bend in the river beyond which lay a substantial hill. They beached the boat, tied it to a big log, and climbed the hill.

To their surprise they found a chert supply. It was clear that others came here, for there were hearths left in several places, and some people had been working the chert into tools at this location. The two men were hungry for what they called real meat after their recent diet mainly of waterfowl. They gathered their spears and walked on dry land, not marsh land into the pine forest. After traveling for a long time, they heard trumpeting. It came from mastodons in the forest. They stealthily approached the location from which the trumpeting had come.

"Thank you, Mother Earth!" Urch whispered. He'd seen a mother mastodon with two small ones. One would be sufficient, he knew. Urch and Wapa made an immediate shift from words. Each spoke with his eyes and head movements. They walked carefully on the pine needles, keeping utterly silent. Finally, Urch and Wapa sent spears into one of the baby mastodons. It screamed and its mother came to its rescue, but she could find no way to help the little one. She watched as his life left, lamenting the death. She was distraught, and she nuzzled the dead twin with her trunk, while the living twin walked about in circles.

For two days the men had to wait, for the adult mammoth had no intention of leaving. Finally, they decided to make her leave and began to poke her. She became angry at the irritation, but after half a day, when they began to poke the other little one, the female mastodon rapidly turned and left with the remaining twin following. It took two trips, to take the meat to their camp. Then, they quickly set up a structure of wind fallen tree trunks that would suffice to smoke the mammoth meat to turn much of it to jerky. They also had a feast that night of *real meat*.

After the meat had been smoked and jerky stored in their backpacks, Urch and Wapa began to explore the area for a good site for a future home. They discovered along the way that wider waters had larger trees and more variety. Along the narrower waterways there were occasional swamps, some scrub trees, and in some brackish locations there were giant lizards that lay on the banks of the river sunning themselves. They would also swim in the water. They had seen these giant lizards eat large animals such as horses and they appeared to be very strong and have formidable jaws. Since the giant lizards were about half the length of their boat, they didn't want to have their boat capsize, when these giants were in the water. Urch and Wapa were curious as to whether these giant lizards were good food.

Urch and Wapa had, as SealEaters did whenever they remained in one place for any time, set up a measuring device that told them when the days would lengthen and shorten. That was the only way they'd know when to meet at the cache as well as have helpful information especially for those living where it became very cold in winter. Urch noticed that the days were shortening somewhat. It wasn't as significant as it had been at the Cove, but there was a difference he could feel without checking his measuring points.

He and Wapa had set up a place where they had a commanding view of the river. Neither had hunted the forest and fished the river. They had not tried the giant lizard as food, but had an increasing curiosity about it. They sat at the large fire that night, enjoying some rabbit and greens.

"I think we should go further south just to see what it's like there. This place is obviously a good place for our people, but we should know what or who is around us, should we not?"

"I agree with you, Wapa. We have plenty of jerky to last us for a long time. If you'd like to leave in the morning, I'm ready. It would be good to know what else is in this place."

By morning they were enthusiastically preparing to leave when two people, apparently indigenous, walked to their camp.

Urch went to greet them with a skin in his hand. He took the hand with the skin and put his fist against his chest. "Urch," he said.

Wapa, arriving moments later did the same thing, calling out his name slowly.

The strangers stood there, and finally one said, "Modoma."

The other announced, "Modulamet."

Using signs, Modulamet indicated they came from a moon's distance upriver. He signed for them to tell their origin.

Urch waved them to follow. In the sand he drew an image of the river. He showed the coast line north. He tried to convey to them the idea of ice and the sea and wondered how successful that would be. Urch said the word SealEaters several times, pointing to both of them. The two men quickly reasoned that these strangers did not come from local areas, and they lost interest but listened.

Modoma noticed Urch's spear point. He was curious how it was made. They all sat. Urch sat with a piece of chert from the supply site downriver. It took a long time, but Urch flaked a spear point and handed it to Modoma. Modoma started to return it, and Urch indicated he could have it. He didn't want it back. Modoma was clearly amazed. Then, Modulamet wanted one. Urch dutifully made the second spear point. The man took it with great delight. They went on their way after leaving Urch and Wapa with a necklace made of snail shells drilled and attached to a narrow leather strip that tied around the neck. Urch gave the necklace to Wapa.

After they had gone, using the path that lined the side of the river across from them, Wapa and Urch finished packing their boat and left to go downriver to explore areas more southern than this one.

Once they reached the sea and traveled for about a moon, they saw a very different land. In this one, the pines had excessively long needles. There was a strange gray moss that adhered to trees and appeared to drip from the tree limbs. Bugs and noise had increased over what they had at their new place. The landscape became fascinating and yet they both felt a sense of foreboding.

As they trekked inland, they crossed forests with deciduous trees and evergreens. Lianas were frequent sights, growing from the forest floor and wrapping themselves in the tops of trees. Wapa climbed one of the woody vines and discovered it would hold his weight. They came across springs with crystal clear water around which scrub trees grew. They saw no giant lizards in the places where the springs were. Spanish moss decorated many trees.

"The clarity of this water is amazing and it tastes good."

"I agree, Urch. I've never seen anything like this. Look at that eel. It's huge!"

"And look at those fish!"

Walking back to the small river they'd traveled, they climbed into their boat to continue.

"What in the world of Mother Earth is that?" Wapa asked forgetting that his use of the expression might offend Urch.

Urch looked into the clear water, moss catching his head as he leaned to find a better view. "It looks like a very poorly made seal," he decided.

They laughed as they looked at the animal. "There are more!" Wapa said with enthusiasm.

The animal surfaced and looked questioningly at the two men. It then slipped back in the water to continue grazing.

"Let's catch the little one to see how they taste," Urch said. "It seems as it is with seals—you have to wait for them to come up for air."

Wapa scrambled looking for the harpoon they used on the sea voyage for seals. He checked it to be sure it was in good order, and then he stood in the boat ready to thrust.

"Here comes the very little one," Urch whispered.

Wapa was ready. He thrusted and secured a good hit and discovered that the little one could thrash around quite a lot. Both were surprised for the strange seals seemed so docile. The small animal headed upstream, pulling the boat after it. Finally, it tired and surfaced. Urch took the bone they used on seals and hit the animal in the head. It took all the strength the men had to pull the smallest of these creatures into the boat. They came close to capsizing twice.

They decided to find a place to camp and retreated back to a good beach they'd passed earlier. They pulled the boat up and dumped the creature on the sand. It landed on its belly. Wapa quickly started a fire. He was eager for something other than jerky. Urch sliced the animal down its back and peeled the skin from the side toward the belly, revealing dark almost purple meat. He cut off a hunk and handed it to Wapa.

While Urch worked on the creature, Wapa started a fire and pulled up two logs for them to sit on to cook and eat the meat.

When Urch brought the meat over, neither could wait. They each took a hunk of meat, cut it in smaller pieces, and skewered it onto a peeled tree limb which they held over the fire. As it cooked they salivated from the smell.

"By the hairs on the chin of Father Sky," Wapa laughed juice running through his beard to land ungracefully on his knee, "This is good. This is better than good!"

"It is good!" Urch agreed. "Wapa, you need to remember that even though you've heard people speak of the gods that way, it's not wise."

"I'm sorry, Urch. I'll control it. I was just astounded that something so ugly could taste so good."

"Are you starting to think what I'm thinking?"

"You mean this might be a better place to have our new home?"

"Yes. This land is full of food, and then, there's this strange river seal!"

Later, Urch rolled the creature on its side and continued to butcher. The meat on the underside was different in color. Urch wondered whether it tasted different because of the color. He would discover the answer to that the next morning.

In the morning, Urch tried the light meat. It didn't taste any different to him than the other meat. Both were amazingly good.

He and Wapa stayed in the location until they'd made jerky of most of the meat and eaten their fill. They did decide to go back to the place above the chert supply on the big river, for winter was coming. They felt they were well provisioned, and that location was exceptional.

As they rowed back, they chatted about the best and worst features of both places. It was significantly warmer in the land of the strange seal-like creature. The environment was more pleasant and more comfortable for temperature by the big river. For once they had found a place they considered too hot. Both knew they could make hunting trips to the far south land to harpoon this odd river seal that tasted so good.

While discussing the virtues of the southern land, Urch began to itch unmercifully.

"I'm going crazy with this itching," he told Wapa. "It's been going on for a while now. I want to know what is on me! Will you look to see what you can find?"

Wapa looked at the back of Urch's leg. "Looks like lots of raw places, little sores. Wait, there's an extremely tiny red bug. There's another. Let me take it off. Don't claw at that place, the skin's all broken, Urch. You could cause it to make pus if you're not careful."

"You have anything for itching?" He asked.

"Let me see what's in this bag my father prepared for me." Wapa returned with the bag. Before he opened it, he said, "Wait, I remember. Let's gather some clay from down here by the river. I'll put some of that on the broken skin and tie a leather strip around it until it dries. It'll draw out the itch. Leave it on until the clay dries. Let me put some on and then I'll tie a strip of leather over it until it dries." During the return trip, Urch would need numbers of applications of clay. He took care of it himself, since he'd learned what to do. Wrapping the leather strip around his upper leg and tying it around his waist was simple.

Back at the big river camp, Wapa and Urch built a stronger storage place for their meat. They chose taller trees and leaned them together to make as much room inside as possible. They constructed a horizontal rack on which to lay the meat so it would have air circulating. Both were almost fanatical about keeping rain out, so they did everything they could possibly think to keep the storage area rain free.

"Hoah," someone called.

Urch and Wapa quickly turned around and saw six men standing behind them. They wore the same style braids as the two other men they had met earlier. Urch reflected that for only two men, they had become lax in watching out for others, since there'd been only the two former visitors. Urch was undone at their lack of wisdom.

Urch put his hand on his chest, "Urch."

Wapa introduced himself.

Each of the others did likewise: Micuit, Tolpurk, Wemetering, Cannta, Utteal, Glatehut. Urch and Wapa were overwhelmed with the names, remembering none of them.

Cannta pointed to the spear tips and signed he wanted Urch and Wapa to join them in their boat to go upstream.

Urch signed his unwillingness. Utteal raised his spear. Cannta gave Utteal a stern look, and Utteal rested his spear back on its end.

Urch stood his ground. He indicated he'd teach them there, but not go with them. Wapa copied Urch's stances, and stood with his forearms parallel to the ground, across his chest, feet at a wider than normal stance, stern face.

Urch was observing every move. It seemed to him they didn't have authority from whoever sent them to bring them back by force, or they'd have done it. They seemed confused as to what to do. He signed for them to go home.

Cannta, the one who appeared to be in charge, was clearly not prepared for Urch's dismissal. He conferred with Micuit. They shook their spears at Urch and Wapa, but they returned to their dugout, boarded, and began to row upstream.

Urch felt the confrontation would likely bring more of the same. There was something about their spears that the men wanted to know. Urch decided it was past time for them to set up a night watch.

"How'd you know to do what you did?" Wapa asked.

"I didn't, Wapa. I didn't want to go with them. I don't like the idea of anyone arriving here and telling us what to do. It appeared to me they were sent by someone who hadn't given them permission to use force or injure us. After I pushed back, they didn't keep pursuing. I guessed my assumption was right, and I just pressed it with more strength. I am certain, however, this isn't the end of it. I think they'll return. They want something. I think it's to learn how to make our spears. We need to be tough with these men, not show fear, but not be unreasonable either. It'll be a careful progress we need to make. I will eventually make it clear that we have more people coming. If we are to bring our people here, they need to respect us."

"All that was passing through your thinking place while they were here?"

"Yes, and another fact. We need to start a night watch."

"I agree. I'll take it first tonight."

"Very well."

That night and many that followed were uneventful, but the men felt better for doing it. A moon later, almost at the winter solstice, three men came back from upstream in a smaller dugout. Three men—all had been there once before.

Cannta, Micuit, and Wemetering approached them, no spears in their hands, with a much more pleasant attitude.

Urch walked over to them. Wapa quickly backed him up.

"What is it?" he asked Cannta, convinced the man had no idea what he said.

"We start bad last time. We want better," he said.

Urch's mouth literally opened with no words coming forth.

"I learn your words Vaima at village there," he said pointing to the north

"I hear my words from your mouth," Urch said humbled somehow that the man would want to communicate badly enough to do what he'd done.

"Vaima your friend our friend. You no have bad man here. We want you visit Hoomuhu. Our land. Our chief wants. We friend like friend Vaima."

"Make picture where Hoomuhu is." Urch showed him how to draw in sand with the end of his spear and drew big waves and said, "Sea." He drew the river with the curves as they were. Urch said, "River," tracing the river and handed the spear to Cannta.

Cannta took it, while both men accompanying him looked on in wonder. They had no idea what was taking place. For a long time Cannta stared at the drawing Urch made.

Cannta drew haltingly the continuation of the river. At one place, he pushed the end of the spear shaft into the sand. "This Hoomuhu," he said.

"You have done well, Cannta." Urch said. "How long to reach Hoomuhu?"

"Not whole day."

"We come before new leaves open."

Clearly, Cannta hoped to hear a better answer, but he received an answer, and he would report that answer. The three men bowed slightly at the waist. The two men returned the gesture. Cannta, Micuit, and Wemetering left.

Wapa was again trying to understand.

"Why did you make the time for us to come so long from now?" he asked.

"I want them to know that we are doing what's best for us, not jumping to serve their desires. But I want them to know we want to be friends. Make sense now?"

"Yes," he said with some doubt.

"I plan for us to go there long before the buds open, Wapa, but I want to reserve the right to carry it that long."

"I see," he said and did.

"Cannta's chief will probably understand what I do."

"You think he will?"

"Yes, for some reason I cannot explain, and I think he will understand and respect us."

Wapa had always thought Urch was worthy of respect, but today and recently his respect for this man had risen much higher. Urch was unaware of the way the younger man felt. He knew Wapa was only twenty-two years of age while he was now forty-five. Age, somehow, had ceased to be anything of importance to Urch since he passed his twenties.

"I think you are a wise man," Wapa said.

Urch looked at him sideways. "Wait, Wapa, return to that thought when we return from the Hoomuhu." He laughed.

Wapa looked at him, realized what he'd said, and joined the laughter.

Urch felt the need for greens, so he went for a trek through the wooded area to see what he could find. Most of the greens he sought lay in the sun, just outside the treed area. He gathered many, carrying them back carefully and took them to the river to let the water wash off anything he might not wish to eat. Urch had found some tubers and dug them up. He held them between his hands and cleaned off the dirt.

While Urch gathered the greens, Wapa took the boat and went up a nearby stream. He pulled the boat up and tied it to a tree. Wapa carried a bag. He went to the edges of the stream and began to feel around with his fingers in the leafy debris. One at a time, he pulled large humpbacked crayfish from the water and slipped them into the bag. When he had enough, he took the bag to the boat, put the boat in the stream, and returned to the camp. They would eat well that night.

Urch had made a fire, and he laid a few large leafed greens on a log. He knew where Wapa had gone since the boat was missing and also knew they'd eat well that night. Sure enough, Wapa arrived back, bag in hand.

"How many'd you find?" Urch asked, eager to eat.

"Forty to fifty," Wapa replied, knowing this was one of Urch's favorite foods from this area.

"Ah, I can't wait!"

"Want a raw one?" Wapa teased.

"I'll wait," Urch said.

Wapa took the crayfish from the bag one at a time and laid it on the leaf to pull off anything that wasn't part of the animal. He placed the cleaned ones into a different bag.

"Forty-eight," he called to Urch as he put the last one in the new bag.

"You have the stones ready?" Urch called back.

"Yes! Ready to go," Wapa said in a raised voice returning from the river with water in the bag. He hooked the bag on a piece of their home where a limb had broken off a tree trunk. He took tongs and put a rock in the bag which instantly set the water to boil. He added another rock. Then, another.

Finally, Wapa said the words for which Urch waited, "It's ready!"

The two men carried their bowls filled with greens to the bag and filled their bowls with crayfish. They carried their bowls to the river's edge and sat. Both began to eat, holding the carapaces and separating them from the tails. They sucked the tails from the shells. All pieces that were not consumed were tossed to the river. Occasionally they'd take a piece of the greens to eat, savoring the crawfish juice that the greens retained.

A moon passed when early one morning Urch said, "I think it time to visit the Hoomuhu."

"I wondered when that time would come," Wapa replied.

"It's here," Urch told him.

They gathered their spears, water bags, and backpacks with sleeping skins. They entered the boat and began to row.

A while after high sun, a village appeared on the right. The village was placed to see well whether anyone came upriver. By the time they reached the village, people were gathered to welcome them. It was a very exciting time for the village.

Cannta came to greet them with a large smile.

Urch noted that he was a different man in his own village. Urch had a fleeting moment of thought that for some reason he may have intimidated the young man.

Cannta led Urch and Wapa to Chief Backtament. They were seated and Cannta prepared to translate.

The chief said, "I welcome you to our home. We would be friends. We can teach you about our land. You can teach us to make large spear points."

Cannta translated.

"Thank you, Chief," Urch said. "There is much we would learn of this land. We are pleased to teach you large spear point making."

Cannta translated.

"I invite you to stay for the rest of this cold season with us. Learn our languages. When the new leaves spring from their buds, you will return to your place and we will be friends. We do not hold you against your will. To learn a language you must live with the language. We offer you a good place to stay and food to eat. You can learn our food here. Also plants to eat and to heal. We hope that you bring young men and women who want to find people as wives or husbands."

Cannta translated sentence by sentence.

Urch listened. He understood the great offer the chief made. He turned to Wapa and said quietly, "I'm inclined to accept."

"I agree," Wapa said.

"Your offer is a very kind one, Chief," Urch said, "We accept. You have much to teach us and we, too, have things to teach. We have left much jerky at our home and are concerned about it."

Cannta translated.

The chief said, "I'll send two of my trusted men. They'll transport your jerky in skins to this place. We will put it in the place we have put aside for you. No one here will touch it or eat of it. Whenever you wish to leave, you are free to leave and to take the food and all your things with you."

Cannta translated.

"Cannta, how do you say, 'thank you,' in your language?"

Cannta told him.

Urch thanked the chief in his language.

There was no need for translation.

The chief told Cannta to show Urch and Wapa to their home in Hoomuhu.

Urch looked about as Cannta led them to their temporary residence. The village was amazingly well kept. Where some places had pieces of food lying about on the ground until either the dogs or ants took care of it, the grounds at Hoomuhu were clean. There was nothing to injure the foot of a careless walker. In some places it was clear that plants had been purposely placed to grow in certain locations along with others of their kind. Some of those plants had leaves used in seasoning, Urch realized. People were not lazy, but they did not run about in the village area. They greeted each other when they met going from one place to another. It was remarkable, for Urch had seen this way of being nowhere else in his life.

Wapa was also seeing the same things and finding them remarkable, but even to him more remarkable was the young woman who looked at him with a shy smile. Her long black hair shone blue in the sun. Her pale colored eyes were striking. He had to control himself not to become lost in her as he walked behind Urch.

They reached a structure like the others made of a frame of wood bent to form an upside down U shape. The structure was covered with bundles of marsh grasses tied tightly to form the bundle and tied again to cross pieces of trees that made up the sides of the structure. Inside there were sleeping places attached to the sides of the structure. There were soft hairless skins folded on the sleeping places atop a fur that was somewhat matted. Urch bent over to touch the furred skin.

"Giant sloth," Cannta said, "They are four man-lengths tall in Hoomuhu lands. North of Hoomuhu they are about half that size. They eat plants. You leave alone. The claws on one of them—aieeeeee!"

Urch was fascinated that he'd go black on the skin of an animal he'd never seen, an animal of four man-lengths. So was Wapa, who leaned over to touch the one on his sleeping place. Wapa's thinking place was better focused since he could no longer see the girl who captivated him.

They put their things away. Cannta showed them how to use the ties to hold their spears upright beside their sleeping places so they could be seized by a single pull on one end of the tie.

Cannta led them back to the place where their boat was pulled up on the shore. He showed them a frame made of tree trunks where Urch and Wapa could turn their boat upside down to store it out of the water, dirt, or mud. They put the boat up and tied the seal head to a tree. They didn't want to permit the boat to be carried off if there were a flood. Cannta thought that a strange thing, but he didn't question them about it.

That night at the evening meal, Urch and Wapa were able to say a few words, for Cannta had been working with them all afternoon. Urch and Wapa were astonished at the array of food.

"All this—there," Cannta waved his hand to the whole area surrounding the village. "Easy gather," he said smiling.

There were crayfish, fish, other meats, greens, root vegetables, fruits of various colors, beans, squash, nuts, some small things that looked like seeds. The array was endless. For people with a limited diet for a long time, this was stupefying. The meats had been seasoned with various crushed leaves. The savor was amazing. It took a long time for Urch and Wapa to eat. They noticed that others went back for more after they finished what was in their bowls. Urch went back for more of what he thought was some kind of water-fowl. The flavoring made the meat taste delicious and unforgettable.

Urch could see in the distance two places in different directions that appeared to be lakes or ponds. Waterfowl would certainly be available there.

Urch and Wapa both went to the chief and said, "Thank you."

"Thank Buowaki, Flumhaha, and Putamoi," the chief told them.

Cannta told them he'd introduce them. They followed him and Cannta took him to where the women stood, still serving the food. Urch and Wapa thanked the women, and then asked Cannta how to say it tasted delicious. He told them. They told the women, who hid their mouths and laughed a bit. Everyone knew the men had meant to say the food was delicious, but they said the food tasted like slime. Cannta told them the word again and they said it correctly.

"It is winter now, Cannta," Urch said. I've seen no snakes recently. I haven't seen giant lizards either. Do they sleep through the winter?"

"You are free of snakes now. They sleep through the cold time. Giant lizards are called alligators. They don't sleep in cold times; they slow down in winter. Don't test them. If they've been sitting in the sun, they can be as active as in summer."

During the winter the men learned the language well. Wapa had learned from Chief Backtament the local plants names and how each could be used for seasoning food and/or for medicinal purposes. Wapa and Urch worked very hard to learn all they could, for the survival of their people might depend on it. Occasionally, Wapa was distracted by the girl. Her name was Yotuimoa. He was terribly shy and so was she, so little developed from his interest.

One day Urch asked Cannta about their first native visit, sharing that they claimed to live a moon upriver.

Cannta smiled. "Generations ago our group grew too large. We divided and came here. We are all one people, but we make better use of land and animals by splitting when we become too large."

Urch had spent time with several groups of men, teaching them to flake spear points like his. He was patient and the men learned.

One morning Micuit, Utteal, and Cannta came to invite Urch and Wapa to hunt. The two men dressed quickly and joined the group outside. Each carried two of their new spears. They had their backpacks. The men waited for the morning meal. They ate and then left. None of the men carried backpacks. Neither Urch nor Wapa felt comfortable without theirs.

They traveled to the west for half a day and then followed the bank of a narrower river that branched to the northwest. They came to a swampy place where it seemed a forest fire might have passed through. The water was blackish.

Wapa saw it first. A great alligator lay in the water, seemingly asleep.

"We are hunting alligators?" Urch asked.

"Best time to do it. They're in their slow time unless warmed by the sun. There's no sun out. The way you do it is to spear through the eye or the back of the head. It's safer to go for the back of the head, as long as you don't step in the water. There could be one under the water that you don't see," Micuit said. "You may not kill the alligator the first time. Don't fight an alligator over a spear. Spears can be replaced. These beasts will snap your leg completely off, even when they're half dead."

Urch took the challenge. He laid down his backpack and took a single spear, handing his other one to Wapa. Wapa knew to stand ready to hand him the second spear. Urch crept up on the beast. His attention was focused, honed. His muscles were tight, ready for command. The beast neither offered an eye nor the back of his head. Urch studied the animal. He touched him in the back of the front leg, trying to cause him to move in a certain way. The alligator paid him no heed. Urch poked it hard enough to break the skin. The alligator moved, eyeing him. It moved slowly, and Urch took aim. He thrust the spear at the exact spot on the alligator's head where he needed to hit it. Cannta was amazed at his accuracy. The alligator still moved slowly as if not affected at all. Urch felt Wapa hand him the second spear. He never looked at the spear or Wapa, he simply whipped it around to the position where he needed it. He thrust the spear into the alligator's left eye. He thrust hard, with as much strength as he had. The second spear thrust finished off what the first one started. Urch was elated and exhausted at the same time. He rested while Wapa retrieved his spears. The first spear point had not broken, but the second one was broken mid-way from side to side.

Urch looked at the broken point. "It's a knife now," he said. The other hunters gave him an understanding look.

Micuit carefully took some heavy cordage to make a loop. He used his spear to hold out the loop over the water, lowering the loop to go over the alligator's snout. He pulled it tight slowly, so it didn't slide off. Then all the Hoomuhu people began to pull the cordage. Urch and Wapa went to help. They managed to pull the alligator to land. There, Micuit, Cannta, and Utteal quickly skinned it. They sprinkled some salt on the skin. They cut the back meat off either side of the spine and then went to the tail, where they cut the large strip of meat from both sides of the alligator's tail. They laid the meat inside the skin, folded it around the meat, and tied it all together with cordage. The remains of the alligator went back into the water. Urch didn't miss a single detail.

"I'll start carrying now," Utteal offered. Cannta and Micuit placed the burden on Utteal's back and they began to make their way home to Hoomuhu.

Urch was excited. The adventure had been educational and fascinating, and he was eager to taste the alligator meat. The Hoomuhu were definitely showing him and Wapa how to live in this land.

"You did well," Cannta told him.

"I have had an exciting experience," Urch replied. "Thank you, Cannta."

"You welcome," Cannta said in Urch's language.

After they had gone a way, Cannta said, "I'll take over now."

He and Micuit took the pack off Utteal's back. Micuit and Utteal placed the pack on Cannta's back. They resumed trekking.

"Don't forget that Wapa and I are here. Please include us in the carrying of the pack. Cannta, when you've done your part, let me have it, please."

Cannta said, "Very well."

Later it was time for Urch to carry the pack. He discovered how heavy it was. Of course, he'd insisted on putting it atop his backpack, which did make for a heavy load indeed.

After a while, Micuit said, "Now it's time for me to carry it." The pack was transferred.

Finally, Wapa touched Cannta's shoulder. He looked with a question. Cannta said, "It's now Wapa's burden." Utteal took Wapa's backpack without asking and put it on his own shoulders. Cannta and Urch transferred the alligator pack from Micuit to Wapa.

Later that night the Hoomuhu gathered around the fire. Each person had a stick to skewer their alligator meat. For all old enough, they took the meat which had soaked in oil and herbs, skewered it, and cooked it over the fire. Parents cooked for the younger children. Then they ate it. The rest of the evening meal was eaten either before or after cooking.

Urch and Wapa liked the alligator meat very much. They didn't know what to compare it to, but they thought it was very tasty. Urch was grateful that the Hoomuhu had reached out to them. These were good neighbors.

While Urch sat in the sun one afternoon, Yotuimoa crept over to him. She had to speak to him, and her shyness was in the way.

"What is it?" Urch asked the timid girl.

"The chief asked me to make something for you. It is a backpack made of the skin of your alligator. I need to show you how to care for it." She was grateful that she'd managed to speak through what she had to say without finding herself caught in silence.

"That is fantastic!" Urch said, frightening her with his enthusiasm.

"Will you come?" she asked.

Urch stood and followed her to a building at the edge of the village. He followed her into it. There he saw the backpack. It was the most amazing thing he ever saw.

"It's beautiful!" he exclaimed.

"I need to let you know how to keep it that way. You should not use this when it will rain heavily. It is not good for it to become wet. To clean it, moisten a soft skin and wring the water out. Rub that soft skin over the alligator leather. Then dry it well. After that you use bees' wax. Not too much. Like this," she said while she showed him. "See how you rub it into the skin?"

He nodded.

"Then you take a dry skin and buff the surface of the skin so it shines."

"I will remember that, Yotuimoa," he said. "This is the most beautiful thing I ever had," he said. "Thank you for doing it so well."

You're welcome," she said blushing brilliant red.

"Am I supposed to take it now?"

She nodded.

Urch took the backpack and shrugged into it. It was exactly the right size. "How'd you make it the right size?" he asked.

"Wapa helped," she admitted.

"Good for him," Urch said meaning one thing, and, he knew, she'd understand it differently from the way he meant it.

He met Cannta outside on his way to put the backpack in his temporary home. "Isn't this the most beautiful thing?" he asked Cannta.

"It is!" Cannta said, touching it and truly admiring it. "We'll have her do more with alligator skin. This is special."

Urch went into his home and put the new backpack beside his sleeping place. He touched the skin once more, then went outside to find the chief.

"I want to thank you," he told Chief Backtament. "The backpack you asked Yotuimoa to make for me is the most beautiful thing I've ever had. I'll remember learning to spear an alligator every time I look at it, and I'll know I learned it from the Hoomuhu."

"Thank you for what we have learned from you. There is a huge world outside our little place about which we knew nothing. Now, we have seen parts of it through your sharing. I will ask you to remain with us until you must leave for your cache and crossing. You are free to leave any time. We have enjoyed you and I am convinced there is more sharing we can do. You have contributed well to our people, and we hope to have done the same. I want you to know that when your people come, we welcome them here. They may come to our village or establish one at your campsite and visit here whenever they like. All are welcome. You and Wapa are good men."

"Chief, I am overwhelmed. I knew it was coming to the time when we should leave, but our lives have been so enriched here, I hated to think of leaving. I will plan to stay here. When we decide to leave for our crossing, I'll let you be the first to know. Know that both Wapa and I are grateful for all you've done for us. I think you've done something special for Wapa that none of us planned."

"Wapa is a fine young man. If he and Yotuimoa come together, I think that is very good."

"Thank you, Chief. I agree."

Urch left to take a walk. He was happy. There was something good here. After all the years of having the young blocked from being able to take a wife, here in this place, things were the way he would have liked to have had them all his life. He felt a fullness that embraced his thinking place and his feelings. It brought all together and gave him a sense of stability. Urch stood with his face to the sun and said quietly, "Thank you Mother Earth and Father Sky.

Thank you Pale-Faced Moon, Water that moves, and Fire. Thank you for letting me know that a place like this exists. Thank you for letting me live among these people. Grant that Wapa and I survive the sea crossing, gather our people, and return here to live. I have not many years left and would like to live them here among these people."

Over the months from winter to the next winter, Wapa and Yotuimoa came closer. The backpack construction requiring her to obtain a size estimate for Urch is what brought them together. Mutual sharing was the glue. Yotuimoa had never shared her feelings and thoughts with a man; Wapa had never shared his with a woman. They talked to each other as they had never talked to anyone.

The seasons passed. One late winter day, Wapa and Yotuimoa walked to the pond where there was a great blue heron rookery. Its chatter was above comfort level. They passed it by and continued on the path thinking of nothing but of each other. Once they passed the noise, they stopped at a grassy spot to rest. They stretched out on the ground and stared at the clouds passing by.

"That looks like a large cat," Yotuimoa said savoring the scent of the man who lay beside her.

"Yotuimoa, you know that soon Urch and I leave to return to our people across the sea to bring them back here to this land?"

"Yes, I know. I dread that time, but I'll be hoping it passes quickly. I will worry for your safety."

"It is a dangerous crossing, but with Urch, I have the best chance of making a safe crossing. He is wise."

"Do you have a girl back there that you love?" she asked the question that had plagued her for a long time.

"No. I did not play with the girls my age as I grew up. I was interested in learning the healing plants in our area and wanted to know how to help people who were sick, so I didn't play much at all. I was shy where girls were concerned when I matured, and I felt awkward. I felt strong when dealing with healing plants."

"I understand. I have been that way with my work—making things."

Wapa took both her hands in his and looked into her eyes. He said, "Yotuimoa, I have come to love you. You are beautiful. You impress me with your amazing work with leather. You create beauty in something practical. It brightens the lives of those who receive your things. You are kind and gentle. Around you, I feel the world is a better place."

"Wapa, I love you also. You are strong in your body but gentle and tender in your care of others. When you took care of Glatehut, when he injured his leg, I was so touched with how gently you treated him. He was so old, but you made him feel he mattered, mattered as much as our hunters. I'll never forget that. I have always been terribly shy, and words failed to come when I needed them to flow. Around you, I am free, and my words flow as they do for others. You give me a sense of freedom and joy."

"Yotuimoa, I want you to know that if I were not about to leave, I would ask you to be my wife. You must know that."

"And I would be the happiest person alive."

"You understand why I don't do that now?"

"Yes, I think so. You know that the sea crossing could take your life."

"True. I would not want you tied to someone who might be dead."

Yotuimoa's pale gray eyes bored into his to the depth of his spirit. "I understand, but I will worry no less not being your wife than I would being your wife. When you love, or at least when I love, my dearest Wapa, it is not about being a wife or not. I have already committed to love you. That happens regardless of what becomes of our lives. If I had to lose you, it would be more to my happiness if you had already planted a seed of yourself within me. That way, I would always have part of you with me."

"That thought had never crossed my mind, lovely Yotuimoa. You would prefer that I take you as wife?" Wapa's thoughts were swirling. He adored this quiet, shy woman and wanted her desperately. "Suppose you are my wife and I die on the crossing. Wouldn't it be harder for you to find another husband if you had my child?"

"Have you not seen how the Hoomuhu live, my dear Wapa? Why would anyone reject my child? We live as a great group, not separately depending only upon each other, but we have a larger group on which we all depend. We all depend on all the others. We are a people that includes, not excludes. You have lived here this long, but you have not understood?"

"I do understand, I just want to be sure you are well cared for."

She leaned over him and hugged him.

He looked long and hard into her eyes. "Will you be my wife, Yotuimoa?"

"Yes." She lay back beside him, reaching for his arm.

They lay there unmoved and knew that they had just taken a huge step while lying down. They would no longer be the same.

Finally, Wapa stood up, offering a hand to Yotuimoa. She stood beside him.

"I must see a chief about a wife," he said.

"Yes, you must," she laughed, "and it's about time."

They walked briskly back to the village and Wapa went to see the chief. The news went out and people planned to celebrate that evening.

Urch was delighted that Wapa had made the decision. He knew that Wapa would never find anyone like Yotuimoa, and he felt his young companion was wise. He also was aware that the change in his life would give him more impetus to make the trip over and back, some of which could cower a brave man.

That evening, there was dancing and Urch was surprised that Wapa and Yotuimoa danced as well as they did. They were tuned together like the drums and flute players. Surely, Urch thought, Mother Earth and Father Sky had a hand in planning this joining of two special people. Urch whispered his gratitude.

During the dancing, Wapa and Yotuimoa left the group to go to their new residence. They did all they could to plant the seed of life.

In the brief time they had remaining, the two young people spent much time together. Wapa told her that if the people chose to move to their campsite, he would come to her to live at Hoomuhu, because he loved it there. He knew that's where he belonged.

She would put her hands on either side of his face and look down through his eyes to his spirit. She would say more without words then than she ever said in many when she spoke. Yotuimoa absorbed him at those times. That absorption had to last for a long time, and she knew it.

The day before Urch and Wapa's planned departure, people from the tiny village began to come bearing gifts. The gifts such as jerky were from the village. Some were from individuals, who brought bladders for filling with whatever they needed, skins of various sizes, a small bladder of honey, various bundles of special herbs, several fire starters, bladders of oil. Others brought services, such as helping to oil the boat, checking the boat for strength of skins and sewing. But the most prized gift was the warmth of the people, the special way they made Urch and Wapa feel. They felt if they could bring their people to this people, they would give a gift greater than any they could have imagined. This is, they both were convinced, how life should be lived.

At the evening meal, Urch asked Yotuimoa to keep the alligator backpack for him while he made the crossings.

"The trip will be very wet. It would ruin the backpack. You did a wonderful work on it and I cannot bear the idea that it could be ruined."

"But it's yours."

"And, I have every intention of returning to claim it. You will take good care of it? Waxing it when needed?"

"Of course."

"And you'll take great care of my new cousin?" he said smiling.

"How did you know?" she asked clearly shocked.

"I am very perceptive," he said.

"Seriously, how did you know?"

"It has to do with how you stand, the look on your face. Does Wapa know?"

"I planned to tell him tonight."

"I won't say anything," Urch promised.

"Good."

Urch took another check of the boat, while Yotuimoa carried the backpack into her home.

"Let's take a quick walk just past the heron rookery one more time, Yotuimoa," Wapa said.

"That's a great idea," she said, needing some way to expend the energy she felt.

They walked down to the rookery and the noise was gone. They passed it and went to the place where they watched the clouds a while ago.

"I have something to share with you, my husband," Yotuimoa said, smiling.

"And what might that be?" Wapa said, putting his arms around her.

"I carry our child," she said.

Wapa had to take her words and pass them through his thinking place. He certainly knew that could be a possibility. To realize that he had a part in a new life overwhelmed him. His words didn't flow.

"Are you disturbed?" she asked with slight alarm.

Finally the words came, "I am overwhelmed with joy," he admitted.

They hugged for a long time in the quiet away from others.

They reluctantly turned and headed back to the village.

The morning of Urch and Wapa's leaving came, and no one wanted to see the time arrive. The men stoically went to the boat, took it from the supports that kept it from damage, and carried it to the river. They put the boat half way into the river. Then they came back to say their parting words. Each went from person to person. Then Wapa and Yotuimoa stood aside holding both hands and talked briefly. They hugged, kissed, and Wapa went to the boat. He turned, waving to her, and boarded. Villagers pushed the boat into the water. Urch and Wapa were on their way.

As they traveled to the cache, the two put markers all along the shore, so if they didn't make it back, the markers would show the people where to go to find their new land.

Chapter 11

The SealEaters' New Land

Whug and Amoroz stood by the shore. Each scanned the horizon looking for the least deviation from normal. Their suntanned faces were creased and deep lines formed in their foreheads and at the corners of their eyes.

"Nothing, as far as I can see," Whug said with a sigh.

"Well, it's not like they're overdue," Amoroz replied. "I'll have to admit, I loved my children before they left, but my awareness of that love is more acute now that I've been without them for so long. Interesting how that happens."

"I know what you mean. To have Urch and Emuka both gone, it's a terrible loss. I hope they find us a new land where we can live well. More than that, though, I hope they return."

"We both can be certain, if there's a way to return, they'll find it. I have to admit I'm terrified to make the crossing they've made. To do it three times . . . ."

"I agree, Brother. If it takes us to a place where our lives will improve, it's worth it, I think."

"We certainly have enough boats prepared, if we are to migrate," Amoroz laughed.

"I think on that we've overproduced."

"The women have a sense of things we don't," Amoroz said. "If they're right, some will return and we'll migrate. They're making pemmican and sewing skins, as if we're about to depart. If it comes to migration, I wonder whether I should remain here."

"Remain here! Have you put your thinking place on the hearth? We have to be where our people are." Whug was alarmed at the thought.

"I was just letting my thoughts into the air."

"Well that thought makes as much sense as drinking sea water!"

"Is Kol starting to watch for the boats?" Amoroz asked.

"Yes. Kol is watching. I know she'll be happy as long as Urch makes it back. That little Aptuk is adorable. What a delight to have in my home," Whug said. "I think she resembles Gemu."

"I'd never even thought of that, but by Father Sky, you're right! Aptuk does look like Gemu."

"If Urch returns, he may see the resemblance. I've never mentioned it to anyone else. Kol has done a good job of raising Aptuk. The little girl already has responsibilities. Before she goes black, she has to fold and stack the leather wiping cloths in our home, and she has to be sure the gourds are all filled. She is so tiny to have responsibilities. Cattu is very fond of her and takes her outside often. Urch would approve of the little one with responsibility." Whug looked at the horizon.

"Yes, he would. You don't suppose he found someone else while over there?" Amoroz let the words out without thinking.

"Urch and responsibilities go together. He knows he could be a parent. From a one-time event, it's unlikely, but certainly not impossible. My thought is that he has left the possibility in front of him, and he'll do nothing until he knows. He may love Kol more than I thought he did. I don't know. He and Kol were not like Litmaq and Lefa."

"Litmaq and Lefa remind me of you and Gemu," Amoroz said smiling.

"Me too. You ready to kill another seal?"

"No, but let's do it anyway—it's our responsibility," Amoroz replied bored.

Momomu and Belah walked the shore south of where Whug and Amoroz talked. Their son, Biez, played in the water at their feet.

"Do you think any will return, Momomu?" Belah asked.

"I think maybe two will return. I doubt more than that. I do not expect Reg to be returning," Momomu replied.

"Why would you say that about my father?" Belah asked horrified.

"Reg is not a normal person. He will press other people too hard, and they'll either chase him away or kill him. We've put up with his nonsense so long, he probably has no idea how abnormal he is."

"Well, the only person who would be very upset if he doesn't come home is my mother. I think she genuinely loves him" Belah said.

"Well, Waywap's the only one he ever treated with any kindness, that's certain. I don't know how she could have lived seeing her children beaten so badly. That's what I mean about his being abnormal."

"Let's gather some sea greens for this evening. Come on, Biez," Belah said.

Biez splashed through the water to them.

Litmaq and Lefa had climbed up the hill to the place where they once hid. They had eaten some jerky and enjoyed the cool breeze and smell of green in the forest. They turned to go down the hill and something caught the corner of Lefa's right eye. She turned her head and, sure enough, out on the horizon was something. She pointed it out to Litmaq.

"Do you really think it's them?" he asked.

"Who else could it be?" Lefa replied. "I do think we need to return quickly to let the others know." They went down the hill faster than they ever had.

They ran into the village shouting, "Someone comes!" The villagers dropped whatever they were doing and ran to the shore. They could just barely make out a dot on the sea.

Out on the sea, Urch said to Wapa, "We must minimize the frightening parts of the crossings. We have to cause them to migrate, and, if we tell what happened, none will move."

"I agree," Wapa said. They rowed stronger now that they could see the Cove.

Knowing that it took a while, women went to cook food as they would for a gathering of all the people. Normally each home prepared its own food. But this was a celebration.

When Urch and Wapa reached the Cove, it was becoming dark. Food was ready and laid out on a log so each person could be helped by the women who prepared the food.

The boat reached shore and Momomu, Smam, Morg, Oppermatu, and Begalit ran to pull the boat to a safe place. The people at the Cove watched Urch and Wapa emerge from the boat. The mariners went to a place where SealEaters had prepared a log so they could sit. They sat. Women brought each one a special plate of the evening's best choices of food. Then others were served.

All wondered where the others were. They wanted answers, but they knew that Urch and Wapa had to be exhausted. They waited in dead silence.

After the SealEaters ate, they did what they'd done countless times in their lives. They took their bowls to empty and rinsed them out in the sea.

They put the bowls where they could dry out near their sleeping places. They returned to the group to sit where they had been sitting.

Urch cleared his throat. "I know you want answers and I wish I had answers to give. We arrived at the cache where we had planned to meet at the proper time. None of the people were there except Wen. Mongwire stopped breathing air, and Wen was taken in by people living near the cache site. Wen wanted to take a wife of those people with whom he'd lived for almost two full seasons. I talked to him and encouraged him to begin his life there. I gave him the reasons I thought he should stay. The girl he met is wonderful. They're a special pair. He would have just been one more in our boat. Of course, there was a risk. Wen's making this trip wasn't necessary. Wen made his own decision to remain behind. I am convinced that he made the right decision."

Guint wept silent tears on hearing that Mongwire no longer breathed air.

"I'm sorry, Guint. At least you know now," At said, putting his arm around the widow.

"We became separated from Vaima, Emuka, Murke, Plak, Torq, and Akla early into the exploration. Before we separated from Murke and Akla, Murke confided in me that Vaima had hidden on his boat when he and Akla went to explore to the south. The son of a chief came to love Vaima, and she loved him. She became his wife. Reg never knew what happened to her. For any of you who worried about Vaima on the voyage, Reg did not abuse her. I am quite serious. He did not do to her what he did to Ipsalu. What he did was to make her row. I will say that Reg's big boat was not a good idea. It slowed us down because we were determined to stay together. His boat kept hanging up on the sea ice. Ours maneuver well on the sea. You might want to know, the best number of people on a small boat is three."

"For the rest of those who went to explore, I do not know whether they breathe air. The land is immense. There is no way to find those who go exploring. What is true is that this land will provide a place for us to live. We have found a place, a warm place. We found indigenous people who welcomed us and will welcome you to their land. They taught us rules of life in that place, rules different from what we have here. Their climate's different; their animals are different; their ways of living together are different. There is no need for heavy clothing in winter there. It rarely snows in the place we found. Food is available in abundance, good food in varieties you cannot imagine. Wapa has a wonderful wife in whom his seed now grows. We plan to return, and we want all of you to join us. You cannot imagine the good things that wait for you on the other side of the crossing. I will not lie. The crossing is frightening. It is not as hard as you might think, however. I urge you to come to a decision quickly. Now is the time to cross. You do not want to wait many days."

Whug stood, "SealEaters, you must leave Urch and Wapa time to rest. Save your questions. For this day, let them go to their homes."

Whug extended his hand to Urch. Urch took his father's hand and stood. They walked home together. Wapa stood to hug Forth and Trupo. He was home but he'd left his love in another land and longed to return.

At home Urch did a double take when he saw Aptuk. For a fleeting moment he thought of his mother. He saw Kol smiling a great smile. She looked beautiful. He wondered whether she was his father's wife.

"Before you wonder, Urch, in your absence we abolished elder permission to take a wife. Women have the right of refusal restored. It now takes the entire council to drown anyone. Things have changed. Kol has been with no one else. She waited for you." Whug thought he needed to know that immediately.

"I have been with no one else," Urch said, looking at Kol, not Whug. "She looks like Mother," Urch said glancing at Aptuk.

"Isn't it an amazing likeness?" Whug asked quietly.

"Her name is Aptuk," Kol said. "She's your daughter."

"She's adorable," Urch said. "And where's Cattu?" he asked looking around.

"I am here," came a voice from the back of the dwelling. Cattu walked out of the shadows and ran to Urch. She was still tiny, still had red hair, but her explosive nature had calmed significantly. She threw her arms around him and hugged him. She began to cry on his neck.

"What's the matter Little One?" he asked.

"I thought you would never return, Urch. I love you so much, but I thought you no longer breathed air."

"You can see, Cattu, I still breathe air."

"Yes, I see. It's just hard to believe even though I see you."

"Would you like me to pinch you?"

"Why would you do that?" she asked, pointedly moving back from him.

"When you dream you don't feel things like pinches. Only in real life does that happen. Shall I pinch you to prove this is real?"

"No, Urch. That's not necessary." Cattu was uncharacteristically serious.

"Where's my funny little Cattu?" Urch asked sensing something wrong but being too tired to think it through.

"Urch, when you left, things changed."

"Something here changed?" Urch showed the inside of the dwelling with his hand.

"No, something changed here," she signed something inside her had changed. "It was two cycles of seasons, Urch! How long does it take to find a new land?"

"Interesting that you ask that. I asked that also. When we reached the new land, we knew immediately that the land was good. We could have turned right around and come back. But most of us felt a need to explore to find where we should locate in this huge land. If Wapa and I had chosen to return here, we'd have missed the place in the south where we intend to go when we return. It's very important there to have good neighbors. We found great ones!"

"Cattu, let me promise you this, if it's all right with Father. You'll be in my boat on the return trip. Would you like that?"

"Oh, yes, Urch. That way you won't leave me again."

Urch looked at Whug, who nodded.

"See, Cattu, Father has given his permission. You'll go on my boat."

Cattu snuggled as close to Urch as she could. For the first time in a long time she felt safe.

In another home, Wapa and his family were reacquainting themselves after the absence. Wapa had left almost a boy and he was now clearly a man. He left at twenty-one, and one would think that was the age of a man, but his years had been spent studying plants and healing. His interaction with people was very limited. He had no experience with women. He returned as someone who had a wife and a baby on the way, someone who had made two crossings, someone who had grown in some ways beyond where most men ever grow.

"Tonight, I feel for the families who are missing people," Wapa said. At and Merian are missing two, but at least Vaima breathes air. Guint must be devastated. Three of her family did not return, and that includes her husband. At least she knows what happened to two of the three of them. Same is true for Waywap, though I cannot imagine anyone missing Reg. She does seem to love him."

"It's a story most people don't know, Son," Forth said quietly. "Let me see whether I can help you understand. Reg was born the third child. He had a testical that was missing. With a missing testical one cannot ever become chief, for a chief must be fully man. His condition turned Reg from a normal kid into a twisted, sick man. Oh, Reg had a part in it. He didn't have to view himself as someone other than perfect, which he seemed to think the rest of us were. He was no different from us except for that missing part. But he let it eat away at his thinking place until there was no substance left in his thinking place. It was all eaten away. He took Waywap as wife when he was young. She was young. They were maybe sixteen or seventeen—maybe younger, even fourteen. Waywap knew his concern about what he considered his deficiency. Instead of supporting his worry over his deficiency, Waywap supported his positive aspects such as his strength and hunting prowess. She gave him support and he was grateful. She didn't do it for any of the wrong reasons, but I'm not sure the effect of it was helpful to Reg. He has a way of taking something that's just simple fact and twisting it into something unrecognizably ugly and sick. Waywap sees the devastation he created, but she knew him before he changed into a man with a broken thinking place. That became a disaster for him and others."

"Your words explain a lot, Father. Thank you for sharing. It seems to me that wouldn't matter, unless he desperately wanted to become chief."

"I think he wanted to be chief, only because he couldn't."

"Oh, I understand. How sad. How sad to twist a life like that."

"Some of us tried in the early time to help. Any attempt to help seemed to make the matter worse, so we quit trying and tried to ignore him. We should never have done that. We learned that the hard way. If he treated people who have lived on the new land the way he treated others here, I expect he no longer breathes air."

"Well, we were run out of one village because of him."

"No surprise there. We never seemed to realize that we could take him on if we did it as a group. We are as guilty of some of his evil as he was, because we did nothing to stop it."

"Do you think that's how the gods measure it?"

"I have no idea how they measure anything. I know how I measure, and I'd call me partly guilty by fear. Fear is a terrible thing, Wapa."

"Well, I think all that is past, Father. I, too, am convinced he no longer breathes. It was he who was pushing to accomplish the exploration so we could start the migration. If he could've been there at the cache site for this return, I'm sure he would've."

"Strange man, Son. He lacked control over the formation of his own body, as all men do, and for him, he strove to control everything. In all aspects, very unreasonable. Now, tell me about the girl."

"I was still horribly shy when I arrived there. Yotuimoa was also very shy. She has long black hair that shines blue and eyes the color of a clouded over sky. She is kind and gentle. She made a backpack for Urch at the chief's request. Urch had speared a giant lizard. Giant lizards called alligators live on land and water and are about twice as long as I'm tall. They can catch and eat a horse."

"You think we should live with creatures like that?"

"Father!" Wapa said, "Those beasts live only in certain places, not in the villages," he paused. "Oh, giant lizard meat is very tasty," Wapa said grinning. "Yotuimoa needed an estimate on Urch's size, so she had to ask me. That's how we came to know each other. Just think, I'd still be without a wife, if Urch hadn't speared a giant lizard!"

"Son, you have grown."

"Yes, Father. I have grown. I'm glad. I'm eager for you and Mother to meet Yotuimoa."

"I am eager, also, Son, but I wish we could travel across the water without the boat trip."

"It offers some things to see that you cannot imagine. Once is enough though. Father, I need to go black."

"Here, your sleeping place is right over there."

Wapa laid himself on his sleeping place, rolled over, and went black.

The next morning there was a great deal of activity at the Cove. Urch was with Whug and Amoroz trying to determine whether they had enough boats for the people. Urch had to laugh, for it appeared they had three boats more than needed. Necessities for the trip were already being stored in the boats.

Just outside Whug's home, Amegulatuga was having a difficult time with Sted.

"I'm not going, and that's how it is, Woman!"

"Don't talk to me like that, Sted!" she barked back.

Sted had no fear of her, and he replied, "You sniveling Woman, I don't have to listen to any more of your yelling at me." He walked off not recognizing the incongruity of his comment with the fact that Amegulatuga was known for her soft-spoken ways.

Amegulatuga grabbed him by the arm to stop him. He swiped at her, scratching her face with his nails, leaving a nasty set of three parallel lines. He hadn't meant to scratch her face. Amegulatuga let go of him and stood bent over with her hand protecting her face. It stung.

Fluga, Amoroz's wife, ran down to Whug and Urch. "You need to see to your wife," she told Whug.

Whug moved quickly to the hut where he could see Amegulatuga holding her face, seemingly stunned.

"What happened here?" he asked as Urch arrived.

She explained. Urch, realizing who did the damage to a woman left. He saw Sted by the boats and walked to bring him back. What he saw troubled him more. Sted was bent over a boat. He had a sliver of stone flaked from a tool. He was using the sliver to slice the hide on a boat. Seeing that, Urch went to the boy and slapped him on the side of his face hard enough that the boy fell to the ground. Urch seized him by the upper arms from the back and forced him back home.

"Thanks to Sted, we have a disabled boat. He cut a hole in the bottom," Urch announced.

Whug looked at Urch in total disbelief. "I knew we were having trouble with him, but I didn't know it had gone this far. Tie him up, Urch, please. I need to tend to the scratches he made in Amegulatuga's face. Then, I'll deal with him."

Urch shoved the boy into the hut and took some strong cordage. He tied the boy's hands tightly behind his back. Then, he tied his feet together. Using the long end of the cord that tied his feet together, Urch tied his hands to his feet. His back was arched just a small amount more than was comfortable. Urch was outraged. He wanted the boy to feel some pain. The boy was certainly complaining.

Sted no longer could control himself, and words began to pour out, words Whug couldn't help but hear. "I hate you brother. I didn't want to go on this voyage. I don't have to go. I am a man. I will do what I will. By Mother Earth and Father Sky, I curse you from this day forward. I hope your boat sinks in the sea and all with you. You stinking pus-filled sore, traveling across a sea where you were not designed by the gods to go. You would take us all with you to drown in cold water far from home. Who are you to decide where we should live. Arrogant whelp of dogs!"

Whug had finished with his wife's injury. He went to where Urch sat with his foot on Sted's back.

"Son, what you've done is unacceptable. You will remain here tied up. Learn this. Be careful what you ask for in life. You might receive it. You will not travel with us. You will be on your own after we leave. You want to be like Reg. You may do all you like after we leave. Until then, I gag you and keep you tied so that you cannot free yourself. You'll receive exactly what you asked for—only it'll be in my time, not yours. You've had too many opportunities to improve your behavior. You have failed each time, becoming worse instead of better. It is you who is a sore upon this people. So we shall cut you off when we leave tomorrow."

Urch's stomach knotted up when he realized his father had just cut off his brother. He could understand the need to do so, but it still came as a shock. It would, he reasoned, be foolhardy to take someone so bent on a suicidal course of action on a trip across the sea. He could injure himself, but he could cause injury or death to others, something that could not be tolerated. Urch had been confident that the SealEaters had seen the last of Reg, only to come home and find him here. Urch wondered whether a group of people always had a Reg. He hoped not. The Hoomuhu certainly didn't have anyone like Reg.

Urch realized his father had said they would leave the very next day. He looked up and said, "Father, your plan is to leave tomorrow?"

"Yes. I think we need give SealEaters no more time than necessary to think about the voyage. We just need to do it."

"Son, help me carry him outside so I can keep an eye on him while we work. I want to be certain he remains tied up until we leave. I'm not sure I'll untie him then."

They each took part of Sted and laid him outside the hut so Whug could keep a watch over him. Sted was furious, but there was absolutely nothing he could do to change anything.

Urch showed Whug the damage to the boat and both agreed the boat was ruined. They took the boat and dragged it to the sea. They set it adrift after walking it out as far as possible. The people gathered after it was set loose, waiting for Whug and Urch to return from the sea.

Whug addressed them, "My son, Sted, cut a hole in the boat earlier. He doesn't want to join the migration, so apparently he resorted to sabotage. For that, he will have his wish. He will not join us on the voyage, which will start in the morning tomorrow. All who will leave will be on the beach at sunrise. We'll load the last of the things and leave. You each know your boats. Have them loaded today so there is no stalling tomorrow. When you pass my hut, ignore Sted."

The people on shore were shocked. Sted might have caused the death of people. That was horrifying. He'd always been a child they avoided, but Whug was right—he was a danger to the people on the voyage and they had to separate him out. Egorgo felt a small amount of sympathy for him. She had been through a tough time growing up and she had behaved very badly, for which she still felt shame, though she had changed her ways. But to endanger the lives of others, that was something she'd never done. It was unthinkable. She shuddered to consider what Sted must be inside his thinking place.

Cattu and Nip were glad they no longer would have to put up with their brother's harassment. He treated them terribly when their parents were not around.

Knowing they had little time to prepare, the people were busily preparing the boats. The assignments to boats had already been made by the

SealEaters before Urch and Wapa returned. The boat Sted was cutting belonged to his father.

Forth came to Whug by the boats. "Brother, my family and I plan to remain here."

Whug looked at him, tired. "Forth, you cannot do that. The ice advances rapidly. You'll be pushed to sea."

"I have thought through this. There are just too many of us. I want to remain here."

"Brother, we wouldn't be leaving, if staying were an option. Stop the silly talk."

"I have made up my mind."

"And your wife says?"

"She thinks we should go. I have authority to keep us here, and that's what I choose to do."

"How many others are in agreement with you?"

"I know of no others."

"Well, do this for me, Brother. Prepare your boats as if you were going. That way you won't trouble others."

"If that'll make you leave me alone, I'll do it," he said and went about preparing his boats.

Whug met with Amoroz, Urch, and Wapa. He explained the dilemma that Forth had just presented. He shared his plan. It would take place just after the evening meal. All continued working hard. It was late and almost dark when the evening meal was ready. The people ate, an edge of nervousness tinging the group.

Late, when it was fully dark and many had gone black in their sleeping places, Whug's plan began. Whug arrived at Forth's home and asked to see him outside. Forth went out, followed by Wapa. Outside, Urch hit Forth in the back of the head, rendering him unconscious. The men carried Forth to his boat, gagged him, tied him up tightly, and put him in the boat. They tied him to the boat and made it appear that the man had gone black in his boat. They returned to their homes. Back at home, Wapa explained that his father would likely be busy most of the night.

The next morning, there was no morning meal. All people were to prepare the boats for departure. Sted still lay outside Whug's hut, tied and gagged. Whug explained to Trupo, Forth's wife, what they had done to make the migration take place as planned. They told Trupo to climb into the boat and act like Forth didn't feel well and she was caring for him. The trick worked.

Before they shoved off, Urch reminded them to stay together and, if any were separated, to look for signs along the coast to point them to where they should go.

All the boats going on the trip were fully filled with necessities and the people were arranged as planned, except, of course, it would be a while until Forth would be prepared to row. With all the preparation and excitement of the launch, everyone including Whug had forgotten to untie Sted. They were well at sea before anyone remembered. Sted managed to free himself after a long time. It would have surprised all to know that he crossed the mountains and became part of a warring tribe. He lived for seven more years and was considered an effective warrior. Sted would be buried with his spears and shield hundreds of miles inland from where he was born.

The voyage began in clear skies with a gentle sea. Urch was grateful that they had good weather at the start. He wanted them well into the trip, so that turning back became less and less an option. There were about eighty-five people migrating in some twenty-five boats. To keep that many boats together was extremely difficult.

Forth had partially regained consciousness that morning but was very groggy as they put to sea. By the first night he was fully conscious, totally frustrated to find himself at sea, but resigned to making the crossing since he had no other choice. He rowed along with the others.

For ten days the weather held. They had made a stop to oil the boat skins and capture some seals primarily for food and making additional oil. The stop went very well. So far, they had lost no boats.

The tenth night brought them great wind. It blew from the northwest, hard but without rain or snow. It lasted for a couple of days and as suddenly as it arrived, it ceased. One boat was missing after the wind.

The SealEaters saw whale killers attacking a young right whale they had separated from its mother, and the children were frightened. After that they were careful to keep their hands in the boats. They could see the size of the teeth of the whale killers.

After they'd traveled for over a moon, there was a great storm that tossed the huge chunks of ice about. It was terrifying after the smooth seas they'd experienced to that point. Many wept and shook in terror. They tried to keep the front of the boat pointed toward the waves, and most were very successful. After the storm, they found they were missing two more boats. They pressed on, not knowing whether the missing boats had capsized or were simply blown away from the others.

Day after day of the sea crossing brought them closer to the new land, but it hardly seemed that they did anything but bob up and down on the sea. Many found the boats somewhat distressing since there was no way to move about. Legs would cramp from lack of use.

Their diet of seals was not tiresome, for it was their normal food. They preferred the organ meat and they included blubber because it was known to build fat on their bodies to keep them warm.

Finally, their direction changed slightly so that they were heading southwest. There was no land in sight and those who were not mariners wondered when they heard of the change. It wasn't significant, for they had many days to go before they would see land. The people knew the ways of the sun, and they began to grow hope of finding the journey's end soon.

Urch thought of how much quicker the voyage was when it was a single boat with the wind behind them. He smiled. There was no interest in his mind to turn about so those conditions would exist.

Women, boys, and girls would all row with the men. Their arm muscles expanded greatly on the trip. They tried to move their leg muscles, but it was difficult on the boats. Children who had been free of any real responsibility suddenly learned what responsibility meant. They participated by scooping water from the bottom of their boat and returning it to the sea.

Eventually, they saw land. All were ready to leap from the boats to the land, but Urch pushed them onward. He knew where the people were the last time he was there. He wanted them to reach land where there would be no temptation to refuse to enter into the boats to continue to their place.

Finally, Urch reached the beach he remembered that had no convenient rivers. He guided the boats to land. They definitely needed to oil the boat skins. People needed to know that they were near their new home. He didn't plan for the biting bugs on this beautiful sunny, almost windless day. They stayed long enough to oil the boats and rest. Then all were glad to return to the sea to go to their new home and to escape the biting bugs. By the time they reached this point, they had a total of twenty boats. Urch felt that was a wonderful accomplishment. The others were very disturbed over the loss. Urch told them that for a long time they could not assume they were lost. It was possible that the boats were still heading their way.

They traveled for many more days watching the coast filled with marsh grasses. Occasionally they'd see a mammoth or a mastodon. They saw birds the like of which they'd never seen. The children were fascinated. Sometimes they'd see fins in the water, either swimming steadily or curving into the water only to surface again and dive back down. They looked a bit like whales, only smaller.

Older children sought the signs that Urch and Wapa had put along the coast. A shout went up when the children sighted the sign that pointed to what they now thought of as their river. They began the trip upstream. They stopped at their old camp site. The little hut was still standing where they smoked their jerky. They constructed lean-to structures and set up a basic camp for the present. They had arrived in the evening and the sunset was of colors they'd never seen in the sky: deep purple, reds, yellows. Some of those colors were in the night lights, which they rarely saw, but these brilliant colors were new, more vivid than any sunset they'd ever seen.

Urch and Whug took on the responsibility of organizing the establishment of the temporary village. Wapa was missing along with his brothers Dupa and Seq and sister Gi from the same boat. Many were also missing, but Urch felt that Wapa had the knowledge to make it back. He refused to consider the worst until he had given it plenty of time.

"Are you going to go upriver to let the Hoomuhu know we're here?"

"No, Father," he said quietly. "I want to wait until Wapa has had plenty of time to arrive. I don't want his wife worried needlessly."

"I understand," Whug said. "I wouldn't have thought Wapa's boat would have been lost."

"That's why I want to wait."

"Look what I found," Cattu said, carrying a turtle.

"Be careful that it doesn't bite you," Urch said.

"They can bite?"

"Yes. Pretty hard bites, too."

People were running about gathering wood and dry grass for fire starters. Hunters were discovering that not having used their legs for so long, they were weaker than normal. They began to run along the river bank looking into the distance to see what food walked about on four legs. Begalit and Lowat, sons of Amoroz, took their spears and headed for a wooded area across the open land. They hoped to eat something other than seal. It was becoming dark, so they knew they needed to move quickly. Begalit noticed something move and pointed it out to Lowat. It was a camel. They were much more careful in their movement, trying to make the most progress while the animal's head was lowered. Lowat and Begalit, despite weakened knees, bent their legs significantly to lower their profiles to avoid detection. As they came closer, Lowat pointed with his head to let Begalit know he'd go after the one on the right. There were two camels.

The two were more careful than they had ever been while stalking the camels. All at once they stood fully up and let their spears fly. They ran in with the second spear to thrust before the animal recovered from the shock. They managed to kill both camels. Begalit lifted the largest one to his shoulders and picked up his spears. Lowat did the same. They returned to their camp overburdened.

The SealEaters greeted them with two big fires. They had cut many sticks for each person to roast his or her meat. The hunters took the camels to the river and made quick work of sharing the meat. Women and men took over the reduction of the meat to portions that would cook quickly on the cooking sticks. To the SealEaters it was a feast.

That night brought a clear sky. After eating, people crawled into their sleeping skins. Many went black immediately. Some lingered grateful that they had their feet on land, not cramped beneath them in a boat.

At the long ago cache site, Wapa made the turn to row along the coast. People in the two boats saw land.

"Let's stop here for the night," Forth said,

"No!" Wapa snapped. He did not want his father to leave for the land.

They kept rowing through the night, as if they were still far out at sea. Wapa was near enough to Yotuimoa not to want to waste one moment. Forth sat back rowing in silence.

After being at the new site for eight days, a dugout from upstream stopped at the camp.

"Urch! Wapa! You are here with your people?" Cannta shouted out, walking toward the group with Micuit.

Urch came running.

"Cannta!" Urch said, hugging his friend.

The two began to converse in Cannta's language, while the SealEaters watched in disbelief that Urch knew the language of the other man.

"Wapa? Where is he?" Cannta asked in the language of Hoomuhu.

"His boat and some others separated from us in a storm. We wait here to see whether he comes late. I did not want to worry Yotuimoa unnecessarily."

"I understand. You made it with so many people. All these people crossed the eastern sea?"

Urch nodded.

"It is so good to see you, my friend," Urch said sincerely. He was glad to be where he considered it home. "How is Chief Backtament?"

"He is well. He is eager to see you."

"You knew we were here?"

"Utteal was coming back from hunting and noticed the fire. We hoped it was you."

"Who else?"

"That's why we came, to be certain it was you."

"You'll eat with us tonight?" Urch invited them nodding at them both.

"Of course, but then we'll head back home. Micuit's wife is likely to have given birth before we arrive back."

"Come, let's have you fed quickly."

Urch went to lead them to the food when he noticed two small boats coming up the river. He strained his eyes trying to discover who was in the boats, but it was very difficult. When they rowed close enough, Urch could see Wapa. He'd hardly known Wapa when they arrived the first time in this land. Now, he almost felt as if Wapa were a son.

"Wapa!" he shouted, waving.

"We made it, Urch!" Wapa shouted back in the SealEater language. He jumped from the boat leaving it for others to pull to the shore. "Cannta, Micuit, how are you?" Wapa asked in the Hoomuhu language, hugging Cannta and then Micuit.

The SealEaters watched and listened as Urch and Wapa would shift between languages depending on the target of their words.

"We both do well," Micuit replied.

"They're staying?" he asked Urch.

"For the evening meal only," Urch said in the language of the SealEaters.

"You leave tonight?" Wapa asked Cannta in the language of the Hoomuhu. Cannta nodded, "We must."

"May I accompany you?" Wapa asked eager to see Yotuimoa.

"Of course, she is eager to see you, too." Cannta laughed at Wapa's eagerness.

While Urch led Cannta and Micuit to the food, Wapa ran to the creek and bathed thoroughly. As soon as he finished, he joined the SealEaters for food. He ate quickly until satiated, but all he wanted was to leave for his wife.

Cannta and Micuit ate quickly as well. Soon the three of them were heading for Hoomuhu.

After the people departed, Urch gathered the older adults so he could explain some of the realities of the area.

"We are different from the Hoomuhu. Let me explain. See this bone that someone dropped here? The Hoomuhu would not permit that to happen. Never is any food dropped on their village ground. They take great care how the place looks and for good reason. Dropped food draws creatures you might not want in your village. It is a risk for injury. Someone who steps on a bone can have a terrible pus-filled mess on his foot, as some of you have had. They carefully throw things like that in a pit they dig outside the village. When the pit becomes too full, they bury it and dig another pit."

"There are no people there like Reg who are unkind to other people. They don't permit unkindness to others."

"They do not have elders as we do. They have a chief. His name is Chief Backtament. He is wise. I like him very much. When he says something, it is the rule. Nobody violates his rules."

"We have choices. SealEaters can build our village here and go on as we have. SealEaters can become Hoomuhu. SealEaters can go elsewhere. I will make a personal choice. I intend to live with the Hoomuhu as Wapa will. We have come to care a lot for them. They took us in when we arrived here, not understanding this land and its demands at all. They taught us. Do you have questions?"

"Why would you choose to live there apart from us?" Afte-ba asked.

"You have asked the wrong question. I do not reject you. I choose them. I have seen how people live when they work together for good. I respect these people for many, many reasons. I prefer what I've seen there to anywhere else I've ever lived."

"Urch, I have a question. What's the purpose of keeping the living place free from what will be thrown away?" Emu asked.

"If you eat meat that has sat out too long, what happens?"

"It can make you sick," Emu replied.

"If you step on a sharp piece of bone with meat attached or fat attached, and it goes into your skin, do you think that is different from eating it?"

Everyone looked at him.

"I would tell you, it's no different. Both can make you sick. Their village is beautiful because they take good care of it. Now, I will also say that the way they take care of their village applies to the way they are with each other. They take it easy with each other. You don't see a lot of people assuming they know what another is thinking. They don't assume all are like they are. Their assumptions are based on long study. They ask, if they don't know and need to know. They are reasoning people. They do not talk about others behind their backs. It's just a different and good place."

"Do people never argue there?" Oppermatu asked.

"They disagree, certainly, but they talk about the differences and where they agree to see how they can come together. They are required to listen carefully to the other's view and to ask questions and answer questions about their own. Questions can become very probing and make one think. You first learn *you* have a problem when they ask questions, and you cannot answer reasonably because you haven't considered your view adequately. They have a goal to live in harmony."

"If we went there, what would we do with our elders?" Morg asked.

"I'm not certain I understand your question? Are you asking whether we'd drown our elders?"

"Oh, Urch, you know that's not what I meant. I mean we'd have a chief, so what would become of our elders?"

"Nothing would become of our elders. They would be people even as they are now, but they would not have power over us. The Hoomuhu chief would have that power."

"One person?" Amoroz asked.

"Yes, one person. I have seen corruption among our SealEater elders. I have seen no corruption in this chief. It is the individuals who rule who make a difference, not the structure. Structure is but a framework as for a house. It's the people who make it good or bad. They could have a corrupt chief, and we could have a more perfect group of elders. We've had what we've had. They have what they have. I would change. You may choose what you wish to do."

"What if some of us want to do one thing while the others want something different?" Whug asked.

"You are free to choose. As I am free to choose and already have chosen, you may choose where you wish to live and whom you want for leadership."

"We have never met these people. How can we choose?" At asked.

"I will take groups of ten each to visit the Hoomuhu. You can see them and talk to them for yourselves. Then, you make up your minds. I don't wish to take all of you at one time. There is a language difference, and it could become confusing."

"When will you take the first ten?" Oppermatu asked.

"Tomorrow is a good day," Urch replied.

"I would like to be among tomorrow's ten," Oppermatu said.

"So be it," Urch said.

"I, too," Momomu said.

Before Urch could rise to his feet, he had the ten visitors for the next day.

The next day the first group of visitors gathered in two boats and rowed carefully upriver, for the boats were a bit overloaded. Urch asked Kol to join him to see the village. Children were not invited on trips, since children would not be making the decision where they'd live.

As they rounded the curve near the village, people came quickly to the river bank to help with the boats and greet the new people. They led the visitors to the central area where they ate in the evening. Urch walked fast to embrace the chief. He called the visitors and they went to meet Chief Backtament. Urch introduced each one. The greeting was formal. Urch translated the chief's words. The chief welcomed them. He told of his village and showed how they ate together. He pointed out their houses and the houses they built for any who chose to come there to live. He said that they'd build more houses if there were others who needed them. His people were as yet unsure how many would choose to come. He encouraged them to look at the houses and to enter the ones designed for newcomers. He told them two were already taken: one for Urch and one for Wapa. He pointed out which was which. Urch wanted to laugh. The chief *knew* him well. His home would catch a breeze on a hot day. He told them to tour with Urch to learn where the privies were and the place for discards of food or other things. He suggested they walk a short distance on the local paths with Urch, who could tell them where the paths went. He told them if there were a need for anything, just to ask someone. He freed them to wander about.

As they walked towards the new homes, Oppermatu asked Urch, "How did the chief know you'd want to live here?"

"The chief and I learned to know one another well while we were here. I told you he was a wise man. While he talks or listens he observes. Rarely does anything escape his gaze. Information sticks to him like the glued sinew that wraps the spear point to the shaft. He is a good man."

Urch reached the home made for him. He walked into it, taking Kol by the hand. He felt strange with Kol after all the time apart. They didn't know each other at all. Nevertheless, she had his child. He needed to spend time with her. She looked inside the airy home. Never had she seen any place as lovely, and to think a single family would live in such a place gave her much to think on. They did not know how to construct places like this.

They went back outside. The visitors were dumbstruck. After all the travel, this place was even better, they thought, than Urch had described. They could imagine living in such a place. The chief was a very special man—that was clear. Each one felt jolted by the chief's eye contact, perceiving that he could somehow peer into their spirit. It would be hard to try to conceal truth from one such as he.

They took the paths and walked some distance on each one. They did visit the privy which each used while there. They visited the throw away place. They walked past the heron rookery. When they returned to the village, they saw Wapa with Yotuimoa. He introduced them to his wife. The people did notice that there was a slower approach to everything in this place. Their speech was slower, and their walking was slower.

When they returned to the gathering place, the chief asked Urch what the people thought.

"They are duly impressed, Chief. One thing that a few people noticed is that the Hoomuhu are slower of speech than we are and you walk slower. We tend to talk faster and hurry about."

"If you go to visit those people who live near the ice sheet, you'll find they speak faster and hurry more. It is a thing of the environment. Where it is hot and humid, speech and movement is slower; where cold and dry, people speak fast and walk fast. It's not custom or anything people plan. It just happens based, I think, on temperature."

"Chief, I didn't realize you had traveled so far."

"I was expected to become chief when I was young. My father had been chief. There is much to being a chief, Urch. You need to be able to see with reason to understand. Too often people see without reason, and they make a quick un-studied decision. They base decisions on assumptions that have no foundation, as if by taking a boat to the grass land, expecting it to float. When a chief makes a decision, that decision can affect a lot of people for a long time. He must reason well and consider all the effects of his decision or risk imperiling his people. An immediate decision that is not reasoned is more likely to hurt the people than help them. That would be unacceptable. Consequently, potential future chiefs are not taught that this or that decision is good or bad. We are taught to think. There must be planning long in advance of creating a chief. We are made to travel, so we can see that others do not think like we do. We can learn from them and they can learn from us. It works when both sides have minds that will listen to the other. When the minds are closed or there are interferences because of hidden desires, there is nothing but chaos. Chaos is good for nothing. When being taught to become a chief, we are taught all the things others are taught, but we spend more time with the wisest of our people and learn from other peoples and experience. It is our way. We try to bring the very best to our people."

"I never heard you say so many words—ever, Chief," Urch said smiling.

"Urch, you have had some of the training of which I speak. You had it from your three crossings. You had it from your exploring places you never saw. You have been blessed with a view of life few have. You have learned well, for your knowledge hasn't made you arrogant but rather humble, the basic substance of human wisdom."

Food was served and the people began to gather. For some time the chief and Urch stood watching them fill bowls, take their food to a certain place they liked, and sit with family to eat. The visitors gathered as a group within the group around Wapa, because he could tell them what they were going to eat, and because he could translate. Finally, the group was seated and they ate. Never in their lives had they had food that was so tasty. Many had to be shown how to eat the crayfish. They were amazed. Each one on this trip wanted to live in this land. They could understand now why Urch and Wapa chose it.

After they ate, the visitors climbed back into the boat and rowed back to the campsite. It was late when they returned. They put the boats away and met those on shore to talk about their visit. The people who had remained at the campsite could not believe the way those who visited described the place. Twelve more people were on the list to go in the morning. No more trips would be needed.

As the second group of people left, the chief told Urch to let them know how many more, if any, places needed to be built. If there were more, they would begin immediately. Urch thanked him and the second group of visitors returned to the camp.

In the morning, the children reverted to their subdued boat behavior. They heard their parents and other older people argue, sometimes quite heatedly, over where they would live. Children were content where they were. They didn't understand the difficulty some adults were having. Urch could hear some words flying off into the air. He was grateful that he had no decision to make. He'd made his before he left to help with the migration. Words kept flying:

"If you could dream a place, it wouldn't be any better."

"We all need to stick together."

"We've given up our land. Must we give up all we've known?"

"Will we ever return to the Cove?"

"The chief is nice, but I like our elders just fine."

"Those homes are wonderful!"

"I'd rather stay right here!"

"I hurt for my children growing up in a foreign land with foreign ways."

"We're the foreigners!"

"I plan to go there. It would be utter stupidity to turn them down."

"Their food is fantastic!"

"You talk as if they're different from us."

"Wapa looks so happy."

"We'd have to learn their language."

"What's wrong with our language?"

"I'm too hot."

The comments went on all day and into the evening. There were women who decided rather than to listen to the heated arguments that erupted from time to time, they would gather what food they could and prepare the evening meal. They didn't have a lot of food from the days before, so much of what they gathered was greens as a soup starter. They discovered wild chives, which they cut and carried back to add to the soup. They made a soup of the greens with all the bits of meat that remained. When it was ready, they called to the group. The adults became quiet and moved to take food. They decided it would be good to go black before anyone reached a decision of this magnitude.

In the morning the discussions began again. They had remembered Urch's telling them that these people reasoned until people could no longer give answers. They realized that giving the same answer over and over was of no avail. As time passed, fewer and fewer people participated. A few men went to hunt knowing their available meat was gone. There was no more soup.

While the discussion continued that day, Urch had called the children and began to teach them the basic Hoomuhu language. Children, he discovered quickly, were easy to teach another language. He remembered his efforts to learn.

Hunters returned with a horse and two large turtles. They butchered them and gave the meat to the women. The remains, since they didn't have the ability to use the whole animal yet, went to the river. The meat roasted filling the air with promises of great taste, and in the distance it appeared a storm was on the way. Urch looked critically at the camp. There was enough elevation for them to be safe, even if it rained heavily. People would, he reasoned, not stay dry in the lean-tos. He did notice that the older boys were busily gathering pine boughs to put under the sleeping skins for the families. That should let water run under the sleeping skins not onto them. At least, he decided, the weather was warm enough for a drenching not to prove a problem.

The meat was ready before the storm hit. They all took their portions and sat under the roof of their lean-to. Urch made a check to be sure the boats were tied adequately. All were fine. He took his food and went to his lean-to.

"You know they'll all do it," Whug said between bites of horse.

"I don't know any such thing," Urch replied watching a brown animal that he didn't recognize on the bank on the other side of the river. It entered a hole in the side of the bank. He could see that it had lots of whiskers, a flexible body, and a fairly thick tail. Moments later another animal of the same type entered the same hole.

The rain fell. It was a heavy rain. Lightning struck and thunder roared. The people hunkered down under their lean-tos. Water ran under the lean-tos which had been made hurriedly without a thought to rain. Urch wished momentarily that he was in his new home at Hoomuhu.

As quickly as it began, the storm ended. People emerged from the lean-tos. Most had put their sleeping skins up on their shoulders when the rain fell to keep it dry. The air smelled so clean, they all noticed, and the colors in the afterlight were vibrant. Tree frogs began a rousing chorus. All seemed good.

In the morning, the older people talked again and then went to see Urch.

"It has been a long, hard decision to reach, but we have decided as a people we must stay together and we would like to move to Hoomuhu. The chief there has been very gracious to accept a group of this size. Will you please tell him, we would like to come?"

"Yes, Father, I will be glad to do it. Do you mind if I take Cattu with me? I plan to take Kol as well, and, of course, the baby."

"Take Cattu. She will be thrilled." Whug looked at Urch. He thought what a wonderful man his son had become.

Urch found Kol and Cattu and asked them to accompany him to Hoomuhu. They would leave immediately. Cattu was so excited she could hardly contain herself. She would soon see her new home. It was wonderful!

They reached Hoomuhu and to Urch's surprise the tree looked wrong. Then, he realized, a whole huge limb was separated from the tree. He almost ran to find the chief. He found him standing in the gathering place. People were chopping into the limb to clear it from the grounds of the village.

"Urch, how good to see you. Look what the storm brought us," the chief said.

"Is everyone safe?" Urch asked, not wanting any bad news.

"Everyone is fine. We had some structure damage in a few homes, but all is well here. How about at your camp?"

"All's well there," he replied. "Can I help?" Urch asked.

"Not at the moment. The men have to cut the limb apart before it can be moved. Come sit with me and bring your family. Now who is this young woman?" he nodded toward Cattu.

"She is my sister. Her name is Cattu. Cattu, say 'Hello, Chief Backtament,' just like I said it," he told her.

She did it perfectly in the chief's language.

The chief took her hand. He patted her shoulder and, looking at Urch, he said, "Isn't it amazing how quickly they learn? Children should learn many languages while they are young."

They reached the gathering place and sat. Cattu took Aptuk by the hand and walked around the village ground where she could still be seen by Urch.

"You have a message for me?" Chief Backtament asked.

"Yes, Chief. Our people took two days to argue what they wanted. It's been decided that all would like to come here to become Hoomuhu. Will you accept all of us?"

"You know I will," he said smiling. "I am so glad they want to remain all together. That is important for now and the future. They are invited to come and make lean-tos here, or to wait until their homes are made. There is no pressure. It might be easier on them to come now rather than wait. Men could hunt and help with the building."

"I will let them know. Chief, I go back now. I see you are busy, and I don't need your time. I am so relieved that none were hurt when the limb fell. It frightened me when I saw it."

"Urch, I find it hard to believe that you were truly frightened."

"Chief, I suppose I should have said dismayed or worried."

"Don't think on it. I was teasing you," the chief touched his shoulder. "Go now and bring your people when you are ready."

"Don't be surprised if we all arrive this afternoon."

"Urch, you are an amazing person. Nothing you do will surprise me."

Urch called Cattu and she came with Aptuk. The four of them returned back to the boat and headed to the camp.

Later that afternoon, no surprise to the chief, the boats arrived at Hoomuhu. SealEaters tied the boats to trees along the bank of the river. They gathered their things and walked to the new home area. There were more homes there than when they first visited Hoomuhu.

Urch put his things in his home. He laughed out loud when he discovered his alligator backpack and a small skin with bee's wax on his sleeping place. Kol and Aptuk joined him inside the new home. He called to Whug, Amegulatuga, Nip, and Cattu. They would stay with him. Eventually, he decided, they'd build onto the side of their home so that Whug, Amegulatuga, Nip, and Cattu had an adjoining home. Realizing what was happening, all the rest of the people did as Urch had done. They filled the available homes so that none needed to make a lean-to. Families would move out to other homes as they were built.

Just outside the home where At and Merlan were, Litmaq and Lefa looked out on the land. He embraced her. "There is no more need of *Little Rabbit*, my dear. You have become such a strong woman—a woman of whom I am so proud—and this is a far, far better place for us to live and bring children. I'll call you nothing but Lefa now, for to me it means a woman who has conquered so much that life gives to fear. A woman of great strength. One with whom not to trifle." They kissed.

The SealEaters over time became Hoomuhu. They loved the warmer land, the variety of food, and the people with whom they had become one. They learned the ways of the Hoomuhu quickly; the language, not so quickly. They became strong in the new land.

Urch took Kol as wife. They had eight children. Urch lived to the age of fifty-nine. Kol lived to the age of sixty-four. Wapa and Yotuimoa had twelve children. Wapa lived to the age of seventy. Yotuimoa lived to the age of sixty-five. Whug died at the age of seventy-five, so very proud of Urch and Oppermatu. He never learned what happened to Emuka, but something inside told him Emuka lived. Whug believed his people would continue through the ages, because of the move. Whug's only regret was that his body in death would not lie with Gemu.

Author To Reader

I hope you enjoyed this look at how Solutreans might have arrived in what is now the United States of America during the Ice Age, bringing their unique spear points with them. Over time, I speculate, those spear points would lead to the development of the Clovis Point. Solutrean's sharing with indigenous people they found in their new land could have been the basis for the conundrum that is the Clovis Point.

I would greatly appreciate a brief (or long) comment on Amazon (http://amzn.to/1ToJVOT) or Barnes and Noble to let me and others know what you thought of this book. It's a contribution you can make as a reader to my future writing.

Bibliography

Please note: This bibliography has not been updated since 2014. I have used my Facebook Author Page to share newly found information, which only lasts a couple of years on the Fb site. These entries, however, do reflect the majority of my research. Research for me is ongoing.

Albino, A., Carlini, A., "First Record of Boa Constrictor (Serpentes, Boidae) in the Quaternary of South America," Journal of Herpetology, March 2008.

Adovasio, J. M., Page, J., *The First Americans: In Pursuit of Archaeology's Greatest Mystery*, Modern Library, Imprint of Random House, 2003.

Alvarenga, H., Jones, W. Rinderknecht, "The youngest record of phorusrhacid birds (Aves, Phorusrhacidae) from the late Pleistocene of Uruguay," N. Jb. Geol. Palaontol. Abh 256/2, April 2010. (in English)

Ao, H., Deng, C, Dekkers, M. J., Sun, Y., Liu, Q., Zhu, R., "Pleistocene environmental evolution in the Nihewan Basin and implications for early human colonization of North China," Quaternary International, 2010.

Bae, C., "The late Middle Pleistocene hominin fossil record of eastern Asia: Synthesis and review," American Journal of Physical Anthropology, supplement yearbook, 143(51), 2010.

Bae, K., "Origin and patterns of the Upper Paleolithic industries in the Korean Peninsula and movement of modern humans in East Asia," Quaternary International, 211(1-2), 2010.

BBC Article Cites Antiquity on Oldest Evidence of Arrows Found (64,000 years ago), http://www.bbc.com/news/science-environment-11086110

Bailey, S., "A Closer Look at Neanderthal Postcanine Dental Morphology: The Mandibular Dentition," The Anatomical Record, 269, 2002.

Bailey, S. E., Wu, L., "A comparative dental metrical and morphological analysis of a Middle Pleistocene hominin maxilla from Chaoxian (Chaohu), China," Quaternary International, 211(1-2), 2010.

Bailliet, G., Rothhammer, F., Garnese, F. R., Bravi,C.M., and Bianchi, N. O., "Founder Mitochondrial Haplotypes in Amerindian Populations," The Journal of Human Genetics, 54, 1994.

Balter, M., "Child Burial Provides Rare Glimpse of Early Americans," ScienceNOW, Feb 2011.

Banks, W., D'Errico, F., Dibble, H., Krishtalka, L., West, D., Olszewski, D., Peterson, A., Anderson, D., Gillam, J., Montet-White, A., Crucifix, M., Marean, C., Sánchez-Goñi, M., Wohlfarth, B., Vanhaeran, M., "Eco-Cultural Niche Modeling: New Tools for Reconstructing the Geography and Ecology of Past Human Populations," PaleoAnthropology, 2006.

Bannai, M., Ohashi, J., Harihara, S., Takahashi, Y., Juji, T., Omoto, K., Tokunaga, K., "Analysis of HLA genes and haplotypes in Ainu (from Hokkaido, northern Japan) supports the premise that they descent from Upper Paleolithic populations of East Asia," Tissue Antigens, 55, 2000.

Bengston, John D., In Hot Pursuit of Language in Prehistory, John Benjamin Publishing Co., The Netherlands, 2008.

Benson, L., Lund, S., Smoot, J., Rhode, D., Spencer, R., Verosub, K., Louderback, L., Johnson, C., "The rise and fall of Lake Bonneville between 45 and 10.5 ka," Quaternary International, 235(1-2), 2009.

Boeskorov, G. G., "The North of Eastern Siberia: Refuge of Mammoth Fauna in the Holocene," Gondwana Research, 7(2) 2004, available in English in ScienceDirect, November 2005.

Bogoras, W., The Jesup North Pacific Expedition, Memoir of the American Museum of Natural History, Volume VII, The Chukchee, Leiden, E. J. Brill, Ltd., Printers and Publishers, 1975 (reprint of the 1904-1909 edition). This publication is routinely referred to as "The Chukchee."

Bolnick, D. A., Shook, B. A, Campbell, L, Goddard, I, "Problematic Use of Greenberg's Linguistic Classification of the Americas in Studies of Native American Genetic Variation," American Journal of Human Genetics, 75(3): 2004.

Bonnichsen, R. Lepper, B., Stanford, D., Waters, M., Paleoamerican Origins: Beyond Clovis, Center for the Study of the First Americans, Department of Anthropology, Texas A&M University, 2005.

Borrell, B., "Bon Voyage, Caveman," Archaeology, 63(3), May/June 2010. (possibility of seafaring by Homo erectus at 130,000 ya)

Bower, B., "Asian Trek," Science News, 171(14), 4/7/2007.

Bower, B., "Ancient hominids may have been seafarers," Science News, 177(3), 2010.

Brantingham, P., Gao, X., Madsen, D., Bettinger, R., Elston, r., " The initial Upper Paleolithic at Shuidonggou, Northwestern China," in The Early Upper Paleolithic beyond Western Europe, Ed. By Brantingham, P, Juhn, S., and Kerry, K., 2004.

Bryan, A. (ed.), New Evidence for the Pleistocene Peopling of the Americas, Center for the Study of Early Man, University of Maine at Orono, 1986.

Cannon, M. D., "Explaining variability in Early Paleoindian foraging," Quaternary International, 191(1), 2008.

Carter, George F., Earlier Than You Think: A Personal View of Man in America, Texas A&M University Press, 1980.

Catto, N., "Quaternary floral and faunal asssemblages: Ecological and tapho-nomical investigations," Quaternary International, 233(2), 2011.

Catto, N., "Quaternary landscape evolution: Interplay of climate, tectonics, geomorphology, and natural hazards," Quaternary International, 233(1), 2011.

Chauhan, P. R., "Large mammal fossil occurrences and associated archaeo-logical evidence in Pleistocene contexts of peninsular India and Sri Lanka," Quaternary International, 192(1), 2008.

Chen, C., An, J, Chen, H., "Analysis of the Xionanhai lithic assemblage, excavated in 1978," Quaternary International, 211(1-2), 2010.

Chen, X-Y., Cui, G-H., Yang, J-X., "Threatened fishes of the world: Pseudobagrus medianalis (Regan) 1904 (Bagridae), Environmental Biology of Fishes, 81(3), 2008.

Chlachula, J., Drozdov, N., Ovodov, N., "Last Interglacial peopling of Siberia: the Middle Palaeolithic site Ust'-Izhul', the upper Yenisei area," Boreas, 32, 2003.

Choi, C., "Denisovan Genome Sequenced, Reveals Brown-Eyed Girl of Extinct Human Species, Researchers say," Huff Post, August30, 2012.

Ciochon, R., Bettis III, A., "Asian Homo erectus converges in time," Nature, 458, March 2009

Cione, A., Tonni, E., Soibelzon, L., "The Broken Zig-Zag: Late Cenozoic large mammal and tortoise extinction in South America," Rev. Mus. Argentino Cienc. Nat., n.s., 5(1), 2003.

Connor, Cathy, O'Haire, Daniel, Roadside Geology of Alaska, Mountain Press Publishing Company, 1988.

Coppens, Y., Tseveendorj, D., Demeter, F., Turbat, T., and Giscard, P., "Discovery of an archaic Homo sapiens skullcap in Northeast Mongolia," Comptes Rendus Palevol, 7(1), Feb 2008. Note: The findings are that the skullcap shows similarities with Neanderthals, Chinese Homo erectus, and West/Far East archaic Homo sapiens. Dating is possible late Pleistocene.

Corvinus, G., "Homo erectus in East and Southeast Asia, and the questions of the age of the species and its association with stone artifacts, with special attention to handaxe-like tools," Quaternary International, 117, 2004.

Coxe, W., The Russian Discoveries Between Asia and America, Readex Microprint Corp., 1966, copy of Coxe's document from 1780.

Cremo, M., Thompson, R., Forbidden Archaeology: The Hidden History of the Human Race, Unlimited Resources, 1996-2011.

Delluc, B., Delluc, G., "Art Paléolithique, saisons et climats," Comtes Rendus Palevol, 5, 2006.

Demske, D., Heumann, G., Granoszewski, W., Nita, M., Mamakowa, K., Tarasov, P., Oberhänsli, H., "Late glacial and Holocene vegetation and regional climate variability evidenced in high-resolution pollen records from Lake Baikal," Global and Planetary Change, 46, 2005.

Derbeneva, O. A., Sukernik, R. I., Volodko, N.V., Hosseini, s. H., Lott, M. T., and Wallace, D. C., "Analysis of Mitochondrial DNA Diversity in the Aleuts of the Commander Islands and Its Implications for the Genetic History of Beringia," The American Journal of Human Genetics, 71(2): 2002.

Derenko, M., Malyarchuk, B., Grzybowski, T., Denisove, G., Dambueva, I., Perkova, M., Dorzhu, C., Luzina, F., Lee, H. K., Vanecek, T., Villems, R., and Zakharov, I., "Phylogeographic analysis of Mitochondrial DNA in Northern Asian Populations," The American Journal of Human Genetics, 81, November 2007.

Dickinson, William R., "Geological perspectives on hte Monte Verde archaeological site in Chile and pre-Clovis coastal migration in the Americas.," Quaternary Research, 76, 201-210, 2011.

Dillehay, T. D., The Settlement of the Americas: A New Prehistory, Basic Books of the Perseus Books Group, 2000.

Dilley, Lorie M, Dilley, Thomas E., Guidebook to Geology of Anchorage, Alaska, Lorie M. Dilley and Thomas E. Dilley, 2,000.

Dixon, E. J. and G. S. Smith, "Broken canines from Alaskan cave deposits: re-evaluating evidence for domesticated dog and early humans in Alaska." American Antiquity, 51(2): 1986.

Doelman, T., "Flexibility and Creativity in Microblade Core Manufacture in Southern Primorye, Far East Russia," Asian Perspectives, 47(2), 2009.

Elliott, D.K., Dynamics of Extinction, John Wiley & Sons, New York, 1986.

Elston, Robert G., Brantingham, P. Jeffrey, "Microlithic Technology in Northern Asia: A Risk-Minimizing Strategy of the Late Paleolithic and Early Holocene," Archaeological Papers of the American Anghropological Association, 12 (1) 103-116, 2002.

Erlandson, J., Moss, M., Des Lauriers, M., "Life on the edge: early maritime cultures of the Pacific coast of North America, Quaternary Science Reviews, 27, 2008.

Etler, D., "The Fossil Evidence for Human Evolution in Asia," Annual Review of Anthropology, 25, 1996.

Etler, D., "Homo erectus in East Asia: Human Ancestor or Evolutionary Dead-End?" Athena Review, 4(1) [Cannot locate year. The author is from Department of Anthropology, Cabrillio college, Aptos, California.]

Etler, D., Crummett, T., Wolpoff, M., "Longgupo: Early Homo Colonizer or Late Pliocene Lufengpithecus Survivor in South China?" Human Evolution, 16(1-12), 2001.

Farina, R., Vizcaino, S. Iuliis, Megafauna: Giant Beasts of Pleistocene South America, Indiana University Press, 2013.

Fell, B., America B.C., Artisan Publishers, 2010.

Fiedel, Stuart J., "Older Than We Thought: Implications of Corrected Dates for Paleoindians," American Antiquity, 64(1), 1999.

Finlayson, Clive, The HUMANS WHO WENT EXTINCT, Why Neanderthals died out and we survived. Oxford University Press, 2009.

Fitzhugh, W., "Stone Shamans and Flying Deer of Northern Mongolia: Deer Goddess of Siberia or Chimera of the Steppe?" Arctic Anthropology, 46(1-2) 2009.

Flam, F.: "Red hair a part of the Neanderthal genetic profile" The Philadelphia Inquirer, October 26, 2007.

Flannery, T., The Eternal Frontier, Atlantic Monthly Press, New York, 2001.

Forster, P., Harding, R., Torroni, A., and Bandelt, H. J., "Origin and Evolution of Native American mtDNA Variation: A Reappraisal," The American Journal of Human Genetics, 59(4): 1996.

Froehle, A., Churchill, S., "Energetic Competition Between Neandertals and Anatomically Modern Humans," PaleoAnthropology, 2009.

Froese, T., Woodward, A., Ikegami, T., "Turing instabilities in biology, culture, and consciousness? On the enactive origins of symbolic mateiral culture," Adaptive Behavior, 2 (3).

Gilbert, M. T. P., Jenkins, D. L., Götherstrom, A., Naveran, N. Sanchez, J. J., Hofreiter, M., Thomsen, P. F., Binladen, J., Higham, T. F. G., Yohe, R. M., II, Parr, R. Cummings, L. S. Willerslev, E., "DNA from Pre-Clovis Human Coprolites in Oregon, North America," Science Express, April 2008.

Gilligan, I., "The Prehistoric Development of clothing: Archaeological Implications of a thermal Model," Journal of Archaeological Method Theory, 17, 2010.

Gladyshev, S., Olsen, J., Tabarev, A., Kuzmin, Y., "Peleoenvironment. The Stone Age: Chronology and Periodization of Upper Paleolithic Sites in Mongolia." Archaeology Ethnology & Anthropology of Eurasia, 38(3), 2010.

Goebel, T., Waters, M., Dikova, M., "The Archaeology of Ushki Lake, Kamchatka, and the Pleistocene Peopling of the Americas," Science, 301(5632), 2003.

Goebel, T., et al, "The Late Pleistocene Dispersal of Modern Humans in the Americas, Science, 319, 1497, 2008.

Goldberg, E., Chebykin, E., Zhuchenko, N., Vorobyeva, S., Stepanova, O., Khlystov, O., Ivanov, E., Weinberg, E, Gvozdkov, A., "Uranium isotopes as proxies of the Lake Baikal watershed (East Siberia) during the past 150 ka," Palaeogeography, Palaeoclimatology, Palaeoecology, 294(1-2) August 2010.

Golubenko, M. V., Stepanov, V. A., Gubina, M. A., Zhadanov, S. I., Ossipova, L. Pl, Damba, L., Voevoda, M. I., Dipierri, J. E., Villems, R., Malhi, R. S., Beringian "Standstill and Spread of Native American Founders," PLoS ONE 2(9): eB29. doi;10.1371/journal.pone.0000829.

Goodyear, Albert C., "Evidence for Pre-Clovis Sites in the Eastern United States," unpublished and undated manuscript, [no longer has active link]

Grayson, D., Meltzer, D., "A requiem for North American overkill," Journal of Archaeological Science, 30(5), 2003.

Grove, C., "Ice-age child's remains discovered in Interior," Anchorage Daily News, 2/24/2011

Hall, R., "Cenozoic plate tectonic reconstruction of SE Asia," from Fraser, L., Matthews, S., Murphy, R., (Eds.), Petroleum Geology of Southeast Asia, Geological Society of London Special Publication 26, 1997.

Hapgood, C., Maps of the Ancient Sea Kings, Adventures Unlimited Press, 1966.

Hardaker, C., The First American: the Suppressed Story of the People Who Discovered the New World, New Page Books, 2007.

Haynes, C,. V., Jr., "Younger Dryas 'Black mats' and the Rancholabrean termination in North America," National Academy of Sciences of the USA, 2008. (See also: for photographs http://www.georgehoward.net/Vance%20Haynes'%20Black%20Mat.htm)

Henry, A., Brooks, A., Piperno, D., "Microfossils in calculus demonstrate consumption of plants and cooked foods in Neanderthal diets," Proceedings of the National Academy of Sciences, 108(2), 2010.

Hoffecker, J. F., A Prehistory of the North: Human Settlement of the Higher Latitudes, Rutgers University Press, New Brunswick, New Jersey, 2005.

Honeychurch, W., Amartuvshin, C., "Hinterlands, Urban Centers, and Mobile Settings: The 'New' Old World Archaeology from the Eurasian Steppe," Asian Perspectives, 46(1) 2007.

Hopkins, D. M., Matthews, J. V, Jr., Schweger, C. E., Young, S. B., Paleoecology of Beringia, Academic Press, New York, 1982.

Huyghe, P., Columbus Was Last: From 200,000 B.C. To 1492 A Heretical History of Who Was First, Anomalist Books, 1992.

Igarashi, Y., Zharov, A., "Climate and vegetation change during the late Pleistocene and early Holocene in Sakhalin and Hokkaido, northeast Asia," Quaternary International, xxx (in process), 2011.

Inman, M.: "Neanderthals Had Same 'Language Gene' as Modern Humans," National Geographic News, October 18, 2007, http://news.nationalgeo-graphic.com/news/2007/10/071018-neandertal-gene.html

Irwin-Williams, Cynthia, "Dilemma Posed by Uranium-Series Dates on Archaeologically Significant Bones from Valsequillo, Puebla, Mexico," Earth and Planetary Science Letters 6 (1969) 237-244, North Holland Publishing Comp., Amsterdam.

Jackinsky, M., "Evidence of woolly mammoths on Peninsula grows," Alaska Daily News, 3/13/2011.

Jackson, Jr., L. E., Wilson, M. C., "The Ice-Free Corridor Revisited," Geotimes, Feb. 2004.

Jiang, Y-E., Chen, X-Y, Yang, J-X., "Threatened fishes of the world: Yunnanilus discoloris Zhou & He 1989 (Cobitidae)," Environmental Biology of Fishes, 86(1), 2009.

Jin, J. J. H., Shipman, P., "documenting natural wear on antlers: A first step in identifying use-wear on purported antler tools," Quaternary International, 211(1-2) 2010.

Johnson, John F. C., Chugach Legends: Stories and Photographs of the Chugach Region, Chugach Alaska Corporation, 1984.

Joling, D., "Warming brings unwelcome change to Alaska villages," Anchorage Daily News, 3/27/ 2011.

Joly, L. G., Guerra, S., Septimo, R., Solis, P. N., Correa, M. D., Gupta, M. P., Lrvy, S., Sandberg, F., Perera, P., "Ethnobotanical Inventory of Medicinal Plants Used by the Guaymi Indians in Western Panama, Part II." Journal of Ethnopharmacology, 28 (1990).

Jones, Anore, Plants That We Eat: Nauriat Niginaqtuat, University of Alaska Press, Fairbanks, 2010.

Joseph, F., Discovering the Mysteries of Ancient America: Lost History and Legends, Unearthed and Explored, New Page Books, 2006.

Khenzykhenova, F., "Paleoenvironments of Palaeolithic humans in the Baikal region," Quaternary International, 179(1), 2008.

Khenzykhenova, F., Sato, T., Lipnina, E., Medvedev, G., Kato, H., Kogai, S., Maximenko, K., Novosel'zeva, V., "Upper paleolithic mammal fauna of the Baikal region, east Siberia (new data)," Quaternary International, 231, 2011.

Kienast, F., Schirrmeister, L., Siegert, C., Tarasov, P., "Palaeobotanical evidence for warm summers in the East Siberian Arctic during the last cold stage," Quaternary Research, 63(3), 2005.

King, G., Bailey, G., "Tectonics and human evolution," Antiquity, 80, 2006.

Klein, H. S., Schiffner, D. C., "The Current Debate about the Origins of the Paleoindian of America," Journal of Social History, 37(2), Winter 2003.

Kolomiets, V. L., Gladyshev, S. A., Bezrukova, E. V., Rybin, E. P., Letunova, P. P., Abzaeva, A. A., "Paleoenvironment The Stone Age: Environment and human behavior in northern Mongolia during the Upper Pleistocene," Archaeology, Ethnology, and Anthropology of Eurasia, 37(1), 2009.

Komatsu, G., Olsen, J., Ormo, J., Di. Achille, G., Kring, D., Matsui T., "The Tsenkher structure in the Gobi-Altai, Mongolia: Geomorphological hints of an impact origin," Geomorphology, 74(1-4), March 2006.

Kornfeld, M., Larson, M. L., "Bonebeds and other myths: Paleoindian to Archaic transition on North American Great Plains and Rocky Mountains," Quaternary International, 191(1), 2008.

Krause, J., Orlando, L., Serre, D., Viola, B., Prüfer, K., Richards, M., Hublin, J., Hänni, C., Derevianko, A., Pääbo, S., "Neanderthals in central Asia and Siberia," Nature LETTERS, 449, 2007.

Kunz, Michael, M. Bever, C. Adkins, The Mesa Site: Paleoindians above the Arctic Circle, U. S. Department of the Interior, Bureau of Land Management, BLM-Alaska Open File Report 86, BLM/AK/ST-03/001+8100+020, April 2003.

Kurochkin, E., Kuzmin, Y., Antoshchenko-Olenev, I., Zabelin, V., Krivonogov, S., Nohrina, T., Lbova, L., Burr, G, and Cruz, R., "The timing of ostrich existence in Central Asia: AMS 14C age of eggshells from Mongolia and southern Siberia (a pilot study)," Nuclear Instruments and Methods in Physics Research Section B: Beam Interactions with Materials and Atoms, 268(7-8), April 2010.

Kuzmin, Y., Orlova, L., "Radiocarbon chronology and environment of woolly mammoth (Mammuthus primigenius Blum.) in northern Asia: results and perspectives," Earth-Science Reviews, 68, 2004.

Kuzmin, Y., Richards, M., Yoneda, M., "Paleodietary Patterning and Radiocarbon Dating of Neolithic Populations in the Primorye Province, Russian Far East," Ancient Biomolecules, 4(2), 2002.

Lam, Y. M., Brunson, K, Meadow, R., Yuan, J., "Integrating taphonomy into the practice of zooarchaeology in China," Quaternary International, 211(1-2), 2010.

Langdon, Steve J., Native People of Alaska: Traditional Living in a Northern Land, Greatland Graphics, 2008.

Lee, H., "Paleoenvironment: The Stone Age. Projectile Points and Their Implications," Archaeology Ethnology & Anthropology of Eurasia, 38(3), 2010.

Lell, J. T., Sukernik, R. I., Starikovskaya, Y. B., Su, B., Jin, L., Schurr, T. G., Underhill, P. A., Wallace, D. C., "The Dual Origin and Siberian Affinities of Native American Y Chromosomes," The American Journal of Human Genetics, 70, 2002.

Lister, A., Bahn, P. G., Mammoths: Giants of the Ice Age, Richard Green Publisher, 1994.

Liu, W., Wu, X., Pei, S., Wu, Xiujie, Norton, C. J., "Huanglong Cave: A Late Pleistocene human fossil site in Hubei Province, China," Quaternary International, 211(1-2), 2010.

Lu, X., Xiong, D., Chen, C., "Threatened fishes of the world: Sinocyclocheilus grahami (Regan 1904) (Cyprinidae)," Environmental Biology of Fishes, 85(2), 2009.

Ma, S., Wang, Y., Xu, L., "Taxonomic and Phylogenetic Studies on the Genus Muntiacus," Acta Theriologica Sinica VI(3) 1986. (Translated by Will Downs, Dept of Geology, Bilby Research Center, Northern Arizona Univ., 1991)

Macé, F., "Human Rhythm and Divine Rhythm in Ainu Epics," Diogenes, 46(1), 1998.

Marwick, B., "Biogeography of Middle Pleistocene hominins in mainland Southeast Asia: A review of current evidence," Quaternary International, 202(1-2), 2009.

Mednikova, M., Dobrovolskaya, M., Buzhilova, A., Kandinov, M., "A Fossil Human Humerus from Khvalynsk: Morphology and Taxonomy," Archaeology Ethnology & Anthropology of Eurasia, 38(1), 2010.

Meltzer, D., First Peoples in a New World: Colonizing Ice Age America, University of California Press, 2009.

Merriwether, D. A., Hall, W. W., Vahine, A., and Ferrell, R. E., "mtDNA Variation Indicates Mongolia May Have Been the Source for the Founding Population for the New World," The American Journal of Human Genetics, 59, 1996.

Mol, D., de Vos, J., van der Plicht, J., "The presence and extinction of Elephas antiquus Falconer and Cautley, 1847, in Europe," Quaternary International, 169-170, 2007.

Moncel, M., "Oldest human expansions in Eurasia: Favouring and limiting factors," Quaternary International, 223-4, 2010.

Mueller, Tom, "Ice Baby: Secrets of a Frozen Mammoth," National Geographic, 215, 5, May 2009.

Naske, C-M., Slotnick, H. E., Alaska A History of the 49th State, 2nd Ed., University of Oklahoma Press, Norman, 1979.

Neel, J. V., Biggar, R. J., Sukernik, R. I., "Virologic and genetic studies relate Amerind origins to the indigenous people of the Mongolia/Manchuria/southeastern Siberia region," Proceedings of the National Academy of Sciences, USA, 91, 1994.

Nikolskiy, P. A., Basilyan, A. E., Sulerzhitsky, L. D., and Pitulko, V. V., "Prelude to the extinction: Revision of the Achchagyl-Allaikha and Berelyokh mass accumulations of mammoth," Quaternary International, 219(1-2), 2010.

Norton, C. J., "The nature of megafaunal extinctions during the MIS 3-2 transition in Japan," Quaternary International, 211(1-2), 2010.

Norton, C. J., Jin, J. J. H., "Hominin morphological and behavioral variation in eastern Asia and Australasia: current perspectives," Quaternary International, 211(1-2), 2010.

O'Connell, L., "Sifting Through Garbage from the End of the Ice Age: It's a LIving for Frontier Scientists," Anchorage Daily News, June 1, 2011.

O'Neill, D., The Last Giant of Beringia: The Mystery of the Bering Land Bridge, Westview Press, Perseus Books Group, New York, 2004.

Oppenheimer, S., "The great arc of dispersal of modern humans: Africa to Australia," Quaternary International, 202(1-2), 2009.

Orlova, L. A., Kuzmin, Y. V., Stuart, A. J., Tikhonov, A. N., "Chronology and environment of woolly mammoth (Mammuthus primigenius Blumenbach) extinction in northern Asia," The World of Elephants – International Congress, Rome 2001.

Osipov, E., Khlystov, O., "Glaciers and meltwater flux to Lake Baikal during the Last Glacial Maximum," Palaeogeography, Palaeoclimatology, Palaeoecology, 294(1-2) 2010.

Palombo, M. R., "Quaternary mammal communities at a glance," Quaternary International, 212(2), 2010.

Park, S., "L'hominidé du Pléistocène supérieur en Corée, L'anthropologie, 110, 2006.

Pei, S., Gao, X., Feng, X., Chen, F., Dennell, R., "Lithic assemblage from the Jingshuiwan Paleolithic site of the early Late Pleistocene in the Three Gorges, China," Quaternary International, 211(1-2), January 2010.

Pietrusewsky, M., "A multivariate analysis of measurements recorded in early and more modern crania from East Asia and Southeast Asia," Quaternary International, 211(1-2), 2010.

Pimenoff, V., Comas, D., Palo, J., Vershubsky, G., Kozlov, A, Sajantila, A., "Northwest Siberian Khanty and Mansi in the junction of West and East Eurasian gene pools as revealed by uniparental markers," European Journal of Human Genetics, 16, 2008.

Pitulko, V., "The Berelekh Quest: A Review of Forty Years of Research in the Mammoth Graveyard in Northeast Siberia," Geoarchaeology, 26(1), 2011.

Ponce de León, M., Golovanova, L., Doronichev, V., Romanova, G., Akazaqa, T., Kondo, O., Ishida, H., Zollikofer, C., "Neanderthal brain size at birth provides insights into the evolution of human life history," Proceedings of the National Academy of Sciences, 105(37), Sept 2008.

Potter, B. A., Reuther, J. D., Bowers, P. M., and Relvin-Reymiller, C., "Little Delta Dune Site: A Late-Pleistocene Multicomponent Site in Central Alaska," Archaeology: North America, CRP 25, 2008.

Powell, E., "Mongolia," Archaeology, 59(1) Jan/Feb 2006.

Pratt, Verna E., Field Guide to Alaskan WILDFLOWERS Commonly seen along the Highways and Byways, 1989 Alaskakrafts, Inc.

Prokopenko, A., Kuzmin, M., Li, H., Woo, K., Catto, N., "Lake Hovsgol basin as a new study site for long continental paleoclimate records in continental interior Asia: General contest and current status," Quaternary International, 205, 2009.

Quade, J., Forester, R. M., Pratt, W. L., Carter, C., "Black Mats, Spring-Fed Streams, and Late-Glacial-Age Recharge in the Southern Great Basin," Quaternary Research, 49(2) 1998.

Ransom, J. E., "Derivation of the Word Alaska," American Anthropologist, 42, 1942.

Razjigaeva, N., Korotky, A., Grebennikova, T., Ganzey, L., Mokhova, L., Bazarova, V. Sulerzhitsky, L., Lutaenko, K., "Holocene climatic changes and environmental history of Iturup Island, Kurile Islands, northwestern Pacific," The Holocene, 12, 2002.

Reich, D., et al., "Genetic history of an archaic hominin group from Denisova Cave in Siberia," Nature, 468, 7327, 2010.

Rose, W. I., Chesner, C. A., "Dispersal of ash in the great Toba Eruption, 74 ka," Geology, 15, 1987.

Rudaya, N., Tarasov, P., Dorofeyuk, N., Solovieva, N., Kalugin, I., Andreev, Daryin, A., Diekmann, B., Riedel, F., Tserendash, N., Wagner, M., "Holocene environments and climate in the Mongolian Altai reconstructed from the Hoton-Nur pollen and diatom records: a step towards better understanding climate dynamics in Central Asia," Quaternary Science Reviews, 28(5-6) 2009.

Russell, Priscilla N., Tanaina Plantlore Dena'ina K'et'una: An Ethnobotany of the Dena'ina Indians of Southcentral Alaska, Alaska Geographic Association, 2012.

Ruvinsky, J., "The Great American Extinction," Discover, 28(8) 2007.

Saillard, J., Forster, P., Lynnerup, N., Bandelt, H.-J., Nørby, S., "mtDNA Variation among Greenland Eskimos: The Edge of the Beringian Expansion," The Journal of Human Genetics, 2000 September; 67(3): 718-726.

27Saleeby, B. M., "Out of Place Bones: beyond the study of prehistoric subsistence," Arctic Research of the United States, U. S. National Science Foundation, 2002.

Sattler, H. R., The Earliest Americans, Clarion Books, New York, 1993.

Schepartz, L. A., Miller-Antonio, S., "Taphonomy, Life History, and Human Exploitation of Rhinoceros sinensis at the Middle Pleistocene site of Panxian Dadong, Guizhou, China," International Journal of Osteoarchaeology, 2008.

Schrenk, F., Muller, S. The Neanderthals, Routledge, 2005.

Seong, C., "Tanged points, microblades and Late Palaeolithic hunting in Korea," Antiquity, 82, 2008.

Shen, G., Fang, Y., Bischoff, J. L., Feng, Y., and Zhao, J., "Mass spectrometric U-series dating of the Chaoxian hominin site at Yinshan, eastern China," Quaternary International, 211(1-2), 2010.

Shepherd, Jill, "Winter Green," Alaska, February, 1999.

Sher, A., Weinstock, J., Baryshnikov, G., Davydov, S., Boeskorov, G., Zazhigin, V., Nikolskiy, P., "The first record of 'spelaeoid' bears in Arctic Siberia, Quaternary Science Reviews, 30, 2010.

Shichi, K., Takahara, H., Krivonogov, S., Bezrukova, E., Kashiwaya, K., Takehara, A., Nakamura, T., "Late Pleistocene and Holocene vegetation and climate records from Lake Kotokel, central Baikal region," Quaternary International, 205, 2009.

Smith, T., Toussaint, M., Reid, D., Olejniczak, A., Hublin, J., "Rapid dental development in a Middle Paleolithic Belgian Neanderthal," Proceedings of the National Academy of Sciences, 104(51), Dec. 2007.

Snodgrass, J., Leonard, W., "Neandertal Energetics Revisited: Insight Into Population Dynamics and Life History Evolution," PaleoAnthropology, 2009.

Starikovskaya, Y. B., Sukernik, R. I., Schurr, T. G., Kogelnik, A. M., and Wallace, D. C. "mtDNA diversity in Chukchi and Siberian Eskimos:

Implications for the Genetic History of Ancient Beringia and the Peopling of the New World," The American Journal of Human Genetics, 63, 1998.

Stephan, A. E., The First Athabascans of Alaska: Strawberries, Dorrance Publishing Co, Inc., Pittsburg, 1996.

Stone, R., "A Surprising Survival Story in the Siberian Arctic," Science, 303(5642): 2004.

Stringer, C., Finlayson, J., Barton, R., Fernández-Jalvo, Y., Cáceres, I., Sabin, R., Rhodes, E., Currant, A., Rodriguez-Vidal, J., Giles-Pacheco, F., Riquelme-Cantal, J., "Neanderthal exploitation of marine mammals in Gibraltar," Proceedings of the National Academy of Sciences, 105(38) Sept. 2008.

Stringer, C., Lone Survivors: How We Came To Be the Only Humans on Earth. Times Books, Henry Holt & Co., LLC, New York, 2012.

Strong, S., "The Most Revered of Foxes: Knowledge of Animals and Animal Power in an Ainu Kamui Yukar," Asian Ethnology, 68(1), 2009.

Sunnyboy, Audrey, Denyaavee: Medicinal Plants of Interior Alaska's People, Audrey Sunnyboy, 2007.

Sykes, B., The Seven Daughters of Eve, W.W. Norton & Company, New York, 2001.

Szathmary, E. J. E., "mtDNA and the Peopling of the Americas," The Journal of Human Genetics, 53, 1993.

Tamm, E., Kivisild, T., Reidla, M., Metspalu, M., Smith, D. G., Mulligan, C. J., Bravi, C. M., Rickards, O., Martinez-Labarga, C., Khusnutdinova, E. K., Fedorova, S. A., Torroni, A., Neel, J. V., Barrantes, R., Schurr, T. G., "Mitochondrial DNA 'clock' for the Amerinds and its implications for timing their entry into North America," Proceedings of the National Academy of Sciences, USA, 91, 1994.

Tarasov, P., Williams, J., Andreev, A., Nakagawa, T., Bezrukova, E., Herzschuh, U., Igarashi, Y., Müller, S., Werner, K., Zheng, Z., "Satellite- and polllen-based quantitative woody cover reconstructions for northern

Asia: Verification and application to late-Quaternary pollen data," Earth and Planetary Science Letters, 264(1-2), 2007.

Tattersall, I., Masters of the Planet, The Search for Our Human Origins, Palgrace Macmillan, 2012

Than, K., "Neanderthals, Humans Interbred—First Solid DNA Evidence: Most of us have some Neanderthal genes, study finds," May 6, 2010 for National Geographic News, http://news.nationalgeographic. com/news/2010/05/100506-science-neanderthals-humans-mated-interbred-dna-gene/

Tianyuan, L., Etler, D., "New Middle Pleistocene hominid crania from Yunxian in China," Nature, 357, June 1992.

Tong, H., Moigne, A-M., "Quaternary Rhinoceros of China," in English, Acta Anthropologica Sinica, Supplement to Volume 19, 2000.

Torroni, A., Sukernik, R. I., Schurr, Tl G., Starikovskaya, Y. B., Cabell, M. F., Crawford, M. H., Comuzzie, A. G., Wallace, D. C., "mtDNA Variations of Aboriginal Siberians Reveals distinct Genetic Affinities with Native Americans," The American Journal of Human Genetics, 53, 1993.

Vasil'ev, S. A., Kuzmin, Y. V., Orlova, L. A., Dementiev, V. N., "Radiocarbon-Based Chronology of the Paleolithic in Siberia and Its Relevance to the Peopling of the New World," Radiocarbon, 44(2), 2002.

Vergano, D., "Modern humanity's ancient cousins, the Neanderthals, lived in small groups that were isolated from one another, suggests an investigation into their DNA. The analysis also finds that Neanderthals lacked some human genes that are linked to our behavior," National Geographic, April 22, 2014.

Vialet, A., Guipert, G., Jianing, H., Xiaobo, F., Zune, L., Youping, W., de Lumley, M.-A., de Lumley, H., "Homo erectus from the Yunxian and Nankin Chinese sites: Anthropological insights using 3D virtual imaging techniques," Comptes Rendus Palevol 9(6-7), 2010.

Viereck, Eleanor G., Alaska's Wilderness Medicines: Healthful Plants of the Far North, Alaska Northwest Books, 1987.

Volodko, N. V., Starikovskaya, E. B., Mazunin, I. O., Eltsov, N. P., Naidenko, P. V., Wallace, D. C., and Sukernik, R. I., "Mitochondrial Genome Diversity in Arctic Siberians, with Particular Reference to the Evolutionary History of Beringia and Pleistocenic Peopling of the Americas," American Journal of Human Genetics, 82(5), 2008.

Wagner, D. P., McAvoy, J. M., "Pedoarchaeology of Cactus Hill, a sandy Paleoindian site in southeastern Virginia, U. S. A." Geoarchaeology, 19(4), 2004.

Waguespack, N. M., Surovell, T. A., "Clovis Hunting Strategies, or How to Make Out on Plentiful Resources," American Antiquity, 68(2), 2003.

Wang, J., "Late Paleozoic macrofloral assemblages from Weibel coalfield, with reference to vegetational change through the Late Paleozoic Ice-age in the North China Block," International Journal of Coal Geology, 83(2-3), 2010.

Wang, S., Liu, H., Zhang, H., Sun, X., Yi, S., Chen, Y., Zhang, G., Xing, L., Sun, W., "Newly discovered Palaeolithic artefacts from loess deposits and their ages in Lantian, central China, Chin. Sci. Bull. (2014) 59(7):651-661.

Waters, Michael R. et al., "Redefining the Age of Clovis: Implications for the Peopling of hte Americas," Science, 315, 1122, 2007.

Waters-Rist, A., Bazaliiskii, V. I., Weber, A, Goriunova, O. I., Katzenberg, A., "Activity-induced dental modification in holocene Siberian hunter-fisher-gatherers," American Journal of Physical Anthropology, 143(2), 2010.

Wendorf, F., Hester, J., (eds.) Late Pleistocene Environments of the Southern High Plains, Ft. Burgwin Research Center, Inc. Southern Methodist University, 1973.

West, F. H., Ed., AMERICAN BEGINNINGS: the Prehistory and Palaeoecology of Beringia, The University of Chicago Press, Chicago, 1996.

Wiedmer, M., Montgomery, D., Gillespie, A., Greenberg, H., "Late Quaternary megafloods from Glaial Lake Atna, Southcentral Alaska, U.S.A., Quaternary Research, 73, 2010.

Woodman, N., Athfield, N., "Post-Clovis survival of American Mastodon in the southern Great Lakes Region of North America," Quaternary Research, 72(3), 2009.

Wu, X., "Fossil Humankind and Other Anthropoid Primates of China," International Journal of Primatology, 25(5) 2004.

Wu, X., "On the origins of modern humans in China," Quaternary International, 117(1), 2004.

Wu, X., Schepartz, L. A., Norton, C. J., "Morphological and morphometric analysis of variation in the Zhoukoudian Homo erectus brain endocasts," Quaternary International, 211(1-2) 2010.

Wu, Y-S., Chen, Y-S., Xiao, J-Y., "A preliminary study on vegetation and climate changes in Dianchi Lake area in the last 40,000 years," partial in English, Acta Botanica Sinica, 33(5), 1991.

Wynn, T., Coolidge, F. L., How to Think like a Neanderthal, Oxford University Press, 2012.

Xiao, J., Jin, C., Zhu, Y., "Age of the fossil Dali Man in north-central China deduced from chronostratigraphy of the loess-paleosol sequence," Quaternary Science Reviews, 21, 2002.

Xiangcan, J., "Lake Dianchi," Experience and Lessons Learned Brief, final version 2004.

Xu, J-X., Ferguson, D. K., Li, C-S., Wang, Y-F., "Late Miocene vegetation and the climate of the Lühe region in Yunnan, southwestern China," Review of Palaeobotany and Palynology, 148(1), 2008.

Yahner, R. H., "Barking in a primitive ungulate, Muntiacus reevesi: function and adaptiveness," The American Naturalist, 116(2), 1980.

Zang, W., Wang, Y., Zheng, S., Yang, X., Li, Y., Fu, X., Li, N., "Taxonomic investigations on permineralized conifer woods from the Late Paleozoic Angaran deposits of northeastern Inner Mongolia, China, and their palaeoclimatic significance," Review of Palaeobotany and Palynology, 144(3-4), May 2007.

Zhang, Y., Stiner, M, Dennell, R., Wang, C., Zhang, Sh, Gao, X., "Zooarchaeological perspectives on the Chinese Early and Late Paleolithic from the Ma'anshan site (Guizhou, South China)," Journal of Archaeological Science, 37(8), 2010.

Zhu, R., An, Z., Potts, R., Hoffman, K., "Magnetostratigraphic dating of early humans in China," Earth-Science Reviews, 61(3-4) June 2003.

Zorich, Z., "Did Homo erectus Coddle His Grandparents?" Discover, 27(1) Jan. 2006.

No author designated. "Bone fossil points to a mystery human species," USA Today, Mar 25, 2010. [Three types of humans lived within 60 miles of each other in southern Siberia.]

WEBSITES

Alces latifrons http://books.google.com/books?id=BQtyg5m1zQkC&pg=PA58&lpg=PA58&dq=alces+latifrons&source=bl&ots=og5L12y8Tq&sig=jrDQlIfRaXGtU2bud_mlupblHww&hl=en&sa=X&ei=ZZe1U8OlKsagigKKhIDIAw&ved=0CEAQ6AEwAw#v=onepage&q=alces%20latifrons&f=false

America's Stone Age Explorers **http://www.pbs.org/wgbh/nova/transcripts/3116_stoneage.html** (8/23/2010)

Ancestral Human Skull Found in China (80,000 to 100,000 ya) http://news.nationalgeographic.com/news/2008/02/080220-china-fossil.html

Ancient bison bones supports theory about Ice Age seafarers being first in Americas http://www.thaindian.com/newsportal/world-news/ancient-bison-bones-supports-theory-abo... (9/5/2010)

Archaeobotany of the Central Aleutian Islands http://www.uaa.alaska.edu/honorscollege/achievements/Competitive_Grants/UnderGrad/upload/Holly-Thorssin-UGR-FA11-Proposal-for-Web.pdf

Archaeology of the Altai Republichttp://eng.altai-republic.ru/modules.php?op=modload&name=Sections&file=index&req=viewarticle&artid=20... (1/30/2011)

Archaic Human Culture http://anthro.palomar.edu/homo2/mod_homo_3.htm (9/9/2010)

As Old Clovis Sites, but Not Clovis, Paisley Caves, Oregon Yields Western Stemmed Points, More Human DNA http://bit.ly/1JJ40ts

The aurochs is about to return to the mountains of central Europe http://www.eurowildlife.org/news/the-aurochs-is-about-to-return-to-the-mountains-of-central-europe/

Back Migration http://www.sci-news.com/othersciences/anthropology/science-back-migration-native-americans-01804.html

Bamboo http://earthnotes.tripod.com/bamboo.htm (9/13/2010)

Berelekh Map http://www.maplandia.com/russia/magadanskaya-oblast/susumanskiy-rayon/berelekh/ (8/31/2010)

China map http://en.wikipedia.org/wiki/File: China 100.78713E 35. 63718N.jpg (8/20/2010)

Chukchi Directions of time and space http://www.cosmicelk.net/Chukchidirections.htm (4/5/2011)

Chukchi Language http://en.wikipedia.org/wiki/Chukchi language (4/5/2011)

Cro-Magnon http://en.wikipedia.org/wiki/Cro-Magnon (8/12/2010)

Denisova Cave (Siberia) http://archaeology.about.com/od/dathroughdeterms/qt/denisova cave.htm (8?31/2010)

Did Ancient Volcano Alter Human History http://www.livescience.com/1661-ancient-volcano-alter-human-history.html

Drum Talk Is the African's Wireless A. I. Good, Natural History Magazine, http://www.naturalhistorymag.com/htmlsite/master.html?http://www.naturalhistorymag.com/htmlsite/editors pick/1942 09 pick.html

Dover Bronze Age Boat http://indigenousboats.blogspot.com/2008/01/dover-bronze-age-boat.html

Earliest Humanlike Footprints Found in Kenya http://donsmaps.com/erectus.html (9/11/2010)

Face of a Neanderthal woman http://www.femininebeauty.info/neanderthal-woman (8/23/2010)

First Americans http://www.nmhcpl.org/First_American.html (8/23/2010)

Four-horned Antelope http://en.wikipedia.org/wiki/Four-horned_Antelope (9/15/2010)

Geography of China http://en.wikipedia.org/wiki/Geography_of_China (9/3/2010)

Historical earthquakes in China http://drgeorgepc.com/EarthquakesChina.html (9/24/2010)

Historical SuperVolcanoes and Archeology Indicate Nuclear Winter Climate Models Exaggerate Effects http://nextbigfuture.com/2010/04/historical-supervolcanoes-and.html (8/20/2010)

Hominid Tools http://www.handprint.com/LS/ANC/stones.html (8/23/2010)

Homo erectus http://humanorigins.si.edu/evidence/human-fossils/species/homo-erectus (8/12/2010)

Homo erectus http://en.wikipedia.org/wiki/Homo_erectus (8/12/2010)

Homoerectus http://www.archaeologyinfo.com/homoerectus.htm (9/5/2010)

Homo erectus Survival http://www.archaeology.org/9703/newsbriefs/h.erectus.html (9/5/2010)

Homo neanderthalensis http://humanorigins.si.edu/evidence/human-fossils/species/homo-neanderthalensis (8/12/2010)

How Two Retirees' Amateur Archaeology Helped Throw Our View of Human History into Turmoil http://blogs.smithsonianmag.com/smart-news/2013/05/how-two-retirees-amateur-archaeology-helped-throw-our-view-of-human-history-into-turmoil/#ixzz2VGdrPFOv

Humans wore shoes 40,000 years ago, fossil suggests http://www.stonepages.com/news/archives/002825.html (8/27/2010)

Hydropotes inermis (Chinese water deer) http://www.ultimateungulate.com/Artiodactyla/Hydropotes_inermis.html (9/8/2010)

Ice Age Climate Cycles http://earthguide.ucsd.edu/virtualmuseum/climatechange2/03_1.shtml (1/29/2011)

Ice-Free Corridor Revisited http://www.geotimes.org/feb04/feature_Revisited.html

Images of Neanderthals http://www.talkorigins.org/faqs/homs/savage.html (8/23/2010) Ki'ti's Story, 75,000 BC The land where the giants played. http://www.youtube.com/watch?v=qgkPb_QfGtg

La Ferrassie Neanderthal Reconstruction http://s1.zetaboards.com/anthroscape/topic/2448167/1/ (8/23/2010)

Late Pleistocene, now-extinct fauna of the southwest http://www.saguaro-juniper.com/i_and_i/history/megafauna.html (8/22/2010)

Maars and Phreatic Eruptions http://geology.com/stories/13/maar/

Meet the Neanderthals http://news.bbc.co.uk/2/hi/science/nature/1469607.stm (8/23/2010)

Moose and Giant Moose http://www.tc.gov.yk.ca/publications/Moose_2007.pdf

Mousterian http://en.wikipedia.org/wiki/Mousterian

Muntjac (barking deer) http://www.itsnature.org/ground/mammals-land/muntjac/ (9/8/2010)

Neanderthal http://www.crystalinks.com/neanderthal.html

Neanderthal culture: Old masters http://www.nature.com/news/neanderthal-culture-old-masters-1.12974

Neanderthals more intelligent than thought http://www.msnbc.msn.com/id/39324819/ns/technology_and_science-science (9/24/2010)

Neanderthal tools http://www.telegraph.co.uk/science/science-news/3345244/Neanderthal-tools-reveal-advanced-technology.html

Neanderthal tools http://www.paleodirect.com/mous1.htm (6/22/2013)

Neanderthal tools http://www.amnh.org/exhibitions/permanent-exhibitions/human-origins-and-cultural-halls/anne-and-bernard-spitzer-hall-of-human-origins/neanderthal-tools (6/22/2013)

New Evidence Puts Man in North America 50,000 Years Ago, http://www.sciencedaily.com/releases/2004/11/041118104010.htm

Origins of Paleoindians http://en.wikipedia.org/wiki/Origins_of_Paleoindians (8/22/2010)\Pedra Furada, Brazil: Paleoindiand, Paintings, and Paradoxes, http://www.athenapub.com/10pfurad.htm (2012)

Pompeii-Like Excavations Tell Us More About Toba Super-Eruption http://www.sciencedaily.com/releases/2010/02/100227170841.htm

Quaternary Period http://www3.hi.is/~oi/quaternary_geology.htm (8/31/2010)

Red hair a part of Neanderthal genetic profile http://seattletimes.nwsource.com/html/nationworld/2003975496_neanderthal26.html (8/26/2010)

Rethining Neanderthals, Joe Alper, Smithsonian.com, Science and Nature, June 2003 http://www.smithsonianmag.com/science-nature/neanderthals.html?c=y&page=1

Sacred Bones, Fields of Stones, Dr. Francis Allard Earthwatch Journal, October 2002. www.earthwatch.org

Savoonga artist to explore traditional native tattoos, Anchorage Daily News

http://www.adn.com/2011/04/02/1788951/savoonga-artist-to-explore-traditional.html (4/5/2011)

Shamanism in Siberia http://www.sacred-texts.com/sha/sis/sis04.htm (4/5/2011)

Shiraoi Ainu Village http://members.virtualtourist.com/m/tt/52254/

Simple techniques for production of dried meat http://www.fao.org/docrep/003/x6932e/X6932E02.htm (9/27/2010)

Snout trout is critically endangered http://www.arkive.org/kunming-snout-trout/schizothorax-grahami/

Solutrean http://en.wikipedia.org/wiki/Solutrean (8/23/2010)

Stone Age Columbus http://www.bbc.co.uk/science/horizon/2002/columbusqa.shtml (8/23/2010)

Stone Age Site Yields Evidence of Advanced Culture http://history.cultural-china.com/en/51History9459.html (9/5/2010)

Stone Me! Spears show early human species was sharper than we thought http://www.guardian.co.uk/science/2012/nov/15/stone-spear-early-human-species

Stone-tipped spear may have much earlier origin http://articles.latimes.com/2012/nov/16/science/la-sci-hafting-spears-20121116

Straight-tusked elephant http://en.wikipedia.org/wiki/Straight-tusked_Elephant (10/3/2010) Synoptic table of the principal old world prehistoric

cultures http://en.wikipedia.org/wiki/Synoptic_table_of_the_principal_old_world_prehistoric_cultures (9/8/2010)

Toothpicks----Homo erectus used them http://phys.org/news/2014-05-tooth-picking-behavior-middle-pleistocene-hominins.html

Transmitting the Ainu wisdom http://www.town.shiraoi.hokkaido.jp/ainu-tradition/yamamaru/index.html

Umiaq skin boat http://en.wikipedia.org/wiki/File:Umiaq_skin_boat.jpg

Volcanic Ash http://geology.com/articles/volcanic-ash.shtml (8/20/2010)

When did humans come to the Americas? http://www.smithsonianmag.com/science-nature/When-Did-Humans-Come-to-the-Americas-187951111.html

Zhirendong puts the chin in china http://johnhawks.net/weblog/fossils/china/zhirendong-2010-liu-chin.html

Zhoukoudian Relics Museum www.china.org.cn/english/features/museums/129075.htm (9/5/2010)